Transmuted

(Dark Landing Series, Book 1)

ROBIN PRAYTOR

A POST-TO-PRINT PUBLISHERS BOOK
PHOENIX

TRANSMUTED

ISBN 978-0-9984685-1-8 (paperback)
Published by Post-To-Print-Publishers, LLC, Phoenix
First Edition: January 2017

ISBN 978-0-9984685-0-1 (ebook)
Published by Kindle Press, Seattle, 2017
Kindle Press is a trademark of Amazon.com, Inc., or an affiliate.

To my husband for his
enduring love and support.

PROLOGUE

Destruction of the last defender belonged by tradition to Sar Mode. None too soon, the appointed principal's next turning was only days away. She directed *Quell's* battle escorts to the rear. The centuries-old tradition demanded that the command ship make the final kill independent of the armada. The Paresee warship turned two-hundred-seventy degrees to *Quell's* right flank, feigning its intention to run. At the last moment it swung back, its cannons positioned for a broadside strike. Perfectly synced with the Paresee, the Diak ship countered its move. Devices planted by the advanced force had infiltrated the planet's military. The Paresee captain's every order was transmitted to the Diak in real time.

She admired the captain's dogged determination to cripple the Diak ship or even, with luck, destroy it. When the ship achieved its optimal attitude the ill-fated captain ordered his cannons to fire, realizing his strategy had failed milliseconds after the command was given. The enemy ship faced him head-on, its lasers fully charged.

Sar Mode waited until the Paresee missiles were equidistant between the two ships. Her lasers ignited the incoming projectiles in succession, right to left, throwing up a curtain of blinding white light. When the curtain fell, the Paresee ship sat, a dark center surrounded by hundreds of escape capsules. The circular wave widened as the capsules accelerated into the void. Some headed into

Quell's shields. All but one disintegrated on contact in a glittering display. The pod carrying the Paresee captain, its momentum stopped by the Diak beam, was held in place until the others blinked from existence.

The remaining capsules continued on their doomed journey. It was doubtful any of the pods' inhabitants would survive, but she hoped one or two might. They reminded her of the farfeni flower when the core burst and its seeds scattered to the four winds — one of the few original memories left to her. *We will not die today.*

She lowered the shields and drew the captain's pod aboard. He was young and virile. Blood still coursed through his veins. Sar Mode was impatient to add his memories to her database. She would replay them slowly, savoring each one as long as possible, and tuck a few away for the dark moments.

When the Paresee ship was destroyed and Sar Mode safely transferred to her new host, she dispatched the landers to the planet below to eliminate any remaining ground resistance. The planet must be cleared in preparation for the colony ships' arrival. While they waited, the colonists would bicker among themselves over the best sites, those with the highest populations. But the colonists would be second to choose. Gunship pilots who'd survived the brief war were rewarded with the first choice of the conquered. To preserve their purpose, only Diak who had fully turned could become pilots, and once rewarded, they were rotated out of the ranks.

The next target had been selected some time ago. Unlike the Paresee system, where only one of its planets supported life, the next objective consisted of multiple planetary systems and five inhabited planets. Preliminary invasion measures had commenced earlier than usual — well in advance of the Diak arrival. Devices were seeding the populations even now.

The armada reassembled at the newly constructed command station to rest, repair damaged ships, strengthen their numbers, and wait for their seeds to take root.

1 DARK LANDING

2519, Zeta Quadrant, Known Universe

Security Chief Drew Cutter leaned his six-foot-three frame over the mezzanine rail and watched the security team herd the cutpurse through the bazaar below. They angled him toward an out-of-the-way spot where they could take him with little fuss. Their target zigzagged around the stalls and merchandise displays, nudging shoppers aside in a half-hearted attempt to dodge his pursuers. He'd been made and had no place to run. Petty thieves and con artists were rare on Dark Landing. Those who found their way to the station also found their stays cut shorter than anticipated.

The three-man security team was in position to take their man unnoticed by surrounding shoppers when the new hire, evidently deciding it was his chance to shine, lunged at the culprit. He misjudged the distance and came up a full two feet short. Unable to check his momentum, he stumbled into the man, shoving him against a display rack filled with decorative glow-globes. They went down together—a tangled mess of shelving and thrashing limbs. Globes scattered across the deck as customers ran to retrieve them for the irate merchant. Eyes on the bouncing balls, several side spats developed as people bumped heads and stepped on each other's feet.

Jones, the team leader, stood back, silently taking in the ruckus while his second endeavored to separate the newbie from the display rack. Jones threw his head back and looked up at Drew. Next in line for shift commander, Jonesy always seemed to know when the boss was watching. Arms out, palms up, with a "do-you-believe-this-shit" expression, he shrugged at Drew before calmly moving into the fray to sort it out.

Confident Jones could handle the mess, Drew turned from the scene below. He surveyed the offerings of the mezzanine food court. It'd been one of those days. Irked whenever the station wasn't lumbering along with monotonous efficiency, he imagined its routine as a length of silk fabric. His job was to iron out the little wrinkles. He'd beat them out if necessary, but that was never his first choice.

He pushed the incident to the back of his mind. If he was smart, he'd grab a quick bite and head back to the office to catch up on his logs. It was Thursday, 1930 station time. Three cargo freighters arrived earlier in the day, joining five others already docked. When their cargos were loaded or unloaded, their crews would clean up for station leave. Eight ships in dock at once meant a hectic weekend.

Still deciding between sauerkraut and bean curd, or reconstituted chicken and rice, Drew's comm implant purred the name Matilda Freelander, his nightshift commander, in his ear.

"Yes, Mattie?"

"You coming back to the office tonight?"

"I'm thinking about it. Is there a problem?"

"No, no problem. There's a lady here."

He waited a beat before prompting. "And . . . ?"

"She asked to speak with you personally. I told her you'd already left."

"This lady got a name?"

Now it was Mattie's turn to take a beat. "Letty Taleen."

Drew frowned. "Has she said what she wants?" It wasn't like Mattie to dance around a point, but he could tell by her measured tone something was up. *Taleen* . . . it couldn't be *that* Taleen.

"I leave it to you, Mattie. Do you think I should come back?" He made no effort to hide his irritation.

Mattie responded with her usual indifference. "It might prove interesting."

"Okay, but I'm gonna grab something to eat first. *End all*." A barely audible tone sounded in his ear, signifying the end of the communication.

There was no line at Long Chow's. He ordered a chicken and rice bowl to go. He'd take the long way back to the office. Whoever she was, it wouldn't hurt to keep her waiting some. She probably had a beef about damaged luggage or rude station personnel. Still, Mattie was holding something back.

He tried to remember the first name of the Taleen Industries woman from the documentaries he'd seen. He thought it was Karen or maybe Katherine. Taleen was an uncommon surname, but anyone of that consequence wouldn't have business on Dark Landing, not in person anyway.

Other than a few scattered mining operations and sparsely populated scientific bases, Dark Landing was the last station in the relay, as far as you could dock from any developed planet in the Known Universe, Earth or alien. Its proximity to multiple, stabilized wormholes made it the perfect hub for hopping between galaxies, but it lacked the luxury accommodations and amenities needed to attract passenger ships, especially those carrying multi-world CEOs. The station catered to inter-planetary trade and was a staging point for space science organizations.

Drew reflected on what he knew of Taleen Industries, a multi-world conglomerate licensed to do business on each of the five MCTT-member planets, and the largest, most diversified outfit in the Known Universe. The founders, an entrepreneurial couple, died in the TuD'wei spaceport disaster, leaving an infant girl as sole heiress.

Karen, or Katherine, an adult now, maintained a low profile. Depending on which version you believed, she was a protected recluse with more looks than brains who didn't involve herself in running the store, or a freak-of-nature brainiac who ran all aspects of the operation from self-imposed exile.

Before entering the conveyer, he reconsidered and instead turned and sought an empty rail bench. To his mind, no good had ever come from surprises. As he sat down, he tapped the small, slightly raised patch of skin behind his left earlobe. *Dock Command,* he mouthed voicelessly, unwrapping his dinner.

The reply was immediate. "Benson here. Yeah, Chief?"

"Benny, can you do me a quick favor?" Drew asked and shoveled a bite of chicken and rice into his mouth.

"I'll try. What's up?"

He spoke around his mouthful. "I need the registries for the ships docked today and the names of the companies they're hauling for."

Benson "Benny" Capone, Senior Dock Foreman, answered without hesitation. "Berth four is co-op-owned, hauling alien and human medical supplies. Berth five, also co-op-owned, is dropping an order here and picking up most of the med cargo from berth four. Both are scheduled to depart in three days. Four's returning back up the line to the Deep Light station, and five's headed to its home port on Fehdeen."

Drew sensed the foreman was speaking from memory and not from a record screen. With little effort, Benny could recall the details of every ship that embarked and debarked from the station on his watch.

The dock foreman continued. "Berth eight is Earth-registry, non-gov. Cane Cargo is listed as principally insured. She unloaded a few cartons of trade goods to barter with the local merchants and debarked four, one-way passengers. She's scheduled to depart in three days, too. No departure destination filed yet."

"I've reviewed the registries for everything docked before today. I don't remember seeing a Taleen Industries' connection. You?" Drew asked.

"Nope, none that's obvious. What with holding companies, co-op interests, and the like, it's hard to say for sure. If you can give me an hour or two, I'll dig deeper."

"Nah, that's okay. You gonna be at poker Saturday?"

"You betcha."

Drew cut the connection. Co-ops owned most of the trade stations scattered at that end of space, and most of the cargo ships. Their shares changed daily, and ownership often proved difficult to determine. Taleen Industries could have interests in any of the ships currently docked. *Only Muck knows.*

Drew tapped his comm implant and mouthed a new

request, *Customs*. A low beeping indicated he'd entered the queue, and the speed of the beep told him he was next. Thirty seconds passed.

"Customs Duty-officer Marcowitz, sir. Sorry to keep you waiting."

"Marcowitz, would you check arrivals for the last few weeks for a 'Taleen'?"

"Searching t-a-l-e-e-n, sir. No results for the past thirty days."

"Thanks. *End all*."

With no more information than when he started, he ate the last bite of rice, dumped his bowl and fork into a waste chute, and headed to the conveyer that would drop him at Security HQ.

Before he could enter the conveyer, he had to step aside to let three Praetorian monks exit single file, heads down. Dark brown hoods concealed their faces, and their long robes brushed the deck. Arms crossed in front, their hands were buried deep in bell-bottomed sleeves.

Why Praetorians would come to Dark Landing and stay as long as these three had, over six weeks now, nagged at Drew. He'd assumed they were only passing through, but they hadn't left. He'd kept a close watch on them. As long as they didn't create the customary disturbances with public demonstrations and doom-provoking prophecy, he'd let them be. It was a free space after all. That they seemed to rush around the station at all hours perplexed him. *Where the hell are they rushing to and from anyway?*

~ ~ ∞ ~ ~

The man leaned casually against the bulkhead outside Security Headquarters, watching for her to come out. She'd been in there for a while. The passageway remained busy, but no one seemed to pay him any attention.

They'd lost track of Speller on Mars after a botched attempt to take him out. She was their best chance of finding him now. Their information said the two were close, *really* close. They spent as much of their personal time together as they did during work hours. Some guys had all the luck. The contact on Earth had followed her for several weeks until she'd boarded the *Temperance*. Her trip to Dark Landing was no coincidence.

The conveyer doors opened, and the chief of security exited and headed into HQ. The man tapped his comm and mouthed a command. "Cutter just returned to HQ. What should I do?" He kept his voice low. "Yeah, okay," he said, and entered the waiting conveyer.

~ ~ ∞ ~ ~

Drew was still shaking his head in puzzlement over the Praetorians when he arrived at HQ. Everything appeared quiet. The duty roster indicated Jones's team had deposited their cutpurse and returned to patrol. The prisoner was being questioned in interview room two.

A kid of maybe eighteen or nineteen was curled up, napping on the two-seater bench in what was generously referred to as the reception area. Drew pegged him as a down-and-out who'd worked his way to Dark Landing but lacked the resources to move on.

He wore the favored travel kit consisting of a multi-purpose wool poncho with long leather fringe. A slouch hat pulled down to his chin, and baggy dungarees with the pant legs tucked into worn, high-topped leather boots completed the outfit.

A small shoulder pack served as his pillow with the strap end clutched in the boy's hand and the upper portion wrapped securely around his wrist. *He may be young, but he's an experienced traveler*, Drew thought.

Mattie and her assistant Kyle stood together at the back of the room studying a wall monitor just outside Drew's darkened office. No Letty Taleen in sight. She'd evidently decided not to wait for him, or perhaps she was in the head. Laughter spilled from the open hatch of the staff rec room. *Maybe she's shooting pool with the night crew*, he thought and chuckled.

Drew heard the boom of a distant explosion a second before the klaxon blared and the emergency lights flashed. He whirled and headed back toward the conveyer. As he passed the bench, he noticed the kid had scuttled under it, still clutching his shoulder pack. *Quick thinker.*

A trample of boots fell in behind him. The main computer transmitted monotone status reports over his comm patch:

Disturbance contained at sublevel two, customs box two, airlock engaged, one fatality, no injured, emergency personnel dispatched.

The message updated with each repeat:

Disturbance contained at sublevel two, customs box two, station-side airlock retracted, one fatality, no injured, fire, environmental, and security personnel on scene. Additional security personnel en route.

Each of the two station sublevels held five docking bays and two separate entrances into the station. While atmospheric shields maintained environmental services for the docks, the box-shaped entrances were twenty-by-twenty-foot emergency airlocks. All station personnel, visiting crew, and passengers entered through the airlocks when passing from dockside to station-side, no matter how many times a day or an hour they made the trip.

Environmental detection equipment scanned everyone and everything in the box during the short crossing. Only when the sensors and the technicians monitoring the displays agreed that nothing in the box posed a threat to the station would the airlock open station-side.

Disturbance contained at sublevel two, customs box two —

"*Pause*," Drew commanded, stopping the transmission. It took him more than twenty minutes to make the trip from Security HQ to sublevel two. Mattie followed with a team of ten men. Security personnel closer to the scene had cordoned off the area. His additional men spread out, confirming no threat remained.

Drew took several minutes to study the scene for himself before taking reports. That there'd been an explosion was obvious, though any residual smoke had been sucked out with the oxygen to suffocate the fire. Simultaneously, ceiling jets would inject the appropriate chemical compound to neutralize any residual contamination.

There was minimal charring, but the box walls were liberally splattered with blood and grisly bits of debris. Drew assumed the grisly bits had belonged to the small mound of remains lying under a damp tarp in the middle of the airlock deck.

He dipped his head toward the fire captain, who'd been glancing in his direction every few seconds, waiting for his signal. Captain Davies spoke to his next-in-command before heading over, shedding the top half of his environmental suit as he approached. Along with security personnel, fire and environmental staff manned a shared substation on each dock level.

"We have everything under control, Chief. The fatality was a crew member from berth eight, the *Temperance*," Davies reported.

"Do we know what caused the explosion?"

"Yes, but you won't believe it. The scan indicated an old fashioned, Earth-grown nitro suspended in the inner pouch of a water skin. Can't tell what ignited it yet."

Drew tried to remember what little he knew about the antique ordnance. "That's bizarre. Nitro was notoriously unstable, and it would take an awful lot to cause any damage. It could never breach the hull of the station."

Davies nodded. "Yeah, if that's what was intended. Plenty of other choices would be safer and easier to come by. Makes no sense."

"Find out if there are other uses for nitro, especially anything that might not be obvious," Drew said, then added, "And try the med-lab database. There might be something there."

"Already on it, sir. It's too early to know for sure, but I don't see anything to indicate a calculated attack on the station."

Drew relaxed a bit. "I hope you're right. We'll talk again after I see the initial reports."

He motioned Mattie over. "I don't suppose you have much on this guy yet?"

She shook her head. "Only his name, Jonas Trammel. We're gathering ship's officers and crew now to start interviews."

"Good. If you've got everything in check here, I'm going back to the office."

He took another quick look around, satisfied the responders had it under control.

On the way back, he issued a general statement to reassure the station populace they were safe and had nothing to worry about.

At HQ, Kyle glanced up briefly from his monitor as Drew passed. He would know as much as Drew by now, maybe more if anything came through in the last few minutes.

Eager for the serenity of his office, Drew called for low lights as he stepped through the hatch and for backup as he drew his blaster and pointed it at a movement in the corner. Startled and already on edge, only his academy training stopped him from pulling the trigger. In two seconds, Kyle fell in at his side, weapon drawn.

"I'll be a jackal's ass!" Kyle lowered his weapon. "I thought she'd left. I'm really sorry, Chief. In all the excitement. . . . Let's go, Miss Taleen. Get up!"

Still brandishing his blaster, Drew stared at the kid he'd noticed earlier. He'd evidently decided to move from the metal lobby bench to the more comfortable lounger in Drew's office. *Wait, did Kyle call him 'she?' 'Miss Taleen?'*

She lay perfectly still, ignoring Kyle's command. Her gaze never wavered from Drew's blaster. Evidently unprepared to take a chance, she gave him the time he needed to absorb the situation. When his thumb reset the safety catch and his arm relaxed, she sat up, pulled the slouch hat from her head and shook out her hair. How had he mistaken her for a man?

He continued staring as he holstered his sidearm, then dismissed Kyle with a flick of his index finger. She stood at five-foot-seven or eight; he figured the boots added an inch or two.

He could tell she was slender, though the loose-fitting poncho revealed no discernible figure. No woman with a face like hers could have anything but a figure to match.

Her hair, thick and jet black, with maroon and navy highlights, barely brushed her shoulders. Her complexion translucent, cheeks slightly flushed.

Drew took a deep, ragged breath.

2 DECKED

"Pretty sloppy operation, Cutter," were the first words out of generously full lips.

Transfixed, mouth already opened, only air whooshed out in place of a coherent response from Drew.

Black, intelligent eyes stared back at him, as black as her hair, and framed by ebony brows.

"You *are* Security Chief Andrew Vincent Cutter, aren't you?" she asked, frowning.

He nodded; his breath and equilibrium returned. He hadn't spoken yet, assessing the situation. Right hand still resting on the hilt of his blaster, he relaxed the arm further, then let it drop to his side.

She took a few moments to study him. "Do you need *medical* attention?" she asked finally, with what seemed to him like genuine concern. When he didn't respond immediately, she edged sideways, closer to the hatch.

Without warning, she erupted. "Incredible! You're the one who's supposed to protect me from the bogeymen? I just remembered I have someplace else to be." She snatched her pack from the lounger and headed toward the hatch.

Composure fully restored, Drew grabbed her arm as she moved past him. "Hold it, lady!"

That was a mistake.

A second later, he was lying flat on his back with Miss Taleen straddled across him. Her hands and knees pinned his arms to the deck. By this point, if she were serious, she should have used a head butt to break his nose. Instead, she stared down at him, panting lightly. While it would've been difficult to convince anyone of it at the moment, she'd employed a move at which Drew was adept. Equally adept at the counter move, he was enjoying the view until he heard chortling outside the hatch.

Despite the pleasure he got from the woman's weight against his thighs, he needed to take control of the situation. He pressed the backs of his arms against the deck for leverage and raised his head and shoulders upward as far as he could, feigning an attempt to kiss her. The tactic always worked against men. As calculated, she wrinkled her perfectly shaped nose and leaned back and away from him, reducing the pressure on his arms just enough and drawing her ankles closer to his hands.

When Drew grabbed her ankles, she instinctively lifted her hands to reach behind and free herself, shifting her center of gravity. He shoved up and backward. Emitting a loud shriek, she flew over his head, landing half-in and half-out of the hatch with a satisfying thud. The staff's chortles turned to roars of laughter.

Drew flipped up and onto his feet in one smooth movement. He lifted her from the deck by an underarm and dragged her through the hatch, issuing the verbal command to close it behind them, shutting out the retreating laughter of his men. He heaved her back onto the lounger, picked up her pack, and chucked it at her. With a steadying breath, he sat down at his desk.

"For the moment, I'll ignore that you just attacked me, but you can bet we'll get back to that. Let's start over. Hello, Miss Taleen, I'm Security Chief Andrew Cutter. Everyone calls me Drew or Chief. I understand you wanted to speak with me. How may I help you?" He leaned back in his chair and propped his feet on the desk. Fingers laced behind his head, elbows akimbo, he gazed at her nonchalantly, or so he hoped.

She glared back at him, rubbing a shoulder, appearing more angry than injured. "You weren't attacked; I checked you." When he didn't rise to the bait, she went on. "*You* grabbed *me,* and I defended myself. It was a knee-jerk reaction. Anyway, I traveled here at the request of my father. He sent me to you specifically for your help. Ha!" She rolled her eyes at the absurdity. "To protect me and —"

He interrupted her; something didn't jibe. "Your father? Before we go any further, can we establish your identity? Who are you and who's your father?"

"You're kidding, right?"

"Humor me."

"Believe me, I am." She smirked and lifted her chin with a proud air. "I'm Katherine Leticia Taleen — Letty — and head of Taleen Industries. My father is George Speller. Well, technically, he's my guardian, but I never knew my biological father."

Drew lowered his feet and leaned forward, elbows on the desk in front of him. Lustful thoughts aside, he watched her intently while mentally arranging his next questions. "You're not making any sense. Why would George Speller, probably the most celebrated CEO in the K.U., send you way out here for protection? And to *me*? Taleen Industries has a security force larger, better trained, and better equipped than most planets. Why aren't *they* protecting you? And protecting you from what?"

"I don't know. I'm sure Dad has his reasons."

"I'd like to speak with Mr. Speller myself."

For the first time, she appeared uncertain. "Y-you can't. He's gone, disappeared — almost two months now. He left me a message. I was supposed to run and make my way here to you."

"Run from what?"

"Again, I *don't* know."

At Drew's disbelieving look, her shoulders slumped, and she looked down at her hands. He thought she might be tearing up. She wasn't. After a few seconds contemplating her nails, she straightened, eyes dry.

"Actually, I thought *you'd* answer those questions. You really weren't expecting me? You don't know my dad?"

He shook his head. "No, and I find it hard to believe George Speller is missing, especially for *two months*. If that's true, the whole universe would be talking about it."

She seemed as perplexed as Drew. He suspected her story was leading to some kind of elaborate con, but he couldn't figure the end game. He'd let it play out. In the meantime, she was something to look at. They sat unmoving for several seconds.

"'Bogeymen,' *really?*" he asked, breaking the tension. She laughed a little. Enough for Drew to know he wanted to hear her laugh more. Not tonight.

"Look, it seems you and I have a lot of ground to cover. But it's getting late, and I've got reports to read and another mystery to solve. We can start again in the morning. Do you have quarters? When did you arrive—on what ship?"

"I arrived today on the *Temperance.*"

"You know about the explosion then?"

"On the *Temperance?!*"

"Not exactly. A member of the crew was transporting an explosive chemical. It ignited in the station airlock." Drew watched her expression for any indication of pre-knowledge. Her features registered only puzzled concern.

"Do you have quarters on board, or do you need a room?" he asked.

"I'll stay here."

"Here on the station?"

"No, *here* in your office. This couch is a lot more comfortable than my bunk on the *Temperance.*"

"Well, you can't stay in my office. That's dumb. If you're the head of Taleen Industries, and I gotta tell you I'm not taking your word for that, couldn't you afford a stateroom instead of a bunk?"

"Of course, but I keep a low profile when I travel."

"Maybe, if you're trying to keep a low profile, you shouldn't be using your real name—if Katherine Leticia Taleen is your name. You may think the poncho and hat make an impenetrable disguise, but what's the point if you're using your own name?"

"I'm not." With another sigh, "I thought we were going to do this in the morning?"

"Yeah. I'll get you a room at Landers Keep."

"I'm staying right here. You have a comfy couch, a private head with a chem-shower. There's probably something to eat in the op's galley."

"I don't think so."

"I don't care what you think! I'm tired and I'm staying here tonight."

"Look, crazy lady —"

"Who do you think you're working for anyway?" she spat out, triumphant, chin high.

Drew fell speechless once more. *Fuck! That's an unexpected twist.* He admired her style. "What are you trying to say?" he asked, recovering faster this time.

"I'm saying, you work for me, and I can prove it."

She joined him behind the desk. The entire desktop, dark now, was a document screen with a palm reader visible under the surface to his right. To activate the screen, several smaller monitors installed in the credenza behind him, and the large monitor on the wall above the credenza, he had only to lay his hand on the reader.

Letty brushed his shoulder as she reached across the desk in front of him, his view blocked momentarily by her poncho. She smelled of leather, stale wool, and orange blossoms, the latter fragrance dredged up from somewhere in his youth on Earth. She placed her right hand on the reader. His desk lit up, displaying the unfinished logs he'd left out earlier. Simultaneously, a mechanical hum sounded from three screens rising to a comfortable viewing angle out of the flat surface of the credenza behind him, and he knew the wall monitor now glowed softly with several columns of menu options.

She removed her hand, leaned back against the edge of the desk, and looked down at him smugly. "As I said, I'm spending the night right *here*. Now, if you don't mind, I'm tired. I'll see you in the morning, say 0700?"

Drew pressed an index finger to a small icon beneath the palm reader, returning all screens to their idle state. He tapped his comm patch. "Kyle, send two men in here—make it four." He was shaken and it probably showed, but he stared evenly back at the woman. "You may be my boss or my boss's boss--whatever. That's just one more thing to sort out tomorrow, but there's no way in hell I'm leaving you in my office with access to station systems."

The hatch opened and his men crowded in with curious looks.

"Take her to holding and have her searched. Disable her comm implant and lock her up. I want someone watching her every second of every minute until I order otherwise."

He expected a scene, but she went quietly without a backward glance, chin lifted. Drew thought the chin thing must be part of her normal carriage.

3 MATTIE FREELANDER

His day now completely turned to shit, Drew strained to keep a conversational tone as he tapped his comm and spoke into the air above his desk, "Mattie, where we at?"

"Just starting my report. I'll have the preliminary in about an hour."

"Can't wait, come on in. I need Kyle too. Ask him to bring coffee, please."

In two minutes, they both entered his office. Mattie pulled a chair from the side wall and dragged it next to his desk. Kyle handed Drew his coffee.

"Thanks, Kyle. Grab the pack on the lounger, it's Miss Taleen's. Go through it for ID, visa, and anything else of interest. Scan it for hidden compartments. Make sure there's nothing she can use as a weapon, then give the rest back to her."

Drew delivered the next request with an intense stare meant to ward off questions. "She said she's the head of Taleen Industries. My access reader captured her palm print. Run it and a full background check. I want to make sure she's who she claims to be."

Kyle darted a startled glance at Mattie as Drew continued.

"She also said she came in on the *Temperance*, but I had customs look for a Taleen earlier and nothing showed. She was probably traveling under an alias." He ran a hand through his hair, trying to think of anything he'd missed. Sandy brown strands curled around his fingers. It was longer than he liked.

"Also, check George Speller's name against my profile. I can't imagine when we would've crossed paths, but I guess it's possible. And have Benny investigate the *Temperance*. I want a complete ownership abstract since her first launch." He paused for a few seconds. "That's it for now.

"Oh, and keep *all* tech gear away from her. I don't want the men chatting her up, either. Tell them to keep a professional distance. Right now, she's in holding; there's no need for an official record. Later, if necessary, we can book her. I'm sure you'll dig something up—counterfeit travel documents—whatever."

Kyle scurried from the office before Drew thought of anything else.

"Wow! I *heard* she decked you," Mattie said with a wide grin.

"That's not the half of it. Between you and me, she has access to station systems!" She replaced her grin with an expression of stunned horror. "You're joking, right? How is that even possible?"

"She said she's our boss. She placed her hand on my reader and the place lit up like a Caxparxt brothel."

Mattie paled, her jaw dropping. "Jesus, Drew, it must be true if she has access. I know we're publicly traded, but the Kettering's still have controlling interest, right?"

All Dark Landing staff were employees of CoachStop Management, MWCorp., a company contracted to operate space stations, mining camps, and other remote outposts on behalf of the owning co-ops.

"Yeah, maybe. Both of us have stock options and we should've gotten some kind of notice. Find out who the other stockholders are. Focus on the corporate shareholders."

"Why? I don't understand. Can't we just contact CoachStop and ask them? If she's the boss now, isn't it risky locking her up?"

"Maybe. Probably. Mattie, there's something else going on here. Access aside, as impossible as it is, I think this is some kind of con. She gave me a crazy story about her dad disappearing, and does she look like the head of the largest corporation in the Known Universe to you? Even if it's true, what the hell is she doing here? Taleen Industries wouldn't give a rat's ass about a trading outpost on the edge of space with two-star accommodations. I don't want to make a total chump of myself by contacting CoachStop before I know she's who and what she claims to be."

"Okay. But I can't lose my job. It's not just me — I got my folks to worry about too."

Mattie's concern was legitimate, but her loyalty to him would trump it, at least for a while. "Yeah, I know. Work on the shareholder information while I look into this, and keep Kyle focused as well. Move someone up to handle the routine stuff."

Once she decided to trust Drew and follow his lead, she dropped her protest. She rarely dwelled on choices after the fact, a trait he admired.

"How are we going to handle Curtis?" she asked.

Curtis Walker was Mattie's dayshift counterpart. He was steadfast, efficient, and a by-the-book company man who could quote policy like the Praetorians could quote prophecy. But Drew didn't trust him. He sensed something snide and sleazy about Curtis that he couldn't pinpoint. Drew wasn't above cutting corners, but Curtis's propensity to remark on the slightest lapse of protocol kept Drew on the straight most of the time. In situations like this, he presented a problem. If Taleen Industries controlled CoachStop Management and Letty Taleen *was* their boss, Curtis would suck up to her. Even on a long shot, he'd throw Drew under the freight loader at the first opportunity.

"Okay, I'm giving Curtis the airlock incident. I'll leave orders that you've been instructed to turn everything over to him and he's to take the lead. That'll puff him up like a Täsorian blow-wart and should keep him out of your hair for a couple days. To be fair, for an asshole, he's not a bad investigator."

Drew rubbed the beard stubble on his chin and went on. "Take him aside in the morning before you leave and let him in on the big conspiracy: 'There's a VIP in holding, a suspected runaway. The chief is juggling eggs and doesn't want anyone approaching her until he hears back from home office.' He'll love that, and it's half true. I need to deal with the Taleen issue quietly until I understand what the hell's really going on.

"Now, where are we on the airlock explosion? I've got a breakfast meeting with Fitz and Doc in . . . *damn* . . . ten hours, and they're going to want a rundown." Drew liked Mattie's reports; she could make the driest subject sound like a rousing campsite story.

"Pretty curious, boss," she started. "The deceased, Jonas Trammel, was working for passage here. The captain said he doesn't usually take on crew under those circumstances, but he found himself short-handed right before departure and the guy was clean, well-spoken, and seemed to know his way around a ship. He did his job, got along fine with the rest of the crew, but kept to himself most of the time."

"What was his job?"

"The ship's carrying livestock. Nothing too exotic, your basic egg birds, some fishy-eely things in a shallow tank of water — waste of good water if you ask me — and a dozen grazers that look like a cross between a tall calf and a short giraffe. Their cookie said the livestock is for ship's consumption. I doubt it. The paperwork leaves something to the imagination. Anyway, Trammel handled their care, feeding, and shit cleanup."

Drew interrupted her report. "The tall calf-short giraffe is a cammeni. They raise them on Fehdeen like we raise cattle on Earth. I doubt they were intended for ship's consumption. Too much trouble. Just butcher and flash freeze the meat. The eggers, maybe, but I'm thinking the livestock is being illegally transported to a colony somewhere."

Mattie shrugged and went on. "Anyway, Trammel told the purser he was going to take a walk-about and spend the night on the station. He'd be back onboard in the morning to collect his kit and clean the pens one final time before debarking."

"I don't suppose you found anything of interest in his bunk?"

"Actually, we did. He had a few pieces of clothing, an extra pair of boots . . . and a monk's robe."

"A monk's robe?"

"Yep. What do you make of that?"

Drew leaned toward her, his interest heightened. "Like the Praetorian robes?"

"Just like them."

"I'll be damned. Maybe he was coming here to join his three friends. They could be planning a demonstration. That might explain what the nitro was for, but it's still an odd choice. The stuff's unstable as hell."

"But Praetorian monks have never been violent," Mattie said.

"You're right. I made inquiries when our brood first showed up. Mostly they've been cited for disturbing the peace, unlicensed demonstrations, trespassing, that kind of thing. The only violence came from spectators throwing things at *them*. If a situation gets out of hand, the Praetorians pack up and leave. I'm going to bring our three in for questioning. What about the airlock scanner log?"

She picked up her report where she'd left off. "The scanner didn't identify the danger until after the explosion. The initial log read clear about a second before it blew. Afterward it was identified as nitro."

Drew rubbed his eyes and stretched his neck, trying to relieve tired muscles. He had too many questions without answers. He needed a few hours of sleep before he could think it through.

"That's all for now," Mattie said. "The scanner tech is reviewing the data, and she'll let us know in the morning what caused the explosive to ignite. Four passengers debarked before Trammel. I'll run them as soon as we're done here. I doubt there's a connection to the explosion, but one is probably your gal, Letty."

"*Miss Taleen*," Drew corrected her.

Mattie raised her eyebrows and put on a playful smirk.

He explained, "Okay, I may have indecent thoughts about Letty, but Miss Taleen scares the hell out of me. I need to keep my edge."

"I'm a little jealous."

"We both know that's not true, Mattie. You keep me humble."

"Someday I may surprise you."

He watched her as she left the office. She was a few years older than Drew, but a fine example of womanhood. Unfortunately, he'd always suspected he wasn't her type, despite their sexual banter. They'd never discussed it, but Letty might be more Mattie's type. *Great!* He'd never sleep with thoughts like that rambling around his head.

There was one more task to complete before he left. He checked the system time stamps for activity at his station between the explosion and his return to the office. He found nothing, but that didn't mean much. If the Taleen woman had the level of access needed to enable his command station, she'd have the means to conceal her presence. He'd order a security diagnostic in the morning.

He stopped by Mattie's desk on the way out. "Anything else before I leave? If you're smart, you'll say *no*."

"Well . . . ," she paused with a pained expression.

Drew waited.

"There's a pigeon."

"A *pigeon*?"

"Yeah."

"I'm leaving now Mattie."

"Yeah."

4 THREE CHIEFS

On his way to the weekly chiefs' meeting the next morning, Drew surveyed the familiar surroundings, nodding occasionally to passersby. The dull metal struts and bolted panels always amazed him. The station was assembled from ships with prefabricated interiors that traveled to the construction site under their own power carrying supplies, equipment, and workers. Once unloaded, the ships were welded into place to become a part of the station whole, but each ship section retained its own environmental systems. In an emergency, each section could be sealed off independent of the others.

Conveyers of wide, corrugated tubes snaked horizontally and vertically throughout the station, serving as both air handlers and inner-station transport, giving the final design a surreal appearance.

The outer bulkhead cells, strap bolted instead of welded in place, still maintained their plasma propulsion engines. With no small effort, they could be made travel-worthy and separated from the main structure. That was the theory anyway. To Drew's mind, a plethora of variables made the process impractical in the event of a station-wide disaster. The thought comforted the populace nonetheless, Drew included.

Dark Landing was anchored to a potato-shaped asteroid by an immense cradle complex. The engineers had unromantically christened the asteroid "Spud" when the station was still in the initial planning stages. Spud's orbit, once every two Earth years around its small sun, ensured stability and the cradle allowed the centripetal acceleration necessary to maintain near-Earth gravity. During building, Spud provided much of the raw minerals used in the cradle's construction, but the mining had stopped when the cradle was completed.

Drew was in the second year of his third tour, and his first as security chief. All command staff signed for four-year tours, with a re-signing option of six months paid sabbatical or a cash bonus. Unlike his fellow chiefs, Drew had never taken a sabbatical.

He'd just turned nineteen when he signed with CoachStop as a security grunt, fresh out of a grueling, quasi-military training program that he'd started at age twelve. He could have opted out at any time for more traditional schooling, but he was hooked from the beginning.

CoachStop made their selection based on his impeccable cadet record and leadership potential. He didn't disappoint. He'd excelled in his first assignment and moved up the ladder at record speed, making shift commander by his second tour. Fast, but not unheard of. CoachStop cut natural-born leaders from the pack early.

Drew's route took him past a bank of observation windows. As usual, several people stood, staring into the dark void. He averted his eyes. He couldn't understand why so many people grew transfixed by looking at nothing. While he'd never expressed such feelings out loud, he held no appreciation for the beauty of space. That incalculable vastness left Drew chilled.

Physical rules that had applied for hundreds of years, thousands in some cases, were rewritten or discarded altogether the farther they traveled and the more they learned. He'd admitted to himself long ago that he was no adventurer. He needed order— imperatives that couldn't be broken.

As he rounded the corner, he was slammed mid-center by a four-foot hellion with a mop of unkempt, black hair. Drew grunted and grabbed the boy by the underarms, lifting him to eye-level. "Toby Greenstein, I swear to God you're going to seriously injure somebody one of these days. What did you do now?" Drew had no doubt Toby was running from something. The boy spent much of his young life waiting inside a holding cell for one of his parents to come get him following some piece of mischief.

Toby squirmed to free himself, kicking his feet uncomfortably close to Drew's crotch. "Let me go!"

Drew extended his arms to avoid the kicks, but that only provided the boy with a better aim. Toby's booted foot grazed Drew on the inner thigh, much too close. He dropped him unceremoniously. Before he could grab hold again, the kid bolted around the bulkhead.

"You're looking at twenty-years-to-life the next time I catch you, Toby," Drew yelled after him, trying to sound serious.

One of the bazaar merchants ran toward him with a furious expression. Drew didn't ask, but inclined his head in the direction Toby had taken, hoping to avoid further arbitration between a merchant and the boy's parents. The man stopped in front of Drew, hands on his hips.

"Hi, Marcus, how's it going?" Drew asked with a weak smile. Though there wasn't a chance in hell the man was going to say *fine* and keep moving.

Marcus crossed his arms over his chest. "That brat was throwing things at the pigeon and knocked over my vid display. What are you going to do about it?"

"The pigeon?"

"Not the pigeon—the brat!"

"I'll talk to his parents." Drew sighed. "What's the damage?"

"I don't know yet."

"Send me a detailed list, and I'll see what I can do."

Marcus spun away, imploring a passing woman, "Do you believe this? *He'll see what he can do.*" She quickened her step, eyes straight ahead. Drew took the opportunity to escape while the man's back was turned.

His fellow chiefs already sat at their corner table when he entered the small executive mess, their faces deep in steaming mugs of coffee.

Drew looked forward to the weekly briefings with Martin Fitzwilliam, Administration Chief, and Dr. Tammy Jameson,

Medical Chief. With Drew, they made up the triumvirate rule on Dark Landing.

Nancy, the mess manager, topped his coffee mug before his butt touched the chair. "Morning," he greeted them and received three "Morning" responses in unison. Nancy hurried off to fill their standing breakfast orders.

Without small talk, Doc asked, "Anything new on yesterday's explosion? Only one dead and no injuries. The body just arrived in med-lab for autopsy. Could have been worse, I guess."

"Right," Drew responded, "but you guys go first. I've got that and something else to go over after."

"Not much from my side," Fitz began without further prompting. "As predicted, we can increase water allotments through the end of the month. That'll make people happy. Scrubber four is back up, but I don't know how long I can keep it running. The replacement is still on back-order and the factory rep on Fahdeen keeps giving me the run-around. I can't figure out what the problem is. We may need to order from Earth and pay the extra taxes and shipping. Anyway, since our backups have backups, there's no immediate concern. Five and six are next on maintenance rotation. We start testing residential airlocks tomorrow."

A renowned space safety engineer, Fitz's responsibility, along with keeping the station stocked, entailed a never-ending series of systems and maintenance tests. Reassuringly, his reports seldom varied. The need to ration any supply proved rare, which always amazed Drew considering the station's permanent population of more than six thousand with another thousand transients, give or take.

"Same old stuff in med-lab," Doc began, "indigestion, cuts and bruises, and a couple of dockside broken bones. We're having our annual common cold outbreak a little early, associated with a mild, atypical rash. About thirty treated so far, and I'm sure there's more just soldiering through. Nothing to do but relieve the symptoms until it runs its course. The rash worries me a little. Everyone's responded to standard treatment though. Isolation isn't called for, and it's too late anyway. That's all I've got, except Nick Carter's wife had her baby — a healthy, screaming boy. Your turn."

Drew made a mental note to pick up a baby gift. He liked babies.

He started with the explosion and relayed what they'd learned so far, pausing while Nancy delivered their breakfasts. "Anyway, I may have more information when I get to the office."

Neither Fitz nor Doc said anything. Drew wasn't holding back and wouldn't speculate without more facts.

The few seconds of silence provided the right dramatic pause for Drew's next report. "One Katherine Leticia Taleen is on board, also from the *Temperance*. She claims to be the head of Taleen Industries, but I haven't seen the proof yet. And it's possible she's our boss. I'm checking that out as well. She has access to station systems. Of course, I locked her up," Drew said matter-of-factly. He paused for a sip of coffee and a bite of eggs and fruit.

Doc was the first to speak. "Okay, I'd pee my panties if I were wearing them." She ignored their looks and went on. "When did Taleen Industries buy CoachStop? Is that why she's here?"

"I don't know that they did. Even so, CoachStop would be the proverbial drop in a universally large Taleen bucket. Why would anyone even close to her level, if she's who she says, and that's a *big* if, come all the way out here?" Drew continued eating.

"So, you locked her up. What now? Are we going to kill her?" Fitz asked, in a rare display of acerbity.

Drew stared, eyes unfocused for a moment. "No," he answered, hesitant, as if still undecided. "She told me her guardian—she considers him her father—disappeared a couple months ago. He left instructions she was to come here to *me*. Go figure. Her guardian is George Speller of all people. Have either of you heard that Speller is missing?"

"Not me," Doc said. She looked from Drew to Fitz.

"Me neither." Fitz closed the circle back to Drew.

"Me neither, and that's my point."

"How long can you keep her locked up? What does CoachStop say?" Fitz asked.

"If I believe she's a threat to the station, and I do, I can keep her locked up as long as I want. I'd have to make it official though. Besides the fact she attacked me . . ." Doc and Fitz exchanged confused looks but didn't interrupt ". . . the only thing I can charge her with is traveling under an alias, which I think is the case. Once I do, and if she's who she claims, legal advocates and judges will come out of the bulkheads.

"I haven't contacted CoachStop yet. I'll tell you what I told Mattie, there's something else going on, and I want to know what it is before I contact the company." Doc and Fitz could override him, but they wouldn't.

On CoachStop-managed stations, chief candidates in the three areas of responsibility were profiled and chosen for their ability to work well together. The security chief had the lead, but administration and medical were consulted on decisions that affected the station as a whole. In dire straits, they could band together to overrule security. What constituted dire straits remained untested as far as Drew was aware. Up to now he assumed the term would apply only upon a security chief's death or incapacity.

"I'd like to meet her," Doc said.

Fitz nodded his agreement.

"I think that's a good idea. I mean, she has to understand our situation. Either of you may get a better feel for what she's up to. She's a kid, sort of. She dresses like a space bum—a hot space bum. But after the display she made in my office, what does she expect? It's life and death out here." That sounded a little dramatic, even to Drew.

Doc tapped her chin with a curled knuckle. "You said her guardian, or father . . . anyway, George Speller . . . sent her to you, and he's missing?"

Drew nodded.

"Well, she may really need help," Doc said. "Why don't we offer it? You can secure the station systems so that's not an issue, can't you?"

Fitz interjected before Drew could answer. "If she said she's our boss, it *has* to be true. She wouldn't have system access otherwise. You don't think she'd harm the station and endanger everyone, do you?"

"I don't know, probably not. Just having the means warrants drastic measures, at least until we can confirm her story. I don't know if I can block her system access either. I'd have to check with our technicians, and I don't want anyone to know about it until I figure out if she's legit. After we meet with her, we can contact CoachStop if we need to."

Doc and Fitz agreed.

"Oh, there's something else," Fitz said.

Drew saw the corners of his mouth twitch as he tried to suppress a smile. He laid down his fork and gave Fitz a meaningful look. "If you say the word 'pigeon' I swear I'll punch you."

The emergency channel toned in his ear announcing *Benson Capone, Senior Dock Manager*. Drew tapped his implant. "Yeah, Benny?"

"Chief, a Camdu trader just limped into berth four. The captain claims another Camdu trader, a competitor, took a potshot at her."

"Since when are Camdu ships armed?"

"Well, this one's not—they ran for it and their attacker didn't follow. Their ship has minor damage. Nothing we can't handle here. But the story gets kinda weird from there. You might want to come down and talk to the captain yourself."

"On my way."

Whether his dock manager needed him or not, Drew wouldn't miss an encounter with Camdulings. They were hands-down the most exotic of the Alliance members, and of the non-aligned races, as well. In the time he'd been on Dark Landing, a Camdu ship had docked only twice. The opportunity to rub shoulders with alien life had trumped his aversion to space and induced him to accept a position with CoachStop in the first place.

To Doc and Fitz, "Sorry, guys—gotta go."

Fitz seemed disappointed at losing an opportunity to nettle him about the pigeon, or something equally aggravating. Since Fitz had never displayed much of a sense of humor, Drew felt almost sorry to deprive him of his fun.

5 CAMDULINGS

In the sublevel one airlock, Drew donned an EMU-lite, pulling the protective hood and breather tight around his head and neck. *Please don't let this day be an extension of yesterday,* he thought as he exited the opposite hatch.

Benny, similarly attired, was waiting for him. Berth four had been sealed and its gravity and air pressure adjusted to slightly above one-third Earth normal to accommodate the Camdu captain and her two crew members. While their suits added weight, both he and Benny skipped more than walked toward the Camdulings.

There was no mistaking the captain. A willowy female, she stood two feet taller than her crewmen, both of whom topped roughly ten feet. Camdulings had two arms and two legs with the attendant fingers and toes but were further blessed with a fifth appendage. Retracted against their lower bodies when not in use, the extra limb served as a third arm or leg, depending on the need. With skin a deep azure and sharp, finely drawn facial features, they appeared more human-reminiscent than human-like.

Benny introduced Drew and the Camdu captain by rank only. Unless phonetically added to the lexicon, Drew's and Benny's implants couldn't translate common names. Drew assumed the translators covering the ear holes of each Camduling suffered the same technical difficulty. While the English translation fluctuated between literal and interpretive, it worked well enough.

The Camdu captain repeated the story she'd told Benny. "A time back of now, my ship was impressed with light projectiles from an associated Camdu ship who should not have done. She is my born sister's daughter, but my trader enemy. This act is against Camdu and Alliance law. My ship cannot project, and so I left with speed. My sister's daughter did not follow."

"Have you reported this incident to Camdu and the Multi-world Coalition for Travel and Trade?" Drew asked.

"Yes. Soon of now."

Drew wondered if that meant they'd just reported it or they were going to report it soon. Regardless, it was taken care of.

"Has anything like this happened before?"

The captain shrugged. "No—not for way, way back from now."

Drew nodded. "Our dock manager assures me we can repair your ship. Is there anything else we can do to help?"

"We are honored by your assistance and thank you. Know that my sister's daughter's ship is joined at Truth. It lives in space twice."

Drew looked at Benny. "Do you understand that?"

"I had to ask a couple times myself. It seems her niece's ship is docked at Verity Station right now."

"That's not even in our quadrant."

"Right. She also claims her niece's ship isn't armed but insists it's not a case of mistaken identity. The ship 'lives in space twice.'"

The Camdu captain nodded approvingly throughout Benny's explanation. Drew expressed his privilege at meeting her and his relief that no injuries resulted from the incident. He apologized that Dark Landing couldn't provide more comfortable accommodation outside the dock area. The captain said she understood the limitations of the station and again expressed her gratitude.

Drew broke the translation link and took Benny to one side. "*Muck* will have to sort this out, but I'll let you know what I learn." The Multi-world Coalition for Travel and Trade, "MCTT" or *Muck* as it was more popularly referred to on Earth, had grown from the Planetary Alliance. Run by a fifteen-member board with three representatives from each planet, it was self-funded through fees and functioned autonomously to enact and enforce space traffic and trade regulations. At times, *Muck* security served as an extension of a member planet's police force, with authority to handle matters themselves or to intercede until planetary representatives arrived. Often, they acted without authority, but few challenged them. While everyone agreed they were necessary, most questioned their trustworthiness. And there were rumors about the legality and callousness of some of their methods. Though, Drew had never seen anything of that nature in his dealings with them.

"Thanks. It's a curiosity for sure," Benny said, shaking his head.

Drew agreed. "And they seem to be coming at us in a steady stream."

6 CURTIS WALKER

In no rush to get to the office, Drew decided to stop for a haircut first. Miss Taleen was probably screaming her head off by now. He didn't want to face her without the other two chiefs, and his dayshift commander would be waiting for him with questions he wasn't prepared to answer. Curtis wasn't stupid. He probably suspected a connection between Letty Taleen and Taleen Industries, but he couldn't know of her claim to be their superior.

As expected, Curtis accosted Drew as soon as he entered the office mid-morning. "Chief, there you are. Your meeting ran long this morning. I need to go over a couple things with you."

It's not always about you, Curtis. "Good morning. I assume Mattie passed on my orders for you to take the lead on last night's explosion?"

As Drew walked toward his office, he had to maneuver around a small crate topped with a military-style duffel bag. The pile filled much of the space in the already cramped front office.

"What the hell is this?"

Curtis turned sideways to skirt the crate as he followed Drew. "Dockside dropped them off this morning with a note from Mattie. They belong to Miss Taleen—the lady in holding. She's one thing I need to discuss with you."

"The staff haven't been asking too many questions, have they? This is a sensitive situation, Curtis. Mattie filled you in on that too?"

When Drew entered his office, with Curtis close on his heels, he made a point of glancing nervously back through the hatch before closing it.

"She just said there was a runaway in holding and you were making inquiries. What's up?"

Drew ignored the question. "Has Miss Taleen been causing any problems?"

"No, she's been quiet. I had breakfast sent in earlier. I thought that would be okay. I mean, it's okay to *feed* her, right? Is she *the* Taleen heiress herself?"

"Maybe, or maybe an impostor. That's what I'm trying to figure out. Listen, Curtis, this situation has career-killing potential. I want you and Mattie out of the line of fire as much as possible. Okay?"

"Absolutely! Appreciate it, sir," Curtis said.

Drew detected a hint of sarcasm in Curtis's appreciation. His side of every conversation seemed to include a subtext that Drew found maddeningly elusive. Still, he'd taken the right approach. "Besides," he continued, "I'm much more concerned about the airlock incident. What do you have for me?"

Curtis never sat down in front of Drew unless invited. For some reason that annoyed Drew. Mattie would have just plopped in a chair. Space facilities were once manned primarily by military personnel. Modern facilities still operated within a loose, military-style infrastructure. Left standing, Curtis uncomfortably shifted his weight from one foot to the other. Drew could tell he was piqued by the slight, but he was never in a generous mood when it came to his day commander. *I should work on the relationship, but he's such an asshole.*

With a fleeting glance at the lounger, Curtis started his report. "I've spent the morning going over the records from last night, especially the crew interviews. We're running background verifications now, but so far everything checks. I'm not sure what to make of the explosive ordnance. The medical database provided a comprehensive report, but it sheds no light on a possible motive. Did you know they used nitroglycerine as a heart medication from Earth's nineteenth to twenty-second centuries?"

"No. So what?" Drew was unclear what connection, if any,

that bit of information had to the explosion. There was a booming drug trade in the outer reaches. Harmless, legal substances on one planet could prove a potent drug on the next. It was impossible to keep track of the drug of the moment, let alone control its distribution. Utopia tablets were the rage now. A form of nitroglycerine might be the next wave.

"Well, I don't know if it's important, but I thought it was interesting," Curtis said.

"Yeah, okay, keep on it. There's one more thing I want you to do. Flesh out my report on the Praetorian monks. Especially their personal backgrounds and anything they were involved in over the last couple of years. Make it a priority. I want to bring them in for questioning."

"Because of the robe?"

"Right. It's all we have. That's it for n — wait, I almost forgot. As if we needed something more going on, the Company wants diagnostic audits completed on all exec command stations covering the last twenty-four hours. A coming upgrade, maybe. Get someone from admin to handle it and make sure the data is in my queue by end-of-business today. I'll submit the report myself."

Curtis nodded.

There was no reason the request would raise suspicions. CoachStop made inexplicable requests all the time to keep them on their administrative toes.

"Anything else?" Drew asked.

"What about the Taleen broad's baggage? We can't leave it in the middle of the office."

"Move it into an empty holding cell for the time being." He'd ask Mattie to go through it when she arrived.

"By the way, there's a citizens' group forming about the pigeon," Curtis said. "They're starting a petition and — "

"Okay, that's it; spread the word. I don't want to hear about that pigeon again unless it's someone explaining how it got past the environmental scanners."

"Yes, sir." Curtis executed a neat military turn and left.

Drew cleared his mind of pigeons and Camdulings that could be in two places at once and thought about the Taleen woman. Doc's approach with Letty may not yield the results she envisioned. Doc always came down on the touchy-feely side of most issues; but it wouldn't hurt, and it might put Miss pointy-chin Taleen a little off balance. He needed to buy time until he could gather more intelligence.

He turned his attention back to the explosion. While he trusted Curtis had been thorough, he wanted to read the crew interviews and reports himself. He worked past lunch and into the afternoon but found nothing out of the ordinary.

The environmental technician on the airlock scanners indicated that minute vibrations caused by the scanners could have ignited a substance as unstable as nitro. But the airlock vids also showed an obviously nervous Trammel tripping over his own feet just before he came literally unglued.

The technician defended the scanner's inability to identify any danger before the explosion. A glass container holding the nitroglycerine was suspended in a water pouch filled with an absorbent gel material. The gel resembled the substance used in modern data vials that confused the scanners. Drew tagged the information as something warranting further investigation.

He checked his in-file for anything else and spotted an inventory of the Taleen woman's shoulder pack and findings from the physical search. The list referenced the data vial on his desk that contained Miss Taleen's travel records. As Drew suspected, she was traveling under an alias: Rebecca Richards, twenty-four, five-foot-seven, black hair, brown eyes, student and pleasure traveler, originating from San Francisco, Oregon, Earth.

He still had no way to verify her identity. Though her system access would be enough for most people, Drew wanted confirmation. There was nothing to prove she wasn't Rebecca Richards as the documents declared. Once Mattie's assistant, Kyle, got back the results of her palm print, Drew would know for certain.

The rest of the inventory listed normal travel accessories and hygiene items. The physical search had also turned up nothing remarkable except for a small dagger in a leather sheath on her right calf, less a weapon and more a tool and *Muck*-approved. Otherwise, she had only the clothes she was wearing and a silver chain bracelet.

The pat down and a follow-up scan both failed to find a comm implant of any kind. Drew considered that suspicious for someone of her supposed standing. Everyone had comm implants. Not having one was as rare as finding a Fahdeenian cave worm. Comm implants synced automatically to a person's location, whether that was a ship, a space station or an entire planet.

As Drew was reviewing the information, Curtis submitted an update to Mattie's initial incident report, identifying the four passengers that disembarked the *Temperance* before Trammel. Letty's alias, Rebecca Richards, was one of the four, along with a medical technician returning to Dark Landing from bereavement leave, a replacement astrophysicist for the Space Science Consortium that maintained a base camp on the station, and a mail-order bride for one of the dock workers.

Drew would ask Kyle to run a background check on the new bride. More likely she was an unlicensed professional, skirting *Muck* taxes and cloaking her activities by pretending to marry some poor schmuck in trade for sex once a week. There'd been an uptick in hooker complaints recently. One filed by Landers Keep and another by the mezzanine bar. Though they'd IDed two Johns and a Jane, they'd failed to flush out the ladies in question. No matter how deep into space civilization traveled, it managed to pack a little vice along with the rest of its baggage.

He continued working throughout the afternoon and into early evening, completing routine administrative tasks and updating his logs.

Doc and Fitz arrived at 1845. They conferred on the correct approach to take with Letty. Doc was appointed the kindly and concerned front man; Fitz would act the suspicious skeptic; and Drew would be the cocky, authoritarian observer. Confident in their roles, they made their way back to the holding cells.

7 LETTY'S CELL

Letty sat curled up on the cot in the corner of her cell staring through the bars. She'd been gifted with the best life offered. Though pampered and protected, she remained unspoiled, with the freedom to do as she pleased. For the first time her beauty, brilliance, and access to the resources of the universe weren't enough.

She felt lost and wretched, and missed her dad — her source of reassurance and sound advice. After finding his note tucked in her makeup case, she'd focused on following his instructions to make her way to Dark Landing.

She trusted her adopted father absolutely and believed him if he thought she was in danger. There was no doubt the note came from him. He'd used their safe word, "gypsy." The word was to be used between them only in dire circumstances. She convinced herself he'd be at Dark Landing when she arrived. At the least she thought Chief Cutter expected her and could answer her questions.

For the hundredth time since she'd left Earth, Letty mentally reviewed everything that occurred before her dad went missing. Not that she had much to go over. It all seemed so normal: a business trip to Mars Settlement for subsidiary meetings. Two of Taleen Industries' subsidiaries were applying for additional operating capital.

They ate dinner together the night before he left. Afterward she sat on the edge of his bed chatting about nothing in particular while he packed a small bag for a two-day trip.

He contacted her on the second day saying he was extending the trip—a common occurrence, nothing to cause concern. A week passed and neither she nor his staff could reach him. The company's Mars office said George left Mars after two days as planned. A Taleen security staffer escorted him as far as the company's private spaceport, but the ship's captain said he'd never re-boarded.

Three weeks later, frantic and despairing of ever seeing him again, she'd received an in-file message addressing her as "Sweetheart." It was his personal endearment for her, and no one else called her that. It said only that there was a present for her in her makeup case, one she used when traveling. The unsigned item was without a date stamp or a return address. When she checked her case she found her dad's handwritten instructions:

> Letty,
> Please leave Earth as soon as possible without anyone knowing. Make your way to the Dark Landing space station and Security Chief Andrew Cutter. Chief Cutter will protect you. Stay with him until I contact you. I'll explain in detail later. Trust only Cutter and me. Be safe, my sweet gypsy daughter.
> I love you,
> Dad

She'd found the data vials only two days out from Dark Landing. They were covered with makeup sponges in a side compartment of the case where he'd left his note. She'd stashed them in a hidden pocket of her duffel bag. Surely, they'd discovered the vials by now; though, without her DNA, they couldn't access them.

Somehow, she must get those vials back and locate a processor. The processor unit she'd taken with her, along with a few pieces of jewelry and a sum of K.U. script, disappeared between the time she'd dropped her duffel off for scanning and when it was delivered to her bunk. Her complaint to the *Temperance* purser only resulted in a these-things-happen shrug.

Petty thievery was rampant on cargo ships which operated without the standards or level of security of high-end passenger carriers. The missing processor inconvenienced her, but neither it nor the jewelry held any real value. Either she didn't leave enough script in her luggage as a bribe, or she'd been robbed by a dishonorable thief.

The processors in the public area offered no privacy. People were always waiting their turn. Interstellar travelers kept to their own time zones until they reached their destinations, and the ship's crew worked in around-the-clock shifts. She thought it unwise to access the data vials until she was alone and with time to explore their contents.

A week later, sitting in a holding cell on Dark Landing, she still hadn't accessed the vials. But she'd found Chief Cutter, who acted a slack-jawed idiot around women. Strange, since he wasn't bad looking, she assumed he got his share. *I easily overpowered him,* she thought, smiling. *But maybe that was due more to catching him off guard than to my rusty combat skills.*

None of it mattered. He didn't know her father and knew as little about why he'd sent Letty to Dark Landing as she did. *There must be a mistake. Dad would never entrust me to someone so clueless. But how many Chief Cutters can there be on Dark Landing? Why here anyway?* Light years from home, she saw no hope of finding her dad on her own. At least his note proved he was alive. She would cling to that knowledge for courage while she waited for contact.

The air pressure changed at the telltale whoosh of the hatch opening, followed by the sound of boot steps approaching her cell. *It's about time. For all they know, I hung myself hours ago.*

Cutter and another man and a woman came into view between the bars.

"Hello, Miss Taleen. I see you're okay and being well treated," Cutter said.

"You're kidding me, right? You've thrown me in jail for no reason and left me here to rot. No, I'm not okay and I'm not being *well* treated!" *Did that sound as whiny and desperate to them as it did to me?*

"You've given me more than enough reason to lock you up. But you aren't being charged . . . *yet.* I want to introduce you to my associates. This is Chief Fitzwilliam, head of station administration, and Dr. Jameson, Medical Chief. Together, we run Dark Landing. We'd like to talk to you, if that's okay?" Without waiting for her response, Cutter palmed the door and the three of them crowded into the cell.

"You mean interrogate me. Sure, I've been expecting it. Doctor, are you in charge of the torture bots?" *Childish! I should just shut up already.*

"You don't have to answer any questions, but it would help us understand your situation better if you did," Drew said.

Dr. Jameson perched at the far end of her cot. The other two stood against the cell walls. Cutter leaned back with one foot crossed in front of the other, hands in his pockets. His casual self-assuredness recharged her earlier anger.

"Miss Taleen," Jameson started, "this isn't an interrogation, and we won't be using torture bots . . . *at this time.*" She smiled at her own little joke.

When Letty refused to acknowledge the lame attempt at humor, the doctor adopted a more serious demeanor and continued. "I assure you, we don't have ulterior motives. We want to hear your story and learn how we can help. Drew said you and your father are in trouble?"

"Yes." Letty paused to consider her situation. Her dad's note said to trust only Cutter and himself. Did that trust extend to the people Cutter trusted? She wasn't sure it did, but she saw no other option or a reason to hold back what she knew — which was precious little.

It didn't take long to relate her story. No one interrupted while she spoke. When she finished, the three of them remained silent for several seconds, processing the information.

She used the time to study the chiefs. Dr. Jameson was older than the other two, perhaps in her mid-to-late fifties. A natural blonde, she was graying at the temples. Trim, with straight posture, and wearing a white lab coat, she appeared kind and parental.

Fitzwilliam had yet to say anything to her. He stood there trying, but failing, to look stern and disapproving. He was shorter than Letty, not over five-foot-five or six, late thirty-something, with a rumpled appearance, as if he was wearing someone else's clothes. She wanted to like them both in the same way she'd instinctively *disliked* Cutter. She considered herself a good people-judge, and her first impressions proved correct more often than not.

Dr. Jameson pursed her lips, about to speak, when Cutter

answered his comm patch.

"Yes . . . I see . . . okay. Why don't you join us? We're having a little party in Miss Taleen's cell."

To the group: "It seems Mattie may have more information for us."

They waited expectantly for the few seconds it took for Mattie to join them. The cell was crowded, so she stopped just inside the door frame. Cutter nodded for her to begin.

"We completed a data search on George Speller and ran a comparison of his profile against yours," she said, addressing Drew directly. "We didn't find a link between the two files or any sign that you'd ever met. But we uncovered a three-month-old request from Mr. Speller to review your CoachStop personnel record and your academy psych profile."

Drew's eyes narrowed. To Letty, he seemed unhappy to learn about the search into his background.

Mattie went on, including the rest of the group. "Also, we confirmed George Speller is considered missing by the authorities, though the public doesn't seem to be informed yet. We only found one press reference." She read from a hand-held processor. "'The always illusive head of Taleen Industries is even more absent from the corporate scene than usual.'"

She looked back to Drew, waiting for his sign to continue. He nodded once more.

"A preliminary review of CoachStop Management shareholders and the *Temperance's* ownership didn't turn up interests by Taleen Industries, but we're still looking into that."

Letty waited for Mattie to get to the meat of her report. As interesting as it was, nothing she'd said so far warranted interrupting her boss's meeting.

She delivered the next bit with a curious look in Letty's direction. "The palm print we ran from Chief Cutter's desk scanner came back belonging to Rebecca Ann Richards, *not* Katherine Leticia Taleen."

Letty grimaced as they each turned to her with suspicious looks. "Try running a local search for the file name but include a dash and the words 'true story' at the end," she offered.

Mattie relayed her instructions to Kyle and asked him to respond to their combined comms. Letty squirmed under intense stares as everyone waited for the results. After several seconds, all four sets of staring eyes widened, and postures relaxed all around.

"Well, that's settled then. It appears you're who you claimed," Drew said, looking mildly surprised.

"But it makes the next piece of intelligence interesting." Mattie glanced at each member of her audience to emphasize the importance of what was to come. "Jonas Trammel, the *Temperance* crewman who died in yesterday's airlock explosion, was an employee of Taleen Industries and worked at their corporate headquarters on Earth."

All eyes returned to Letty.

8 INTERROGATION

"I need to speak with Miss Taleen alone. I can fill you all in later, if you don't mind," Cutter said.

Without comment, Dr. Jameson and Chief Fitzwilliam left with Mattie in the lead. Dr. Jameson gave Letty a sympathetic glance over her shoulder as she went.

Cutter hadn't altered his position against her cell wall, feet still crossed, hands still in his pockets, but his countenance darkened. Letty suddenly felt threatened. She disliked the man from the first, but she hadn't been afraid of him until now. If anything, she'd thought he seemed like a harmless buffoon. He'd imprisoned her, but that was understandable after her little display in his office.

The trick with Chief Cutter's desk had been a stupid mistake. She shouldn't let her pig-headed emotions get the better of her. But he'd made her so angry. And she was scared and close to losing it, realizing she'd come all this way to find he knew less than she did. She'd felt an inescapable desire to prove to herself and to Cutter that she was in control.

Letty tried to hold his gaze without blinking, but when he shifted his weight from one foot to the other, she jumped tellingly. She was alone in a cell with a total stranger. Even if he'd looked harmless when they first met, he could still have a cruel streak, and she *had* made him look the fool in front of his men.

After a few more seconds of silence, he stepped away from the wall toward her. She gasped, drawing her legs up and hugging them against her body, pressing herself as tightly as possible into her corner. Despite her apprehension, she couldn't seriously believe he'd physically attack her. Still, she calculated the space between them as well as her options. It was too close to draw on hand-to-hand combat, and she wouldn't catch him off guard a second time. An ineffective groin kick would only incite him.

Without slowing, he reached past her to palm the processor panel above her cot. He issued verbal commands to activate the recorder, then stood back and looked down at her stonily.

"You're a little jumpy, aren't you? Now *this* is an interrogation. You're not required to answer my questions, and you can have a legal advocate present during questioning."

Letty considered it for several seconds and shook her head. "Not now, but I might ask for one later." She saw no reason to bring a third party into the mess she'd made.

"Okay," Drew continued, "let's hear your story again from the top, and this time include Trammel's part in it." His tone was disarming, even menacing.

"I don't know Mr. Trammel. I really don't."

"How can you be so sure?"

"I . . . I can't, I guess, but I don't remember ever meeting anyone by that name."

Cutter tapped his comm patch. "Mattie, send Trammel's image to Miss Taleen's monitor for me."

The wall monitor resolved into an image of a Taleen employee profile, including the picture of a pleasant-looking man in his mid-forties. His title read "Research & Development Engineer II."

She gave Cutter a slight shrug, then shook her head. "I've never seen him before."

She couldn't tell if he believed her or not. "Look," she continued defensively, "Taleen Industries and its subsidiaries have millions of employees. If you include ex-employees, well, this is just a coincidence."

"You don't recognize him from the *Temperance* either?"

"No. But it's possible Dad had someone keeping an eye on me. He might not have told me. He knows how I hate that. We've gone to a lot of trouble so I don't have to have security tagging along everywhere I go. But if he thought I was in danger . . . ."

He studied her for a few moments. "All right. Again, what

brings you here?"

She told her story again and twice more at his prompting. He kept pressing for minor details, trying to catch her in a contradiction. She quickly ran out of patience and decided she would refuse to go through it all a fourth time, when he changed the subject.

"How is it you have system access at Dark Landing?"

She flinched. "I'm not able to discuss that with you. But I'm sorry, I shouldn't have done it, and I promise it won't happen again. *Please* believe me." She was in dangerous territory now.

"Since you apologize so politely, I'll ignore that you have the power to destroy this station and everyone on it."

Letty knew Drew's sarcasm was for effect only. System safeguards wouldn't allow her to destroy the station. She also knew it would be gross negligence on his part to dismiss her system access based on her apology alone.

"You understand I'm responsible for the more than six thousand souls on Dark Landing?" he said.

With a nod, she studied the cell deck to avoid looking at him. To tell the truth would violate Taleen's confidentiality agreement with the Earth Technology Oversight Commission and possibly make public an inconceivable security breach which could endanger Earth, the Alliance, and Taleen Industries. She'd never been so ashamed of herself.

As disappointed as she was in herself for misusing that access, she knew her father would be even more so. Worse, Cutter would soon sort it all out and learn she'd been lying.

When she entered his office yesterday evening, she recognized the desk immediately as one of Taleen Industries' tech pieces. It was the only Taleen-designed product, or any tech product since the end of the twenty-fourth century, that had suffered a security breach. They'd deployed code to check every desk sold for foreign nanoids like those found in the same model unit at Taleen Industries' home office. It was assumed the nanoids were of alien design since none of the company researchers could discern their origin. They had little to show for months of investigation.

Perhaps taking her silence as a refusal to answer his question, Cutter continued. "Letty, you give me no choice. I'm filing preliminary charges against you for unauthorized access to station systems and your suspected connection to the airlock explosion and death of the *Temperance* crewman. In my experience, once Earth authorities review the charges, in situations as grave as these, they'll send a deputation to escort you back to Earth for arraignment and trial. You'll stay in custody here until then. I can keep the press away, which isn't a problem this far out, but that's all I can promise."

The press! Somehow that, the use of her common name, and his softening tone, brought into clearer focus the severity of her situation. Once again, she found herself without options.

"I'll try to explain," she said, nervously glancing at the processor recording her statement, "but only to you."

Cutter issued a cease recording command and disabled his comm.

"It's the desk," she said immediately.

"The desk?"

"The specific model of processor desk in your office. You must have requisitioned it within the last year."

He nodded and shrugged.

"It's designed and sold by a Taleen Industries subsidiary." She sighed. "You're not going to believe this."

"I'm sure I won't but keep talking."

She cast a furtive look around the small cell, trying to compose a plausible last-minute explanation that wouldn't expose the entire truth. She couldn't. She *had* to trust him or accept that her father trusted him. The word *trust* suddenly became alien to her in the way repeating any word over and over seemed always to do.

Resigned, she shook her head and looked at Drew. "About eighteen months ago we discovered something . . . someone . . . breached the security protocols of that model processor desk. Fortunately, it was one of our company units and not a customer's."

He snorted. "Impossible."

Letty went on. "Right, that's what we thought. We located and disabled the offending nanoids, but not knowing who put them there meant it could happen again. And we still don't know their purpose."

All existence depended upon technology. The success or failure of each planet in the K.U., its security, the strength of its economy, and the health and wellbeing of its citizens, as well as the sustainability of the Planetary Alliance, was measured in direct relationship to their combined ability to secure their technology.

Without tech security and the stability it provided, there could be no advancement, no sharing between civilizations, and no peace. While the occasional authorized user might act unethically or with criminal intent, those instances were rare, and modern tech was thought to be airtight against external attacks.

"How could you keep anything of this magnitude a secret? You're right, I don't believe it."

"I've known about it for over a year now, and I still can't believe it. But it's true."

"And that breach allowed you system access through my desk?" he asked.

"Not directly. You can imagine the consequences. We notified the Earth Technology Oversight Commission and, with their authorization, made excuses to examine all the units sold for what we've been calling a 'virus,' in case they were similarly infected. We've been working with the ETOC ever since—without success unfortunately—to discover how it could happen and who could have pulled it off."

Letty rubbed the fatigue from her eyes and continued. "Again, under ETOC authority, we developed a subroutine and pushed it out to each unit as an upgrade. A nanoid search commences each time a user logs in. It runs continuously throughout the session and again at logout. Every action is tracked. Only Dad and I and the ETOC head, Secretary Rostenkowski, know about it, and we're the only three who can recover the data from each unit. Though, even then, we need a warrant." She mumbled the last sentence and reddened.

"Come again; I didn't hear you."

"Yes, you did," she said, louder. The clearance was never meant to be used as the cheap parlor trick she'd pulled on Cutter. She straightened her shoulders and went on. "Of course, the tracker can't be hidden. Anyone could find it, but who would think to look?"

"That part about you being my boss?" Drew asked.

"That ... I might have ... that may have been an exaggeration." Taleen Industries *could* own Dark Landing for all she knew. They had holdings in every corner of the Known Universe.

In the same quiet tone that so alarmed her before, he said, "So, when you were in my office, with, according to you, the future of

Earth and the Planetary Alliance at stake, you were showing off, running a bluff?"

"Pretty much." Though her words sounded flip, she regretted her actions and averted her eyes from his gaze.

In silence, Chief Cutter secured the wall monitor and walked out of her cell. The cell door closed and locked behind him.

As his footsteps continued down the corridor, she whispered, *"You may be in charge of this hick station, but I'm one of the most powerful people in the K.U."* But he couldn't hear her, and that fact failed to comfort her. Just thinking it made her feel mean and petty. For the first time since her father disappeared, she sobbed uncontrollably.

9 GEORGE SPELLER

When Drew returned to his office, he was thankful Doc and Fitz had left. He sat at his desk, head in hands, physically and mentally exhausted from the events of the last twenty-four hours. *Hell,* he thought, *it hasn't even been a full twenty-four hours.*

His comm purred. "Mattie, I need a few minutes to myself right now."

"Sorry, Chief, Doc tapped while you were in with Miss Taleen. She asked you to contact her as soon as you came out. It sounded important. *End all.*"

Give me a break. He tapped his comm — *Dr. Jameson.*

Doc answered immediately. "Drew, we have a problem."

"More of the same or something new?"

"Both. They delivered Trammel's body early this morning. I've scheduled the autopsy for tomorrow. The blast almost decapitated him and mangled his facial features."

"It was in the reports along with some grisly images," Drew replied. "I'm not surprised. He was carrying the nitro on his back, just below the neck."

"Right. But his ship's identification vial survived the explosion, and a little while ago Mattie transmitted Trammel's employment profile from Taleen Industries. The image on the *Temperance* ID and the image on the Taleen employment record don't match. They're two different men."

"Huh?"

"It gets worse. He'd shaved his head on the *Temperance* ID, but I pulled an image of George Speller —"

"*No!*"

"I ran the DNA to confirm. It matches Speller's Earth Citizen Record."

"There's *no* way you could be wrong?"

"I'm afraid not. Listen, Drew, when you tell her . . . I mean, if you need me . . . ." She paused.

Drew was on emotional overload. The security issue Letty described angered and terrified him. It would be cataclysmic if...*when* the public found out. Simultaneously, he was overcome with compassion for what she faced next. There was no time to process either set of feelings. He focused on what needed to be done, pushing his conflicting emotions to the background.

"I can't tell her and then leave her in that shitty cell. I'll take her to the inn. It might be a good idea to send some tranqs over. Also, Doc, submit your preliminary report tonight and complete the autopsy as soon as you can." Then, more to himself, he added, "This whole scenario is freaking insane."

With heavy foreboding, Drew tapped his comm and requested *Landers Keep*. When he'd finished making arrangements, he called in Mattie.

"Have you had a chance to go through Miss Taleen's baggage?"

"Yes, but only a quick search. No inventory yet. There's mostly clothing and shoes. She has a little of everything — casual, business, warm, cool. Also, she packed a few pieces of men's clothing. She must have expected to find her father. And there's three data vials, but they're all user encrypted."

"Pack it up, including the vials, and have it delivered to Landers Keep. I've booked a room for her."

"You're *releasing* her? I thought —"

"I don't know who Jonas Trammel is, or if he even existed, but it was Letty's father, George Speller, who died in the airlock explosion. Doc confirmed it."

"Seriously? Could this get any more bizarre?"

"I don't know how. I'm gonna take her over to the inn now

and break the news."

"Poor kid," Mattie said. "It's hard to lose one family, but two! That's not fair, not even for a twit like her."

Determined to remain focused, Drew went on. "No reason to keep it from Curtis now, so fill him in. Set up an incident database merging everything we have on Miss Taleen's visit and the airlock explosion, *except* her station access. I'm still researching that, and I don't want it on the record yet. It's not clear anymore what crimes have been committed, but it all intersects somehow.

"I'm naming you and Curtis co-leads. Arrange the schedules so everyone, including Doc and Fitz, will have a couple of hours shift overlap in the late afternoons to meet for situation reports. My number one concern is what does any of this have to do with Dark Landing."

After Mattie left, Drew spent several minutes reviewing Curtis's diagnostic reports. There'd been no activity at his station from when he'd left to get something to eat early yesterday evening until after he'd returned to find Letty in his office. There was no mention in the report of finding a tracker either. Letty'd been right. Who would think to look for one? He'd never given it much thought before, but as tech-reliant as the Alliance was, perhaps they'd become too security-complacent over the last half-century of peace and prosperity. He scanned his in-file for new information and, finding nothing critical, reluctantly headed for Letty's cell.

She was sitting where he'd left her an hour earlier: on her cot, pressed into the corner, her knees drawn up and her head down. Her uneaten dinner sat on the pop-up tray at the end of the cot. When she lifted her head, he could tell she'd been crying. Already miserable and afraid, and missing her father, this news would crush her.

"Come with me," he said, opening the cell door.

"Where?"

"I've arranged quarters for you at Landers Keep."

"Why?"

"You should have more comfortable accommodations."

"Why?" She hadn't moved an inch from her spot in the corner.

"Letty, please, come with me. I'll explain when we get there." He could see the apprehension building in her eyes. "Relax. I'm not going to touch you. We're moving you to someplace more comfortable. These cells aren't meant to hold anyone long term."

She seemed persuaded by the last. She untangled her arms and legs, reached under the cot to retrieve her shoulder pack and hat, and stood, a little wobbly at first. Drew didn't move to assist her but let her steady herself against the wall.

Neither of them spoke as they traveled one level down to Landers Keep. Drew sat her in a chair in the small lobby. He kept a watchful eye on her while he confirmed with the desk that the hatch to her room was reprogrammed for Security access and egress only, and the room's processor disabled. This wasn't the first time they'd sequestered someone at the inn until a ship arrived to transport them off Dark Landing. The clerk handed him a small package sent over by Doc.

As they crossed the lobby, a security employee arrived with Letty's baggage. She looked surprised to see it. The man accompanied them to the room, delivered her belongings, and left quietly.

When they were alone, Letty took a defensive stance. She appeared prepared to bolt if he came closer, though she had no place to go. Under different circumstances, Drew might have laughed. But he only wanted to take her in his arms and console her. Why was she so threatened by him? She'd been suspicious since she'd arrived. Not remarkable now that he knew her story.

"Please sit down. There's something I need to tell you."

She sat gingerly on the edge of the chair next to a small desk.

He pulled the only other chair from the side of the room and set it a few feet in front of her. "What I have to say is very difficult. It's about your father."

She sprang to her feet. "You found him?"

"Yes, but it's not good news. Please sit."

She remained standing, arms held rigid at her sides, hands balled into fists.

Realizing she wasn't going to sit back down unless he forced her, Drew reluctantly continued. "The man in the airlock explosion . . . it wasn't Jonas Trammel, Letty . . . it was your father."

For a few moments she stared at him as if she hadn't understood his words, and then she charged. "You lying bastard! I don't believe you," she screamed.

Drew grabbed her arms when she came at him, pushing her

back and awkwardly standing up.

"Let me go. It's not true. Why are you lying?"

He held her arms tightly, afraid to let go. When she kicked his shin, he pulled her roughly against him, pinning her arms between their two bodies, wrapping his own arms around her while she squirmed frantically and stamped at his feet. He held her that way for several seconds as she struggled. Suddenly her body went limp against his. He continued to hold her, afraid to release her in case it was a ploy.

She spoke haltingly, sobbing, gasping for air, her forehead pressed against his shoulder. "I ... d-don't believe you. You're lying. I w-want to see him."

"No, Letty, you don't."

"Y-yes, I d-do. It's not true. There's been a mistake."

He relaxed his hold enough to see her face. "Doc checked the DNA of the man in the airlock." He avoided the word *body*. "It matched your father's Earth Citizen Record. There's no mistake."

He backed her toward the bed. It sat in an alcove, away from the small lounge area. "I'm going to let go now, okay? Can I trust you?"

"Y-yes."

He gently maneuvered her against the edge of the bed and down until she was sitting, then sat next to her. He kept one arm wrapped securely around her waist.

"If I can see him for myself to be sure," she begged.

"I won't stop you if you insist, but I don't think it's a good idea. It was an explosion, Letty, his head and face . . . there was a lot of damage."

Her crying turned into a low mewling, the most heartbreaking sound he'd ever heard. More than anything he wanted to fix it for her and make everything all right, but he couldn't.

They sat like that for several minutes. Sure she wouldn't become physical again, he left her side and poured a glass of water from a pouch on the desk. He took a small phial from the package Doc had sent over and emptied its contents into the glass. The water turned lavender to indicate it'd been altered. He offered her the glass and she drank it submissively. Her eyes were so swollen he doubted she could see what she was drinking or cared.

He spoke in a calming tone. "Lie back on the bed. I've given you a mild sedative. It'll relax you. I'll stay here for a while and check back in the morning. Doc will stop by sometime tomorrow to answer any questions."

With no struggle left in her, she lay back on the bed as he'd asked and pulled her legs into a fetal position, crying quietly. Within ten minutes she was asleep.

Whatever Doc sent over was more than a mild sedative, thought Drew.

He tapped his comm. "Mattie, would you send someone down to stay until morning?"

"Of course," Mattie said.

He was grateful she hadn't asked how Letty had taken the news. "Thanks."

He pulled a light blanket over Letty and moved his chair next to the bed. He sat, his eyes never leaving her until the relief staff arrived.

10 MORNING AFTER

When Drew entered Letty's room the next morning, a different woman was standing in front of a mirror putting the final touches on her hair and makeup. Dressed in a tailored gray jacket over darker slacks that draped loosely from a wide leather band at her waist, she appeared every bit the professional superstar one would have expected of the head of Taleen Industries. Her jewelry comprised of a silver chain around one slender wrist.

She turned from the mirror to face him. The only remaining evidence of last night's tragic news was a deep sadness in her eyes and a lingering puffiness to her eyelids that makeup failed to hide. She stood straight, looking at him with authority and a sense of purpose. All traces of the silly little girl he'd met earlier were gone.

"Did you make arrangements for Dr. Jameson to meet with me?" she asked without a customary greeting, as if Drew were her personal assistant and not her jailer.

"She said she'd be by after she completes the aut—other business."

"My father's autopsy?" she asked in a strong, sure voice.

"Yes."

"Good. She'll be able to answer my questions. Did she say when I can expect her?"

"She'll come when she's available," Drew spoke sternly, trying to gain control of the conversation. Then softer, "How are you feeling?"

"How do you expect?"

Well, not this, he thought, but he didn't answer her. "You look as if you were going out."

"It's the first opportunity I've had to shower and change since I arrived," she said matter-of-factly.

"I see. Have you had breakfast?"

"No, I'm not hungry."

"Maybe not, but you should eat something — even just fruit and toast. I have additional questions, and it might be more comfortable for us both over breakfast. We can eat in the inn's café if you want."

"If that's what *you* want."

"Well, I thought . . . since you're dressed and everything. You'll be spending a lot of time in this room and maybe . . . if you'd like. . . ." His control was short-lived. He felt like he was asking her out on a date instead of an interrogation. *Why on Earth does she affect me like this? I've never been timid around beautiful women before.* Remembering their circumstances, he winced inwardly from embarrassment at his inappropriate musing.

"Fine," she said, without emotion.

Drew opened the hatch. They moved into the corridor and boarded the conveyer for the lobby.

"About that — spending a lot of time in the room — is it possible for me to have a processor? I'll remove my access from your desk. I need to be physically at the unit to pull the user data anyway, and I'm restricted from entering system commands or searching for unrelated information.

"So *you* say--maybe, maybe not. I'd have to confirm that with our tech engineers first, and I'm pretty sure you don't want me to do that. We could feed entertainment vids to your room if that would help."

"No, that *won't* help. You said I could contact my legal advocate, and I need to talk to my office."

They'd entered the café from the inn lobby and Drew steered her toward an empty table next to an invisiwall with a view of a busy main corridor.

"By the way," she continued when they'd sat down, "what exactly are the charges against me? You can't still believe I was involved in the explosion that killed my father." Her jawline clenched, but otherwise she appeared emotionless.

"Final charges are up to the Earth prosecutors once they review the case. There might be MCTT charges as well, if they suspect you knew your dad was transporting a dangerous substance," he said. "Personally, I don't think you're responsible for the explosion, no. But I think Speller sending you here, you both traveling on the same ship, his death, and maybe the security issue you described are connected."

"It's all connected. Just how, I don't know. But I intend to find out," she said, chin lifted in determination.

"Then, that's something we have in common."

They placed their orders through the document screens set into the table in front of each seat. After ordering, Drew picked up the conversation again. "I'm required to remind you, you don't have to answer my questions. You can wait until you talk to your legal office if you want." She shook her head resignedly, and he went on. "It's hard for me to understand how you and your father could travel on the same ship for a month without running into each other. Can you explain that?"

"No, except he wasn't a regular passenger. I stayed close to the passenger quarters. They're on the same level with the mess and common areas. I had no reason to go exploring. The *Temperance* is a cargo freighter, not a luxury liner. Look, I learned early on that ships' crews can be rough, and I avoid interaction as much as possible."

"How could he know you'd be traveling on that particular ship unless someone told him?"

"I'm not sure he did. It might have been a coincidence. I waited several days to catch a ship heading this far out, and only my senior assistant knew about it. He wouldn't mention it to anyone."

"You realize how far-fetched this sounds."

"I know it does. But if Dad knew I was on the ship he would've contacted me. Or . . . maybe he knew but avoided me for my own protection. Without more information, I think he meant to *meet* me on Dark Landing, not *escort* me here."

Her theories relied too heavily on coincidence and speculation for Drew's taste.

"Was your dad a religious man?" he asked.

"No, of course not. That's an odd question. Why would you ask that?"

"Just curious—it's not important." Drew changed the subject. "The explosive was nitroglycerine. Nitro is an Earth compound that no one's used for at least a couple centuries. Do you have any idea where your father might have gotten it or why he had it?"

"No. I've never heard of it." She looked genuinely baffled.

"Okay." He decided to let that one go for this session. "How does someone of your prominence hop a transport and leave Earth without people noticing? If your assistant never explained your absence, wouldn't the authorities, or at least your security staff, be looking for *you* as well as for your dad?"

"I come and go as I please, and no one questions me, though I always keep in touch with Dad and my assistant. I don't travel with security because it's safer to remain anonymous. There are exactly ten people on Earth who know me as Letty Taleen—and now more than that number on Dark Landing do as well. I broke the rule here because . . . because . . . ." Her voice wavered. "I was more focused on finding Dad than keeping up a disguise . . . even though he warned me. That's not important anymore. Without him, I'll have to be the visible head of the company."

She stared over his shoulder, distractedly watching the foot traffic in the corridor. "Dad and I share . . . shared . . . control of Taleen Industries. Dad was the public face—CEO and board chairman. He attended meetings, gave press interviews, and dealt with regulatory authorities. When my parents died, he kept me sheltered from public contact from early childhood throughout college and boot camp—"

"Boot camp?"

Her gaze returned to him. "Well, you said it yourself when we first met . . ." She blushed, perhaps remembering her childish behavior then. "Taleen Industries has a security force larger, better trained, and better equipped than any army in the Known Universe. They're structured along military lines. After college, I did a year of training, including self-defense and combat skills.

"Everything till now: school, boot, personal life, I did under an alias. I pretty much live my life in the open, the same as anyone else, with no more concern for my safety than the average citizen. For the last two years I've posed as Dad's research assistant and more recently, department head. Those who know my true identity — a few of my close friends from grade school and my two Taleen assistants — are also trained security staff. They'd die before they'd expose me."

A polite attendant delivered their orders. They assured him they had everything they needed, and Letty continued. "Anyway, it was easier to keep me out of the public eye than you'd think. I attended Taleen-owned schools, including our universities. My education was accelerated, and I had a private tutor while I traveled. Dad thought I needed to experience the scale of the company firsthand — and to get a feel for each of the Alliance planets and their cultures.

"I guess there was a lot of curiosity right after my parents' accident, but Dad held everyone at arm's length and eventually people lost interest — or gave up." She paused and took a bite of fruit. "Every once in a while, someone will make inquiries or want to meet me, but they're given the runaround until they go away. Once Dad had to prove I was still alive. We thought that was funny at the time. Sometimes I'm ordered to appear in person at a hearing or some legal inquiry, but we ignore those requests or procrastinate. I'm not ashamed to admit people are occasionally paid off."

Drew must have looked unconvinced.

"You need to understand how large a company Taleen Industries is," she continued. "It's difficult to even estimate the company's net worth to within a googolplex of accuracy. I tried once to calculate how long it would take to dispense with it — to divest of every interest I hold in the company. I guessed it would take twenty years just to prepare the paperwork. Well, short of offing myself." She took another bite of fruit, watching Drew's reaction as he struggled with the enormity of her statement. "Believe me, there are times — fleeting maybe — when I'd let it all go."

"So, the two of you basically own the K.U.?"

She smiled. "Just me. Dad's an employee."

With the knowledge of George Speller's death so fresh, they both struggled with tense as they spoke of him, mixing past and present.

"I'm sorry, but I don't understand how two people can run a

business that gargantuan," Drew said.

"But that's the secret to our success." She lowered her voice conspiratorially. "We can't. We don't even try. There's no such thing as a perpetual motion machine, but Taleen Industries comes close. Dad has more executive responsibilities, but we tend to focus on tech development projects, and both of us oversee our security force. Everything else is held by subsidiaries with their own boards and CEOs."

"Why's maintaining such a large fighting force so important?" Drew asked, as concerned as he was curious.

"It's not our intent to use it as an army, an offensive weapon, though I'll admit it has that potential. It's our means of collecting information, networking really. At the same time, we serve the K.U. We freely offer the Taleen Security Force to all of the aligned planets in times of crises. They step in to put out fires literally and figuratively in response to any disaster, natural or otherwise."

As she talked, it became obvious to Drew that this was a practiced speech. She'd probably given it a hundred times.

"TSF personnel include medical professionals, engineers, technicians, and trades experts in every field and specialty. Their humanitarian efforts are legendary. And in return, they are our source of trans-Alliance information unavailable to any other entity, government or civilian. Our knowledge base is massive." Her eyes shone with pride.

"We nose around a bit—read reports, analyze statistics, and Dad attends meetings. But day-to-day control is superficial. We don't have any, really. Occasionally we'll dissolve a subsidiary or divest of a financial interest. Enough to keep people looking over their shoulders, we hope. Though I doubt it lasts long."

Drew shook his head. It sounded like Taleen Industries had been surreptitiously manipulating the Known Universe for years under guises of philanthropy and compassion. That kind of power was never a good thing.

"So, to everyone back on Earth, other than a handful of close associates, you're Rebecca Richards?"

"Yes, for the most part. I use other aliases occasionally. But I used one for this trip that my dad would recognize."

"And Jonas Trammel, is that an alias?"

"I'm sure it is. We both have a bank of identities with well-developed backgrounds to draw from. We wait to switch out the head shots, DNA, and palm prints until the last minute to keep some clerk from stumbling across multiple files with the same identifiers. I'm surprised Dad didn't make the switch. Maybe he ran out of time or wanted to avoid accessing the system."

More speculation, Drew thought. He couldn't fault her for trying to make sense of it all.

When they returned to her room, he promised to look into giving her access to a processor and told her he'd compile formal allegations by the next morning. He didn't say so, but he wanted to wait until after the command staff met that afternoon.

Drew contacted Doc and assured Letty she'd be by to talk with her shortly.

As he turned to leave, she put a hand on his arm to stop him. "I . . . I want to thank you for the way . . . for last night. You were very kind."

"I'm sorry about your father, Letty, I really am. I promise to do everything I can to find out what's behind all this."

He left then, his arm warm where she'd touched him.

11 INVESTIGATION

At the top of the meeting, after Drew made sure everyone had reviewed all the reports filed so far, Doc summarized George Speller's autopsy results.

"I'll keep it short. Speller was a human male, early sixties, and in reasonably good health. His injuries and cause of death were consistent with the explosion specifics provided by environmental. Only two items of note, probably unrelated: He was missing one kidney, and he didn't have a comm implant."

"How could he be missing a kidney? Aren't kidneys replaced before they go bad? I mean, is there any reason someone wouldn't have one replaced?" Drew asked.

"New kidneys are easily cultivated in a lab. There are a few situations when a surgeon might postpone the transplant surgery, but none apply here. Mr. Speller's kidney was surgically removed with a precision I've never seen before, by human or robot. Normal healing takes six to eight months, maybe a little longer, and Speller was completely healed. He had no visible scar even under a microscope. I might have thought he was born with one kidney, except the renal artery and veins are all present and ligated."

Doc shifted in her chair. "I asked Miss Taleen about it this morning, but she was unaware of his condition. Once all the interested parties are notified, I'll request his medical history. There may be something that explains the irregularity, but for the life of me, I can't imagine what."

Doc seemed unusually agitated. Drew made a note to speak with her alone after the meeting. "Moving on. Miss Taleen doesn't have a comm implant either. Curtis, start a list of areas for investigation. Why neither of them is implanted should be easy to answer.

"I have a question," Mattie said.

Drew nodded.

"Do we care that no one but us and the Taleen broad even know we found Speller? Shouldn't we send an announcement to Earth officials and Taleen Industries so they can stop their search? And are we charging Taleen with anything or just keeping her locked up in the local inn like Rapunzel for the heck of it?"

Mattie had always been outspoken, but she was displaying more attitude than usual. He didn't appreciate it in this setting. He addressed her questions nonetheless with a monotone calmness that he knew everyone would recognize as his *I'm-in-no-mood-for-this-crap* voice.

"I wanted to wait until after this meeting to bring charges, if there are any. I'm not sure she committed a crime other than traveling under false documents. Do any of you really think she had something to do with Speller's death? I don't. As for unlawful access to station systems — well, she's given me a plausible explanation for that, but I still need to confirm her story."

Out of the corner of his eye, Drew saw Curtis's head snap to attention. He alone was unaware of Letty's breach. Drew figured it would come out. He might as well be the one to introduce it.

"When we're done here and everyone's signed off, and when I've decided to bring charges or not, I'll send reports to Earth and CoachStop. Then Miss Taleen can inform her office of her father's death. Any objections?"

"I'd like to know her explanation for having access to station systems," Doc said dryly.

Drew picked up on the challenge in her tone. He hoped the others had missed it. The three chiefs never challenged each other in front of staff. Differences of opinion occasionally surfaced, but they aired them privately. Again, Drew sensed Doc's uncharacteristic agitation.

He disliked the direction the meeting was taking. Everyone

seemed touchier than usual. On the other hand, his command staff were pretty straight arrows. He was asking a lot of them to disregard proper channels and keep all that'd happened under wraps for much longer.

He had a reputation, and some of his off-hand comments may have led them to believe he had feelings for Letty. They were right to question any prejudice that might influence the investigation, especially an investigation of this magnitude. However, even to people he trusted with his life, which he could say with certainty about everyone in the room, he couldn't reveal the information Letty had shared with him about the security breach. Somehow, he needed to confirm her story. But how to do that and still keep the details confidential was a problem.

"Look, I get what some of you are thinking. Maybe I made some offhand comments, but my feelings for Miss Taleen are nothing more than a natural *affinity* toward a beautiful woman and sympathy for the spot she's in." He paused. As soon as he spoke the words, he realized he was trying to delude himself. In the short time since meeting her, his attraction to Letty had progressed beyond physical desire. He took a quick breath and continued. "I need you to trust me. I can't tell you why she has system access. I promise you my judgment hasn't been compromised. *And*," he added, looking pointedly at Mattie, "she's still detained because she admitted lying about being our boss. I believe her story, but I won't risk putting the lives of everyone on Dark Landing in jeopardy by allowing her to wander freely about the station. I'm asking for you guys' support for a few hours longer." He looked at each of them in turn.

Curtis spoke first, though, as usual, his phrasing was suspect. "Chief, I figure you have a good reason to withhold information. I trust you."

"Thanks, Curtis. If anyone feels different, speak up. I won't hold it against you. I expect to hear whatever's on your minds if it's in the best interest of the station." Heads nodded assent all around, and Fitz gave Drew an endearing thumbs up.

"Good. Let's keep going." His comm purred before they started. "Cutter here—what is it, Hernandez?"

"I'm on the Taleen detail, Chief. She says it's urgent she speaks to you."

Considering the discussion they'd just had, Drew wanted

everyone to hear what Letty had to say. If she meant it for his ears only, she'd need to sit on it until later. "Okay. Tell her I'm sharing the tap at our end, and you do the same." He paused for a second while Hernandez opened his end of their conversation.

"Miss Taleen, I'm currently meeting with my command staff and this conversation's being recorded."

"Thanks, Alberto," Letty said to Hernandez. It appeared she was on a first name basis with her guard. Drew needed to conduct remedial training with his staff on becoming too familiar with suspects. *Do as I say, not as I do . . . or want to do.*

Letty continued. "Chief Cutter, Dr. Jameson told me you were meeting to discuss everything that's happened over the last two days. I'd like to be there. I'll submit to any questions that might speed up your investigation. Plus, I want to know what you're charging me with."

"We were just discussing that. I'll file charges in the morning if there are any. Maybe you should wait until then to speak to us if you still want to."

"No, I want to know what's going on as much as you do. Even if you don't believe me, I've done nothing wrong . . . illegal . . . well . . . anyway, I behaved badly, and I apologize for that."

"I'll discuss your request with the others and get back to you," Drew said. He didn't think they could conduct the investigation effectively without her help, and he'd planned on suggesting her participation himself. This was better; the idea wasn't coming directly from him. Surely the others would agree that she could provide valuable information and save them a lot of time.

"Hernandez, I'm closing this tap." A slight initial increase in volume indicated that Hernandez had done the same at his end. "You understand, when you're guarding Miss Taleen, you should do it from the *exterior* of her quarters?" Drew asked.

"Yes, of course, sir. But she—"

"*End all*," Drew said, cutting Hernandez off.

Doc spoke first. "She's got a point, Drew. I have a lot of questions for her."

Fitz nodded his usual agreement to any suggestion made by the other two.

Drew tried to look contemplative. "Okay, I agree with Doc. First, let's finish building our investigation. We have questions that fall into each of your areas of expertise."

They worked another forty-five minutes then took a break.

When they returned, Drew tapped Hernandez. "Chief?" he answered immediately.

"Bring her up," Drew said.

More than twenty minutes passed while they discussed different approaches — and they were still waiting for Letty. Drew was pissed. He pictured her changing clothes or messing with her hair. This had been her idea, even if he did agree with it, and her disrespect was maddening. Finally, he ran out of patience.

He tapped Hernandez again but got no response. Drew's annoyance turned to alarm. "Mattie, have two men meet me at the Inn, and check if Hernandez' comm is enabled. Keep trying to reach him. Everyone stay here."

~ ~ ∞ ~ ~

An hour passed before Hernandez came for her. Letty was relieved Drew had agreed to let her join their meeting. She wanted to learn the direction the investigation was taking and any details he may not have disclosed earlier. Though she doubted there was much she could contribute. Surely Drew understood there must be no mention of the Taleen Industries security issue.

With a quick check of her hair and sparse makeup, she stepped across the hatch rim and breathed deep, relieved to be out of her room. How could they leave her sitting by herself for hours at a time? All she did was pace and think about never seeing her dad again, never sharing the serious or silly episodes of her life with him, never hearing another of his dumb jokes, never getting another hug . . . . She forced back the tears. *If I don't stop this, I'll go crazy.*

The air in the passage seemed fresher, more invigorating than the stale air of her room. From the inn lobby, they entered the main corridor. It was an hour to dinner break and several hours before a shift change, so pedestrian traffic was light, but still noisy. Conversations and laughter echoed the length of the hallway.

~ ~ ∞ ~ ~

When the woman and her guard exited Landers Keep, he fell in close behind. He needed to pass them unnoticed. This was his first opportunity since he'd waited for her outside security HQ. But he didn't like it, it was stupid risky. There were too many people around. The money was good, yeah, but for the rest of it—what a bunch of bullshit. Now that he knew she was Katherine Taleen, the famous heiress—famous *rich* heiress—that might pay better than killing her. It was *his* ass on the line for a lame, *ad lib* plan. If he got caught, and the boss seriously thought he would keep his mouth shut for the promise of a reward he would never see, the fool had a surprise coming.

~ ~ ∞ ~ ~

Letty slowed her pace to prolong their walk. She raised her voice above the din hoping to engage Alberto in conversation. "So, Alberto, you're originally from Earth?"

"No, I was born and raised on Mars. I've never been to Earth. Funny thing is, I was on my way there with a transfer from Dark Landing when I learned that CoachStop was having a job fair. I extended my stay on the chance an interview might turn into something. As you can see, I'm still here. I've been saving my vacation time. Pretty soon I'll have three months. From what I've heard, there's a lot of Earth to see."

Letty nodded. "Good for you. Do you think it's strange that we don't know where we are? I mean a wormhole just goes somewhere and, as long as our probes find a way back, we follow it. We have no idea how many light years we are from Earth or any other developed planet. But after a string of hops, we'll be back, or at least close to where we want to be."

Hernandez seemed to enjoy the conversation, and as eager as Letty to extend their walk. He slowed the pace even further. "You know what's really strange? Wherever we are right now—and they think it's mega-distance from our home galaxy—I'm closer to Earth here, travel-wise, than I was on Mars."

"It's all so incomprehensible," Letty said. "Incomprehensible but still commonplace—how does that work? Thinking about it is exhausting. Do you miss Mars?"

"Truthfully, no. My dad's an impassioned separatist. Talk about exhausting, his rhetoric could put you into a coma, and he never stops."

"Really? Mars separatists are a rare breed these days. I don't understand their arguments."

"You're not alone. As a teenager I thought Dad was crazy. His constant campaigning embarrassed me. But I've come to realize he's a futurist. He believes if the seeds are planted now, in a hundred years or so, when . . . if . . . the terraforming is successful and Mars becomes self-sustaining, the movement will have had time to take root. They want to smooth the path to independence for later generations. But I still can't take it twenty-four-seven. And it's not like it's ever going to really happen."

"Hmm, I—" Letty was jostled by someone passing on her left. She instinctively moved to one side, bumping shoulders with Alberto as she continued their conversation. "I'll have to reconsider my position. Of course, that assumes one-hundred percent success with the terraforming projects, which seems unl—" She was looking at Alberto when he abruptly jerked to his right into a dimly lit side corridor. Letty followed him, perplexed by the sudden detour.

"*Alberto?*" He seemed to have lost his balance; he was falling backward. She took several steps into the corridor after him before realizing someone stood behind him, trying to prop him up—no, not propping him up—dragging him. Hernandez' eyes filled with confusion and fear. He pulled at the arm around his neck. Letty lurched forward to help him. She was inches from him when there was a quick movement and the flash of light on metal. The unintelligible clamor from the outer corridor dulled to a subdued roar as the scene in front of her shifted into slow motion. Warm liquid sprayed her face and down her front. It filled her eyes and mouth.

~ ~ ∞ ~ ~

Drew waited less than a minute for the conveyer. He shoved roughly through a boisterous group of people entering as he exited. The inn lay less than fifty meters down the main corridor from the conveyer. The only passage intersecting it was a twenty-foot length hallway, which led to a maintenance tube hatch. As Drew passed the opening, an almost imperceptible sound caused him to stop and look in. For the second time in forty-eight hours, he drew his blaster and pointed it at Letty Taleen.

12 SMOKING KNIFE

Hernandez lay on his back at the end of the passageway, his head bent to one side at an unnatural angle. He was beyond help. The wound to his throat gaped raggedly from one ear to the other. Drew recoiled at the sharp, metallic smell of blood. It was everywhere; much of it covered Letty, who stood frozen over his body. She stared down at Hernandez in apparent bewilderment.

In her right hand she held a security-issued combat knife with a ten-inch serrated blade. Drew thought it must have belonged to Hernandez, but why would he carry it on guard detail?

With his blaster pointed directly at her, he shouted an order, emphasizing each word carefully. "Put . . . the . . . knife . . . down!"

She stood motionless, still staring at Hernandez.

Extreme, stress-evoking situations often impaired the senses, particularly hearing. He ordered her again, this time using her name. "Letty . . . I said . . . put . . . the knife . . . down!"

She turned toward him in slow motion with a blank stare and then looked back at Hernandez — the knife still clutched in her hand. At least he'd gotten a response, though he wasn't sure she'd consciously heard him. He called to her a third time. "Letty . . . Letty, look at me."

When she turned toward him again, he saw a flicker of recognition.

"Letty, listen to me," he said softly, as if speaking to a child.

"Put the knife down, please."

She raised her arm and looked at the knife, seemingly confused at how it got there or even what it was. Then, with a jerk of awakening, she cried out, dropping the weapon. She looked back at Drew in horror and ran the few feet between them and into his arms. She either didn't see or chose to ignore his blaster. As he held her, the thought came fleetingly that, had it been anyone else running at him under the same circumstances, with or without the knife, he might have fired.

Two of his men stood directly behind him. He'd registered their arrival as he was trying to get Letty's attention. He glanced back, realizing they hadn't fired at her only because he was blocking the narrow passage entrance.

He wanted to shield her from hurt, but for the second time, he was helpless to protect her. For a few brief seconds, he closed his eyes and surrendered to emotions from upheaval and apprehension to a burgeoning allegiance to this woman.

With no other viable choice, he gave her over to his men who restrained her wrists behind her back. She looked at him pleadingly, but he couldn't afford to show compassion. He kept his voice steady and avoided returning her look while he instructed the men. "Take her back to her cell at headquarters. Have someone stay with her until I get there."

"Yes, sir," the two men answered in unison. They turned with Letty between them and headed for the conveyer.

One of them must have already tapped headquarters because others were arriving now, including Mattie and Curtis, with Doc and Fitz trailing them. Out of habit, Doc knelt next to Hernandez to check his pulse. She was wasting her time.

Other security staff closed off the corridor to keep gawkers at a distance and preserve evidence.

Fitz stood at the entrance to the passageway wringing his hands. Abstractly, Drew wondered if Fitz's distress stemmed more from an uncontrollable need to tidy up the station than from the horror that lay in front of him.

Both Mattie and Curtis seemed to recognize that Drew — usually assured and in command — was acting uncharacteristically preoccupied. They took charge of the scene in a rare display of teamwork. After issuing only a terse and unnecessary command in

Mattie's and Curtis's direction to search the maintenance tube, Drew announced he was returning to HQ to question Letty. He ignored the glances of shared concern that passed between his command staff.

He went straight to his office, fighting his desire to go to Letty first. Every foot of common area was monitored around the clock. He wanted to look at the vids from the main corridor and maintenance passageway. With the station blueprint opened on his desktop, he overlay it with a second plan showing surveillance lens positions and their asset numbers. There were two lenses with overlapping views of the main corridor and another that was aimed directly into the maintenance passageway between them.

From those three views he would be able to see exactly what happened, leaving no room for doubt. He hesitated for only a moment, staring at the vid request form, then entered the information. Letty hadn't killed Hernandez—of that, he was sure. Even with her combat training, she couldn't overpower him, take his knife, and slit his throat. More importantly, she *wouldn't* have. He submitted the form with a verbal command and waited as a new and disturbing thought nagged at him.

Drew reviewed the vids twice. He selected three frames and attached them to general orders for a station-wide search, despite having little hope for positive results. Too much time had passed, and without facial ID, the search would be based solely on a description of the man's clothing. The killer would be all kinds of stupid if he hadn't at least ditched the jacket he'd been wearing. Waste chutes scattered throughout the station emptied into a chemical vat that disintegrated everything but metals.

In the detention area, he was relieved to find a female staffer, Teresa Zamora, standing guard at Letty's cell. Letty was sitting on the cot, facing forward, legs together, feet flat on the floor. She stared at her hands resting in her lap, without acknowledging his arrival.

She wore the same gray jacket and slacks she'd had on that morning, but now the front of both were stained with Hernandez' blood, already dried to an ugly brownish red.

Drew spoke quietly to Zamora, though he didn't think it made a difference to Letty. She seemed oblivious to anything going on around her. "Take her to the showers and find something in the lockers for her to wear. Put her clothes in an evidence bag. When you're done, bring her to my office."

He turned to Letty and unlocked her cell door. "This is Teresa, she's going to take you to clean up and find a change of clothes. We have vids of everything that happened, Letty. It's all right — don't worry. I know you didn't do it. We'll talk after you've cleaned up, okay?"

Letty looked up at him then, her face distorted. "It was horrible. It happened so f-fast. I didn't even know — "

"I saw it all. Go with Teresa now. We'll talk when you come back. Everything will be okay, I promise."

"How can it be okay? Dad's dead. I'll never see him again. I can't do this alone. I don't know what's happening."

"You're not alone. I'm here, and we'll figure it out together."

Letty stood. Teresa took her arm gently and escorted her out of the cell and down the hallway.

When Drew returned to his office, he viewed the vids once more, isolating and enhancing several frames, looking for anything that identified the killer.

The man wore dark pants and a hooded jacket that obscured his facial features. The deep hood reminded Drew of those worn by the Praetorians, only it was attached to a short, dark blue jacket, not a robe.

Hernandez and Letty came into view from the direction of the inn, at an easy stroll. They were chatting as if they'd known each other for years. The man in the hood came up behind them and hurried past. He reached the side passage about twenty feet in front of them and turned in, flattening himself against the wall just inside the opening. To Drew, it looked as if he was holding something — certainly the knife — by his side, away from the lens.

Hernandez and Letty had shifted to one side as the man passed them but otherwise continued chatting. Drew was enraged by Hernandez's incompetence. That he was distracted and enchanted by Letty was obvious. He was supposed to be protecting her . . . guarding her. Either way, he'd failed in his duty and paid the ultimate price, nearly getting Letty killed as well.

Whether the man's objective was to kill Letty, which Drew was certain was the case, or to free her, it would have worked if not for a group of seven people who came down the corridor less than a minute later. They were coming from a celebration. Several held opened packages with remnants of brightly colored paper and loose hanging ribbons.

As Hernandez and Letty drew even with the passage entrance, the man grabbed Hernandez from behind and dragged him several feet into the passage. He sliced Hernandez' throat from one ear to the other with practiced expertise. Blood sprayed from the wound. Hernandez had no time to understand what was happening before it was done.

As if on autopilot, Letty had followed Hernandez into the passage. Seconds passed on the vid before she appeared to understand and react. Instead of turning and fleeing, she threw herself at Hernandez in what could only have been an attempt to pull him away from the attacker. The man continued to drag the now-dead Hernandez deeper into the passage with Letty tugging at the body.

At the maintenance hatch, the man dropped Hernandez and grabbed for Letty. He brandished the knife in a gloved hand. Clearly, he intended to use it on her. Letty, evidently realizing his intent, took several steps backward beyond his grasp. Suddenly the man froze, looking past her into the main corridor. No part of his face was visible from the depth of the hood.

The group of partiers passed in front of the lens, blocking the view into the passage. They talked and laughed with animated gestures. They must have made quite a bit of noise. If any sound came from the passageway, they hadn't heard it. Focused only on each other, not one of them looked into the opening.

In the next clear view, Letty stood alone over Hernandez' body, but now she held the knife. The killer was nowhere in sight. The only exit was through the maintenance tube hatch. A minute later, Drew entered the frame, paused at the passage entrance, and drew his blaster.

He sent copies of the vid triptych to each of the command staff. Though relieved at Letty's obvious innocence, he was nonetheless deeply troubled. How did the killer know Letty would be coming down that passageway at that moment?

13 SUSPENDED

Drew tapped for Mattie. "You about done down there?"

"We're finishing up now. Doc's accompanying Hernandez to med-lab, and Fitz and Curtis are back-tracking Hernandez' and Miss Taleen's movements, interviewing anyone they might have seen on the way. We're dotting all the i's."

"I'm counting on it, Mattie. I need you and Curtis back in HQ as soon as possible. We have a killer loose."

"From the images you attached to the search order there's not much to go on," Mattie said.

"No, but it's possible someone saw something. A group of people came down the corridor just after Letty and Hernandez. We need to identify them for questioning. I want Curtis to coordinate the search teams while you help me file reports with Earth authorities and CoachStop."

"On my way. Jones is here; I'll have him deal with the final touches."

"You thoroughly searched the maintenance tube?" Drew knew she had but couldn't stop from asking.

"Just a preliminary search. The forensics team is going back over it with glasses and a sweeper now. I don't think there's much to find. I also have three, two-man teams tracking all exits out of the maintenance tube from this point. Drew, you know as well as I do, maintenance hatches require a code and palm print for entry. You don't think it's possible our killer's an employee?" Concern was evident in her voice and from the use of his given name. Her suspicions headed in the same direction as Drew's, but she hadn't thought it through.

"He must have used Hernandez' palm on the reader," Drew offered. "If he were an employee, he wouldn't want his own print logged. It's the only reason Letty's still alive. If he suspected he'd been seen by someone in the passing group, he only had a few seconds to wrestle Hernandez' body up, place his palm on the reader, and enter the code to make his getaway. Any blood on the hatch controls?"

"He still had to have the code, but yeah, there's blood on the hatch controls and everything else. You'd think the guy would be covered in it himself, but he didn't leave any in the maintenance tube that we could see. Maybe the sweep will turn up something."

"Let's hope so. We're going to be slammed for the next couple of hours. Get up here as soon as you can."

Drew had no sooner ended his conversation with Mattie when Kyle tapped him. "Quadrant Representative Wellington is on a live feed from the *Golden Tracer*."

Albert Wellington—a name adopted for Earth's convenience, his Bahdane name, like most alien races, being unpronounceable by humans—was the MCTT Enforcement Representative for Dark Landing's quadrant of space. Drew had made a special effort to become Bertie's friend. He thought it wise to stay on the good side of *Muck* and, besides, Drew genuinely liked the Bahdaneian.

Wellington visited the station every ninety days to inspect the docks and warehouse level and to audit traffic records. He always scheduled his visits over a Saturday evening so he could sit in on the weekly poker game.

While several of the known alien races appeared humanoid—not surprising considering the efficiency of the design—Bahdane's environment and the Bahdaneian physiology were closer to Earth's than any other planet supporting intelligent life. Because of this, the two races interacted more with each other than with the other Alliance races. Wellington had last visited three weeks earlier. Drew couldn't imagine what he wanted now.

Bahdaneians made excellent administrators and civil servants. They were natural-born linguists who needed little exposure to a new language to become fluent. They held positions of authority throughout the K.U. and were a particular favorite of *Muck*. It helped that their appearance was non-threatening in the extreme.

Drew had Kyle patch him through. Wellington's image resolved on the large panel above his credenza. Short, velvety facial fur, bright, liquid-brown eyes, and a snout protruding between luxurious whiskered cheeks, if it ended there, might have given him the appearance of a charming stuffed seal one might win at an arcade game. But the long, spindly ears that folded forward and hung on each side of his head, resembling an English counselor's wig, added a comical element. Drew always thought Bahdaneians looked like a seal had hooked up with a bunny rabbit.

Wellington wore his uniform jacket, with MCTT patches on each sleeve, and as stern a look as he could pull off given his furry facade.

"Hello, Bertie! You popping by for tonight's poker game?" Drew knew this wasn't the case. He could see from the feed source that the *Golden Tracer* sat two hops out.

"Security Chief Andrew Vincent Cutter..." Wellington began in formal English, without the slightest accent or underlying hum that for decades was thought to denote a casual conversation between friends. Earth linguists only recently learned the hum was the Bahdaneian translation occurring just under whatever other language they were speaking. Fluted tongues and four active vocal cords (unlike humans, for whom only two were active) allowed them to speak two languages simultaneously, as long as one was their own. Humans found this complicated series of hums difficult to imitate, let alone master. But Bahdaneians considered it rude to translate a reprimand, or words said in anger, into the accompanying Bahdaneian.

Drew sat straighter in his chair; something was off. Wellington had only addressed him by his full name and title once — the first time they'd met. "Yes?" Drew said. •

"It has come to the attention of the Board of the Multi-world Coalition for Travel and Trade that there was a security breach with the potential for serious consequences to all Coalition members. Further, your failure to bring this matter to the Board's attention yourself, and in a timely manner, is a violation of Earth's membership agreement. Earth authorities and your employer have been informed and requested MCTT to intercede." Wellington paused, either for dramatic effect, or in expectation of a retort from Drew.

When Drew sat, quietly waiting, Wellington continued. "The *Golden Tracer* will arrive at Dark Landing in three days. Upon arrival, by order of the MCTT Board, and with the aforementioned cooperation of Earth authorities and CoachStop Management, I will assume temporary command of the station and initiate a formal investigation. As of this transmission, you are relieved of your position. Chiefs Jameson and Fitzwilliam are being notified as we speak that they are to assume co-command until my arrival.

"Copies of the allegations against you, the official orders from the MCTT Board, and letters of authorization from both Earth and CoachStop, promising full support and ordering your cooperation, are attached to this feed. Do you understand?"

Drew understood all right. He nodded and held the Bahdaneian's gaze for several moments while he composed himself to speak. "Can you tell me the nature of the security breach?"

Wellington's demeanor remained stolid. "I think you know its nature, Chief Cutter. Regardless, it would be inappropriate to discuss over a live feed."

"Well, at least you can tell me who gave you the information?"

"No."

"Okay, then. I'll see you in three days." Drew ended the feed himself. It was a hollow gesture, but it gave him immediate, albeit short, gratification.

Drew sat for the next ten minutes, staring at the now-dark viewing panel. It was sobering how fast his circumstances changed in less than three days. And Letty was linked to everything.

She was unaware of his intensifying feelings for her, and she certainly didn't share them. Why would she, in light of all that'd happened? She'd traveled light years from her home only to be locked in a detention cell. Her father had died in an unfathomable manner under mysterious circumstances, and she'd witnessed a gruesome murder and suffered an attempt against her own life. Though he doubted she'd recognized it for that. The only feelings she could reasonably have were horror, grief, and fear.

His comm purred. *Bad news travels fast,* he thought.

"Yes, Mattie?"

"Curtis and I are back, and Doc and Fitz are on their way to the conference room. They want you to join them as soon as you're free. Do you want Curtis and me there as well?"

"No. Tell Doc and Fitz I'll be about thirty minutes. You and Curtis come in here. *End all.*"

Mattie and Curtis entered his office before the last "l" in *End all.* Mattie was speaking to the air, relaying his message to Doc and Fitz.

Drew called toward the open hatch, "Kyle, if you're out there, you can hear better from in here."

Kyle entered and nodded at him with a sheepish look. The three stood in front of his desk with expressions of children who'd misbehaved. Uncertain of what they'd done wrong, they waited submissively for punishment. The feed from Wellington and simultaneous packets addressed to Doc and Fitz, were enough to alert his staff that a new element had been introduced to recent events.

Not wanting them to see his inner turmoil, Drew sat back in his chair, doing his best to appear relaxed. But he got right to it. "I've been relieved of my position. Doc and Fitz are taking over for the next three days until Albert Wellington arrives, then he'll be in charge."

They didn't say a word. *What could they say?* Still, he'd expected some show of protest, or for someone to ask why.

He continued after an awkward pause. "So, from this point on I won't be giving any orders."

The three still showed no movement and gave no response. Drew was pretty sure he'd been speaking out loud. He started to repeat himself when Mattie bobbed her head in his direction.

"Yes, Mattie?"

"Zamora is waiting outside with Miss Taleen."

Drew passed a hand over his face as if clearing away cobwebs. "Okay, tell Zamora to take Letty back to her room at the inn. I'll —"

Curtis coughed delicately.

"Curtis?"

"No disrespect, sir, but wouldn't that be giving Zamora an

order?"

Now Drew stared speechless at the three of them.

"Oh, screw it!" Mattie burst out. "I'm giving Zamora an order to take Letty back to the inn at no one in particular's suggestion. Does anyone have a problem with that?"

Curtis and Kyle shook their heads.

"Thank you, Mattie," Drew was relieved she'd taken the initiative. "Would you do that now? That is . . . if you want to. When they've left, I'll head over to the conference room to join Doc and Fitz."

They filed out of his office.

He might have suspected one of them had turned him into MCTT, but while all three, along with Doc and Fitz, knew that Letty had accessed Dark Landing's system, he'd kept secret the circumstances behind her access.

Wellington specified a security breach at Dark Landing *with the potential for consequences of a serious nature for all Coalition members.* Surely, he hadn't meant Letty's access to station systems as much as to the underlying security breach at Taleen Industries, and its potential consequences to the Coalition. MCTT must know Letty was on the station and the one who'd told him about the breach.

The timing confused him. The incidents on Dark Landing all occurred over the last seventy-two hours. Somehow, in the same timeframe, *Muck* learned of the security breach, whether on Dark Landing or on Earth or both. They'd deliberated and formed a plan on how to handle the situation, then notified Earth authorities and CoachStop to receive their blessings, and dispatched Wellington and the *Golden Tracer.* Quite the ministerial feat, even for *Muck.* There had to be a leak . . . and a close one. He refused to believe it came from one of his command staff, even Curtis, but at the moment, he saw no other possibility.

Mattie's instruction to Zamora could be heard from the outer office. Not ready to face Letty just yet, he'd explain everything to her later, once he learned how Doc and Fitz would react to the news.

He spent the next fifteen minutes completing a series of tasks and packing his processor bag with a few personal items before heading to the conference room.

As he walked, Drew continued to ponder Wellington's feed. Wellington made no mention of Letty, the explosion in the airlock,

George Speller's death, or Hernandez' murder. Even if he knew nothing about the deaths, certainly Hernandez' since it'd just happened, he had to know about Letty. He seemed focused only on the security breach. No surprise there; the significance was far-reaching and would be of greater concern to *Muck*.

Maybe Wellington's instructions to his two co-chiefs mentioned Letty. *Muck* would want to interrogate her, and their methods were renowned for their lack of subtlety. Wellington couldn't know Letty's life was in danger—or maybe he did. With Drew's instinctive distrust of *Muck* taking over, he made a leap: *What if the MCTT were somehow involved in everything?*

Instead of answers, he found more questions. Drew, trusting his own instincts, and accepting his evolving feelings for Letty, decided he'd handle matters his way.

14 ESCAPE

When Drew entered the conference room, Doc and Fitz were sitting next to each other on one side of the long table. Without a greeting, he plopped heavily into a chair opposite them. Eyebrows raised questioningly, arms folded across his chest, he signaled them to begin.

With half his attention still dissecting Wellington's message, Drew tried to look attentive as Doc took the lead. She proclaimed their bewilderment and outrage at MCTT's action, declared their loyalty and support, and expressed their assurances that the whole thing was a huge mistake that would be resolved in his favor — *and he better damn-well get an apology when it was*. Fitz remained silent, vigorously nodding his agreement to everything Doc said in true bobble-head fashion.

Drew appreciated their sincerity and support, but he was anxious to learn if Wellington's instructions mentioned Letty.

Her speech apparently at end, Doc glanced sidewise at Fitz. Fitz continued to nod his head several times before realizing that Doc was no longer speaking. He stopped nodding and cleared his throat.

His discomfort was obvious. "Ah . . . Wellington . . . er, *Muck* . . . MCTT, that is . . . has instructed us to reduce your security level to civilian and restrict your access to Security HQ."

"Am I being detained?" Drew tensed.

"Absolutely not!" Doc said, indignant. "They have no right as it is to treat you this shabbily. They wouldn't dare order us to lock you up."

Nodding once more, Fitz went on, "No, no . . . you can come and go as you please. They only said you had to stay away from HQ. I think it's more to alleviate awkwardness and confusion on behalf of the staff than a concern about something you might do."

Drew relaxed a bit but remained eager to get to the meat of the situation.

Fitz continued. "I'm going to move into your office temporarily to keep the staff focused on their duties until Wellington arrives. Nothing was said about the ongoing investigation into the airlock incident. We're a little baffled about that." He studied the tabletop and avoided looking at Drew. "Evidently *Muck* hasn't been informed yet?"

"I would've been filing the incident report on that now and on the Hernandez' murder. If they have the information, they got it someplace else, not from me," Drew said, rushing his words. He wanted to ask about Letty. One leg bounced impatiently under the table, waiting for Fitz to broach the subject. He didn't have to wait long.

Fitz continued. "Er . . . about Miss Taleen . . . while our orders didn't mention the explosion and Speller, the MCTT wants to speak to her about a security breach. It wasn't stated directly, but clearly, they assume she's here at headquarters. We — Doc and I — think it's best so as not to muddy the waters any further . . . not that it would necessarily . . . anyway, it would be best to bring her back here until Wellington arrives. Of course, we would make her as comfortable as possible and provide every courtesy. She's been through so much."

That's an understatement. Drew wouldn't let Letty spend another night in a cell if he could prevent it. He ran his fingers through his hair. The gesture of frustration was becoming a habit. "I guess all I can do now is wait until Bertie arrives to see what MCTT has in mind," he said resignedly. "I'm sorry to put you guys through this, and I promise I won't make it any harder on you than it is now. It means everything to me that you've got my back. You know I'd feel the same if it were either of you. Can I ask a favor?"

"Anything," Doc said.

Fitz nodded.

"I'd like to be the one to tell Letty. I owe her that much, and maybe if I talk to her, I can make her understand why she has to come back here. I mean it when I say I want to make this as easy for you guys as I can, and for her, of course. If you can give me about an hour, after I'm done explaining the situation, I'll have her security detail escort her back here."

"Well . . . I don't know—" Fitz started.

Doc interrupted again. "I agree, Drew. You should be the one to tell her. It's the only civilized thing to do." She scowled challengingly at Fitz.

If Fitz had any objections, he held them back. "Sure, that's fine."

"Thanks, guys. I appreciate it. Oh, one more thing. Would one of you please cancel tonight's poker game?"

With a hug from Doc and a firm handshake and arm squeeze from Fitz, Drew left them discussing how best to word the staff announcement.

He needed to stop by his quarters to pick up a few things. He hoped he'd given himself enough time. The hardest part would be convincing Letty to go along with him. He'd have to make up a good story to gain her cooperation. If he told her the truth, he doubted she'd agree to his plan.

Jonesy was in the corridor arguing with an irate resident as Drew passed. All he heard was, " . . . scaring the pigeon and . . ."

"Shoot that damn pigeon, Jonesy!" he ordered over his shoulder. The complainant's voice rose several octaves, but the words faded as Drew rounded the bulkhead and doubled his pace.

In his quarters, he stuffed a change of clothing into a military-styled duffel similar to Letty's. He added two flashlights, four two-liter water pouches—he would need to pick up more—and the few dried meat and fruit packs he had on hand. He crammed a wool blanket on top, then rolled and secured a second blanket to the outside, making the pack bulkier than he liked.

At least Doc and Fitz hadn't asked him to surrender his weapon. He grabbed his security knife and started to strap it to his thigh but instead added it to the duffel. It was a twin to the one the killer had used on Hernandez. Better if Letty didn't see it.

Mentally reviewing a list of anything else he might need, he added a heavy sweater and left for the inn.

~ ~ ∞ ~ ~

He didn't go straight to Letty's quarters but stopped by the front desk first. The clerk greeted him with a welcoming smile.

"Hello, Chief. What can I do for you?"

"Hi, Mona. How's your lovely self?" *Keep it short Mona – I'm in a hurry here.*

She tipped her head coquettishly. "I'm well, and you?"

Drew only smiled in response. "I need a room for a couple nights. The environmental controls in my quarters are off-line. Just put me on the same level as Miss Taleen if something's available there. We should probably keep our security presence contained to one level, don't you think?"

"Of course." After consulting her monitor, and with a twinkle in her eye, she offered, "The room adjoining Miss Taleen's is available."

Drew started to protest but stopped himself. *It's a little late to worry about people's perceptions.*

"Great, that'll work. I'm going up to check on Miss Taleen now. Could you have someone deliver my duffel and case to my room and send up three or four water pouches?"

Remembering that he wouldn't have station-wide access much longer, if it hadn't already been removed, he added, "Oh, and you'd better give me guest access. This is a personal stay, not job-related. CoachStop would stick me in a bunk in the staff quarters before paying for a room. Their budget outranks my comfort." Drew winked.

The clerk extended a palm reader for imprint.

He thanked her and left. *I hope the rest goes half as well.*

Once on Letty's level, he tried to remember the name of the staff member standing guard in front of her hatch. The man's posture straightened as Drew approached.

"Simmons, isn't it?" Drew asked.

"Timmons, sir."

"Sorry, Timmons. Everything seems quiet."

"They delivered her dinner about twenty minutes ago."

"Good. I'm here to escort her back to headquarters. We're releasing her."

"That's great!" Timmons responded, a little too

enthusiastically. "She's very nice, sir."

"Yes, she is. When does your shift end?" He didn't have time for chit-chat, but he didn't want to raise suspicions either.

"Another hour-and-a-half, sir."

"Why don't you take off now? I'll tell Curtis when I get back. You won't be docked."

"Thank you, sir. If you're sure?"

"No problem. Just don't stick your head back in HQ tonight unless you want Curtis or Mattie to find some busy work for you."

"Right. Thanks again. Much appreciated."

"Go ahead then. Have a nice evening."

"You too, sir." Timmons headed toward the conveyer.

"Two down too easy," Drew mumbled. As soon as the conveyer door closed, he entered his room and palmed the shared hatch to Letty's room; a click indicated his side was unlatched.

He returned to the corridor and knocked on Letty's outer hatch, trusting they hadn't pulled his security clearance yet and he could still access her quarters. Once he collected Letty, he'd have no more need for station-side access. Hearing her muffled "Come in," he pressed his palm to the reader, relieved at the soft, opening whoosh.

He was startled to see Teresa Zamora sitting on the edge of Letty's bed.

She jumped up when he entered. "Sir?"

He covered his surprise. "Zamora, I want to thank you personally for staying with Miss Taleen. When does your shift end?"

"I'm on overtime now, sir."

"Well, you're relieved. And thank you again."

"My pleasure. Good evening, sir." She turned to Letty, her voice softening. "Goodnight, Letty."

"Thank you, Teresa," Letty said.

Drew wondered if there was anyone Letty couldn't charm. Everyone who met her personally became captivated, himself included. If only half the rumors about *Muck* were true, they might be the exception. He had no desire to find out.

When Zamora left, Drew moved quickly to the reader that opened the hatch to the adjoining room and pressed his palm once more, hoping his luck hadn't run out. It would prove awkward to make another request to the desk and would waste valuable time.

The seal released and the hatch popped open an inch.

Letty sat at the small desk and stared at him quizzically, her half-eaten dinner pushed to one side. Even with dark circles and red, puffy eyelids, she was stunning.

Without a credible story, he dove in, hoping something brilliant would come to him. "Change into your travel gear and pack your kit. I'm taking you out of here."

"What?"

"We don't have much time. An MCTT agent is on his way now to arrest you. They want to get to you before Earth authorities arrive. They're convinced you're involved in a conspiracy to disrupt the Coalition and seize control of trade commerce in the K.U." *What a load.*

Letty agreed. "That's absurd. Why would they assume that all of a sudden?"

Drew piled it on. "They see a pattern in everything you've been doing. And somehow, it's tied in with the security breach. Trust me, Letty, if they get their hands on you, you'll never be seen again."

She smiled weakly. "MCTT can't do that. Why would they?"

"Let's see—you have an army under your command. You're wealthy enough to finance a hundred coups, and Taleen-staffed offices are strategically located throughout the K.U. They're afraid of you, and they want you under their control. And don't forget, your identity was hidden until now."

Her look said she wasn't buying it. The brilliant thought he'd been waiting for came to him then. "They're going to charge you with Hernandez' murder for starters."

"But the vids prove—"

"They're only electronic files. Did I mention they fired me for defending you? MCTT now has unrestricted access to station records and backups. They can do anything they want with those files."

"Hasn't everyone else seen them . . . Mattie? Doc and Fitz?"

Of course they have, but she can't know that for sure. "I never had the chance to share them with the command staff. Letty, you've got to trust me. I'm trying to protect you, and we're wasting time."

Muck's game remained a mystery, but he was convinced they were up to no good. Once she was safe, he could tell her the truth.

So, maybe she wasn't in as much danger from *Muck* as he'd suggested. Still, someone wanted her dead, and that was no exaggeration. If she thought he'd over-dramatized events and insisted on returning to face MCTT, he'd confess to tricking her.

She stared at him for a few moments, as if unsure he wasn't just carrying a bad joke too far. Then, evidently having made up her mind, she moved to the small wardrobe fitted into the wall and pulled out her poncho and boots. From the drawer next to the wardrobe, she grabbed a shirt and her dungarees. When she began to unfasten the security jumpsuit Zamora had provided her, Drew turned his back, giving her privacy. As she was dressing, he heard the attendant enter the adjoining room to deliver his bag and the extra water pouches.

"Where exactly are we going?" Letty asked.

"I have a plan."

15 THE PLAN

Drew and Letty exited the inn. If anyone spotted them leaving the conveyer and making the hard right through the café, it didn't matter, security would tag them AWOL soon anyway.

The residents, used to seeing Drew wandering about, waved and nodded as he passed but seemed otherwise unfazed. That would change if Doc and Fitz issued a station-wide alert for him. Letty received little attention from passersby, who probably identified her as a boy. *If they knew what was under the poncho, they'd pay attention for sure*. What they needed to avoid was security staff.

He counted on Doc and Fitz sending a team to search for them at the inn and perhaps his quarters before they issued an alert. They might not issue an alert at all. They were on a space station for Pete's sake. Where were they going to go? And issuing an alert for the chief of security would be embarrassing. Still, Drew disabled his comm and its locator before leaving his office. He'd also disabled the surveillance cameras along their escape route and dozens of others throughout the station to further confuse a search. An added layer of passwords would keep them offline for a while. *Those* actions wouldn't go unnoticed.

He was relying on Doc's trusting character and her inability to think the worst of anyone, particularly Drew. If Fitz's typical acquiescence to Doc's suggestions held firm, they'd be okay for the short term.

They headed to the west end of the station, which consisted of supply and equipment storage and saw little traffic. Even better, a limited-access conveyer separated it from the public thoroughfare. This time of day most workers were off shift or on dinner break. It was likely they'd pass unseen.

They both carried duffels slung across their backs. Letty struggled with an extra shoulder pack filled with the water pouches and dried food packets that Drew had her purchase on the way. He'd provided her with hard script so the purchases couldn't be traced. He might have done the gentlemanly thing and carried it for her, but it looked more believable this way. To her credit, she didn't complain.

There was no one around when they reached the entrance to the conveyer, which required palm and code access.

Letty stared at the palm pad. "What do we do now?" she asked. Her tone conveyed the suspicion that Drew hadn't considered when he palmed the conveyer their escape would be traceable.

"Press your palm to the reader," he said.

"*My* palm?"

"Uh-huh."

When Letty put her hand to the reader, the right half of a horizontal light strip across the top of the pad turned green.

"Now punch in Charlie-November-Kilo-Eight-Zero-Quebec-Three."

She entered the code. The left half of the light bar turned green as well. The conveyer doors slid apart.

He shot her a superior smile. "A little something I whipped up before I left HQ."

"What else did you whip up?"

"You'll see."

The conveyer traveled only a short distance before it stopped, and the doors on the opposite side opened. Letty stepped out ahead of him while Drew hung back in the shadows. Corridors formed an upside-down "T" to the right and left of the conveyer doors and straight ahead. Letty looked in each direction before motioning for him to join her. He nodded forward, and they proceeded down the passage in front of them.

The facility was a metal cavern, two levels high. They traversed a corridor roughly sixty meters long. Free-standing storage cells packed tightly together lined each side, giving the appearance of permanent structures. If anyone stepped into the corridor in front or behind them, they would have no place to duck out of view.

The cavern echoed each step, making it impossible to move quickly and quietly at once. Still, they were covering the distance in good time. To anyone watching, they'd look ridiculous tiptoeing down the corridor in heavy boots, their arms arched out stork-like for balance. Drew could think of no excuse to explain why they were there. Simultaneously with the thought, he heard the whoosh of the conveyer doors open at the head of the corridor behind them. The voices of at least two men echoed loudly. Drew and Letty froze.

One of the men called out to them. "Sorry we're late, Matt. We'll be right back with the loader."

Drew dared to look behind him. The men had moved out of sight. He and Letty were only a few meters from the end of the corridor. Letty had the lead. In the dim light, the worker saw him but not Letty. And he'd seen what he expected to see: "Matt." Drew didn't take time to worry about where Matt really was.

He pushed Letty toward the end of the corridor and motioned to her hand. She moved quickly and placed her palm on the reader next to a hatch access. He pulled a flashlight from his duffel and relieved her of the shoulder pack. A nearby loader came to life with a deep thrum, its tread hammered against the metal deck. Drew yelled the access code.

Letty shook her head at him. She hadn't heard.

He put his mouth to her ear and repeated the code as she punched it in.

Drew shoved Letty backwards through the opening hatch and hit the red emergency control positioned above the palm reader as he fell in after her. An alarm sounded one strangled half whoop before the hatch resealed behind them. He lifted weightless from the deck, still facing Letty. She floated in front of him wearing a terrified expression. Her hair and slouch hat hovered comically above her.

He pushed off the closed hatch and held out his elbow as he passed her. She grabbed on, and he pulled her along the side of the airlock toward the palm pad at the opposite end. She nodded in understanding and palmed the reader as soon as they reached it. Drew recited the code, and she punched it in. The hatch opened, and they dropped heavily through into pitch blackness on the other side. Artificial gravity restored, bodies and duffels hit the deck with heavy thuds. The hatch sealed automatically behind them. No alarms sounded on that side.

~ ~ ∞ ~ ~

Drew pointed his flashlight at Letty. Spread-legged on the deck, leaning back on locked arms, she looked like a mad woman, saucer-eyed, hair disheveled.

She shouted questions at him rapid fire. "Are you insane? What the hell was that? Where are we? My hat . . . where's my hat?"

"Relax, relax, we're fine. Sorry, that airlock is a no man's land between the station and Spud. It has its own gravity inductor but activating it would trigger a light on someone's panel." He smiled at her boyishly.

"Where . . . are . . . we?" She pronounced each word as if she were speaking to a toddler.

"In the west cradle arm."

"Why are there environmental services here?"

"Because I enabled them before I left my office."

"Won't *that* trigger lights on someone's panel?"

"Nope. There's a stand-alone setting to activate or deactivate Spud's environment, but Spud's operating system from this side of the hatch forward was never integrated with the station systems. The cradle arms operate under Spud's self-contained system — *unmonitored* system."

"I hope by system you mean there's a light control somewhere."

"We need to move along the arm and into the mining facility. A second airlock opens into an anteroom. Back when they were still mining, the anteroom and airlock served as the transport dock. There's a main control panel there. The facility itself is huge. There are admin offices, living quarters, mess halls, social areas, and the mine, of course. When I was assigned to Dark Landing, I took a tour of the facility. It's been closed for years."

As Drew talked, he offered Letty a hand and pulled her to her feet. Still holding her hand, he led her along the gently sloping arm toward Spud — almost two kilometers.

"The mining equipment is still intact, but they stripped most of the personnel areas," he said. "There should be enough left to make ourselves comfortable."

Drew detected an element of disbelief bordering on fear in Letty's voice when she spoke.

"So . . . *what*? We're going to set up housekeeping on Spud?" She jerked her hand away. "Seriously, I don't think you've thought this through. How long did you plan on hiding out here?"

She was questioning the soundness of her decision to come with him. *No surprise there. So am I!* "Until we can get some answers. If I share what little we've learned so far, maybe you can fill in a few of the blanks. And I need to figure out what *Muck's* up to."

"Why do they have to be up to something? You don't think I believed half the crap you were feeding me earlier?" she asked.

"It worked, didn't it? You're here."

"The part about being charged with Hernandez' murder sounded plausible enough, though not for the reasons you so dramatically outlined."

"The truth is, Letty, I'm trying to protect you. Hernandez' killer was after *you*, not Hernandez. He just needed to get him out of the way first."

"Wasn't he taking a big chance? I mean, he couldn't possibly have known how I'd react. I could have just run. I *should* have run, but I couldn't leave Alberto."

"I've thought about that. It was the first opportunity the killer had to get to you. You've been locked up under guard since you arrived. I think he had to take the risk because he might not *get* another chance." He didn't mention his own concerns about the timing of the attack, and how the killer knew she'd be in that corridor. Which went to validate the likelihood that someone — and probably a higher-up someone — knew about everything and was the one who contacted MCTT.

"Okay. But why would anyone want to kill me?"

"It might be something to do with your little security problem which, by the way, I'm pretty sure *Muck* has learned of."

"Only if you told someone," she said accusingly.

"Not me. Someone else maybe."

"Like who? You're one of four — with my dad gone, one of

three—who knows about it. You've kept me away from all comm devices and processors. Anne Rostenkowski at the ETOC certainly wouldn't leak it."

"You're forgetting the others."

"What others?"

"The bogeymen," he said.

That silenced her for several minutes. Finally, she asked, "So, what's your plan?"

"I created profiles for each of us with CoachStop executive roles. When they remove my access from the security database, they may not think to look under the corporate accounts. Still, I couldn't use my palm print station-side without setting off alerts. That's where you come in. Your profile is under Rebecca Richards, and I added your print to the system as a CoachStop officer. I spelled your name 'Rebekah.' They'll trace my print, but it would never occur to the system techs to trace yours unless they were ordered to. As far as I know, the technicians don't know who you are or that you're traveling under an alias. Regardless, they can't track the access or movements of anyone on Spud."

"They'll find us eventually, Drew."

"*Eventually*, yeah . . . and probably soon. We just need some time to work on plan B."

"You realize . . . I mean, after everything you've done . . . your career on Dark Landing is probably over?"

For the first time, Drew abandoned his lighthearted posture and considered the consequences of his actions. In the darkness of the armature, he felt insulated, freer to talk about his feelings. It didn't come easily to him. "Honestly, I should be wrecked. I have . . . *had* . . . everything I ever wanted. Or, at least, I thought I did. If this goes south, I don't know what I'll do. I don't have family on Earth anymore. I have a little savings. I can always find a shipwreck somewhere, fix it up, and become an independent trader." He shuddered at the prospect of life as a space-dwelling, nomadic.

"But I'm feeling a strange . . . I don't know . . . *emptiness*." *Emptiness doesn't begin to describe it . . . dread? . . . panic? . . . Jesus, what have I done?* Drew reined in his verbal and internal ramblings. There was no turning back. Well . . . there was, but it wouldn't change things.

They walked the rest of the distance in silence. As they

approached the end of the arm and the airlock, the glow of the light indicating it was fully pressurized became visible. No code was needed to open the hatch, and Drew turned the manual wheel. There was a satisfying whoosh as the seal broke. They crossed and opened the opposite hatch.

Drew and Letty stepped from the blackness of the airlock into the blackness of the miner's anteroom. He directed his flashlight clockwise around the room, searching for the control panel he vaguely remembered being somewhere near the eleven o'clock position.

"Stay here," he said, when he spotted it. "I'll see if I can find the lighting menu."

Drew crossed the room and placed his palm on the pad to the left of the panel. The panel glowed softly with a multi-colored display of options. After studying the choices for a few seconds, he pressed several icons in succession. A muted blue light emanated from narrow soffits located around the perimeter of the ceiling. He'd selected the evening illumination option.

Suddenly exposed and self-conscious at having shared his feelings earlier, he reverted to his customary flippancy. "Sexy, huh?"

"We need to talk, Chief. I came with you so that I wouldn't be arrested for murder, and so I'll be free to figure out what happened to my dad—and to Hernandez as well now—but that's all. You're insane if you had anything else planned."

Drew measured his response. It was pointless to deny his attraction, but he wanted to reassure her they'd come to Spud for her protection. "Don't worry. You're safe from me for as long as you want to be."

"Good," she responded quickly. Then she paused, her eyes narrowing as if she were considering what he'd said.

He gave her no time to dwell on it. "So, let's figure out where we want to set up operations, and then have a snack. Slinking around like a criminal is making me hungry."

They searched the outer offices and administrative quarters for anything useful. In one of the storage lockers they found an overlooked folding cot and carried it into what was probably a VIP suite with a back office and a front reception area. While Letty set up the cot in the office, Drew searched for something he could sleep on softer than the deck, though he doubted they would stay hidden more than a few hours, if that. Finally locating a broken lounger, he wrestled the cushions off. Pushed together, they were short for his frame but better than nothing.

He found two small tables in the rec room. Placed end-to-end in the reception area, they formed one longer table against the wall opposite his improvised bed, and directly under conveniently situated built-in shelving. Chairs proved more difficult. He finally settled on cable spools which were about the right height, though a little wobbly.

Once he'd created a workable space, he unpacked his duffel and Letty's shoulder pack, placing their limited food and water supply, along with what little gear he'd brought, on the shelves. He set his processor on the table and stood back to survey their new quarters. Not bad, considering. He pulled a water pouch from the shelf along with a package of dried meat and another of dried fruit, then called to Letty in a sing-song voice, "Dinner's on."

She entered and walked to the makeshift desk, laying three data vials next to the processor.

"What are those?" Drew asked.

"I'm not sure. Dad hid them with his note instructing me to come to Dark Landing. I haven't had a chance to look at them until now."

"I should have brought popcorn," Drew said.

16 DATA FILES

Letty straddled the nearest spool and picked up one of the vials. Positioning it above the processor, she paused before slipping it into the drive port. "Here goes."

"No idea what's on these?" Drew asked.

"No. We were nearly here when I found them. Someone nicked my processor when my baggage was stowed on the *Temperance*. I tried several times to use the public terminals, but there were always too many people hanging around. Then, when I arrived . . ." She cast a sideways glance at him without finishing.

An audible click sounded as she pressed the vial firmly into the port. A short rod, about a half inch in diameter, made of a clear, synthetic material, swung out from the processor's side. Letty wrapped her fist around it. With her user identity confirmed, a picture of her and Speller materialized on the screen, both smiling, heads cocked toward each other. A muted sob escaped her, and unchecked tears rolled down her cheeks.

Drew laid a comforting hand on her shoulder, but she shrugged it off, sniffling. She wiped the tears from her eyes, dried her hands on her dungarees, and took a deep breath.

"*List files by most recently modified*," she said in a shaky voice. The image morphed into two columns of file names. Letty leaned closer to scan the lists. She opened and quickly closed several documents.

Steadier, she said, "These appear to be a history of the

investigation into the security breach—copies of shared reports between Dad and me and the ETOC. Nothing I haven't seen, but I'd have to study them closer to be sure." She pressed a narrow ring inset around the port opening, and the data vial popped up above its edge. She replaced it with another and grasped the rod once more for the required DNA access.

A new image appeared of her and a man, about the same age or a couple years older, both wearing caps and gowns and holding degree certificates on each side of their beaming faces.

"Who's that?" Drew asked.

"That's Travis—a friend from college."

Drew winced at a sharp stab of baseless jealousy.

The file list spanned longer than on the previous vial, with several more columns. Letty scanned the columns quickly without opening any files.

"Taleen Industries business," she said as she popped the vial out and replaced it with the last one. There was no image this time. The vial opened to a short list of four files. Each file title was nothing more than a long string of meaningless symbols, letters, and numbers.

To Drew, some of the symbols appeared to be of alien origin. "Encrypted," he said, stating the obvious.

Letty nodded and studied the coded words. "*Tiger traffic*," she said. The screen didn't waver. "*Tiger traffic two four nine.*" Nothing happened. "*Middle Earth two—*" She stopped and bit her lower lip as she concentrated on the screen. "*Gypsy daughter*," she said finally. The letters, numbers, and symbols changed into legible Earth English:

Compilation
Confirmed Data
Personal Notes
Raw Data

They bent close to the screen and then pulled away self-consciously when their heads bumped. "Open *Compilation*," Letty commanded. Words filled the screen.

ED2519.01.15
Virus (simplification) Detection & Transmission

Taleen labs have isolated the virus[1] infecting the biomaterial gel in tech victim zero: desk model 2500.5A, SN4032-909-09509, as well as the biomaterial gel of data vials inserted into the subject desk during the critical timeframe[2]. The virus subsequently infected three human technicians[3] who came into direct contact with the biomaterial gel during the course of their research.

Initial human viral infection presented with cold-like symptoms[4]. Two of the subjects also presented with a mild rash[5] on their necks and chests. Each subject responded to standard treatment, and all were symptom-free within 72 hours of onset; however, it was discovered that nanoids of unknown origin[6], seemingly identical to those found in the desk and vial gels, had adhered to the subjects' DNA[7]. To date, it is unknown what objective, if any, the nanoids have or to what extent they might affect humans. Attempts to remove, or disable and decode[8], the nanoids from the human subjects have failed. Nanoids extracted with blood or other bio samples disintegrate upon extraction; replacement nanoids re-construct in the subjects' bodies at roughly the same speed[9]. Inactive nanoids found in data vials are shielded[10]. Attempts to breach the shielding have resulted in disintegration. Spectrogram analysis[11] has proved unsuccessful.

It is believed (and maybe one possible objective) that the virus can be transmitted human-to-human through exchange of bodily fluid[12]. Other than through direct exposure to already infected biomaterial gel, all tests for machine-to-human transmission[13] have returned negative. However, once infected, humans can pass the virus to technology requiring DNA access verification. Though attempts to replicate resolution in humans have failed, reformatting and reprogramming[14] has successfully disabled nanoids in infected technology.

The combined findings from multiple research teams confirm tech victim zero: desk model 2500.5A, SN4032-909-09509, contracted the virus through an infected data vial. Investigation into the company's source[15] of data vials during the critical timeframe revealed that, due to a shortage caused by as yet unsolved cargo scow hijackings[16], Taleen Industries Corporate Center requisitioned one shipment of unformatted vials from a local boutique manufacturer owned and operated by a branch of the Praetorian religious sect[17].

Suitable safeguards have been implemented, and further transmission has been contained[18]. The human subjects continue to be held in quarantine under observation. All technology at Taleen Industries headquarters is currently being examined through scripted diagnostics[19] presented as R&D product development testing[20].

The remainder of the report consisted of footnotes with links back to detailed information in the *Confirmed Data* and *Raw Data* files.

Letty, hands pressed together to control their shaking, issued the command to open the *Personal Notes* file.

ED2519.01.25

Letty, sweetheart,

I assume since you are reading this, you received my instructions and you're safely on the way to Dark Landing. If not, do as I say! I'll join you as soon as I'm able. Until then, seek the protection of Andrew Cutter, Chief of Security. My research indicates he's of good character and I believe we can trust him. Tell him all will be explained as soon as I can make myself known.

"Huh . . . interesting. See, your dad knew I was trustworthy." Drew said, reading over her shoulder. Letty continued reading without comment.

> *I opened an investigation into the Praetorian sect (which led me to Chief Cutter; he initiated a similar investigation only days before me). I discovered that several members of the sect had been dispatched to Dark Landing. Since it's the furthest trading station from Earth, I believe our project may be widerspread and more dangerous than we imagined. We should stay together from now on.*
>
> *Our research teams are looking into the chemical character of the bio gel from the data vials supplied by the Praetorians. It differs (even ignoring the nanoids) from the gel in a typical vial. They've isolated one chemical, and I'm bringing a sample with me to research personally. I have my own suspicions as to the reason for this anomaly.*
>
> *Letty, I can't stress enough the importance of secrecy and the possible danger to both of us. I don't want to scare you, sweetheart, but I believe I was followed to Mars, and there may have been an attempt on my life. I'm anxious to discuss all my findings and suspicions with you as soon as we're both safe. I miss you terribly. Stay alert. I'll see you soon.*
> *All my love, Dad*

Drew and Letty (both ignoring new tears streaming down her cheeks) spoke excitedly in unison, neither comprehending what the other said.

"Stop!" Drew shouted.

Letty's mouth snapped shut at his volume and tone of command.

"We'll take turns. You go first," he said in a more normal tone.

Letty wiped her tears and runny nose on a sleeve. "In the café, that's why you asked if my dad was religious. You knew, didn't you? Why were you withholding that information?"

"I wasn't withholding anything then or now. Remember, we haven't had a chance to compare notes. We have three Praetorian monks on the station. I've been watching them since they arrived, trying to figure out what they're doing here. After the explosion, we found a monk robe in Tram . . . your father's locker on the *Temperance*. It could have meant nothing. I was just fishing. He probably thought it would come in handy if he needed to snoop around."

He took his turn. "You mentioned earlier that only three people knew about the breach, but the compilation report and your dad's note talks about teams of research technicians. Any one of them could have informed *Muck*," Drew said, mirroring her accusing tone. It was obvious they still had trust issues.

"It's possible, but unlikely," she said. "The research team members don't know the nanoids were discovered as part of a security breach. We presented a scenario to them as a training exercise. If they suspect anything, it's that we're researching new product prototypes."

Hyped on adrenalin, she stood from the stool and paced the small reception area as she spoke. "We have three teams of technicians from different disciplines. Each team researches an aspect of any problem we present. When Research and Development design a new product, its components are divided between the teams to test and break. Theoretically, no team knows the others exist.

"Sometimes . . . well, these are brilliant men and women, well-known in their respective areas of research, sometimes they put things together. On the other hand, they're overpaid, coddled and perked, and perform challenging work in their chosen fields. We make sure they get individual credit where it's due. They're fanatics really, but in a good way. We compile psych workups and background checks before anyone is added to a team, and we monitor their personal and professional lives. They're loyal to a fault and, believe me, we know what buttons to push. I'm sure the information didn't come from one of them. "Did you question the Praetorians?" she asked.

"No. We were preparing to bring them in when Hernandez was murdered. Then, I was suspended."

He continued, abandoning the give and take and postulating out of order. "Some of it makes sense now. Your father came to Dark Landing following our particular Praetorians. After he checked up on me, he sent you here to join him and to keep you safe."

"He doesn't mention nitroglycerin specifically, but that must be the chemical anomaly he talks about," Letty said. "But it's not mentioned in the *compilation,* unless there's something in the individual reports." She sat back down at the processor.

Drew watched as she began opening and scanning files. "The environmental report confirmed your dad's findings. The scanners didn't identify the nitro until it exploded because it was encased in a gel like the bio gel used in data vials. But that still doesn't explain its purpose." Drew leaned close, absentmindedly nibbling on pieces of dried meat and fruit as he read along. After a few minutes, he jerked upright. "How can I be so stupid?" he said, slapping his hand against his forehead.

Letty glanced over her shoulder at him with a telling look.

He ignored her. "I know what the Praetorians are doing here," he said. "They're carriers!"

"Carriers?" she asked, eyebrows raised.

"At our last breakfast meeting, Doc reported there'd been an outbreak of colds on the station with an atypical rash."

As soon as he said it, Drew saw the flaw in his theory. "That doesn't make any sense, though. The monks wouldn't have access to our tech and the virus can only be spread human-to-human through bodily fluids. Unless. . . maybe it makes you sneeze and spreads just like a normal cold. I'll have to ask Doc. Could a synthetic virus infect both humans and technology? Wow!"

"You're going off the rails, Cutter," Letty said. "I need to contact the ETOC immediately. If there's any chance this thing has spread . . . *is* spreading . . . that's what Dad would want me to do."

"They moved the long-range relay servers to the station when the facilities here closed. Local transmissions or even remote data inquiries from Spud won't be any problem. They'll get lost in the daily traffic. But a live interstellar transmission originating from here would be red flagged. We'll figure something out."

They started trading questions again.

"Why would the Praetorians come *here*?" Letty asked.

"Who brought *Muck* in? What's their involvement?" said Drew.

"I keep coming back to the nitroglycerine. Why nitroglycerine? Dad suspected the answer." Letty's tears started afresh.

"We need to focus on the bigger questions," Drew said. "Who

are the bogeymen behind it all and what are their motives? Yes, there's profit in knowledge. If the tech nanoids let them eavesdrop on everyone's business, it would be immensely profitable, but also dangerous. If it got out—and basically, it has—it could mean the end of the alliance between planets and even war. That can't be the end goal. Can it? If it is the goal, who stands to benefit, or even survive for that matter? And why would they infect humans? I don't get it." He looked at Letty, shaking his head. Then he had another thought. "The comms. That's why you and your dad don't have comm implants."

"Until we found the source of the breach, Dad said it would be best to remove our comms. It's been damn inconvenient."

With emotional and mental energies heightened to frenzied levels, Drew needed physical relief. He didn't think Letty would accommodate his first choice. "I'm taking a walk. You want to join me?"

Evidently suffering the same over-excitement, she popped up from her spool with enough force to overturn it. "Yeah, I do. Are we going anyplace in particular?"

"I need to check the oxygen generator and scrubber settings."

The walkway outside their new quarters ran in a half-circle, beginning and ending on opposite sides of the anteroom. Four similar, half-circle walkways, nothing more than tunnels with natural rock walls, were excavated an equal distance from each other, expanding deeper into the underground facility, like ripples in a pond with the anteroom the stone. Three cross-section tunnels, one through the center and one along each side, joined the passageways together in a time-tested design.

Offices, public areas, executive living quarters, and mess lined the first ripple. The second contained operational and environmental equipment, storage, and admin crew quarters. The last three ripples provided access to miners' quarters and common rooms, and large caverns furnished with rock crushing and separating equipment. The mine itself consisted of caverns excavated above and below the complex. Each side spoke ended in a space dock, now capped, where raw materials were loaded onto smelting and refining ships.

Drew's and Letty's new quarters sat at one end of the first passageway, close to the anteroom. Drew headed there now to consult the map kiosk and refresh his memory of the location of the environmental equipment and controls. He entered the room ahead of Letty and stopped abruptly.

Unable to check her forward motion in time, she bumped into him. "Hey! You need to be fitted with caution beams. A little warning, please."

"Look." He pointed to the information counter.

She stepped from behind him to see where he was pointing. The hat she'd left floating in the station-side airlock was perched neatly in the center of the counter.

17 FOUND

They weren't alone. Tiny hairs on the back of Drew's neck stood to attention at the sound of fabric brushing fabric. It came from the deep shadows by the armature hatch where the glow of the soffit lights failed to reach. Instinctively, his hand moved to his blaster. He paused, unsure if whoever lurked in the shadows had a weapon already pointed at them. To make matters worse, Letty stood between him and the sound, blocking his line of fire. She was still staring at her hat, unaware they had company.

Drew swung his free arm, shoving Letty behind him and turned to face their intruder full-on. His blaster hand hovered above his holster.

"What is *wrong* with y . . ." Letty's question trailed off.

Curtis stepped from the shadows into the dim light of the anteroom. "Relax, it's only me." He held his arms away from his body, palms up to show he wasn't holding a weapon.

"What are you doing here?" Drew challenged, still poised for action.

"I haven't come to take you in if that's what you're worried about. Hello, Miss Taleen." Curtis dipped his head politely at Letty as she peeked out from behind Drew.

"How did you know where we were?" Drew relaxed his posture, standing straight, letting his blaster hand drop to his side.

"When you didn't come back to HQ, and with Miss Taleen disappearing too, there were only so many places you could be. I've made a lot of trips over here in the last few months. I'm thinking of opening a nightclub. *The Mine*. Catchy, yeah?"

Drew didn't respond. He was bewildered at the odd direction Curtis's dialog was taking. He'd hoped command would thoroughly search Dark Landing before looking on Spud. It was the next obvious hiding place but, if Mattie was leading the search, he'd also hoped she'd delay coming to Spud to buy him a little time. As usual, the worst-case scenario was Curtis.

Curtis was outlining his nightclub plans. "The rooms at the front of the complex are partitioned and too small for my purposes. One of the larger caverns back by the miners' quarters would be perfect, but they're filled with massive equipment that'll be hell to disassemble and move out. I'm still working on the idea. Anyway, I give environmental a heads-up whenever I come over. So, when they caught a transitory blip indicating the interior hatch to the west armature opened, they contacted me first. Lucky you."

"A nightclub," Drew said, dumbfounded. It revealed a side of Curtis he'd never expected.

"Yeah, and eventually, maybe a hotel and casino, but that's not why I'm here. I've got some information you might find interesting."

"What information?" Drew wasn't buying this laidback, amenable Curtis. A security team on the other side of the hatch was probably waiting for a signal.

Curtis took a couple of steps toward them but stopped when Drew tensed and flexed his blaster hand. He scoffed. "We both know you're not gonna shoot me. Anyway, the *Temperance* has requested clearance to depart on schedule tomorrow morning. Chief Fitzwilliam granted the request. I was a little surprised at that. What's really interesting is the Praetorians booked passage."

"No one's questioned them yet?" Drew knew the answer.

"No time. Besides, Fitzwilliam suspended the investigation until the *Golden Tracer* gets here. Odd that he's letting the *Temperance* go before then."

"Does he know the Praetorians are leaving?" Drew asked, similarly puzzled.

"He should. It was in my shift report. I assume he read it — maybe not."

Letty stepped out from behind Drew. "We can't let the

Praetorians go before they've been questioned. They may be murderers as well as technology terrorists. We've got to stop them. Maybe if we turn ourselves in and tell Fitz . . . ."

Drew was about to caution her not to act too fast without considering the ramifications when Curtis offered a suggestion.

"You could follow them onto the *Temperance*," he said flatly.

"How would we do that?" Drew asked. "The minute we step foot back on the station we'll be taken into custody."

"There are extravehicular mobility units in the miners' area. They used them to inspect the armature during construction. They appear to be in good shape. You wouldn't *need* to return to the station."

"Okay. But how exactly do we board the *Temperance* from space? Even if we could sneak on, where would we hide?" Drew asked. He was still suspicious of Curtis's motives, but willing to give him the benefit of the doubt for the short run. He glanced periodically at the hatch, still expecting it to open at any minute and a security team to file in.

"You got a processor?" Curtis reached slowly into the inside pocket of his jacket, keeping his eyes on Drew as he did. He pulled out a data vial and offered it to Drew. "This is Miss Taleen's travel documents . . . *Rebecca Richards'* travel documents, to be more accurate. She can just book passage back on the *Temperance*. No one on the ship ties her with the explosion or anything else that's happened here over the last three days. She could book a double for herself and her brother . . . *or* husband."

"Brother," Letty said quickly.

Too quickly, Drew thought, with an internal sigh. "Security is sure to be watching every ship departing. As soon as Rebecca Richards books passage, and with a *brother*, they'll be waiting."

"Right, but they'll be waiting dockside. When the two of you don't show, they'll think they scared you off."

Curtis still hadn't said how they'd board the *Temperance* from space, but he had something in mind. "Where would I get documents?" Drew asked. "I can't travel under my name. Besides, my records are frozen by now."

"Actually, I can fix that," Letty said. "I told you Dad and I have multiple aliases ready to go. I'll pull one from the company's database and substitute your image, DNA record, and Ver-i-Palm

Print." She looked at Curtis. "Can you provide those records?"

"I *could*."

Drew detected the *quid pro quo* in Curtis's response. "You still haven't said how we'd get on the *Temperance*."

"I have an associate," Curtis said carefully.

Here we go, thought Drew. He gave Curtis a disgusted look.

Curtis shrugged, outwardly unfazed by Drew's opinion of him. "I'm holding a package for my associate. But, since the crew's been confined to the ship, I couldn't deliver it without exposing myself. Just before they depart, they'll need to pay their water fee. There'll only be two crew members in the ship's cargo bay manning the coupling controls. My friend can pressurize the maintenance airlock on the opposite side and let you in unseen. From there you can check in with the purser. The purser will think you boarded from the station. If he bothers to look at the passenger manifest and finds you didn't register, he'll chalk it up to crew error."

"What's in the package?" Drew asked.

Curtis pulled a tightly wrapped package of about four-by-six inches from another pocket. "Is that really important?"

"Utopia tablets," Drew said, scrutinizing the package.

Curtis shrugged again, his bland expression neither confirming nor denying Drew's guess.

Letty tugged at Drew's sleeve. "We can't stay here, and if we go back there's no guarantee we can persuade Fitz to delay the *Temperance*. We'll be detained, and the Praetorians will get away." She stopped abruptly, morphing into her self-assured, mega-mogul persona. She let go of Drew's sleeve, turned to Curtis, and stepped forward, shoulders squared, chin up, her hand held out to accept the data vial and package. "We'll do it."

Curtis handed the items over, wearing the smug smile of a man who knew he held the winning hand.

~ ~ ∞ ~ ~

"What's wrong?" Letty frowned and watched Drew apprehensively.

They were back in their temporary quarters. With Curtis's help, she'd downloaded alias files from the Taleen Industries database. As promised, Curtis had provided Drew's official DNA and print records, and she merged the two sets of documents to complete his new identity. She'd pay for their passage using the generous expense account of the vice president in charge of interstellar promotions, whatever that was. The documents indicated that David Jacobs had held his position for three years, reporting directly to Rebecca Richards. She liked that bit of irony.

While she was at it, Letty created her own new identity. She thought it unwise to continue using the Rebecca Richards cover. Mr. Jacobs would be traveling with his personal assistant, Tina Kingsbury.

Drew hadn't heard her. They sat on their respective cable spools, Drew watching Letty while she worked, apparently deep in thought.

"What's wrong?" she repeated, nudging him with her foot.

His eyes focused. "What's wrong? You mean what's wrong besides what's wrong?"

"Yes."

"I don't trust Curtis."

"Do we have a choice?"

"No."

"So . . .?"

"What's wrong is, assuming the EMUs are still functioning, and we make it to the *Temperance* alive and undetected, assuming Curtis's associate is where he's supposed to be and we board without being caught, and assuming the purser doesn't suspect anything, what's the next step?"

"We question the Praetorians."

"Under what guise? Are we going to attack them and drag them back to our quarters? We'd have to take on all three at once. As far as I can tell, they never leave each other's side. Someone might question us dragging three monks around by their hoods, so force is out. What's left?"

"Well . . .," Letty considered their options. "As a representative of Taleen Industries, it would make sense that you'd want to talk to anyone who'd been on the station when the CEO died in such a bizarre manner." Her breath caught in her throat, and she blinked rapidly to ward off more tears.

Drew's expression softened. "That might follow if people knew that Jonas Trammel was George Speller in disguise. Or if they knew about the robe we found, *and* its connection to the monks," he said. "No one on the *Temperance* is aware of those things. And what possible excuse could we give for Speller traveling as a humble ship's crewman, cleaning up after livestock no less? The two of us questioning the Praetorians without an official capacity isn't going to elicit any major revelations, especially if they're guilty of something. Besides, you're missing the obvious."

"What's that?"

"The monks, and anyone else who boarded from Dark Landing, will know me. Even if my suspension goes unannounced officially, it's not a secret, and word travels fast. The minute someone spots me, they're going to bring it up to their friends back on the station. I won't be able to leave our cabin."

"You can stay in the cabin for the first day or two while I poke around and find out who besides the Praetorians would recognize you and know about your suspension. If we're lucky, the monks won't socialize that much. There are two sittings for each meal, one for passengers and one for crew. But passengers can eat with the crew if they want. We just need to be careful. Maybe we can figure out a disguise." She closed her eyes and rubbed her forehead. Letty's weariness and frustration were taking their toll. Events were unfolding too fast to form a solid plan, or *any* plan. They were improvising, and too many obstacles blocked their ability to act freely.

Drew seemed to sense her frustration. "For now, we'll focus on following the Praetorians. Any idea where they're going?"

"I assume Earth. Hold on a sec, I'm almost done here, then we can book our own passage." When she completed the documents, she accessed the *Temperance's* scheduled route.

"I'll book passage through to Earth, but it won't be a problem if we have to follow the Praetorians off-ship somewhere before then," she said absently, studying her screen. "We're headed to Bin first, then to the Camdu moon colony, Prosse. Short stops—only long enough to unload cargo. Then we have a tentative stop at . . . oh, crap!" Letty looked at Drew, eyes wide, "Minerva Station."

"Minerva Station! I thought we were running *from Muck*, not *to* them. If the monks get off there, we can't follow. But it'll confirm *Muck's* involvement. No one boards Minerva Station uninvited.

Where do we go from there?"

"We head back with stops at . . . one . . . two . . . three mining operations. That's interesting, two of these are owned by Taleen Industries. After that . . . ." She stopped. "Crap!"

"More crap?"

"Yes. We come back here before a straight shot to Earth."

"How long?"

"Eleven days out and three back."

Stabilized wormholes provided one-way shortcuts through space. While light years measured real distances, travel distances were calculated in days and weeks, or hops. Wormholes appeared in clusters, and in greater numbers than believed centuries earlier. When one was located, there were often others at the opposite end to carry a ship, if not precisely in the reverse direction, then to another cluster with a wormhole headed the right way. As a result, travel times could vary significantly between going to a location and returning to the starting point. The Known Universe resembled a patchwork quilt with vast areas of space still unreachable in real time, and where wormhole access would never be discovered. Try as they might, in the face of such enormity, life-kind would explore only minute bits of the cosmos before the Big Freeze.

"Okay," Drew said, thinking aloud, "if the monks debark at Minerva Station, we can't follow. Our only option will be to stay onboard and come back here."

Letty listened, still studying her screen.

"Once back here, our choices are to continue to Earth or return to Spud. Since there's a chance we'll need the EMUs again, and we can't walk around the *Temperance* in them or carry them with us during check-in, we'll tell Curtis's associate he'll get his package when he delivers the suits to our quarters."

"Sounds like a plan," Letty said. After a few seconds, she turned back to Drew. "Actually, this could work in our favor. It's our excuse to make the trip out instead of just waiting on Dark Landing for the *Temperance's* return. I'll book passage with brief visits to the two Taleen mining concerns. Taleen representatives would want to visit such remote operations before returning to Earth."

"Maybe that's why Fitz is letting the *Temperance* go, knowing she'll be returning so soon," Drew said. "Still, why would he let the monks leave before questioning? They're central to the investigation. He must not know they're leaving. I'm curious if *Muck's* approved the *Temperance's* excursion."

Letty could only shrug.

She booked a two-bedroom family suite, one of only three suites on the *Temperance*. Let the other passengers and crew think what they would. The smaller passenger cabins were taken, and the alternative meant bunks or hammocks, which didn't provide the privacy they needed and wouldn't fit Mr. Jacobs's demographic.

When she'd finished, Drew said, "That's settled then. The game's afoot."

"Huh?"

"Never mind. Let's find the EMUs and make sure they're space-worthy."

The units were in the mine storage area near the materials loading dock, as Curtis said. They would exit the airlock on the open-space side of Spud, just outside the east cradle arm. Drew explained that when the larger dock, used to move ore to the refinery ships, had been capped, they'd installed smaller airlocks as emergency exits. The facility served as headquarters and dorms during station construction after the mining ceased.

When viewed from a distance, Dark Landing, the armatures, and Spud, resembled a small crab with unnaturally long claws extended in front of it holding a rock—or in this case, a large potato. The armatures bowed out slightly. Rungs and handholds peppered their exteriors every few feet for tethering to the structures—looking just like a crab's bumpy shell. Anything in the space between the crab's arms sat in the cradle or the pocket. Anything outside the cradle was open-side or spaceside. Ships docked at the station protruded from the back end of the crab.

Drew inspected the row of eight suits and their compact oxygen/propulsion tanks, going over each one inch-by-inch. Despite the dated design, they looked in good condition. An hour passed before he pulled two complete sets from the rack.

"These will do," he said, folding the flexible suits over one arm and then slinging the strap for one of the tanks over the opposite shoulder. He motioned for Letty to take the second tank.

She followed him back to the front offices, taking one and a half steps for each of his longer strides. He moved with confidence, and she admired his lean physique. His hair was thick, sandy brown, and probably naturally wavy if he let it grow; instead, a recent trim kept it conservatively short.

She smiled to herself. For now, she'd let him continue thinking he was in charge. To be fair, he hadn't been cocky about it. That was more *her* style. Other than duping her to come with him, he'd solicited her opinion at every step. Not that they'd had a surplus of options. He'd given her the lead where she was more knowledgeable, such as with creating fake identities. They made a good team.

Despite finding him attractive, he wasn't her type romantically. She favored men more clued into the larger universe. While she didn't know Drew well, he seemed intellectually limited to his personal corner of space. *Only Muck knows.*

He stopped in front of her, breaking her reverie. They were back at their makeshift quarters.

"Okay, let's try these babies on and make sure all systems are nominal." He seemed uncharacteristically nervous.

"Don't tell me the big, bad security chief's afraid of taking a walk in space," she said, with a malicious wink.

"It's only that I like more than a few millimeters of fabric between me and minus 455 degrees. I saw a desiccated, popsicle-man once in an academy training accident. Not something you forget easily."

After trying on and testing the equipment, then double- and triple-testing it until Drew seemed satisfied, they packed their duffels and grabbed a bite to eat. He'd suggested they try to catch a couple hours of sleep. Neither of them was successful, judging by the continuous tossing and turning noises that came from the outer office.

18 SPACE WALK

Ships docking at Dark Landing paid a water fee in addition to berthing and MCTT regulatory fees. The water transfer from the ship to the station was made an hour or so before departure. Without access to station records, Drew couldn't know if the *Temperance* had enough water reserves to pay its fee. They accommodated any ships unable to make their water payments, with the understanding the delinquency must be made up on subsequent visits. Meticulous records were kept.

If the *Temperance* was unable to pay, with no crew manning the coupling controls for the water transfer, there might not be environmental services in the ship's cargo bay. And Curtis's contact wouldn't be there to meet them. He thought about messaging Curtis but was undecided how to word his inquiry without implicating him if the message fell under the eyes of someone else. Not that he cared a blow-wart's fart about Curtis, but he'd turn them over to *Muck* at the slightest pressure. He foresaw other problems.

"Look, we need to go over a few things." Drew held Letty's EMU up so she could step into it without dragging it across the rough rock surface of the corridor outside the east airlock.

She placed a hand on his shoulder to steady herself as she stepped into the suit. "Like what?"

Normally, he'd find such close proximity to her distracting, but he was too anxious about their outing. Letty had been spot-on when she teased him about his fear of extravehicular activities. He didn't like venturing so close to space he could touch it.

"For one thing," he said, "we won't be able to communicate through our suits' open circuits. Someone on the station or a docked ship might intercept our conversation. Since you don't have a comm implant and mine is disabled, that leaves only hand signals."

"Sounds simple enough." She pulled the suit to her waist, reached back and inserted her arms into the armholes, then shrugged it up over her shoulders with difficulty. It proved bulky in Spud's gravity. Drew helped her secure the neck piece.

"If our man's not on the other side, we turn around and head back here. Understood?"

Letty nodded, preoccupied with sealing one of her gloves.

Drew slid into his own suit as he spoke. "Another thing. Since normally we'd be tethered to the station or to a ship, and not free floating, it's important only one of us navigates so we don't overshoot. You'll be tethered to me, and I'll control our direction and momentum. You won't need to do anything unless there's an emergency and you have to cut me loose."

She stopped struggling with the glove and looked at him. "Like what?"

"I don't know, like if I spontaneously combust." Drew felt foolish even suggesting such an absurd possibility. But all sorts of weird things happened in space—everyone knew that.

"I thought you were afraid of freezing into a man-sickle. Is there a chance you might burst into flames?"

"I'm trying to make a point."

"Yeah, I get it. Don't use my propulsion jets unless I cut you loose first." She taunted him with an exaggerated grin.

It seemed she looked forward to their upcoming adventure. He was learning she could be impulsive and a risk-taker, but Drew found it hard to imagine she'd ever seen real peril before coming to Dark Landing. Neither had he, but she didn't need to know that.

They stood close together. As he held her gaze, Letty's expression changed from a teasing grin to one of confused unease. He wanted to kiss her, and in that moment, he felt certain she wanted him to. Words hung in the air unspoken. Drew hesitated too long; whatever passed between them was fleeting. Her attention returned to securing her glove.

After double checking the seals, they attached their helmets and tested the environmental settings one last time. That done, they tethered their duffels on a short lead behind Letty and stepped into the airlock. The interior hatch closed behind them and the cabin depressurized. Drew faced the outer hatch, took a deep breath, and pressed the release.

They drifted into open space. Drew's stomach lurched, and he swallowed hard. He'd purposely avoided food and drink that morning, so he'd have nothing to come back up. The intermittent contractions of the EMU soothed him. Its gentle massage facilitated an even distribution of bodily fluids to counter the headaches and blurred vision associated with weightlessness. He concentrated on modulating his breathing. After a few seconds, his panic subsided. He engaged the miniature propulsion jets located on the back of each arm, depressing one slightly longer than the other to angle them away from infinite space and toward the armature. Since the docks sat on the side of Dark Landing facing away from Spud, Drew and Letty could travel spaceside along the armature and be hidden from view until they reached them.

The *Temperance* rested on the second sublevel, berth eight, the third berth when approaching from their side of the station. Once they rounded the station and headed toward the *Temperance*, anyone in the ships docked in berths ten and nine could spot them, but that wasn't a serious problem. Suited crew commonly carried out inspections and made repairs. No one would be close enough to tell they weren't tethered to a particular ship.

Drew kept his eyes on the armature exterior, avoiding the view out to space. They were making good time and were within a few meters of the junction between the arm and the station when he felt a tug on his tether. Their forward motion stopped. He reached for the nearest handhold on the armature and turned. Letty had one arm through a second handhold up to the crook of her elbow, anchoring her. She gestured frantically with her free hand at the three-by-three-inch display on the opposite wrist. Drew pulled in closer to determine the problem.

She had roughly a minute of oxygen left in her suit; nothing was coming from the tank on her back. Drew had tested her oxygen supply and flow multiple times. It was sufficient to make several trips between Spud and the *Temperance*. The tank connected directly to an aperture on the back of the suit with nothing to kink or become disconnected. He had no time to diagnose the problem. *What was I thinking? The EMUs are too old to risk our lives on.* He glanced nervously at his own wrist display, relieved his reading was nominal. *We have to return to Spud.*

He turned away from her and reached his free arm over his shoulder to point at the coiled hose secured to the back of his tank. Solely for sharing oxygen in an emergency, when extended, the capped hose reached two feet long. Removing the cap exposed a vulnerable diaphragm, which kept oxygen from escaping. The front of each suit held a female aperture with a matching diaphragm. When connected, a small, manual lever would break the diaphragms to allow the exchange of oxygen. He'd walked through the procedure with her once. Hopefully she'd been paying attention. He realized too late they should have practiced using two of the spare suits.

Drew could feel her releasing the coiled hose from the back of his tank. He fought the urge to turn around and see if she was successful. Fifteen seconds passed as he watched his flow gauge. Precious seconds later he realized he was holding his breath. He let it out and took in a fresh lungful. His gauge leapt double the previous level, and a tap on his shoulder communicated she was set.

Over his shoulder, he jerked a thumb backward toward Spud, then pushed gently out from the armature. Letty pulled at his suit, stopping him. He angled his head around and saw she'd grabbed the handhold again. He pointed toward Spud.

She made angry jabbing gestures in the opposite direction, toward the station and the docks. He shook his head. He . . . *they* needed to return to the safety of Spud. She alternated pointing forward and slapping the back of his helmet. They were getting nowhere. Panic rose when she wouldn't let loose of the handhold. He was afraid to pull too hard and disconnect the oxygen hose. He placed his gloved hands in front of him, palms pressed together, eyes closed and fought for control. Letty put a hand on each of his shoulders. He could barely feel her thumbs massaging his back through the thick fabric, but it calmed him. She activated her propulsion jets, and they moved forward once again.

With the two of them so close together, traveling would be awkward. More problematic, if a crew member from one of the ships spotted them now, with Letty essentially riding Drew piggyback, it would be obvious they were in trouble. Someone would be dispatched to assist them.

They reached the armature junction and rounded it, hugging the station as they approached dockside. A bluish glow emanated from the lighted cargo bays, and the bulk of a ship protruded from the end berth. Letty probably saw nothing but the back of his helmet. This was the part of their journey he dreaded the most. They now had to leave the security of the station toward open space, then around the bows of the docked ships and down the line to the third bay and the *Temperance*.

Even with Letty's suit malfunction and his panic attack, they'd made good time. They would arrive well within the timeframe Curtis arranged for his man to be waiting by the airlock—assuming he'd be there at all. Drew shuddered at the thought of making the return trip to Spud. He tapped his propulsion controls and angled them away from the station toward open space. He bit his bottom lip to stave off a new wave of panic and steadied his breathing.

When he was even with the bow of the first ship, he maneuvered the jets so that they were traveling midlevel between corresponding viewports. If no one had seen them approach, they wouldn't be in view again until they made the crossing between it and the ship in berth nine.

Time slowed. It felt like they'd been in open space for hours, though Drew's wrist display indicated they left Spud only thirty-five minutes earlier. According to his gauges, they had enough oxygen to continue for two more hours, even sharing resources. He wondered what the opposite of claustrophobia was—agoraphobia? He wasn't sure. He thought he recalled a phobia for being lost in the cold emptiness of space. As he pondered possible names for his fear, he kept one eye on his wrist display and watched for anyone else out for a stroll, or a shuttle launching from one of the ships.

He remembered: *astrophobia*. He hadn't faced it since the academy. He'd hidden his problem well during training exercises and psych exams, graduating with the harmless notation of "mild initial anxiety" on his final record, but he was out of practice dealing with it.

As they rounded the bow of the second ship and headed across to the *Temperance*, Drew sensed more than felt Letty bobbing along behind him. Every so often she shifted her hand from one shoulder to his other, inadvertently assuring him she was okay. Once closer to the *Temperance*, they would have to travel down her port side toward the docks to reach the cargo bay airlock. Dark Landing's atmospheric shields would blur the view of anything outside the dock's contained environment.

Halfway between ships, he caught a movement to his right. A suited crewman had exited a hatch of the second ship and waved to signal help was on its way. Drew responded with the universal rigid arm, palm outward signal for stop. He elbowed Letty to indicate she should do the same. She caught on and repeated the gesture. The crewman hesitated, hanging close to the ship's hatch, watching them. Drew couldn't increase their momentum since they were already moving at maximum speed. He brought them in closer to the side of the *Temperance*, simultaneously letting the watching crewman know they had maneuverability. Once within a few feet of the airlock hatch, Drew reached out to grab the handhold. If no one was there to let them in their little adventure was at an end.

19 THE TEMPERANCE

Drew peered through the viewport hoping to see someone staring back at him from the other side. It was a waste of effort. Layers of grime obstructed his view into the airlock interior. He suppressed the temptation to see if the crewman from the other ship was still watching, certain that was the case. He could feel the crewman's eyes boring into his back.

A keypad to the right of the hatch held a large square button, which glowed green to indicate the airlock was empty and depressurized. Had someone occupied the airlock, suited or not, the button would be red, and the hatch could only be released from the inside. Green or red, if Drew pushed the button before entering a code, an alarm would alert security of an unauthorized boarding attempt.

It seemed silly, but the only thing he could think to do was knock. At the third rap, the hatch slid up, out of sight. Drew and Letty entered the airlock and pulled the duffels in after them. As soon as they cleared the opening, the outer hatch closed, and the inside keypad flashed intermittent red. They faced the interior while they waited for the airlock to pressurize. Anxiety at what awaited them shipside replaced Drew's sense of relief at surviving the spacewalk. He imagined *Temperance* security, or perhaps his own men, were dispatched to return them to Dark Landing. When the button turned green, the hatch slid open, and they stepped into the

Temperance's cargo bay.

The man who greeted them was huge, taller than Drew in his EMU, a mass of muscle . . . and he was in a hurry. In seconds he had unattached Letty from Drew's oxygen supply and had her helmet off. Just as fast, Drew's helmet seal popped, and he was breathing *Temperance* air as well. While Drew fumbled with his gloves, the big guy set both tanks down and stripped back the top of Letty's suit. He watched in trepidation as the man grasped her by the waist and lifted her out of the bottom half, then set her gingerly down on the deck next to it. He did the same with Drew. In no time they stood in front of him in their civvies with the EMUs puddled beside them.

The man's smile was as big as he was. In a thick Earth-Eastern European accent, he introduced himself as Nikko and shook both their hands. Drew and Letty mumbled, "Nice to meet you," in turn. Nikko had none of Curtis's slime quotient but, by his bearing and sheer size, Drew was certain the man could be as dangerous as he was polite. Without being asked, he directed them to the purser's stand, announcing he would deliver their duffels and the EMUs to their cabin and wait for them there.

"Well, that went slick as snot on a gold tooth," Drew said as soon as they entered the passage Nikko had indicated.

"Did he just pick us up like dolls?" Letty asked.

"Yes . . . yes, he did."

With Nikko's accent, his directions required some interpretation. But after weaving through back corridors and up two levels, they successfully found the passenger area of the ship. Drew hung back, head down, and let Letty take the lead. She strolled up to the purser's stand as if she owned it and introduced herself as Tina Kingsbury, Mr. Jacobs's assistant. She advised the woman whose badge read "Melissa, Assistant Purser" that she and Mr. Jacobs were unable to access their suite. After checking her screen, Melissa flashed Letty with a look of annoyed bureaucratic superiority, quickly followed by a sequence of facial expressions that needed no subtitles. She started to speak, hesitated, reconsidered, smiled, and apologized.

Melissa is definitely management material, Drew thought.

"I'm sorry. I'm not sure how that happened, Miss Kingsbury. I've corrected the error. Is there anything else I can help you with?"

"No, that's all. Thank you *so* much." Letty returned the

woman's smile.

"My pleasure. If you need anything at all, please contact the purser's office. Refreshments will be served in the passenger mess along with a short orientation, exactly one hour after we debark."

Letty nodded her acknowledgement and preceded Drew down a carpeted corridor behind the purser's station. When they moved out of ear shot, she said, "Well, that went slick as snot on a gold tooth."

Their cabin was tucked away at the end of the corridor. Drew palmed the access panel, and the hatch slid open. He couldn't squelch the uncomfortable feeling that things were falling into place too easily.

Nikko waited in the small lounge of their suite, the EMUs and duffels in a pile next to him. How he'd made it there before them, Drew couldn't fathom. He pulled the infamous package from the inside pocket of his jacket and handed it over. Nikko accepted the package and, flashing another face-wide smile, exited the cabin, ducking through the hatch. No words were exchanged.

~ ~ ∞ ~ ~

Letty stored her duffel and EMU in one of the bedrooms, freshened up, then joined Drew in the lounge. He was scrolling through a list of menu options on a wall-mounted monitor.

"They're transmitting the orientation to our cabin. I may be able to see most of the passengers from here," he said.

"Good. When I come back, we can compare notes. Do you think someone from the station would recognize me?"

"Possible, but I doubt it. Even so, only command and a handful of security staff know who you are, especially in connection with all that's happened. What about passengers you traveled with on the way out?"

"No chance. I avoided contact as much as I could. When I had to interact, I kept my hat on, head down, and said as little as possible. Cleaned up, in a business suit and without the hat, they'll never give me a second glance."

Drew looked like he wanted to comment. After a moment, he winked.

Now what does that mean?

"Smile for the camera," he said as she left.

On familiar ground now, Letty headed to the mess. To further distinguish herself from the reclusive Rebecca Richards who'd made the trip out, she decided to act the extrovert Taleen Industries ambassador. She nodded and smiled at everyone she passed, sprinkling in "Hellos" here and there.

In the mess, she accepted a glass of wine and hugged the back bulkhead, giving her full view of the room. She raised her glass in the direction of the empty podium where she thought there might be a camera and toasted Drew, then looked around for monks.

Letty recognized a few faces of passengers continuing on from the first half of the trip, and noted they were few in number. Since the ship was returning to Dark Landing, most must have opted to stay on the station. There were no monks. Among the passengers she didn't recognize was a distinguished gentleman who Letty guessed worked in the sciences. He looked like every physicist she knew—a preoccupied tour guide. A family—father, mother, and a boy of about eight—stood by themselves looking out-of-place. A businessman had been at the canapé table stuffing his face since Letty arrived.

She noticed two women at the bar with exaggerated hair and makeup, and tight-fitting clothing that revealed a lot of skin. Another woman stood nearby, chatting seductively with a male passenger. Openly staring, she realized the two at the bar were now staring back at her wearing sardonic expressions. Fortunately, the head purser stepped to the podium and diverted everyone's attention.

After the purser's short welcome speech came mess schedules and safety announcements, and then the crowd dispersed. The monks were a no-show. Letty wrapped several canapés in a napkin, grabbed another glass of wine, and headed back to their quarters.

As she entered, she offered the snacks and wine to Drew. "Well?"

Drew unfolded the napkin and sniffed at the appetizers suspiciously. "Thanks. I didn't recognize anyone from the station except the kid and his parents, the Greensteins. The boy, Toby, is a problem child. We've pulled him into HQ a dozen times for various mischief. The family and I are well acquainted. If Toby's onboard, this ship's in imminent danger."

Letty ignored his comment. "What about the scientist-type and the businessman? They weren't on the first half of the trip with me. Did you recognize them?"

He shook his head.

"What about—"

"—the hookers?" Drew finished her question. "We've had several recent complaints of prostitution. Since we serve such a wide variety of races and cultures, we don't permit hookers, licensed or otherwise—and I think these are otherwise. It was only a matter of time until we IDed them. They must have felt us closing in and decided to pack it up. My guess is they're getting off at one of the mining operations."

"They seemed as interested in me as I was in them."

"You were sizing them up based on their appearance. They were doing the same. It's a woman thing, isn't it?"

"Men don't size people up?"

"Okay, it's a *human* thing."

"Whatever. I'm taking the first meal with the crew. It seems likely the monks will do the same if they want to avoid socializing. I don't remember ever seeing monks before."

"There's not much to see but brown robes. Their faces are hidden by hoods, but they must lower them to eat."

Letty spent the afternoon reviewing her dad's data vials for more clues, while Drew tried unsuccessfully to find the source of her EMU malfunction. Neither of them had mentioned his bout of panic during their spacewalk to the *Temperance*, but she could tell by his manner he was brooding over it. Failing to uncover anything new, she still had several files to go through by dinnertime.

Only one of the continuing passengers (who appeared to be acquainted with a crew member) ate in the crew mess as well. No monks. She would take breakfast in the passenger mess in the morning. The *Temperance* didn't offer room service, so the monks had to show sometime.

On a bulkhead just outside the mess hall, a row of hooks held an assortment of hats, jackets, and aprons that crew members had hung up on their way to dinner. As she passed, she grabbed a black, stiff-billed cap with a soft crown worn close to the skull. The caps were common among the crew.

In their quarters, she handed Drew a meal container from the mess buffet, a water pouch, and the hat.

"Thanks," Drew said.

"You can eat in the crew's mess. No one there would recognize you. You're going to go stir-crazy if you can't leave this cabin."

She went to her bedroom and returned with a brown sweater. "I brought along Dad's favorite cardigan. I've been trying to get rid of it for years and must have bought him a half-dozen replacements. He would never give it up. It's stretched out and has holes. With the sweater and hat, you'll look like a crew member. The other passengers should ignore you. As long as you avoid the Greensteins, you'll be okay."

Drew put on the cap, adjusting it at a rakish angle so the brim cast a shadow across his forehead and one eye. He flashed a boyish grin. The dark cap made his eyes an even deeper green than usual.

He knows he's adorable, Letty thought. "Just stay away from the hookers," she said.

"I beg your pardon?"

"You're just their type."

"What's that mean?"

"Okay, don't take this the wrong way, but . . . you're cute . . . cute-*ish* anyway. If you're passing a woman, keep your head down and don't look at her."

"Why, Miss Taleen, that's the nicest thing you've ever said to me."

"I wasn't trying to be nice." She turned abruptly to hide her smile and headed to her bedroom. "I'm going to scan the rest of Dad's files then hit my bunk early. See you in the morning."

~ ~ ∞ ~ ~

Drew reached for his blaster on the table next to his bed, realizing instantaneously that there *was* no table and that it was Letty standing by his bedside.

"Wake up!"

"Why? What?" His head cleared, and he remembered where

he was. "What's wrong?"

"Nothing's wrong. It's the hookers!"

He relaxed and tried to make sense of what she was saying. "The hookers aren't here, Letty. You may think I'm their type, but I guarantee they're not mine. On second thought, if you want, I could probably invite them—"

"*Idiot!* The hookers are the monks."

"The hookers are with the monks?"

"No. Listen carefully, Drew. The hookers ... *are* ... the monks."

"The hookers are the monks? The hookers ... *are* ... the monks. *The hookers are the monks!*"

"One more time and maybe you'll get it."

"Come to think of it, I've never seen their faces or any other part of their bodies, and—"

"Here it comes."

"*Ho-ly* shit!"

"Right

20 BIN

Drew wore his chinos, George Speller's ratty brown cardigan, and the crewman's cap Letty had swiped pulled low on his forehead. Letty figured no one would recognize him from a casual glance. He hunched his shoulders slightly and turned to one side to present a profile view. He'd let his beard grow the last three days. The dark shadow completed his scruffy appearance.

She appraised him carefully. "Don't look anyone in the eyes and mumble a little if you have to speak, and I think you're good. At least for meals in the crew mess. Going down to Bin is pushing it, though."

"I just want a quick look-see."

"Yeah, well, this isn't a site-seeing trip. Anyway, you should stay here and keep your eye on the hookers."

"The hooker monks aren't going anywhere. I checked with the purser and there's only one other passenger going down with us, a biochemist by the name of Cooker ... er ... Crocker. I've never heard of him. If he's the same scientist-guy you pointed out on the orientation feed, I've never *seen* him before, either."

"That doesn't mean he won't know who *you* are. He wasn't a passenger on the trip from Earth, so he had to come from the station. And can you please stop saying 'hooker monks'? It sounds like the title to a theological porn vid."

"I've met all of the scientists stationed on Dark Landing," Drew said. "More likely he transferred to the *Temperance* from another ship. Anyway, Crocker is getting off at Bin. If he recognizes me, I'll just say I'm on holiday. And 'prostitutes disguised as monks' is too long. 'Hooker monks' says it all."

Letty shrugged, abandoning her effort to modify Drew's terminology. "How would you explain using an alias *and* the disguise?" Letty asked.

"You're over-thinking this. It's not like I'm wearing a wig and fake mustache. It'll be fine. Besides, I've never been on an Alliance planet except Earth. I don't want to miss the opportunity."

Other than the Bahdaneians and, to a lesser extent, the Fahdeens, their distant relatives, Earth citizens rarely made physical contact with aliens. Only scientists and the occasional capitalist might venture beyond an alien planet's arrival and departure lounges.

She knew it was a wasted effort, but Letty tried to dissuade him from making the side trip anyway. "Well, except for the view from the Earth lounge, you aren't going to see much. If you want to interact with a real, live Bindian, you'll have to do it through an invisiwall."

"Have you met a Bindian before?"

"I spent a month with them. Taleen Industries has trade partnerships with several Bindian enterprises. We've hired and trained two legions of security personnel there as well."

She downplayed the experience. "They look like all the vids you've seen: squat, big-jointed, with shiny exoskeletons. Most people don't know they can stand upright if they want to, but it's a sign of aggression. Even standing, the tallest wouldn't be over four feet. The difference between Bin and Earth gravity is brutal. I had to wear an anti-g suit whenever I left the controlled Earth environment," Letty said.

"I'm only going in order to contact the ETOC and my assistant and fill them in about . . . everything. With Curtis's friend knowing who we are, our quarters may not be secure." She raised her voice on the last few words so if someone was listening, they'd know she was on to them.

Drew laughed. "By now, *Muck* or Fitz has already informed your company and the local authorities about everything," he said. "I'm curious to know where your people think *you* are, though. You're sure you can trust your assistant?"

"Yes, and with your life as well as mine."

"I wish I felt as certain. What time is it? We don't want to cut boarding too close."

"We can head there now." Letty started to pull her travel poncho on then, remembering her current identity, reached for her suit jacket instead.

The passenger lift was empty going down. When the doors opened onto the shuttle bay, two of the hooker monks stood a few feet from them, chatting coquettishly with Dr. Crocker.

The three turned at Drew and Letty's arrival. From their expressions, there was no doubt in Letty's mind that the ladies not only recognized Drew but were surprised to see him.

Before any words could be exchanged, the pilot appeared around the shuttle bow. "All aboard that's going down." He looked startled to see a group of five people. "I was told there would only be three passengers. The way the freight's been distributed there's no extra seating. If there's been a mix up—"

"No worries, hon," the bustier of the two women said. "We were just saying goodbye to the doctor." She smiled and leaned closer to Dr. Crocker. "Too bad you're not going all the way with us, sweetie."

Crocker had the decency to blush at her innuendo and uttered a hasty "Goodbye" as he stepped backwards through the shuttle hatch, tripping on the lower lip and catching himself awkwardly.

Letty fought the urge to turn around and get back on the lift but allowed Drew to usher her past the ladies and onto the shuttle. The women watched with tight smiles.

Their seats lay just inside the opened hatch, and Letty heard the two speaking in low tones as she and Drew strapped in. She couldn't make out what they said before the pilot directed them off the shuttle bay, but she heard the word "contact" and "react"—or maybe "deact"—nothing that made sense without more context. Letty looked at Drew questioningly. She started to ask if he'd heard anything, but he shook his head slightly to indicate *not now*.

Crocker sat opposite them across a wide aisle. A row of neck-high crates down its center separated them, making casual conversation difficult. Crocker, seemingly still embarrassed, avoided eye contact.

The pilot entered the control cabin by the forward hatch, closing it as well as the one next to their seats. The shuttle bay depressurized, lights on the pilot's control panel flashed, and the bay doors rumbled and opened to space. As they moved out, Letty looked at Drew. He swallowed hard. His knuckles shone white on the hand grasping the armrest between them. She had suspected as much before, but since the EVA episode, she felt certain. Drew was more than just nervous walking in space; he was terrified of space in general. *What the hell is he doing in charge of a space station?*

Crocker was evidently expected. He disappeared from the Earth lounge through a side hatch immediately upon arrival.

Along with environmental obstacles, the fear of disease inhibited close contact between alien races and demanded lengthy quarantine, both upon arrival on an alien planet and return to the home world. Alliance planets were required to provide environmentally compatible lounges and short-stay quarters for member visitors. Non-aligned planets proved far less accommodating. If there was a need for an extended stay on any alien world or colony, *Muck* regulations dictated the visitor must obtain prior approval from both the home and host authorities.

Drew and Letty split up. Drew headed toward the transparent enclosure where a Bindian sat crab-like on a carpeted platform. This put him—or her, Letty could never tell with certainty—close to eye level with most humans.

She nodded toward the Bindian as she passed, her head tilted at the proper angle to denote respect but not esteem. Bindians who worked in the alien arrival lounges did so as punishment for minor offenses. To them, casual conversation and personal questions were an insult, to which they would often respond by asking about the visitor's mother, an even greater insult.

She sought the furthest lounger. It took twenty minutes to open a clear connection to the ETOC. Rostenkowski was out of the office, so she left her a message: *Contact me on the freighter Temperance. I'm not feeling well. I caught a virus on Dark Landing. It's spreading fast there.*

Her transmission to San Francisco found more success. Stephen, her senior assistant, took it in Rebecca Richards' private office.

Without the usual salutations, Letty asked, "Stephen, you've learned about Mr. Speller?"

"Yes. I'm at a loss for words . . . Tina." He obviously wanted to offer his condolences and express his own feelings of loss, but he upheld her Tina Kingsbury cover.

"I understand. It could be a while before I make it back. We're on Bin now and soon we'll be dropping in on two of our mining operations near the Schwarzschild Cluster. Everything all right with you guys?"

"As all right as possible under the circumstances. Evans has stepped up, and we're grateful to have a steady hand on the tiller." Carl Evans was Taleen Industries CFO and next in the line of succession. "You said 'we'?" Stephen asked, with an arched eyebrow.

"Yes, I'm traveling with David Jacobs our V.P. of Interstellar Promotions for this quadrant. I believe you may need to update my itinerary. I'm not sure where you show me right now."

"We understood you were at Dark Landing working on a delicate project involving *Muck*."

"Another commitment made it impossible for me to accept that assignment. Please have Mr. Evans extend the company's apologies. Perhaps the head of legal could work with *Muck* in my absence?" Letty wanted her legal office to pave the way, in case she wound up being questioned by MCTT.

"Of course; I'll see to it. I can't imagine what Miss Taleen is going through right now. Mr. Evans is eager to speak with her about arrangements but, understandably, she's been in seclusion."

Evans had never met Katherine Leticia Taleen as far as he knew. Though he'd worked with "Rebecca Richards," George Speller's *assistant*, for several years. He must have been shocked when he learned Rebecca's identity.

"Under the circumstance, I believe she would prefer that Mr. Evans and you handle the necessary arrangements."

"Yes ... certainly. Do you have any suggestions for an appropriate service?"

"Whatever Evans decides will be fine. I'm very sorry I can't attend. Even if I headed back today, I'm over a month out. Leaving now is impossible regardless."

"I see. I have a bit of other business if you don't mind?" Stephen said.

"What's that?"

"Secretary Rostenkowski of the ETOC has been trying to reach you. She asked me to tell you the recent tech schematics you provided are very similar to schematics she received from Camdu, and she needs to speak with you personally about supporting documentation. Is there anyone else I can refer her to?"

"No. I tried to reach her before I contacted you, but she was unavailable. I left her a message. Please tap her and, if she and I haven't already spoken, ask her to be available in five days—Sunday my time—for a transmission from the Resolution Mine on Caffrey. Anything else?"

"No, everything's being handled. I wish you could be here with us."

"So do I, Stephen. I miss you all. Please give Mr. Evans my best. Tell him Taleen Industries is very fortunate to have someone with such commitment and passion in charge. I'll talk to you again as soon as I'm able. Use your best judgement about telling people where I am. Goodbye." Letty broke the connection. She couldn't be there for Dad's memorial service but, if possible, she would accompany him back to Earth and arrange a proper funeral.

Letty shared her and Stephen's conversation and Rostenkowski's enigmatic message with Drew on the way back to the *Temperance.* "I don't know what to make of it. I never sent her any schematics," she ended.

"It sounds like one of your desk units with hacker nanoids may have wound up on Camdu. Do you trade tech with them?"

"We barter tech with all Alliance members, but we've located and updated every processor desk out there and none were on Camdu." She sighed. "There's no point guessing. We won't learn anything until I talk to Rostenkowski." Noticing Drew had made a purchase in the Bindian gift shop, she asked, "What's in the package?"

"A stuffed Bindian." He pulled it out. "See, its pronotum plate has the Bin emblem on it."

"You collect stuffed characters?" Sometimes Drew Cutter was outright baffling.

"It's a gift. One of my security staffers just had a baby."

"Ah, that's thoughtful of you. So, how *was* your first encounter with a Bindian?" she asked archly.

"Great! It was interesting. He answered all my questions about himself and his life on Bin. Though, I got the feeling the translator unit wasn't always accurate. He seemed eager to learn about my family too, particularly my mother."

"Really?" Letty pinched off her smile and turned to look out the shuttle port.

~ ~ ∞ ~ ~

Drew was sitting on his bunk, still working on Letty's EMU, when the monitor chimed in the lounge area. Letty answered the chime before he could get there. He stepped to his open door to see who it was.

Transmission External Relay to: Tina Kingsbury, Passenger, Temperance Freight Carrier, Regristry-RMD5H2. From: Earth, Oregon, San Francisco, Taleen Security Force, Commander Travis Barnes. Will you accept transmission?

"Yes," Letty said.

The same man who'd been standing next to Letty in the graduation picture on her father's data vial appeared on the screen.

"Le—Tina? *Jesus*, I've been so worried about you. Don't be mad; Stephen told me how I could reach you. I've been going crazy, honey. I'm so sorry about George. Are you okay? I hate it that you're there all alone."

"I'm doing okay. It's good to see you, Travis. I told Stephen he could share my whereabouts. It's just been so crazy here. I guess everyone knows?"

"Yeah, and it finally made the news. We're all devastated. I . . . I can't believe it. I won't ask for details now. When are you coming back?"

"I don't know. It could be a while—weeks, maybe a couple months. I'm bringing him home and we'll have a private service." Her voice wavered, but she maintained control.

"What on earth were you two doing all the way out . . . never mind. Sorry. I just wish I could be there for you, or if Stephen was with you. One of us anyway." Travis looked past Letty and spotted Drew in the doorway. "Who's that?"

Letty glanced over her shoulder. "Oh, Drew. Travis, this is Drew Cutter, Chief of Security on Dark Landing . . . *oh—shoot!* I mean—"

Drew cut her off. "Nice to meet you, Travis."

"Yeah, good meeting you, too."

It was obvious to Drew, if not to Letty, that neither man was sincere. "Sorry. I wasn't trying to eavesdrop, but I want you to know she's not alone."

"I see that." Travis's look dismissed Drew. He turned his attention back to Letty. "Listen, babe, I just wanted to make sure you're okay and let you know how sorry I am, and how much I want to be there for you."

"Thanks, Travis. I know—I miss you. I miss everyone . . . and

Dad. But I'm okay. I'll be okay."

Drew returned to his room to give them privacy but stood next to the door and listened.

"I'm going to let you go," Travis said. "I promise not to bother you again, but *please* contact me as soon as you can. I want to know what's going on. Don't make me beat it out of Stephen."

"As if you could." She laughed softly. "I will, I promise. And if I can't talk to you directly, I'll leave a message for you with Stephen . . . or whoever."

"I guess that'll have to do. Take care. Love you."

"Love you, too. Bye."

When she ended the transmission, Drew returned to the lounge. "That was nice of him."

"Yes. We're old friends. I've known him since I was nine. We went through school and most of college together. We're like brother and sister . . . now. Like I said—just friends."

"You don't have to explain your relationship to me," Drew said.

"I know. I know that. I was just telling you how we knew each other. That's all."

"He seems like a nice guy." Drew went back to his room and closed the door behind him.

21 THE GOLDEN TRACER

Curtis stood in front of Drew's desk at parade rest, his feet roughly ten inches apart, legs straight, hands clasped against the small of his back. His blue eyes fixed forward. At five-eleven and 185 pounds, he might be described as compact or sturdy, but never overweight. Though he disliked most things military, he understood the value in a level of regulatory fastidiousness on outposts such as Dark Landing. His auburn hair was cropped short; his uniform spotless and unwrinkled, with knife-edge creases across the back and down the sleeves and pant legs.

He doubted Fitz understood the stance's meaning — and he would never think to put Curtis *at ease*, but it amused Curtis anyway. He played tiny mind-games most days to keep himself from imploding of boredom. It might simply be moving someone's coffee cup from one side of their desk to the other, back and forth during the day. Or answering a question with a subtle double entendre. Someone, usually Drew, would inevitably grow suspicious, but that just made the games more challenging. If Drew commented, it provided Curtis an opportunity to practice his earnest, innocuous expression.

He disliked Fitz. He disliked Mattie Freelander even more. To be honest, he disliked most people, usually because they were dolts. A person needn't be brilliant or accomplished, they just had to be interesting. He'd come to space for adventure and excitement — and maybe to escape a bit of trouble back on Earth — but until the last few days, he'd found only tedium. *Torture me, kill me, just don't bore me to death.* He let his thoughts wander. *Mattie thinks she's clever, but she's wrong. And there's something going on between her and Fitz. Couldn't be romance*; he grimaced involuntarily at the thought.

Curtis liked and respected Drew Cutter, even though he saw through his lame attempts to deflect Curtis's attention. *What's the big deal with the Taleen chick anyway?* If given the chance, he and Drew might become friends. He'd tried to ingratiate himself with Drew, but nothing seemed to work. He'd like an invite to the weekly poker games, but Drew had ignored those hints as well.

"Curtis, are you listening to me?" Fitz said, breaking Curtis's trance.

"Yes, sir. I'm sorry, sir. I may have missed . . . the middle . . ."

"I received an urgent message from Minerva Station." Fitz appeared frazzled and out-of-sorts.

"Minerva Station — right."

"Can you get in touch with Drew?" He watched Curtis intently.

"What? No, of course not, why would you even ask that? If I knew where he was, I would tell you immediately, sir."

Fitz waved his hand in front of his face as if shooing away gnats. "Mattie seems to think you know where Drew is. That there's something you're not telling us. Is he on the *Temperance*?"

"On the *Temperance*, sir? How *could* he be? I resent the implication that I would withhold . . . if anyone, Mattie . . ." Caught off guard, he was sputtering.

Fitz sighed. "Mattie and her team searched Spud and found signs Drew and Miss Taleen had been hiding there. The environmental logs show the airlock to the armature was accessed the afternoon they went missing, and that you went over later that same day. They're not anywhere on the station or Spud, and the *Temperance* was the first ship to leave after they disappeared."

"I was searching Spud for them myself, sir. I saw no sign someone had been there. I don't know about the *Temperance*."

"Okay, we'll play it your way. I don't have the time to spar with you right now. If you know where Drew is, tell him the *Golden Tracer* was attacked and destroyed early this morning. All souls on board were lost. The *Temperance* is delivering cargo to Minerva Station in two days. He needs to stop this silliness and turn himself in to *Muck.*"

Curtis's smarmy facade deteriorated. "You're shitting me? Who would . . . why would anyone attack the *Golden Tracer*? *Muck* can't think Cutter's involved."

"I don't know who thinks what. I'm leaving tomorrow morning on the *Essovius* for Minerva Station. Mattie's in charge. You're dismissed."

"Mattie? What the—?"

"You're *dismissed!*"

Stunned, Curtis left the office. *Where did Fitz suddenly find his balls? Something turned on his* el hefe *switch. It must be that bitch Mattie's doing. And, who'd have the nerve to attack the* Golden Tracer. *Why?*

It was forty-five minutes until the night shift, but Kyle was entering HQ as Curtis came out of Drew's office.

Curtis spoke to him in an undertone. "You know about the *Golden Tracer?*"

"Yeah, Mattie filled me in. That's why I'm here early."

"I just heard. You got any details?"

"Only that they got off one transmission identifying it as an Earth-design light cruiser, nothing else. I mean, except, it had to be armed to destroy the *Golden Tracer.* How would a raider get a hold of an Earth light cruiser?"

"I don't know, and there's been no raider activity in this quadrant in our lifetimes. Not since Earth joined the Alliance, anyway. *Muck* audit ships are only midrange commuters. They don't carry cargo. The only thing of value would be the ship itself, so why blow it up? It couldn't fire back at them."

"Maybe someone has a grudge against *Muck*?" Kyle offered.

"Everyone has a grudge against *Muck.*"

Mattie walked up behind Kyle and addressed Curtis." You heard what happened, I see."

"Mattie . . . er . . . sir. Congratulations."

"Don't get your pantaloons in a bunch. It's only temporary."

What is going on with everyone? Curtis tried to look affronted. "Hey, you won't have any problems with me. I get it. You have seniority and someone has to be in charge. Drew would have picked you as well."

"Good," Mattie said. "Did Fitz talk to you about Drew?"

"He did," Curtis said stiffly. "But I couldn't help him. Since you're here, if you two will excuse me. I need to finish my shift report." He left them standing in the middle of the room and sat at the shift commander's desk he shared with Mattie. *Let her lurk around with her thumb up her ass. It's my shift and my desk for another forty-five minutes.*

Curtis worked until a little after shift end. Fitz and Mattie had left to grab dinner. He spoke to Kyle on his way out. "I'm going. Tell Mattie I'll be on call if she wants me back."

He wouldn't risk contacting Drew directly, but he could get in touch with Nikko. If anyone tracked his transmission, he'd say he was following Fitz's lead and asking his friend on the *Temperance* to keep an eye out for Drew and Miss Taleen.

~ ~ ∞ ~ ~

Drew and Letty retired to their individual rooms after the last dinner mess. The *Temperance* had made a brief stop on the moon colony of Prosse earlier in the day. Drew was relieved to learn the Greensteins debarked there. Though Prosse was a Camdu protectorate, it housed a human colony. He wished the authorities good luck with Toby. They would need it.

The *Temperance* would put in at Minerva Station in two days. He wondered what the hooker monks would do. The impropriety of three hookers getting off at, essentially, an Alliance police station, would be remarkable. He smiled at his unintended pun. Even if they put their robes back on, who would they be fooling? But then, the last eight days had been one surprise after another.

A muted gong sounded from the lounge, and it took him a few seconds to realize someone was at the entry hatch. He and Letty came out of their rooms at the same time. No part of a face was visible on the monitor. It displayed only a chambray shirt covering an expansive chest.

"It's Nikko," Drew said, opening the hatch. With his ever-present smile, the big man handed him a data vial, then turned and left.

"Nice seeing you again," Drew called after the retreating hulk.

He inserted the vial into the wall monitor. The image of Curtis Walker materialized on screen. Drew and Letty moved to the two-seater lounger. Curtis had evidently transmitted from his personal quarters. He was sitting in a relaxed position at a table filled with dirty food containers.

"Nikko, buddy, the guy in charge here seems to think there are two people from the station – a dopey looking guy with a super-hot woman – who got on the Temperance *to avoid questioning about a local matter."* Curtis looked to be enjoying himself. *"Keep your eyes out for them, will you?*

"You're scheduled to stop at Minerva Station in a couple days, right? Our chief of administration is heading that way himself, but he'll be about a week behind you. He thinks the two I told you about should turn themselves in. It's likely Muck *security will board the* Temperance *to search for them otherwise.*

"Speaking of security, three monks boarded the Temperance *from Dark Landing at the same time as those two. That's assuming those two did board . . . which I don't know they did. Anyway, I've been looking into the monks' backgrounds – don't ask – and I'm pretty sure those guys are not monks. They're probably not even guys. Anyway, I thought you should know.*

"Oh, and did you hear about the Muck *ship, the* Golden Tracer? *It was attacked and destroyed early this morning. I don't have any details yet except all hands were lost."*

"So, that's it. Take care, buddy. Catch you later." Curtis's image froze and then faded out.

Drew's stomach sunk. He was stunned by the loss of the *Golden Tracer* and its crew. Why would anyone attack a *Muck* audit ship? It made no sense. And that meant Bertie Wellington was dead. He would miss his friend despite the current strain on their friendship. He turned to Letty. "Well, the jig's up," he said without emotion.

"Why do you do that? Why do you say things like, 'the game's afoot' and 'the jig's up'? People have died. My *father* is dead."

He reached out to comfort her, but as usual, she pulled back from his touch. "I'm sorry, Letty, I'm being insensitive. It's just . . . when I'm in these situations, I tend to be flippant. Don't ask me why. I had a friend on the *Golden Tracer*." Chastised, he was genuinely sorry he'd reacted so callously. It hid his true feelings.

"No, I'm the one that's sorry. You're right, the jig is up, and we're back where we started. We haven't learned anything," Letty said.

"We've learned who the monks are and how the bogeymen are spreading nanoids," Drew offered.

"Yes, but we still don't know who's in charge. It's not the hookers for sure. And who killed Hernandez? And now we don't know who or why someone would blow up a *Muck* ship. Everything that's happened . . . happening . . . is connected. We were foolish to think we could figure this out ourselves. I'm contacting Rostenkowski tonight."

Drew silently added his own items to the list of things they didn't know. Like how Hernandez' killer had known precisely when and where Letty would be. And why was Fitz on his way to Minerva Station? Invitations to Minerva Station were infrequent and only offered to politicians and other VIPs. What could possibly be the connection between the loss of the *Golden Tracer* and Dark Landing? What did they need to speak to Fitz about that they couldn't discuss over a live feed? The list grew longer, but Drew withheld his contributions, not wanting to add to Letty's defeatist mood.

"First," he said, "we didn't really have a choice in making this trip — we were following our only lead. Second, go ahead and call Rostenkowski. I'm going to reveal myself to the *Temperance* captain and enlist his help in detaining the hookers. At least they can take them back to Dark Landing for questioning. Look on the bright side."

"What's that?"

"We'll get to visit Minerva Station. How many people can say that?"

"You're being flip again and, actually, I've been there before."

"Of course you have." Drew looked at the monitor. "Well, there's no reason to wait," he said. "*Transmit Internal: Pursers Office.*" The message, *Holding for Pursers Office*, flashed on the screen, quickly replaced with the image of the assistant purser.

"This is Melissa. Good evening, Mr. Jacobs. How may I help you?"

"Melissa, my real name is Drew Cutter. I'm chief of security on Dark Landing. I've been traveling on the *Temperance* under an alias because I'm tracking three suspects wanted for questioning." Drew hoped Melissa was unaware of his current shaky status on Dark Landing.

"Oh, my God!"

"I'm sorry to spring it on you, but I want to meet with the captain first thing in the morning if that's possible."

"I'm sure he'll take time to see you under the circumstances. But I need to check with his admin first. As soon as I get a firm appointment, I'll message the information."

"Thanks. I appreciate it," Drew said.

"Are these suspects dangerous?" Melissa glanced nervously over her shoulder as if someone were creeping up on her.

"I don't think so. But I can't have them debarking at one of our stops."

"I see. I'll get back to you."

"Thanks again." Drew ended the transmission. "Okay, Letty, you're up."

Letty squared her shoulders and addressed the monitor: "*Transmit External Relay: Earth, Washington, DC, Earth Technology Oversight Commission, Secretary A. Rostenkowski.*"

A message appeared on the screen in response to her request: *Connecting to external transmission relay. Approximate wait ten minutes. Please state your name and/or affiliation.*

Letty looked at Drew. "*Katherine Leticia Taleen,*" she said, shrugging.

"Does she know who you are?"

"No, but it's 2:00 a.m. there. I'm betting that name will prompt a transmission transfer from her office to her personal comm." Letty was right, several minutes later the image of Anne Rostenkowski filled the screen. She was evidently used to people waking her in the middle of the night. Dressed in a meditation robe, with her hair neatly coiffed, she appeared alert.

"*Rebecca*? What on Earth?"

"Actually, it's Letty Taleen, not Rebecca. I'm sorry to have deceived you, but, considering my new circumstances, there's no longer a reason to conceal my identity. To confuse you further, I'm traveling now under the name Tina Kingsbury," she said, with an apologetic smile.

"I'm . . . I'm astounded. All this time I thought you were George's assistant. I'm so sorry for your loss, Miss Taleen." The Secretary was noticeably unnerved but managed to stay focused. "I received your message, and you evidently got mine. We need to talk. We've made some headway here, not all of which we can discuss over a live feed. And I see you're with a friend?" Her gaze shifted to Drew.

"Anne, this is Drew Cutter, he's chief of security on Dark Landing. He's also fully familiar with our situation."

Drew nodded at Secretary Rostenkowski.

The secretary's countenance immediately changed from perplexed wonder at Letty's true identity to stern dismay. "You had no right. This is a serious breach of confidentiality."

"I think when you hear the details, you'll understand that I had no choice." Letty summarized the series of events since she arrived on Dark Landing, maintaining the loosely coded references they'd employed in their earlier messages. Secretary Rostenkowski sat quietly through Letty's narration.

"If I understood your earlier message," Letty finished, "Camdu is experiencing an outbreak of a similar cold virus?"

"Yes. At least that's what I was advised by Mr. Diak, a . . . a *paid consultant* who contacted us independently. We haven't confirmed the information but, unless we learn otherwise, I'm acting as if his report is factual."

Letty interrupted her. "The name sounds familiar. How are you spelling it?"

"D-i-a-k," Rostenkowski said and went on. "I've since received veiled inquiries from the other Alliance planets, which lend credibility. In line with what you just shared with me, the Taleen research teams have made some explosive discoveries of which you may not be aware. At this point I need to brief Earth Governor Fitzwilliam-Bennett." Rostenkowski turned her gaze to Drew. "It occurs to me now. You work with the governor's brother don't you, Chief Cutter?"

Drew stiffened. Rostenkowski's shock at learning Rebecca Richards' true identity couldn't compare to his shock at being told his chief of administration, Martin Fitzwilliam, a man he'd known for years, was brother to Earth Governor Eleanor Fitzwilliam-

Bennett. *How is it possible I don't know this? Yeah, the names are the same, but it's a big universe. People share last names, and Fitz has never said anything. There's nothing in his personnel file.* In those few seconds, Drew tried desperately to reconcile the revelation and his long-term friendship with Fitz. *Does his sister have something to do with his trip to Minerva Station?* He wondered how many other people he knew were concealing their true identities.

"Drew?" Letty prompted.

The sound of his name broke through his disjointed thought process. He looked at Letty, mouth slightly open then, collecting his wits, back to Secretary Rostenkowski. "Yes, right, Fitz, our chief of administration and Governor Fitzwilliam-Bennett's brother." Mercifully, the moment passed.

Rostenkowski addressed Letty, "What's your schedule?"

"I'm not sure. We're evidently to be questioned by *Muck*. As I told you, Chief Cutter thinks they already know about the . . . cold virus . . . but we won't confirm that for them. That's Governor Fitzwilliam-Bennett's job."

The responsibilities of the governor's office included maintaining goodwill and setting policy for day-to-day interactions with Alliance-member and non-member planets, as well as the appointment and oversight of Earth's *Muck* representatives.

"There's a good chance we'll be detained for several days, possibly longer. With my dad gone, how are you coordinating with our research teams?" Letty asked.

"Each team lead contacted me and advised that Mr. Speller had left instructions for them to work directly with our agency to whatever extent I needed. Without further information, that's how I've proceeded."

"Good," Letty said. "It seems Dad covered all the bases. I'll contact you again as soon as I'm able, but I don't know how long that might be. By the way, ask the governor about *Muck's* ship, the *Golden Tracer*. She'll explain the situation, and she'll probably want to investigate the possibility the two matters are connected." Letty ended the transmission.

She turned to Drew, excited. "Her reference to 'explosive discoveries' by the Taleen research teams means the nitroglycerine."

"Absolutely."

"'Paid consultant' must mean informant."

Drew nodded.

"I'm pretty sure the Mr. Diak Anne mentioned was also mentioned by the hooker monks outside our shuttle hatch while we waited to go down to Bin."

Drew nodded again, distracted by his own thoughts.

Letty switched topics. "You had no idea about the relationship between Chief Fitzwilliam and Governor Fitzwilliam-Bennett, did you?"

"Not a clue."

22 BY ANY NAME

The presence of unlicensed working ladies on the *Temperance* had not gone unnoticed. Without the proof to take action himself, the captain happily conceded jurisdiction and, at Drew's request, offered assistance in the form of Nikko. The ladies had booked lower class bunks under the gender-neutral names Tammas Cameron, Chris Stevens, and Michael Gautier, the same names they'd used on Dark Landing.

Nikko was a man of few words, but he knew his ship, including, without consulting the passenger list, where the three women were bivouacked. However, upon arrival, they found only empty lockers and containers of fresh, neatly folded linen at the foot of stripped bunks awaiting new occupants. With breakfast mess already ended, they tried the passenger common areas next with the same results.

"Maybe they're on the job," Drew postulated. Though, to his mind, it was too early in the day. He assumed hooker monks worked the nightshift. But since the ship's crew worked around the clock, it made sense the ladies would accommodate all three shifts.

Nikko grunted and headed in a new direction with Drew on his heels. He followed him up one level and down a narrow corridor with six close-set hatches lining each side. Drew guessed they were crew quarters a couple notches above hammocks. At the far end of the corridor, Nikko pounded on the first hatch. The sound shot up the narrow hallway like a bullet in a gun barrel. Several hatches opened, heads popped out and just as quickly disappeared inside again.

The hatch Nikko was pounding on opened to reveal a man in a sleeveless tee and boxers. His surly expression turned to alarm as he looked up at Nikko's smiling face, two feet above him. Still smiling, Nikko grasped the man's head, his hand covering the entire crown, and pulled him forward. The man's arms dangled passively at his sides, his face pressed into Nikko's expansive chest. Nikko craned his head and peered into the quarters. Not finding what he was looking for, he pushed the man back inside and closed the hatch, then pounded on the next one.

Drew wondered if crew with their own quarters out-ranked Nikko, but that didn't seem to present an issue. When his pounding went unanswered, Nikko entered what Drew figured was the master access code and opened the hatch uninvited, squeezing his massive frame inside the quarters. Again, finding nothing, he backed out and pounded on the next hatch.

As Drew watched, it occurred to him he didn't know what Nikko did on the *Temperance*. When he asked, he received a two-word response, "Compliance officer." That made sense and covered a broad spectrum of responsibilities. Nikko probably would have offered his assistance without Drew asking for it.

They continued down that side of the corridor with Nikko pounding on hatches one after the other, using the master code to open it if no one answered. As each hatch opened, musty aromas of sweat and dirty linens drifted into the corridor and lingered.

At the sixth hatch, a stout man met him wearing nothing but a head of wild gray hair and one bushy, black eyebrow that underscored his forehead. He growled something to Nikko in a language that seemed to match Nikko's accented English. With the wide smile Drew now suspected was surgically fixed in place, Nikko stepped back a few inches, replying respectfully to the man in their common language. Whatever he'd said set the man off. He shook his fist at Nikko, issuing a string of what could only be curses, but allowed him to pass.

High pitch screams and more cursing, this time in English, followed as the big man emerged through the hatch, bending low to allow clearance for the squirming woman draped over one shoulder. He dropped her unceremoniously face-down on the deck and, with a foot planted firmly on her back, tossed Drew two restraining ribbons. Nikko held her while Drew tied her hands behind her back and wrestled her flailing feet together long enough to secure them at the ankles. They left her squirming on the deck and moved to the other side of the corridor. The hatch pounding started again.

In short order, all three ladies, with hands and feet secured, lay squealing and squirming on the deck. After they'd bound the last woman, Nikko went back into the quarters where he'd found her and returned with a dirty sock and a bandanna. Bending over the loudest of the three, he balled up the sock and stuffed it into her mouth, tying the bandanna around her head to hold it in place. The other two, seeing what lay in store for them, quieted.

Drew picked up the woman with the sock in her mouth, carrying her rescue-style, her body wrapped around the back of his neck. He followed Nikko, who had the other two slung one over each shoulder, down to the ship's holding cell. When they entered, the pungent odor of animal manure and urine overtook Drew. He noticed that even Nikko's eyes were watering. Drew felt certain he'd located George Speller's workstation, and it appeared no one had cleaned up after he'd left the ship. Drew didn't hear any animal noises though, and didn't bother to nose around to confirm his guess.

The *Temperance* had one large cell with a half-dozen cots, reminiscent of drunk tanks back on Earth. It was tucked into the corner of a storage area filled with cartons stacked to the deck above. Nikko and Drew deposited the ladies one to a cot. The only other occupant awoke from a nap to gape at his new cellmates. Nikko nodded toward the open door, motioning for the man to leave.

The man shook his head. "Pero, tengo más de seis horas para completar," he pleaded, anxious to serve his full sentence. Nikko's smile widened ominously, his head still cocked toward the exit. The man mumbled what were certainly Spanish expletives, crawled off his cot, and slunk out of the cell. He glanced back over his shoulder at his lost opportunity. Drew noted that, in a short period of time, he'd heard curses in three languages.

As Nikko and Drew removed their captives' restraints, the questions and profanities started anew along with complaints about the accommodations. Drew spoke over the racket to Nikko. "Can we just leave them here for a couple hours? It's close to lunch, and I want my partner with me when I question them. Will I be able to get back in?"

Nikko nodded. As they exited the outer hatch, he punched a code into the palm reader and motioned for Drew to press his palm on the pad.

"Is that all I need?"

"Keelo-Alpa-Sulu-doo-Yonkee-vive," Nikko said, then he disappeared, leaving Drew to find his way back to his quarters while translating Nikko's code into English.

He found Letty sitting cross-legged on the lounger with the processor in her lap. "Well?" she asked.

"Mission accomplished. The ladies are relaxing in a luxury suite. I thought we'd grab a bite to eat. I want them to stew a little. Afterward we can question them together. But I need to contact Doc first."

"Doc?"

"Yeah. The ladies are contagious. In case we can't accompany them back to Dark Landing, Doc needs to keep them isolated until the ETOC collects them."

"We'll be at Minerva Station early in the morning. I think we should skip lunch and question them now. We may not get the opportunity later."

"Okay, but I'm still hungry. Be a doll and grab me a fruit pouch," he said. Sitting down heavily on the cushion next to her, he addressed the wall monitor. "*Transmit External Relay: Zeta Quadrant, Sector 1701, Dark Landing Station, Chief of Medical, Dr. Tammy Jameson.*"

A confirmation message displayed: *Connecting to external transmission relay. Approximate wait three minutes. Please state your name and/or affiliation.*

"*Drew Cutter.*" Drew faced the screen but watched Letty out of the corner of his eye. She hadn't moved. "Well, it was worth a try." He got up and crossed the room to where their remaining food pouches lay on a side table.

His conversation with Doc proved awkward. She was surprised and confused at receiving his transmission and questioned the reason for the detainees being thrust into her care.

"Why is the ETOC interested in prostitutes on a remote space station? I insist you tell me what type of contagion I'll be dealing with. Otherwise, I cannot let them debark here."

"Look, I can't tell you exactly. It's not airborne or even a *real* disease, it's something . . . else."

"Not good enough." Doc crossed her arms, staring unblinking from the monitor.

Letty interjected. "Doctor, when the women arrive, perform a DNA scan and search for chromosomal aberrations. I'll send you specifications. You'll understand the problem and why the ETOC is involved. There's no danger as long as you keep them isolated from other residents and away from tech devices."

Evidently accepting that was all the information she was going to get, Doc shifted her gaze back to Drew. "How much trouble are you in?"

"I don't know. We're docking at Minerva Station shortly, and I'll find out then. It's possible I won't be returning to Dark Landing just yet. I know I'm asking a lot, but can I count on you, Doc?"

"Not like you're giving me a choice." Her features softened. "Of course, Drew, you know Fitz and I always have your back."

"Thanks, Doc. Speaking of, any idea why Fitz is headed to Minerva as well?"

"They didn't want to send another ship after they lost the *Golden Tracer*—you know about that?" Drew nodded and she continued. "They wanted to question Fitz, but who knows why they couldn't do it over a live feed."

"*Only* Muck *knows*," Drew responded fittingly. He was tempted to ask if she knew who Fitz's sister was, but decided to wait until he could talk to Fitz face-to-face. He was sure the simple answer was Fitz didn't want to be constantly compared or approached because of the relationship, but that didn't excuse him for keeping it from his fellow chiefs.

"I'll talk to you again as soon as I can. Thanks for taking care of my girls."

"Take care of yourself, Drew. Things will work out. You're a good man."

"*End transmission.*"

He turned to Letty, who was busily chewing the last piece of his dried fruit. "It's hooker monk time."

~ ~ ∞ ~ ~

Drew would have preferred to question the women separately, but the storage area lacked an interview room. As he entered this time, he peeked around a pallet of cartons and saw a corral area, its deck covered in filthy straw. Though empty now, there was space for a dozen smallish animals if they were crowded together. A stack of small cages that probably held the eggers, sat next to a water trough. He started to point out to Letty the place where her father had worked, then decided against it.

When they approached the cell, one of the women stepped forward. "Where are you putting us off? This place stinks."

Ah, we have a leader. "You're going back to Dark Landing and eventually into the arms of the ETOC," Drew said.

"The ETOC?" The woman looked as confused as Doc had been.

"Which one are you?" Letty asked.

"I'm the pretty one." All three laughed.

Letty ignored the quip. "What's your name?"

"Tammas. What's the ETOC got to do with anything?"

"We'll ask the questions," Drew said. "Who do you work for?"

"We work for ourselves; we're free agents." The other two left their cots and joined Tammas at the bars.

Drew decided to try a more direct approach. "What's the objective of the nanoid programming?"

The three of them stared back at him as if he were speaking Bahdaneian. "Do we look like tech geniuses to you?" Tammas replied. "Ask me how much pleasure I can give you in an hour, Chief. I'll double that figure for you, sweetie." She winked at Letty.

Drew went for the jugular. "You're aware treason carries the death penalty."

That cracked their streetwise facade. "Treason? Since when is hooking treason? Who do you think we are?"

Drew kept up the pressure. "I think you're working for a religious cult that's spreading tech viruses across the K.U."

"That's crazy. We're not working for anybody. I told you, we're free agents." A sliver of alarm flashed in Tammas's eyes.

"If that's true, tell us how you came to be at Dark Landing

dressed as monks." They seemed honestly perplexed by his accusations. Even so, they knew more than they were saying.

The three exchanged glances, seemingly reaching a silent consensus. Tammas spoke once more, dropping her street edge. So far, the other two had remained silent. "We were working in Arizona. The LAPD picked us up for not having a license."

Prostitution wasn't a crime; it was a business, with licensing, taxes, and requirements for regular physicals and continuing health education. But the law made a distinction between street ladies or those soliciting in bars and hotels, and high-end, licensed professionals with their own security and accounting staff. And there was no middle rank.

"We weren't together then, we only met in jail," she continued. "It wasn't our first time, so the judge set our bails super high. Since we couldn't pay, they scheduled us for mandatory reeducation and forced licensing. That goes on a lady's permanent record you know. Then this monk came in and said he would bail us out on condition we leave Earth. He gave us travel documents and fare to Dark Landing, and the robes to use as a disguise. The robes worked swell. You never figured it out, did you? We should have worn them here too."

Drew didn't comment.

"Anyway, it was time to move on, so here we are. That's it. I don't know nothin' about nanoids or treason."

"What was the monk's name?" Letty asked.

"Brother Diak."

Letty shot a look at Drew. "Brother Diak gave you tickets to Dark Landing specifically?"

"Right, he gave us everything. Our documents, tickets, walking script, our shots—"

Drew interrupted, "Shots?"

"Yeah, shots against space diseases—that sort a thing."

"What did this Brother Diak look like?" Letty asked.

"I don't know, with the hood and all. He was youngish, nothing special."

One of the other two spoke for the first time. "He was nice. He told us there were hookers in his bible and this man, Jesus, loved hookers."

"All right," Drew said. "Here's what's going to happen. You'll be dropped back on Dark Landing and held for the ETOC. Doc Jameson will be in charge of you until they arrive. They'll ask the same questions we did and a lot more. Tell the truth, and if it checks out, you'll be okay."

"We weren't the only ones," Tammas said.

"What?" Drew asked.

"Yeah, there were at least a dozen others he bailed out too."

"Where did they go?"

She shrugged. "I don't know."

23 MINERVA STATION

Drew contacted the *Temperance* captain and thanked him for his cooperation. He considered warning the captain of the possible contamination by the hooker monks but, since they were contained, decided to risk waiting to see what *Muck* had in mind. On that front, it seemed only fair to tell him what to expect when they docked at Minerva Station the next morning.

"Captain, it's likely *Muck* security will want to . . . ah . . . *speak* with me tomorrow. There was an incident on Dark Landing that they feel I didn't handle according to protocol."

A moment of silence passed before the captain replied. "I see. Perhaps it's best if you, and Miss Kingsbury as well, are in my office when we arrive, so as not to keep *Muck* waiting. I'll send Nikko to accompany you just before we dock."

"Thank you." The captain was a wise man. Or he didn't want *Muck* snooping around his ship.

Nikko arrived at their quarters at 0700 the next morning. As the three of them made their way to the captain's office, Drew assured Nikko that his personal troubles with *Muck* had nothing to do with the package they'd delivered. Nikko smiled and nodded, seemingly unconcerned. This reminded Drew, even though he was no longer chief of security, Curtis had to be dealt with. *Is Curtis the traitor?* Drew still struggled with that possibility.

The captain wasn't in his office when they arrived. Drew assumed he was personally greeting *Muck* dockside. He and Letty sat in the chairs facing the captain's desk. Nikko stood blocking the hatchway, all *friendly escort* pretenses abandoned. Soon the captain arrived, accompanied by a uniformed Bahdaneian. Drew noted the starburst pips on his shoulders indicated a mid-rank *Muck* security officer. As soon as the men entered, Nikko ducked out. The captain introduced the Bahdaneian by his Earth pseudonym, William William, and then left the office as well.

Sitting in the captain's chair, William's whiskers rippled as he assumed his best imitation of a human smile. "Good morning, Miss Taleen. Please accept my personal condolences and that of the MCTT on your recent loss." He addressed Letty in unaccented English accompanied by a soft hum that reminded Drew of Bertie. With a renewed pang of loss, Drew regretted the way things had ended between them.

"Thank you," Letty said.

He turned to Drew. "And thank you, Chief Cutter, for agreeing to meet with me."

The warmth with which they were being greeted, particularly the hum of amity, was unexpected. Drew was more than willing to play along. Encouraged to be addressed as "Chief," Drew nodded and smiled.

William William began with an uncharacteristic obsequiousness for a *Muck* officer. "I hardly know where to start. It appears someone claiming to be an ETOC representative contacted us regarding the security issue that precipitated your suspension. Because of the serious nature of the accusation and our affiliation with the Earth Technology Oversight Commission, we failed to verify the report and were far too hasty in our response. Within the last twenty-four hours, we have been contacted by Taleen Industries legal advocates and Secretary Rostenkowski of the ETOC, advising us of our error. They provided related information of which the two of you may or may not be aware, but I'm not at liberty to discuss. We're working closely with the ETOC to discover the perpetrator."

William William squirmed in the chair, clearly ill at ease. "On behalf of the MCTT, I apologize for any embarrassment and inconvenience you have suffered as a result of our actions. We have notified your employer of the mix-up and offered them our apologies as well. Of course, your suspension is immediately and unconditionally rescinded. Chief Cutter, I hope you will accept my personal apology as well as that of the Multi-world Coalition for Travel and Trade."

"Yes, of course," Drew said. "But if it's suspected someone on my staff—perhaps a disgruntled employee—is the perpetrator, you'll coordinate your investigation with me, won't you?"

"I don't have the authority to agree to that, but I believe it's a reasonable request, and I'll see that it's brought before the board." William William stood. "Again, thank you both for your understanding."

"Before you go," Drew said, "I want to express how sorry I am about the loss of the *Golden Tracer* and its crew, particularly Albert Wellington. I considered Bertie a friend."

"You're very kind. It seems we have all suffered losses recently. Now, if you will excuse me, I must return to my duties."

Letty and Drew sat silent for several seconds, staring at the empty desk chair.

"Well," Letty said, "that's that... I guess. But I don't understand. He mentioned Dad, but he never said anything about Hernandez. You think they're missing the connection?"

"They see it alright. But they're just now clued-in and struggling to grasp the bigger picture along with the rest of us."

"So, Hernandez' murder is going to be swept to the side. Doesn't anyone care about that?" Her voice cracked in anger.

"I care about that. Hernandez has to take some of the blame for his own death, but he was killed on my watch. Don't forget, whoever killed Hernandez was after *you*. We need to redouble our efforts to make sense of everything. We're short too many steps to build a staircase."

"From what Secretary Rostenkowski said, our research teams made headway. I'll request updated reports when we get back to our quarters. Maybe they'll explain the nitroglycerin."

"One thing's for sure," Drew said, "while we focus on what's in front of us, now that things are coming out in the open, the Alliance and the K.U. are dealing with a lot bigger issues."

As if on cue, their conversation was interrupted when the captain returned to reclaim his office. "Please stay seated. There's some disturbing news. *Muck* has advised us that a Fahdeen water tanker heading for one of their survey bases was attacked and destroyed a couple hours ago. Earlier in the week, an agro-colony on the outer rim was also attacked. A Taleen security ship two hops out heard the distress call, but before they could reach them, the settlement was completely wiped out and one hundred twenty-five colonists lost. I doubt they could have saved them at any rate, since your security ships are unarmed." The captain paused, raising his eyebrows questioningly at Letty.

She hesitated a moment before responding to his unasked question. "That's not *entirely* true, Captain. Many of our security ships do have minimal defensive weaponry—approved weaponry, of course."

He nodded as if he suspected as much. "Regardless, all Alliance planets have suffered attacks on ships and remote settlements in this quadrant. Unfortunately, some attacks appear retaliatory, and it's difficult to distinguish who was the initial aggressor. It's a mess, and *Muck* is trying to act as intermediary before things take a nastier turn—though they're in the middle of the fray themselves."

"No one's IDed the attackers?" Drew asked.

"Not definitively. Three of the attacks were reportedly committed by ships of Earth, Bahdane, and Bin designs. A ship with *Muck* markings made an unsuccessful pass at a Bin moon colony. Each member is pointing fingers and crying foul."

The captain's forehead creased, and his shoulders slumped. "I've received orders from Cane Cargo to return directly to Dark Landing to deliver you and your prisoners and to pick up the rest of our passengers and then head straight to Earth. *Muck* is providing an armed escort as far as the station. I assume your issue with them has been resolved?"

"Yes," Drew said. "It was a minor misunderstanding. I'm impatient to get back to Dark Landing. Thanks for the use of your office."

As soon as they returned to their quarters, Letty headed to her room with the processor while Drew contacted HQ to speak with Mattie. He got Curtis instead. He told Curtis he'd been cleared by *Muck* and was on his way back to the station.

"Yeah, Doc already told me."

"Okay. So, what's happening there?" Drew asked, surprised that Curtis had known about his reinstatement before he did.

"Well, I'm in charge. Mattie's disappeared along with Fitz and his senior engineer. Doc keeps mumbling about hookers. You know . . . routine stuff. What's happening there?"

"What do you mean Mattie and Fitz disappeared?"

"Mattie just never showed up this morning and her comm was disabled. I checked her quarters, but they looked abandoned. Fitz is supposed to be on his way to Minerva Station on the *Essovius*. But when one of the scrubbers broke down again, his staff couldn't find Justin Ruble, the guy who fixes it. When I tried to contact Fitz to see if he knew anything, I was told he'd transferred off the *Essovius* at her first stop. But no one seems to know where he went from there. Turns out he wasn't expected at Minerva Station after all. I filled Doc in, and she contacted CoachStop who told her you were on your way back. We haven't found Mattie or Ruble either."

Drew had a sinking feeling at even the remote possibility that Fitz or Mattie, or worse, Fitz *and* Mattie, might be responsible for Hernandez' death—*and what else?* But, even in the face of the evidence, he refused to believe it. It was inconceivable he'd misjudge Fitz's, and possibly Mattie's, characters so completely. He had to be wrong. There must be another explanation. And if so, were they in danger, or lying somewhere with their throats cut like Hernandez?

"Jesus!" he said.

"Also missing." Curtis seemed completely unruffled by his predicament.

"Look, I'm still three days out. How are you holding up? Is the staff cooperating?"

"Yeah . . . more or less. Jones is taking the nightshift. Everybody's doing their job. If there's no explosions or murders, we should be able to hang in for another three days."

"Curtis, thanks. You've really stepped up and I appreciate it. Thank Jonesy for me too. Tell him I'll check back with him tonight. I'll touch base with you again in the morning."

"Aye-aye."

Drew ended the transmission. He still needed to talk with Curtis about his extra-curricular activities, but in light of all that occurred since then, his transgressions seemed inconsequential.

Letty had entered the room for the last part of his conversation. She was wearing her CEO persona. "I just messaged my assistant to request updated reports from our research teams, and I asked him to initiate a K.U.-wide search for the name 'Diak.' Then I checked the news feeds. The headlines are all screaming about tech breaches and alien attacks. The Alliance Stock Exchange crashed an hour after opening today."

Drew's chest tightened as he sensed what was coming next.

"When we get back to Dark Landing, I'm taking Dad and continuing home on the *Temperance*."

Drew stepped close and rested his hands on Letty's shoulders. His fingers lightly kneaded the muscles at the back of her neck. The warmth emanating from her drove him crazy, but he suppressed the urge to pull her body against his. "Listen, I know you have to return to Earth, but before—"

"Drew, please don't." She held his gaze. "I think I know what you're going to say. But now . . . *right* now . . . there's just too much turmoil in my life."

Up to this time, Drew had never met a woman that he needed—or *wanted*—to have this talk with, plus he'd never had to convey his feelings in words before. And he definitely wasn't ready to say he loved her. Even if he felt that strongly, she *clearly* wasn't ready to hear it. "There's a lot going on for both of us, Letty. You don't feel the same. I get it. But I need you to know, under all my joking around—"

Their cabin was located in the center of the ship, but the laser blast rocked them as if they'd been leaning against an outer bulkhead. Both Drew and Letty fell to the deck. The deafening *awoogas* of a klaxon filled the room, assaulting their ears with almost the same impact as the blast itself. The klaxon's blare was followed by an announcement from an obviously shaken crewman:

> *All hands to their stations. Passengers, please return to your quarters. Seal all hatches behind you. The captain will make an address shortly.*

The message repeated three times.

Back on his feet, Drew helped Letty from the deck onto the lounger, then went to his room to retrieve his sidearm. Though useless in this situation, he felt better with its weight against his hip. She was gone when he came back but reappeared after a few seconds with a frightened but determined expression, outfitted in her dungarees, poncho, and boots. She pulled her hat on, and, without a word, they headed to the bridge.

24 ENCOUNTER

The ship took two more hits before they reached the bridge, both times throwing everyone in the corridor to the deck, including Drew and Letty. The klaxon had finally silenced to allow intermittent announcements over the comm. But the sound of running boots, shouted orders, and screams, which increased after each laser strike, drowned out all else. When they arrived, an armed crewman stood guard outside the bridge hatch, his eyes so wide Drew was afraid his eyeballs would fall out. "Stop there . . . you can't enter the bridge!"

Drew approached him with assumed authority. When their faces were only inches apart, he yelled over the din, "Drew Cutter, Chief of Security." He conveniently left out *where* he was chief of security.

The guard, though he appeared confused by Drew's pronouncement, made only the slightest hesitation before stepping to one side, motioning them to pass. "Yes, sir."

Drew suppressed the urge to give the guard a dressing down, reminding himself that the *Temperance* crew consisted of cargo handlers and service personnel, most lacking military or even security training—and evidently, common sense.

The bridge was a compact, circular space. He and Letty crowded in with the captain and two instrument technicians, who called out a steady stream of coordinates and damage reports in shaky voices. Only the captain looked as if he knew what he was doing and was equal to the challenge. Though, since the *Temperance* was an unarmed freighter, the only actions he could take was to follow the attack and swear.

Their presence went unnoticed. Hands clasped behind his back, spine flagpole straight, the captain's posture suggested a military background. His attention remained riveted to a large screen that seemed to display a wide view into space. However, the images that alternated across it at three-second intervals were multiple-angle views from all sides of the ship. At the captain's command, an individual image would pause momentarily and then the series recommence. The speckled paths of pulse lasers etched across several views, syncing with the rocking of the ship and accompanied by appropriate expletives from the captain.

A waist-high rail encircled the room, with a gap at the hatch opening. Drew and Letty each clung to the rail to stay upright, Letty with one hand on the bar and the other holding tight to Drew's arm.

Drew caught brief glimpses of their attacker. It was a gunship, surprisingly small and extremely maneuverable. It darted in and out of several frames, never providing a clear view. With each pass, it drew closer to the *Temperance*, limiting the freighter's ability to take evasive action. Not as quick as the attacker, their two *Muck* escorts moved steadily to intercept it. The *Muck* ships returned laser fire but, lacking its maneuverability, they'd only managed to chip away at the edges of the smaller ship's shields. Muted rainbow waves undulated across the gunship each time a *Muck* laser made contact. As Drew and Letty watched, the two *Muck* ships gained their desired attitude, placing themselves between the *Temperance* and the gunship. A laser pulse from the lead *Muck* ship finally broke through the shields to its target. Apparent damage to a thruster sent the enemy spinning out of range.

The gunship was not Earth-engineered. After ten years on a space station, Drew was familiar with most alien and Earth ship designs. There was nothing remotely like it in the Known Universe, at least in *his* known universe. While the weapons seemed contemporary, the ship's appearance was anything but. It looked like something out of a novel—futuristic, with a surface that intermittently rippled and changed shape. Drew couldn't be certain though, since the ship never stayed in view long enough to study, and the rippling was subtle.

The damage to its port side was noticeable but must not have been severe. Their attacker regained control. Losing its enthusiasm for the fight, it shot off at sub-light speed. The *Muck* ships didn't pursue but maintained their positions alongside the *Temperance*. She continued plodding along on course toward the Schwarzschild Cluster and the nearest hop to Dark Landing.

The captain ordered one of the technicians to open a channel for an announcement and turned, seeing Drew and Letty for the first time. Spewing expletives that took Drew aback, but didn't seem to faze Letty, he ordered them off his bridge and back to their quarters.

" . . . and don't fucking come out again until you're back at your own fucking station you fucking idiot. And take that brat with you."

"Er . . . sir, the open channel . . ." the technician said timidly.

Drew and Letty exited into the outer passage and headed to their cabin with the captain's diatribe still echoing over the ship's comm system. Two crew members and a passenger stood in the corridor as they passed, staring into the air above them with open mouths.

Letty turned to Drew as they hurried on their way. "What brat?"

"I don't know. Maybe he meant you."

She countered, "Or, maybe he was talking to me, and he meant you."

They spent the next hour in the cabin, helplessly pacing the small lounge, anticipating the return of their attacker at any moment. At one point, Drew interrupted his pacing long enough to send a request to the captain for copies of the skirmish vids. He didn't know if the captain would share them, but it didn't hurt to ask. He wanted to compare multiple static frames of the gunship to see if his impressions had been correct.

Continued announcements instructed passengers to remain in their cabins or at their hammocks.

"Screw this," Drew said. "I'm going down to check on our detainees. I doubt anyone bothered to tell them what happened. I'm sure they're terrified."

As he moved toward the hatch, a subdued gong sounded, announcing a visitor. The wall monitor displayed Nikko's broad chest. When Drew opened the hatch, Nikko reached one muscled arm behind him and dragged out a squirming Toby Greenstein. The boy rained ineffectual punches against Nikko's thigh, all the while kicking him in the shins with the same lack of result. Effortlessly picking Toby up by his shirt collar, Nikko thrust him at Drew.

"Capteen zey you dake hem."

"Ouch!" Grabbing Toby, Drew held him at arm's length in an effort to escape his flailing limbs. With a sense of *deja vu* when that didn't work, he shoved him roughly into the cabin, sending him sprawling on the deck at Letty's feet. "You two introduce yourselves." He stepped into the corridor and closed the hatch behind him.

"What the hell?"

"Boy stole on board. Capteen dold parents ve'd turn hem ofer on vey back, but don go back. Transvission to Prosse no goot now. *Muck* dinks zey been het. Capteen zey hem you proobloom."

That was by far the longest speech Drew had heard Nikko make, and for the first time, he wasn't smiling. Speechless with surprise, Drew's lack of a response allowed Nikko to make a clean getaway.

"Son of a bitch," he said and returned to their cabin. If he could, he would have slammed the hatch shut behind him, but it slid effortlessly into place, its seals making only a soft sucking noise.

"Drew! Language, *please*." Letty sat on the lounger with one arm around the boy. Toby cast a smug, malicious sneer in Drew's direction then turned and, with a cherubic countenance, gazed adoringly up at Letty. Drew hissed, causing Letty to glare at him again with increased intensity.

"I'm going down to check in on the hookers. If you're smart, you'll lock him in the head." He turned and left before either Toby or Letty could say anything further and before he received any more scathing looks.

He was right; the girls were terrified. They huddled together on one cot, sobbing and sniffling. As soon as they saw him, all three scrambled up to the bars.

"Let us out."

"We're going to die in here."

"What happened? Who's shooting at us?"

"Relax, ladies. You're not going to die, and I'm not releasing you. *Muck* advised the *Temperance* might be targeted by a raider and provided armed escorts. The raider wasn't expecting a fight. It got in a couple sloppy shots, but when *Muck* returned fired, it took off. We're on our way back to Dark Landing."

As he spoke, a crew member delivered container lunches of sandwiches, fresh veggies, and fruit. Since the trip had been cut short, there were plentiful rations, and the captain evidently knew food went a long way to calm the human soul. The ladies returned to their individual cots still mumbling but distracted by the normality of lunch being served.

Drew stopped by the mess on his way back to the cabin and picked up lunches for himself, Letty, and Toby. Toby was napping on the lounger when he came in. He left a container on the side table for the boy, but didn't wake him.

He knocked softly on Letty's door. "I'm back, and I brought lunch."

"It's open."

Drew entered her room and handed her a container. "You mind if I stay and eat with you?"

"Of course not. How are the ladies?"

"Scared, but better now I think." He pulled a chair closer to her bunk, unwrapped his sandwich, and sniffed at it. "Toby's sound asleep. Did he say anything about his situation?"

She smiled. "He called Prosse a 'back water crap hole.' While his folks were collecting their luggage, he told them he was going to find their new quarters. Somehow, he snuck back onboard and hung out in the passenger lounge. He was a familiar face there, and no one gave him a second thought."

"Smart kid."

"Yes. Anyway, the ship debarked before his folks realized he was missing. He avoided capture for a few hours but was eventually found by that 'thick headed muscle monster.' They stuck him in with the mess crew when the ship was attacked."

"Where was he going? Earth?"

"No, he wants to go back to Dark Landing. He says that's his home and, by the way, you're his hero."

Drew laughed. "I doubt that. Do you know how many times I've had to bust him for his shenanigans?"

"Even so . . . his goal is to become a station chief someday, just like you."

"Trust me — he's playing you and he's trying to play me."

"What are you going to do with him? There's no way to return him to his parents right now."

"I'll take him to the station until things settle down and I can put him on a ship back to Prosse." He changed the subject. "I've been wondering. With your security forces scattered across the K.U., and your so-called *massive* database of ill-gotten information, how did you miss the current turn-of-events?"

"Other than my dad's vials, and with all that's happened, I haven't read reports for the last eight weeks or so. Drew, I think the security breaches, the attacks on the outer colonies, the *Golden Tracer*, and now the *Temperance*, is all to weaken or disrupt the Alliance. Whoever's responsible wants Taleen Industries, specifically Dad and I, and maybe even you, out of their way. But for the life of me, I can't imagine why or who's orchestrating it all."

Drew nodded. "You and your dad maybe, and it's got something to do with your research. But there's no reason they'd worry about me. By the way, did you notice anything odd about the gunship that attacked us?"

"No. I mean — you know — it was kind of weird looking."

"You don't think it changed from one view to the next?"

"Changed? In what way?"

"I don't know exactly. I got the impression it was physically changing its shape. I'd need to study the vids to be sure. I think whoever's responsible may come from outside the K.U., certainly outside the Alliance. But it seems obvious they have inside help."

He took the last bite of his sandwich and chewed slowly. "Concerning that, there's something I need to talk to you about," he said.

"Let me guess: How did the killer know Hernandez and I would be in that passage? Someone had to tell him. And, if you take you, me, and Hernandez out of the equation, that only leaves your command staff. I knew you'd have to face that sooner or later."

"You're as smart as you are beautiful."

"Now who's being played?"

25 REFUGEES

Dark Landing was in chaos. Drew had conversed with both Curtis and Jones the day before the *Temperance* docked and knew what to expect. Outer colonies and bases of every Alliance member were suffering random attacks with no discernible motive. Evacuees who'd abandoned their remote colonies and outposts now crowded the station's public areas. Drew judged the evacuees alone exceeded the station occupancy level by more than two thousand souls.

While it appeared an unorganized mess at first glance, he soon detected a loose line comprising newcomers and residents alike. All carried their belongings and were queued for first available transport off the station to Earth or larger, more established colonies, in hopes their defenses would hold. The situation was ripe for disaster, but security staffers moved continuously through the throng to comfort and reassure everyone they were safe and to dampen petty arguments before they flared up.

The news feeds reported the Alliance governments had stopped communicating with one another except to hurl accusations and threats. Member planets recalled their *Muck* representatives. Many of the *Muck* security staff stayed and acted independently to patrol and provide escorts where they could. But their fleet numbers were woefully insufficient to protect the entire quadrant.

For almost two hundred years, alliance members, including Earth, though they'd only been a member for the last fifty, had focused on the three Es: exploration, entrepreneurship, and enlightenment, while letting their defensive forces wither. The universal consensus that a reduction and de-emphasis on military assets was fundamental in building peaceful relationships between diverse civilizations seemed foolish in retrospect. Drew had happily surfed those peaceful waves along with everyone else, and now he couldn't shake the feeling of shared responsibility for the tsunami that seemed bound to overwhelm them.

Drew and Letty met with Doc and Curtis immediately after debarking. Back in his office, Drew couldn't believe how good it felt to be sitting behind his desk, once again in charge despite the growing turmoil surrounding him.

"What's the situation, Doc?" Drew began.

"Actually, Curtis will need to give you details. The last couple days, it's been all I can do to keep up with the steady stream of people coming into medical."

"Curtis?"

Curtis held Drew's gaze for several moments, obviously savoring his bump in prestige. Drew expected a snarky comment, but when Curtis spoke, he was organized and professional.

"Right now, we're at about eight thousand souls. Since the influx of refugees is declining and more people are catching rides out, that figure should go down. That's good, since our supplies are dwindling. And restocking is going to be a bitch. Most freighters have stopped running, at least in this direction. Several evacuees from the outer reaches brought rations with them and that's helped. Also, for ships already here, I've been waiving docking fees and *Muck* tariffs in exchange for food goods. I estimate shortages will reach critical in about seven days. The place will start to stink as well, since I implemented water use restrictions and rationing."

Curtis yawned, and Drew wondered when he'd last slept.

"We're reaching out to nearby ships, letting them know we have people looking for rides and asking for whatever rations they can spare. A couple have detoured in, but neither of them had a lot of room for extra passengers and only minimal surplus food and water."

"What's CoachStop saying?" Drew asked.

"They understand our situation and are working with the co-ops to send supplies our way. They keep saying they'll get back to me, but so far nada. Rumor has it our own co-op lost a freighter this morning. At this point, it's hard to separate fact from fiction. We also heard the financial markets on all Alliance planets are on the verge of crashing if they haven't already."

"Drew, does the station have defenses?" Letty asked.

"Not really. We have shielding capabilities to protect from debris and small asteroids, but they're a huge power drain and haven't been deployed since . . . ever, I think. I don't know how they'd hold up under serious fire. I assume Fitz kept the system in peak condition at least." At the mention of Fitz's name everyone but Curtis avoided eye contact with Drew. *It's time to discuss the gargantuan Bindian lizard in the room.*

"Have we learned anything more about Fitz's and Mattie's whereabouts, or the engineer's? What's his name?" Curtis and Doc exchanged glances, neither speaking. "Would you like me to flip a coin, guys?" Drew asked.

Doc finally stepped up. "Fitz and Mattie are gone; no one seems to know where. All our inquiries have reached dead ends." She winced at her unfortunate phrasing and continued. "But," with another quick look at Curtis, "we found Justin Ruble last night. His throat was cut and his body left in a maintenance tube. I bagged and stored him. He's been dead for a while. I don't know when I'll have the chance to complete an official autopsy. We were waiting for you before notifying his family and Earth authorities. Drew, I really need to get back to med-lab. Can you stop by later?"

"Of course." Drew got the impression she would prefer to speak with him in private. He'd gotten the same feeling when Doc delivered the summary of Speller's autopsy at the last command staff meeting. With Hernandez' murder and his own suspension, he'd forgotten all about it.

"Wait a sec, Doc. Were you aware — or you, Curtis — that Eleanor Fitzwilliam-Bennett is Fitz's sister?"

Curtis's mouth opened slightly. He looked back at Drew with a blank expression.

"*Governor* Fitzwilliam-Bennett?" Doc asked.

"So . . . no."

Letty intruded. "Do you mind if I use your conference room? I want to contact my office. I might be able to arrange protection for the station as well as scrounge up supplies."

"Miss Taleen," Curtis said, "check with Kyle on your way out.

He's prioritized the shortages, but right now water is my main concern."

"I will. And please call me Letty."

Doc followed Letty out of the office shaking her head. Left alone, Drew and Curtis sat in awkward silence.

Curtis broke first. "So, Nikko—a cool dude, yeah?"

"Yeah," Drew agreed. "Look, Curtis, we need to have a conversation at some point about your side businesses. But now's not that time. I want to commend you on the job you're doing. I don't think I could have handled things better myself." Seeing the relief and pride in Curtis's eyes only reconfirmed to Drew that he'd been an across-the-board ass at judging people's true characters. "This is overstepping my authority, but I'm naming you acting chief of administration. Understand that CoachStop won't approve a field promotion without further consideration, even under these circumstances. I'll let you choose a temporary successor for your command position."

"I appreciate that. Thanks. Since Jonesy's covering the nightshift, Kyle is the obvious choice," Curtis said.

"Agreed. Make that appointment before the end of the day if you can. The first thing I want him to do is initiate a station-wide search for Mattie . . . or her body." It made Drew sick to think of Mattie as either a victim or a traitor.

"Actually, after we found Ruble, we searched every crack and corner again. I'm confident she's not on the station or on Spud, dead or alive. If you want, I'll order another search."

"No, sorry. I should have known you already did that." It occurred to Drew how easy it would be to replace him. *Hell, I've already been replaced.* Drew shook off his feelings of irrelevance. "So, a couple things . . ." He filled Curtis in on the security breaches, the possibility the hooker monks contaminated Dark Landing residents who in turn contaminated station technology, and the ETOC's oversight of that situation. Curtis accepted the new information with remarkable calm.

Their meeting finished, they swung by the conference room to check on Letty. Drew wasn't surprised to see Toby sitting at the table next to her while she worked. Not knowing what else to do with him, he'd left the boy in the security rec room with a warning: "For every tear I find in the pool table felt, I'll yank out a lock of your hair." Toby had just laughed in his face. *Hero my ass.*

"Any luck?" Drew asked, ignoring Toby.

"Of sorts. I ordered a Bin TSF unit to provide two corvette-class ships to protect the station until replacements arrive. They'll be here as soon as possible if Bin authorities allow them to shuttle up to our Taleen space port. They may be Bindians, but they're also Taleen employees — Earth employees. I'm still working on the supply issue. Bin has only limited human provisions. Toby's been helping me." She smiled at the boy.

"I'll bet," Drew said. "I'm headed over to med-lab to see what Doc's up against. I'll talk to you later. Maybe we can scare up dinner." As he left, he gave Curtis a *carry-on* nod and stuck his tongue out at Toby. The boy flipped him off in reply, careful that Letty didn't see his gesture.

~ ~ ∞ ~ ~

As Drew made his way to med-lab, he had to skirt groups of refugees camping out in the passageways. The newcomers wouldn't know who he was, but he nodded and smiled as he passed anyway. The security staff seemed relieved he'd returned. He stopped and greeted each one with a slap on the back and words of appreciation.

In med-lab, interns and nurses scurried from one exam station to the next. Fortunately, Dark Landing served as a residency training facility for med grads bound for the colonies. Since various Earth foundations subsidized their salaries, the station had more medical personnel than would otherwise be assigned.

He found Doc in her office relaying instructions to a nurse. She motioned him in, inclining her head at the chair in front of her desk.

"Thanks, Becky. Just keep a close eye on him and let me know of any changes."

The nurse closed the door behind her.

"Thanks for coming so soon. We really need to talk." She looked weary and, it seemed to Drew, a little scared.

"What's going on?"

"Earlier I told you I hadn't had time to do an official autopsy on Justin Ruble, Fitz's engineer."

"Yeah—so?"

"Well, emphasis on the word *official*. Since we knew the cause of death, I asked one of the interns to do a preliminary autopsy for me to sign off on. It's not like me to take shortcuts, Drew. But we were so busy, and Ruble—"

"Doc, I get it. You don't have to explain yourself. Just tell me what you found."

"He had no internal organs."

"Huh? Wait—what?"

"No kidneys, no liver, no lungs, no heart, *no brain* . . . you name it. What he did have was a skeletal structure, muscles, connective tissue, and skin, of course, a partial vascular system of arteries and veins, and so on. But what's the point without a heart or lungs? Remember, I told you that George Speller had only one kidney; the other had been removed with a surgical precision I've never seen before? It was the same for Ruble, except on a massive scale."

Drew was struggling to understand. "So, you're saying his throat was slit, then—whoever—removed his organs too?"

"No. Somehow, incredibly, it had to be done before death, and it wasn't the *cause* of death."

"Okay, I never had any medical training, but I feel sure that's impossible."

"*Way* beyond impossible; there's no plausible explanation. And I found no sign of associated incisions."

Drew thought about it for a few seconds, then asked, "Was Ruble one of the patients who came in with cold symptoms and a rash?"

Doc voiced a command to her processor. Justin Ruble's medical records displayed. "*Next . . . next . . . stop.*" She turned back to Drew expressing her surprise. "How did you know?"

"There may be an explanation after all," he said.

~ ~ ∞ ~ ~

Drew, Letty, and Curtis stood to one side while Doc instructed Tammas Cameron to lie still on the exam table, reassuring her that taking a blood sample and doing a body scan wouldn't hurt a bit.

Tammas chewed her bottom lip but otherwise lay motionless while Doc entered the desired scan settings.

When the procedures were completed, Curtis summoned a security staffer to return Tammas to her holding cell.

"Well?" Drew asked Doc.

"I don't believe it. There's been a . . . transmutation. Every organ in her body has reconstructed from what, without more study, appears to be multi-modality nanoparticles, that seem to perform all the requisite life functions while still preserving individual intellect and personality. Her blood and DNA samples are devoid of nanoparticles. The DNA aberration — the missing chromosomes I noted when she first arrived — is still there. So, the nanoparticles must disintegrate as soon as a sample is drawn. I'm sure the same will happen if the subject dies, which explains the missing organs from Speller and Ruble.

"I need to do further analysis to determine what residual compounds are left, if any. And help — I can't do this by myself, at least *here*. I'm not a laboratory scientist. We don't have half the equipment needed. And time! It'll take lots of time — months — years — I don't know. This isn't something that can be understood in a few hours." Doc's excitement was palpable.

"This is astounding! I can't begin to imagine what a boon this could be to the future of mankind and probably alien-kind as well. Her brain . . . my God her brain . . . and the heart! Basically, we're talking potential immortality."

Drew and Letty exchanged looks.

"What?" Doc's gaze shifted anxiously between the two.

"It may not be the boon you imagine," Letty said. "The only thing we're sure of is that the nanoids, or *nanoparticles*, are not of Earth design. At first, we thought they'd infected only Earth technology. More accurately, Taleen Industries technology. Then, during our research, three Taleen technicians were cross-contaminated. All three presented with cold-like symptoms accompanied by a rash. Sound familiar?"

Doc nodded. "Feeling ill with cold or flu-like symptoms can be early indications of transplant rejection, though that's rare. The rash is not as easily explained, but may be a mild allergic reaction? What amazes me is how quickly the subject's bodies acclimated to the nanoparticles; or, perhaps, the nanoids adapted — "

Doc's thought processes were ricocheting like a pinball. Letty cut her off. "Anyway, Drew and I identified the hooker monks as carriers who someone specifically dispatched to spread the virus to Dark Landing. And from here . . . well, everywhere, I guess. When we questioned them, Tammas indicated similar groups were sent to other locations. The ETOC believes the infecting nanoids may have arrived on every Alliance planet at roughly the same time. And we have no idea where they originated."

"I need to examine the other two 'hooker monks' — are we really calling them that?" She grimaced. Letty cast a superior look at Drew. Doc continued. "Anyway, I don't get the impression that Tammas knows what's happened to her."

"No, I don't think the victims are aware," Drew agreed. "But I can't vouch for Ruble or, as much as I hate to accept it, Fitz and Mattie. When I speculate on the end game of whoever's responsible, it makes me want to space myself."

Doc looked pensive. "It may be a little late, but I'm issuing a quarantine order for Dark Landing and any docked ships until we can scan everyone. This can't be too far spread or physicians and medical labs would have already discovered and reported it. Though, this is so crazy no one would want to report unless they were absolutely certain, and even then — "

Drew interrupted her. "How long is it going to take? There's well over five thousand still waiting for passage, and we're running low on supplies."

She refocused her attention. "We can easily reset the four dockside airlock scanners to do the job. I would estimate, with sufficient supervisory personnel, we could finish in three or four days. No reason to restrict unloading food and water stores."

"If we find a few people, or a lot of people, who've been contaminated, what do we do with them?" Letty asked.

"Isolate them," Doc said, "at least in the short term. We'll start with the four of us, my staff, the security staff, anyone still on the station who self-reported symptoms, then . . . ." She continued to outline an impromptu plan.

They spent the balance of the day implementing Doc's plan and discussing ways to minimize the inevitable panic.

~ ~ ∞ ~ ~

Drew and Letty met in the officers' mess for a late dinner and to play catch up. Drew smiled when Letty ordered a small salad and a large hot fudge sundae.

"What? I've been running my ass off all day." Her look dared him to disapprove.

"Honestly, it sounds good. I'll have the same." It made no difference. Neither fresh vegetables nor ice cream were available. They settled for stale sandwiches. He changed the subject. "Doc should finish up the staff scans by midnight. So far, she's found three people in different stages of . . . I guess we're calling it *transmutation*. One from medical and two from security, both isolated now. When we start the civilian scans, we'll probably see more cases. Curtis is worried we may be splitting up families soon. *Curtis* is worried — go figure." Drew shook his head, still astonished at his own empathic deficiencies.

He went on. "With Fitzwilliam missing and Doc overwhelmed, CoachStop is abandoning any attempt to oversee management of the station and has transferred full command to me. They're redirecting their efforts to keeping Dark Landing and their other contracted stations supplied and helping with evacuations. By the way, they've received offers of assistance from Taleen Industries. They asked me to thank you."

Letty nodded.

"In our spare time we're still trying to track Fitzwilliam and Freelander, but so far no luck." Drew had taken to using Fitz's and Mattie's surnames in an effort to curb his feelings of loss and betrayal. "How about you?"

"An ETOC contingent headed by Rostenkowski herself is on its way here. I spoke to her only briefly, but she solved the nitro mystery. I'll get to that. Anne said she'd be here in a week; they're taking a shortcut. Seriously, a week! She cut me off before I could get more information. What shortcut?"

"They must have stabilized a new wormhole," Drew offered.

"But they make a big deal when they find new clusters. Shouldn't we know about it?"

"All bureaucracies have their little secrets, especially

189

considering our current circumstances."

They sat several moments in silence, considering the ramifications of the station being so much closer to Earth.

Cutting three weeks off the journey from Earth was huge. Its discovery would be momentous, and the lead news story for weeks when they announced it. No surprise they'd only found it now. Most wormholes were pinpricks, appearing and disappearing in an instant. Even considering the sheer volume, finding and stabilizing *any* was the miracle of science that allowed human and alien-kind to venture so far from their home worlds. No one knew where an uncharted wormhole led, or what they'd find at the other end. But as long as one of the thousands of nano-probes sent through could safely trace a path back within a reasonable time period, all advanced races were eager to follow, explore, and claim new territory. The map of known space was spotty — with more *Unknown* regions than charted ones. Filling in a blank spot on the map caused universal celebration.

"Tell me about the nitro," Drew said.

"Did you know the human body has enough electricity to charge an old-fashioned, coin battery?"

"It sounds vaguely familiar. What does that have to do with it?"

"The nanoids need an electrical or thermal charge to jumpstart them. Humans provide the charge naturally if they come in contact with inactive nanoids; but, due to their super coolants, processors don't. The gel formula for the contaminated data vials the Praetorians used was infused with a small amount of nitro. Just enough to ignite a teensy spark when anyone inserts the vial into a processor drive, but not enough to be noticeable. The modified gel also acts as a shielding agent for both the inactive nanoids and the nitro, making them undetectable by most scanners unless they're specifically calibrated for them. Transmission from a data vial is a one-way, onetime-only process." She sobered from her otherwise enthusiastic explanation. "Dad must have been carrying several ounces of nitro when he entered the station."

Drew didn't let her dwell on her father's death; he was getting good at redirection. "So, another mystery solved. Do we have any idea what purpose the tech nanoids serve?"

"Not yet."

Drew sighed. "So . . . what about the ships from Bin?"

"Resistance from the Bin authorities caused a day's delay, but they should be here in seventy-two hours."

"Any luck locating supplies?"

"Yes and no. The human Taleen security ships coming to relieve the Bin squadron will be escorting a supply frigate. But they won't arrive for more than three weeks, which is why I was wondering about the ETOC's shortcut and if we could use it as well. No luck reaching Anne again. It seems the *Reagan's* gone silent."

"That makes sense. Ships in route anywhere in the K.U. right now must feel like targets. If we found a new wormhole cluster — and it can't be anything else — it's possible your TSF ships already traveled past the origination point. All we can do is keep trying to reach Rostenkowski and wait it out.

"Anyway," Drew continued, "the station's had some luck in the supply area so we're not as bad off as we anticipated. This afternoon we diverted a passing water tanker. They'd just delivered to one of the evacuated colonies but, with no one there, they only left a quarter of their load. We got the rest. And Curtis raided the warehouses for edible cargo. There wasn't much but, if we continue rationing, no one will starve over the next three weeks. So, for the short term, we're in okay shape."

26 LOST AND FOUND

First thing the next morning, Drew headed toward med-lab for a status report on Doc's overnight scans. Curtis walked beside him, delivering his own report. When they exited the conveyer from HQ, they ran into a large knot of about twenty evacuees waiting to get on. Drew nodded courteously in acknowledgement. As his gaze passed over them, an individual in a wide-brimmed hat standing in the center of the knot quickly turned away and looked down at the deck. His cop-senses kicked in and he slowed for a closer inspection. There was something vaguely familiar —

"Mattie!"

At his shout, the figure broke from the group and bolted down the corridor. The others shuffled around looking for the cause of the commotion, temporarily blocking Drew's pursuit and giving the runner several seconds head start. Shoving one of them aside, Drew took off with a bewildered Curtis on his heels; both drew their weapons.

"Are you sure?" Curtis yelled as they ran.

"Yes!"

Well ahead of them, the figure entered the bazaar, which was packed with evacuee families, some still curled up asleep on the deck. As she pressed into the throng, a pigeon rose from the deck directly in front of her. Its flapping wings knocked the hat askew, and it fell from her head, confirming what Drew already knew. She ducked low. He lost her momentarily as he and Curtis danced around bodies and baggage. One of the bodies scooted to get out of Drew's way, managing only to drag himself directly in front of Curtis. At Curtis's expletive, Drew glanced over his shoulder and watched with admiration as Curtis dropped, rolled, and came up again still running.

Drew scanned the crowd ahead of them, trying to reacquire Mattie. He finally spotted her on the west edge of the bazaar, heading toward the supply and storage conveyer. She stopped in front of the doors and turned back toward him. She had her blaster drawn and, in that split second, he realized she intended to fire into the crowd to create a panic. There was a small crate on the deck to his right, next to a startled mother clutching her crying toddler. Without hesitation, Drew jumped on the crate. It held just long enough for him to take aim over the heads of the crowd and fire.

~ ~ ∞ ~ ~

As he stood looking down at Mattie, Drew was relieved she remained unconscious from his stun shot. He only now considered how hard it would be for him to face her. Security staff who'd joined the chase secured her wrists and ankles.

"Take her to HQ. I'll have someone sent over from medical to check her out. No one, and I mean no one, talks to her when she comes to—not one word. Do you understand?"

With grim expressions, each man nodded.

"Are you all right?" Curtis asked.

Drew nodded then shook his head. "Yes. No. I don't know."

"I'm sorry, Chief. This is my fault. I swear we searched everywhere."

"Don't sweat it, Curtis. If anybody could stay hidden on the station for this long, it would be Mattie . . . or Fitz. Go on back with her—I'll join you later. She knew this is a limited-access conveyer. She must still have access. Have engineering complete a palm search for her and disable any hidden user accounts." Drew winced; they both should have thought of that earlier. Unconsciously, he guessed neither of them believed she was still alive. "In the meantime, keep her restrained and remove all access to her cell except for you and me."

Two of the men grabbed Mattie's unconscious body by the

legs and underarms and, with Curtis clearing the way, carried her back through the crowded bazaar. Drew tapped medical and asked for an EMT to report to HQ. It occurred to him he'd pursued and stunned her for leaving the job without giving notice. He had nothing concrete to charge her with. As obvious as it seemed to Drew, no evidence connected Fitz's and Mattie's disappearances, let alone linked them to current events. *Fuck! How did things get so screwed up so fast?*

Doc was waiting when he arrived at med-lab. "You found Mattie? Why does she need an EMT? Is she hurt?"

"Jesus, word travels fast around here. I don't think so. Just following procedure and having her checked out."

"What did she say?"

"Nothing. I saw her. She ran. I shot her. She's unconscious. I came here. Now you know as much as I do. As soon as the EMT looks her over, I'll have her brought in for scanning. I'll let her soak until I get the outcome . . . or figure out what to say to her. And I'd appreciate it if you don't ask her any questions. In fact, I'd rather someone other than you complete her scan. Now, can we review last night's results?" Drew was angry at the universe, and it showed.

"Of course. I only found one additional victim on top of the three from yesterday afternoon. So, that makes two security staff and two medical staff. They're being counseled and interviewed now to determine who they may have infected in turn. The two medical personnel are husband and wife. No surprise there. All four are confined to their quarters with no access to technology. Our engineers working with Taleen Industries have already scrubbed our systems, but they're checking the workstations and personal processors of those four again, just in case." Doc appeared relieved that they'd found so few victims.

"We started resident and evacuee scans this morning. No positive results so far. Curtis's team is working to track those who have already left the station. We don't have data on the evacuees who passed through, but we should be able to locate most of the ones who were living here, which includes almost all of those who displayed symptoms. Then there are the crews who took leave here and passenger stopovers. I'm not even going there. I'll mention those in my report to the ETOC. That's all."

"Thanks, Doc. There are fewer than I expected. Make scanning the *Temperance* crew and passengers a priority. The ladies were doing a brisk business before we detained them. Keep me posted and let me know as soon as you get the results of Mattie's scan."

"You okay, Drew?"

"No. You?"

"No."

~ ~ ∞ ~ ~

Mattie's scan revealed that her internal organs had transmuted. Drew kept her "soaking" for forty-eight hours longer. He was tempted to wait to question her until Anne Rostenkowski arrived, but the ETOC would probably take jurisdiction, and he'd lose the opportunity.

He and Curtis stood in Drew's office watching Mattie on the monitor. She'd been moved to an interview room. At Drew's orders, no one had spoken to her, and she hadn't spoken to anyone other than the occasional "thank you" when food trays were passed in to her. Drew had withheld entertainment vids and K.U. news feeds.

He outlined his plan to Curtis. "Let's keep it simple. We tell her we have Fitz in custody and we're comparing her testimony to his. Somehow, we need to work in the name *Diak* to see what reaction that gets. It's possible, even probable she's unaware of her physical transmutation. We can save that to use if she refuses to cooperate. Do you have a better idea?"

"Mattie's no dummy. What if we tell her Chief Fitzwilliam is dead? That might shake her up," Curtis offered.

"Yeah, that's good," Drew said.

"No offense, but can you handle this, Chief? I mean, it's not a secret how tight you two were."

Drew nodded. "It won't be a problem. I've had some time to get used to our new circumstances." He hoped that held true. He recalled a quote his academy trainer had been fond of reciting, usually in the quiet that followed her request for a volunteer: *And a shiver ran along the bench looking for a spine to run up.*

Drew shivered as he watched Mattie on the monitor. She looked tired and oddly different from the uber-competent, wise-cracking dayshift commander he'd known so well . . . *thought* he'd known so well. She'd cropped her hair short and dressed in men's clothing, but it was more than that. Her countenance had changed. The posture and facial expression of the woman sitting quietly with her hands clasped on the table in front of her didn't belong to *his* Mattie. He was struck again by how wrong his perception of those closest to him had been—people he'd accepted as friends and trusted for years. *Face it, Drew, in different ways you've underestimated Fitz, Mattie, and Curtis. You're a rotten judge of character. You have no business leading others.*

He'd thought a lot about what he would say to Mattie and decided to avoid opening comments and jump into the middle of the interrogation as if they'd been talking for hours. She knew the routine and that they were watching, and she obviously had a better take on him than he had on her . . . or himself.

Drew felt Curtis studying him. "Okay, okay, I'm going in." He opened a tap between them so they could communicate.

Mattie looked up when he entered the room. Drew held her gaze and sat down opposite. "So," he started, "who killed Hernandez?"

"I don't know. Ask Fitz."

"Fitz is dead."

"I don't believe it."

"I don't care whether you believe it or not. I'm talking to you right now anyway, and I want to know who killed Hernandez."

"I don't know." She shrugged then slouched in her chair and stared back at him with a *bring-it-on* look. She seemed prepared for a long session.

Drew was silent for a few seconds, his gaze never wavering, then he stood and stepped to the door. Before opening it, he looked back at her. "I'm not going to waste my time if you've decided not to talk. Oh, by the way, Mr. Diak says 'hi.'"

"*Mister* Diak . . . ?" She laughed. "You don't know what you're talking about."

"Maybe not, but now I know you do. Anyway, that part of it is the ETOC's concern, and they'll be here in a few days. You can *not* talk to them."

Curtis spoke to him over his comm. "*Now would be a good time, Chief.*"

"I am curious about one thing, though," Drew continued smoothly. "Can you feel the nanoids crawling around inside you?

Does your heart still beat like it used to, or does it clank? It's got to be really creepy knowing you no longer have human organs. Especially knowing, by entering a single line of code, you can be turned off just like Fitz and the others." He hoped throwing in "the others" would add a layer of uncertainty. Whatever the conspiracy was, it didn't start and end with Fitz and Mattie. There had to be others.

He could tell he'd struck a chord. While she didn't respond, he noted a tightening around her eyes, and her lips parted slightly. Drew thought she looked scared, but he couldn't be sure. He shrugged and left the room.

Jones was waiting outside the door. "Leave her in there for another thirty minutes before you take her back to her cell."

"That was quick," Curtis said when Drew returned.

"She was ready for me. She's not going to talk, but it surprised her when I packed it in so quickly after the question about Hernandez. I'm hoping she thinks I'm only interested in Hernandez' murder and don't really need to question her otherwise. Maybe that'll give Rostenkowski an edge."

~ ~ ∞ ~ ~

Several hours later, his comm beeped, slowly growing in speed and volume in order to wake him gently. Drew waited a few beeps until his grogginess subsided.

"*Time?*" The beeping stopped and the time and caller was announced in a low, even tone: *Two-thirty a.m., Mitchell Jones.*

"Yes, Jonesy."

"Sorry, Chief. I thought you'd want to know that Mattie . . . uh, Freelander, wants to talk to you."

"Now? She wants to speak with me now?"

"Yeah, well, she seems a little beaten and I—"

"That's okay, Jonesy. You're right. Tell her I'll be there in twenty, and make sure the coffee's fresh."

When he arrived at HQ, Drew poured two cups of coffee, one black and one with cream and headed to the cell block. Mattie sat on her cot, shoulders slumped. *Jones is right, she looks beat. Why the sudden change?*

As soon as she saw him, she asked anxiously, "Is Fitz really dead?"

Drew kept quiet as he juggled the coffees and opened her cell door. Handing her the one with cream, he decided to go with the truth, "Not as far as we know."

"I didn't think so. So that bit about my organs . . . you just made that up too, right?"

"No, Mattie, that's true."

"Yeah, I was afraid of that. I don't really feel any different, but I knew they'd done something to me. I just didn't know exactly what or how."

"They?"

"The Diaks."

"*The* Diaks?" Drew leaned back against the cell wall and removed the lid from his coffee, blowing on it gently and then taking a sip. He replaced the lid. "Why don't we go to my office where we'll be more comfortable? Then you can start at the beginning."

"Drew . . . I, I just want you to know, I'm really sor—"

"Don't, Mattie, just don't."

"Yeah. Okay."

In his office, Mattie chose the lounger instead of pulling the chair next to his desk as she normally would. Drew sat with his feet propped up, holding his coffee in both hands for warmth against a sudden chill. When they'd settled, Mattie started without prompting, reminding him how much he used to enjoy hearing her reports.

"Fitz approached me the first of last year. He told me his sister, Governor Fitzwilliam-Bennett, had asked him to help her. Did you know the governor was Fitz's sister?"

Drew nodded. He wanted to keep her talking, and he wasn't ready to admit he'd only recently learned about Fitz himself.

"Huh?" She looked surprised. This was the type of station gossip they would have shared. "Anyway, he said there was a new alien race petitioning for Alliance membership. But they were technologically advanced beyond the existing members and, while Earth gov knew about them for a while, they kept that knowledge from the rest of the Alliance. So that created a problem."

She kept her eyes on her coffee cup as she talked. "By keeping the Diaks a secret, Earth had breached the accord and couldn't just all of a sudden introduce them. That's where we came in, Fitz and I.

I forged records from the early days of the station, showing that we'd done business with the Diaks a long time ago. You know, the normal entries, acting as intermediary for trade goods and that kind of stuff. That way no one could accuse Earth of keeping their existence a secret. I even created old lease records showing the Diaks had rented office space for several months here. Fitz wanted a lot of detail to make it all seem real.

As she talked, Mattie displayed an enthusiasm for her story that disturbed Drew.

She went on. "In the meantime, Fitz and I also started auditing the station's actual archived records and sending updated files to both CoachStop and Muck, asking them to copy over the old files. The first few we sent them were legit. We corrected accounting errors and miss-categorizations, minor things. After a few weeks, it became so routine that neither CoachStop nor Muck thought anything about it.

"Everything we created about the Diak predated Earth's membership in the Alliance and the Coalition. Supposedly, the governor was going to slip an entry for them into the Known Races Concordance, but in the wrong category, as if it had been entered incorrectly. That way, if the other Alliance members made a fuss, Earth could say, 'Sorry, we thought you knew.'"

She cast a quick glance at Drew, then back to the coffee cup and continued. "This went on for about eight months, and then Fitz said the governor had stumbled on the fact that her predecessor— you know, the guy who died in office—continued conversations in secret with them long after first contact. Some of the advanced technology he described in his personal notes intrigued the governor, and she was negotiating a side deal with the Diak. Fitz hinted at an advancement that would make us wealthy beyond imagination. He couldn't give me the particulars without the governor's authorization. I know now most of what he told me was bullshit, but there was some truth to this part. He seemed genuinely excited—like he needed to talk to somebody about it."

Drew interrupted her. "Mattie, how could you be so stupid?"

"It was Fitz, Drew. I mean, really, *Fitz*. And it felt special to work on a classified project for the Earth governor. I was being paid too. Not a lot, but enough. When I started to suspect something more was going on, I assumed it was on the part of the governor—that

Fitz was the one being duped because she's his sister and he's such a milquetoast. Anyway . . . it was garbage from the beginning, and I was the sap.

"I didn't get really scared until Hernandez was killed. Fitz always approved each new batch of corrected records before I sent them. When I went back and looked more closely at my transmissions, I found encrypted attachments and that all sorts of people were being copied — some on Alliance planets. There was one attachment that Fitz must have miscoded. It contained a map of the Schwarzschild Cluster with coordinates for each wormhole. He'd been using me as a patsy to cover his ass. I realized then that I was a traitor — me, a traitor — and probably an accomplice to murder. When I confronted him, he told me about the big Diak tech advancement that was going to make us rich: immortality."

Drew interrupted her again. "That's what Doc said. The nanoid transmutation might mean near immortality. At least freedom from disease and aging."

"Fitz never mentioned nanoids. But I knew for sure I was involved in something way beyond my understanding. He tried to sell me on the notion that he and the governor were heroes. They were saving millions of lives by collaborating with the Diak. That may be true, but I don't think saving lives was Fitz's motivation. He and his sister are just greedy and power hungry. You think they were being duped too?"

Drew ignored her question. "And Hernandez?"

"Honestly, Drew, I don't know. I figured after Hernandez' death it was all connected with Taleen and Speller, but I never figured out how."

"We suspect it was Fitz's head engineer, Justin Ruble, who killed Hernandez," Drew said.

She shrugged. "If you say so. So, that's what you call it, huh? Transmutation?"

Drew was sickened by how easily she was able to dismiss Hernandez' murder. He kept it from showing. "That's what Doc calls it. You didn't know what was happening to you?"

"Just before Fitz left for Miranda Station, he told me I was already on my way to immortality. I thought maybe something I ate—"

"Have you met a Diak?"

"Nope. And Fitz said he hadn't either. All I'm sure of is they must be oxygen breathers. When I created the fake lease agreement, Fitz said it should specify that their quarters required a nitrogen-oxygen environment within human tolerance."

"Jesus, Mattie."

Mattie looked at her hands in her lap without saying anything further.

After a few seconds of silence, Drew asked, "And the hooker monks?"

"The *what*?!"

The look on Mattie's face convinced Drew she had no idea what he was talking about. He had a hundred more questions but decided to withhold his speculations about the connection between the Diaks, Letty, and the recent series of events. He'd leave that to the ETOC. He knew they'd have a hundred questions times a hundred more, but no way did Mattie know the full story of what the Diaks, or the governor, were really up to.

27 REINFORCEMENTS

Two Bin TSF, light-armored, corvette-class cruisers arrived and began patrolling around the station and Spud. Drew felt somewhat secure knowing that, between the station's shielding and the two cruisers, Dark Landing would enjoy short-term protection. So far, only similar light-armored ships have led the attacks. The morning after the Bin ships arrived, the ETOC's *Reagan* docked, carrying Anne Rostenkowski and a much heavier armory. The new arrivals contributed to the station's food and water stocks. Their local problems, at least, continued to improve.

~ ~ ∞ ~ ~

Secretary Rostenkowski took notes while the Dark Landing command staff, along with Letty, filled her in on events over the last two weeks.

When they finished, she looked up from her processor. "So, Speller . . ." She paused and glanced at Letty, then started over, her voice softening. "When George connected the nanoid vial gel to the Praetorians, he suspected a wider-based conspiracy and broadened his investigation, literally following the clues to Dark Landing. He instructed Letty to join him here for her protection. George was carrying a sample of nitro. He either didn't realize the danger or thought he'd neutralized it. For what it's worth, I agree with your assessment. The airlock explosion was a tragic accident. The ETOC has since learned that infected data vials were shipped to every Alliance planet and Earth concerns beyond Taleen Industries. We're rounding up members of the Praetorian sect for questioning, and to be scanned as well now, but it looks like they were infiltrated. Their membership had no knowledge that their data gel formula was tampered with."

She glanced back at her processor. "The Diaks learned of George's investigation, possibly through his research on the Praetorian monks, which triggered an attempt on George's life when he was on Mars. When George died, they needed to take out Letty in case he'd shared what he knew with her. They missed Letty but killed Hernandez. Hernandez' killer was Chief Fitzwilliam's engineer, Justin Ruble, who Fitzwilliam may have in turn dispatched before he left Dark Landing."

Drew interjected. "We're guessing about Ruble and Fitz. It's possible Fitz wasn't the one in charge here." Eyebrows rose around the room. "*What*? We don't know for certain. Yeah, it looks that way, but . . ." Drew's face scrunched in frustration, and he waved at Anne to continue. *Why am I defending Fitz?* He promptly dismissed the thought. He wasn't defending Fitz, he was defending himself for being an idiot. Anne was still watching him. Drew threw his hands up—*what are you waiting for?*

Secretary Rostenkowski nodded. "The Diaks, or their co-conspirators, possibly Fitzwilliam himself, . . ." she tossed a quick glance at Drew, then went on " . . . contacted *Muck* impersonating an ETOC officer to further deflect inquiry. That's an awful lot of speculation, but some version of it makes sense. With the Taleen research into the data breach, George's personal investigation, and his and Letty's arrival at the station, the bad guys—Diaks, co-conspirators, whoever—"

A calmer Drew spoke up again. "We're calling them "bogeymen."

Rostenkowski smiled. "Okay then, the Diaks and whoever is in bed with them, hereafter collectively known as the *bogeymen*, stepped-up attacks on outlying colonies and ships. Up to this point, we assume the bogeymen were operating on a less aggressive timeframe toward disrupting the Alliance, pitting us against one another and destroying our economies along the way. The ETOC believes, after studying vids recovered from several of the attacks, particularly the attack on the *Temperance*, that Diak nanotechnology is sufficiently advanced to equip their ships with . . . I guess you'd call it *shape-altering* . . . capabilities to imitate Alliance member and *Muck* ships.

"I've sent each of you a list of the attacks which we now attribute to the Diaks, along with fatality numbers. Of primary concern is that we've got survivors on several outposts cut off without supplies. Letty, I'd like to speak to you about that a little later."

Secretary Rostenkowski took a deep breath, letting it out slowly. "So . . . we can guess that the Diak's goal is to divide in the short term and ultimately conquer. About their race, we know only that they are aggressive, technologically advanced, have successfully recruited human and probably alien conspirators, most likely by promising immortality and riches—a heady inducement. They also displayed a cheeky conceit by disclosing their identity through Brother Diak and our informant, *Mr.* Diak. Perhaps they're the same person. There are likely other instances of which we're unaware. Oh, and we believe the Diaks are oxygen breathers, but we don't have a clue what they look like. My men are questioning Mattie Freelander and the three, uh . . . *monks?* . . . but I doubt we'll learn more. We haven't had any luck decoding the attachments Fitzwilliam added to Freelander's audit reports either, except for the one Mattie was able to open."

She sat back in her chair and surveyed the group. For a second her facial features sagged, revealing acute levels of exhaustion and dread. She quickly regained composure and continued. "When it comes to the nanoids, the Alliance, and perhaps the entire K.U., has been invaded to an extent still unknown. Spreading their nanoids through sex and technology might have been a *fait accompli* if we hadn't caught on when we did. Though, it would have come to light soon. Medical communities across the Alliance, to larger and lesser extents, are discovering the nanoids presence—*transmutation* as you're calling it—and reporting it. The growing consensus is that an Alliance member developed the technology and somehow accidentally released it. So far, no one's enlightened them otherwise. And as far as I know, no one's made the connection with cold/rash symptoms yet. The ETOC's main concern is discovering the extent of the invasion and stopping its spread."

Her manner changed from monotone briefing mode to a more sobering delivery. "I received intelligence a few hours ago on the high probability the Diaks can remotely control the nanoids. Taleen researchers believe the ones infecting our technology serve as communications *boosters* for transmitting commands to infected biological subjects. Much like the superconducting communication relays we deploy. Smart. If their nanoids had spread undetected, they would have control links in every corner of the K.U."

Rostenkowski paused a few moments to let the new information sink in, then continued. "Where does that leave us? Bin, Camdu, Bahdane, and Earth are talking to one another. Fahdeen seems to be the hold out, but Earth is sharing information with them as we learn it, and they'll come around soon. For all intents and purposes, *Muck* has disbanded except for roughly half of their security forces. Those remaining are operating independently to aid evacuees as much as they can with limited resources. Good for them. If . . . when . . . the Alliance re-alliances—is that a word?—the Coalition will probably be back in business as well."

As he listened to Rostenkowski, it occurred to Drew he needed to reassess his opinion of *Muck*, or at least their security division. They evidently weren't the evildoers he suspected. *That's one more example of poor judgment on my part.* He refocused on her sum-up.

"We're reaching out to the unaligned planets to warn them. But due to the distances involved and our cultural and biological differences, we couldn't come to each other's aid regardless. We don't know yet if, or to what extent, they may be suffering the same crisis.

"With internal chaos and distrust between members, all five aligned worlds are experiencing economic setbacks, and each has weak militaries and defensive capabilities. Every member is struggling to find resources to strengthen those capabilities, as well as to scan entire populations for nanoid infection. And we haven't agreed on how to inform our populations. Plus, we still need to deal with infected technology which, from my, the ETOC's, official standpoint, is the easier task. Then there's the *biggie*: How much time do we have to accomplish all of the above?

"I'm sure you won't be surprised to learn that Governor

Fitzwilliam-Bennett is missing. Have I left anything out?"

The room was silent.

~ ~ ∞ ~ ~

Doc and Curtis excused themselves to return to their offices. Rostenkowski pulled Letty aside for a private conversation about continuing support from the TSF in aiding stranded colonists.

Drew scanned the ETOC's list of locations and ships attacked by the Diaks. One location jumped from the screen. *Prosse! No survivors. Aw, Toby . . . poor kid. What are we going to do with you now?* His thoughts dwelled on Toby's misfortune for several minutes then wandered to Fitz and Mattie. *Are the Diaks controlling them through the nanoids? Is that why Mattie was so callous about Hernandez' murder?* He hoped so. He wanted to believe neither had acted on their own volition.

Letty called to him from across the room. "It's just like we said, Drew. There's a new wormhole cluster. Only one has been probed and stabilized so far, and I couldn't reach Anne because communication relays aren't deployed."

Drew joined them at the other end of the conference table.

Anne looked annoyed. "Letty, you didn't let me finish. Ordinarily there would be an Alliance-wide announcement, but with everything else going on we need to keep the discovery as quiet as possible."

"Oh . . . sorry."

"It's okay here. With Dark Landing now in greater contiguity to Earth, the command staff will learn of it by necessity, along with local TSF staff, but we don't want it to be general knowledge."

"Understood," Letty seemed only marginally contrite.

Ignoring their exchange, Drew looked at Anne with a saddened expression. "Prosse?"

"Yes, I'm sorry. Were you acquainted with someone there? Camdu commissioned an Earth ship to evacuate anyone who wanted to leave, but they arrived too late. They scanned and found no survivors."

"Oh, no!" Letty cried, "What are we going to tell Toby?"

"Toby?" Anne asked.

Drew explained the boy's presence on Dark Landing. Tears

streamed down Letty's face. Her grief over the death of her own father was still fresh. Toby's loss rekindled it.

"Letty, sweetheart, we should tell Toby right away, but you need to be strong for him." As soon as he called her *sweetheart*—her father's endearment for her—Drew realized his mistake.

Letty leaned on the table and buried her face in her arms.

Anne went to her and motioned Drew out of the room. As much as he wanted to be there for her, Anne was right. Letty had brushed him off more than once, and she would respond better to another woman than to him. He left the conference room and sought out Curtis at the shift commander's desk. He'd been offered Fitz's office but preferred to work closer to the action and keep an eye on Jonesy and Kyle.

"Where's Kyle?"

"There was a dust up in the mezzanine bar. He went to sort it out."

"You seen Toby Greenstein?"

"Yeah, he left with a couple of the guys to get something to eat. What's up?"

"His parents were killed in an attack on Prosse."

"Aw, that's harsh. What are you gonna do with him?"

"Keep him with us short term. Will you find out if he's got other relatives somewhere?"

"Sure, I'll look into it."

"Anything new?"

Curtis rubbed his face and yawned. From the shadows under his eyes and his sluggish movements, Drew could see he was spent. Curtis was not only performing Fitz's duties, made harder by the added strain of the evacuee population, but also overseeing the shift commands to relieve Drew of much of the daily routine.

"I just chatted with the ETOC reps," Curtis said. "They haven't learned anything from Mattie we didn't already know. I doubt they're going to."

"I agree. Listen, on second thought, why don't you take off and get some sleep? I'll watch the shop until Kyle or Jonesy gets here and have one of them look into the Toby thing. I don't want you back in HQ until morning."

Curtis didn't argue. "Thanks, boss. I'm bushed."

~ ~ ∞ ~ ~

Drew reviewed provisioning records until Toby returned to HQ. He preferred to wait for Letty before talking to the boy but, under the circumstances, he didn't think she was up to it. He couldn't handle the two of them if they broke down at the same time. He brought Toby into his office and sat next to him on the lounger.

"Look, maybe we aren't the best of friends," he began, "but I want you to know I do care about you. There's something really tough I need to tell you."

Toby looked down and shuffled a foot against the deck, "Yeah, I figured. You're sending me back to my folks, right? It's okay — I sorta miss my ma."

Drew felt stinging behind his eyes. *Jesus!* "Toby, I have some really bad news. You heard about the colonies and ships that were attacked?"

Toby's head snapped up and he looked hard at Drew, fear building in his eyes. "Yeah . . . so?"

"I'm so sorry, Toby, but Prosse was one of the places attacked. A ship arrived afterward and didn't find any survivors. Your mom and dad died in the attack."

The boy's eyes filled with tears and his bottom lip quivered. Before the tears fell, he jumped from the lounger and ran out of the office.

Drew tried to catch up to him, but Toby had always been too quick. Letty stepped out of the conference room as Drew was sprinting past, and he stopped.

"What's happening?" Her eyes were red, but otherwise she seemed to have recovered.

"I told Toby about his parents, and he took off."

Letty blinked rapidly and squared her shoulders. "I'll help you find him."

Drew tapped his comm and issued an alert to keep an eye out for the boy. "There's a couple places we can look first. He hangs out around the bazaar or down at the docks," he said. "You take the bazaar; I'll take the docks."

Before Letty could respond, the emergency siren sounded, repeating in long, closely spaced whoops. Hatches began to close automatically. The hatches would remain operational as long as environmental services were functioning on both sides. Even though Drew had override authority, he needed to be in HQ in the event of the catastrophe which would cause that hatch to lock even him out. When the siren paused and a canned announcement came over the speakers, it was clear the threat extended station-wide:

> *All essential personnel report to your emergency stations. Commercial enterprises are ordered to close. Non-essential staff and residents proceed to your quarters. Emergency procedures are now in effect. Further announcements will follow. Remember your training. Thank you for your cooperation.*

The announcement repeated and the sirens blared once more. Drew grabbed Letty's hand to bring her with him, but she pulled away.

"I'm going to find Toby," she said, and headed toward the outer corridor without waiting for his response.

Drew couldn't follow her. His responsibility was in HQ. *Now what?*

28 ONSLAUGHT

Curtis groaned. His arms and legs thrashed against the sirens assaulting his slumber. Only when he knocked the bowl off the end of his bunk dumping the remains of popcorn from three days earlier, did he come fully awake.

"What the hell!"

As the announcement played, he grabbed the uniform pants he'd worn that morning, making a face at their wrinkled condition, and reached for his boots. He tapped security dispatch. Three unidentified ships were approaching the station, ignoring Dark Landing's hails. Station shields were activated. Drew's orders were to check on the evacuees camped in the corridors and the bazaar on his way to HQ. Their guests had no training in emergency procedures, and no assigned stations or quarters to go to. Curtis could imagine their panicked state and was curious exactly how he was expected to handle the masses alone.

As soon as he entered the corridor from his quarters, he knew the situation was as bad as he'd envisioned. Evacuees were crammed against the far hatch to the public areas, attempting to pound it open. Curtis yelled above the siren whoops. "People . . . listen to me!"

The crowd turned and, seeing his uniform, came at him shouting questions.

"Shut up!" Curtis reached for his blaster with no intention of drawing it. The motion slowed them down, and they quieted somewhat.

"I'm as in the dark as you are," he lied. "I won't know what's happening until I get to headquarters, and there may be another announcement explaining the situation long before I get there."

Other than a few scattered whispers, they were now listening to him, though they looked ready to erupt at any moment.

Curtis continued in a more even tone. "You're in the middle of the station and as safe here as anywhere. The hatches are closed, but they're still operational if you use the manual keypad, but not by pushing and pounding on them."

Two women broke from the crowd and headed back to the hatch.

Curtis raised his voice again. "*However*, I'm advising you to stay here until we know what's happening. Try to stay calm. Chief Cutter does not believe in withholding information—"

The siren cut out as Cutter's voice came over the speaker:

Could I have everyone's attention? Dark Landing is being attacked by unidentified ships. So far, two Bin fighters and a heavily armed ETOC ship are holding the attackers off. We've sustained no damage, and I expect the attack to end soon. Remain calm and stay where you are. I'll keep you advised.

The announcement ended abruptly, and the two women opened the hatch and hurried out. Curtis didn't stop them. He had the others' attention, but their expressions had changed from fear to terror. *Great timing, Drew.*

"Okay, I know you're frightened, but don't panic. Wait for the all-clear announcement. I'm reporting to my station." He pushed through the crowd, ignoring questions, and opened the hatch. As it closed behind him, a laser blast shook the station.

The hit, though too weak to throw anyone to the deck, managed to send them into the frenzied state they'd been barely containing. The hatch reopened, and Curtis was jostled to one side as the evacuees piled out to join the pandemonium in the main corridor. Without more men, short of shooting someone, he couldn't think of a way to regain their attention, let alone contain the panic. *But it couldn't make it any worse,* he thought.

The Diak ships matched the design of the one that attacked the *Temperance*. Evidently, they stopped bothering with disguises. An enemy laser pulse had breached the shields and hit the east armature. Drew's display showed debris from a missing chunk blown out midway between Dark Landing and Spud, rendering it impassible. With redundancies upon redundancies, Dark Landing had no single point of failure. However, to any attacker, the armatures securing it to Spud would appear a weakness.

Without the correct code, shared only by ships approved for travel within Alliance territory, the Diak would be unable to detect the shielded threads of Pohang steel alloy. Pohang alloy was stronger than titanium, stronger even than uru. They might destroy both armatures in their attempt to separate the station from the asteroid. But twenty slender threads strung between Dark Landing and Spud, stacked at varying intervals (five above and five below each armature), would have to be individually severed.

Drew watched as one of the Bin ships entered the edge of Drew's display, atmosphere streaming from one side. Severely crippled, the ship was still attempting to defend the station. Despite the damage and, Drew was sure, fatalities, it maneuvered to face the Diak ship and continued to fire its forward lasers from its undamaged side. The second Bin ship joined its crippled twin. The *Reagan* did not appear on the display. The station shook again, but less violently in Security Headquarters this time. They'd sustained a hit from outside his display field.

He expanded his display to encompass the station and Spud in their entirety. Instead of a live-action view, all components of the battle were now rendered as icons. Bin ships and the *Reagan* appeared as green squares with ID tags off to the side. The enemy ships displayed as red squares. One of three red squares tagged E-1, zig-zagged, forward and back, side-to-side, and fired laser salvos at the two Bin ships. The undamaged Bin valiantly defended its crippled partner, but gray concentric circles representing its shielding strength dimmed with each successful hit from the Diak ship. Its refusal to move from its partner's side hampered the healthy Bin ship.

The *Reagan* faced danger as well. Though more heavily armed and shielded than the Bin ships, it was outflanked. Two red squares, E2 and E3, moved in similar zig-zag patterns against the ETOC ship, keeping up continuous fire. So far, the *Reagan's* shields were holding, but its defensive fire was ineffective as the Diak corvettes darted in and out close around it.

Another hit shook the station more forcefully than the previous two. Diak ship E1 had fired past its Bin targets and connected with Dark Landing. The main display indicated that the station shields, though activated, appeared to be failing. *Either the shields are ineffective, or Fitz re-configured them before he left.* Drew tapped engineering and ordered them to check the settings and run a diagnostic on the shielding programs. He didn't know how long that process would take, but he hoped not long.

Sirens recommenced their whooping as he zoomed back to a live view of the station, catching the last of the escaping atmosphere from the passage immediately behind dock sublevel one as it dissipated into surrounding space. His breath caught. As many as a dozen bodies floated amid the debris. A mental image of Letty's face, bloodied and broken, flashed in front of him and his stomach flipped. He fought the urge to leave HQ to look for her.

~ ~ ∞ ~ ~

The sirens blared once again as Curtis picked himself up from the deck. He looked through the port of the hatch he'd been about to open. A small airlock five feet across marked a seam between two ship sections. Normally the two hatches would stand open, unnoticeable to the foot traffic passing through them. The hatches on both sides had closed automatically at the onset of the attack. Now, through the opposite port, he saw bits of debris and body parts drifting away from the station. A circle of red lights flashed around the perimeter of the far hatch, confirming it was impassable, though the strip of green above the control pad indicated the airlock was still pressurized. The laser hit took out a section of the corridor that skirted the back of the upper dock level. Curtis had detoured to the docks to make sure they'd evacuated, checking the corridors along the way. Dock workers were a stubborn bunch with a stand-your-ground devotion to *their* ships.

Curtis headed back the way he'd come. He could do nothing

for the poor souls on the opposite side of that airlock. He tapped dispatch to provide a first-hand report of the damage and request the safest alternate route to HQ. The sirens quieted as he ended the connection. A dull thudding noise sounded behind him. He spun around. A small fist pounded on the hatch window then dropped from view, reappearing a second later to pound again. In quick succession the fist appeared and disappeared three times. *Thump . . . thump . . . thump.* Someone, a child, was caught in the airlock.

Curtis palmed the control pad, initiating a security override. The hatch didn't respond. The green light strip above the pad now flashed to indicate oxygen depletion. There had to be a leak. He tapped environmental, glancing at the small lettering centered above the hatch.

"Acting Chief Curtis Walker here. Hatch SL268-H is not responding to my override. At least one person, a child, is caught in the airlock between SL268-H and SL269-H."

After a brief silence, the tech responded. "I'm sorry, sir, but the atmosphere is leaking from a damaged seal on 269, and the 268 hatch cannot be opened."

"But I need to get in there."

"There's nothing I can do, sir. Opening that hatch would endanger the station. The system won't release the controls until the damage is repaired."

"There's got to be a work-around. We can't let this kid die."

"There's not one I know of, sir. And if you managed to open the hatch, it would just trigger a domino effect. The section you're in would seal as well, and both of you would be trapped along with anyone else in that section."

"This is ridiculous. Do something, you idiot!" Yelling at the tech wouldn't change things. He ended their connection. The hand no longer appeared in the window. The light still flashed green, indicating some atmosphere remained, but he had no way to tell if it was enough to sustain life. When the light turned red there would be no air left.

As he stood helpless, trying to think of something to do, the small hand appeared once more. This time the fingers dragged against the glass and down out of sight, leaving three red smears.

"Shit . . . shit . . . shit!"

Curtis frantically surveyed the corridor for something to open the hatch, but with little hope. He needed a mechanical wedge to pry the door open and, even then, the bulkheads would likely give before the hatch. Its small port window, constructed of triple-paned quartz glass to withstand cosmic extremes of heat and cold, was shatterproof. Even a pile-driver wouldn't make an impact. And environmental was right: breaching the hatch could endanger the whole station.

The green light was still blinking. As he watched it, afraid to take his eyes away in case it stopped, he accepted an incoming tap from Jared Barlow in environmental services.

"Look, Barlow, I'm sorry. I had no business attacking you."

"No worries, sir. I understand. We've been working on the problem at this end. Sensors show two people in the airlock — a child and an adult. The adult is unconscious. The child is conscious, but probably not for much longer. The air is pretty thin. Neither of them has comm implants if you can believe that."

Shit, Curtis thought, *it's got to be Letty Taleen, and if it's Letty, then the child is Toby — bet on it.* "Is there *anything* we can do?"

"Well, maybe, whether we can do it in time is the question. There are two techs in the crawl tube above the airlock right now."

Curtis listened for noises from above the corridor but heard only Barlow's recitation. He refocused on what the man was saying.

"Our men are going to drill a small hole into the seam to feed oxygen through. Once we locate the leak, with the child's help if he or she is still . . . is able to, maybe we can seal it. Then the control panel should reboot, and you'll be able to open the hatch. But even if we can't get in right now, the oxygen feed will keep them alive until we can get outside and panel off the damage. The airlock bulkheads are still generating heat, so that's not a problem unless the exterior hatch blows . . ."

Curtis was only partially listening to Barlow now. He'd understood the plan about three sentences in. He concentrated on the rattles and dull humming noises coming from above the corridor and thinking of all the things that could go wrong. He figured whatever they used to weld ships together was too strong to drill through. After all, if the welds were vulnerable to a common drill, the station would always teeter on ripping apart at any time, wouldn't it?

"Chief Walker?"

"Yes, Barlow, I can hear them working now. What's happening?"

"They're almost through. Can you see the occupants?"

"No. The space is too short." He peered through the hatch port, standing on his tiptoes and craning his head down, but he still couldn't see the deck. He rapped on the port to get Toby's attention—if it was Toby. No response. As he watched, the control pad light changed from flashing green to solid red.

"You guys need to hurry. There's no more oxygen."

"Just another minute. It's slow going," Barlow responded.

"A minute's a long time if you're not breathing." Curtis banged on the hatch port.

The station shook again, this time more violently, throwing Curtis off balance. He fell on his back, hitting his head hard on the deck. The siren whoops restarted. After dragging himself up, he looked through the aligned ports for new debris. That hit had been close. He pressed his face against the window, straining to spot the flotsam that might identify the extent of the damage. A hand popped up and slapped the glass directly in front of him. Startled, Curtis jumped backward and tripped over his own feet. He fell again, this time on his ass. The hand continued slapping the glass. From the deck, Curtis glanced to the control panel. The light blinked green once more. The chamber was getting oxygen, but it must still be leaking through the damaged seal. The hand waved energetically, so the kid was breathing.

"Barlow, are you there?" His connection to Barlow had broken. Back on his feet, he slapped his side of the port and yelled.

"Is that you, Toby?" The hand waved furiously as the boy jumped up and down. An arm and the crown of his head were intermittently visible.

"If you can hear me," Curtis yelled, "make a fist."

The hand balled into a fist.

"Great! Okay, if the answer's yes, open your hand wide. If it's no, make a fist. Okay?"

The hand opened *yes*, and Toby spoke, his voice faint, but clear, "If I can hear you, can't you hear me?"

Curtis laughed out loud at his stupidity. "Yeah, yeah, I can hear you. Is Letty there with you?"

"Yes, she's here. Her head's bleeding, but only a little. And she's been moving a little too, and mumbling."

"Those are good signs, Toby. How are you? Are you hurt?"

"No, I'm okay. Can you get us out of here?"

"We're trying, kid. Just hang a minute while I get environmental back and see where we are."

When Curtis reconnected with Barlow, he provided Curtis with the location of the leak. It was a pinprick-sized hole at the top of the exterior hatch, well above Toby's reach.

"The leak was larger a few minutes ago," Barlow said. "The hatch managed to self-seal, leaving just the smaller hole. Still enough to keep the interior hatch in lockout status."

"So, what do we do?" Curtis asked. "Miss Taleen is only semi-conscious, and the kid is too short to see through the port, let alone reach the top of the hatch."

"Hold a sec," Barlow said.

Curtis called to Toby, "You hanging in there, kid?"

"Yeah, I'm okay. Letty said something a minute ago, but I couldn't understand her."

"Try shaking her a little, but not too hard."

"Okay."

Barlow came back on the connection. "We have a possible fix. It's not very scientific, though."

"What is it?"

"Have the boy take off his shirt and try throwing it up to the top of the hatch. Even with a small leak, the vacuum pull might be strong enough to suck the fabric against it and seal it. He'd have to hit it dead-on though."

"Okay, I'll have him try." Curtis stepped up to the hatch port. "Toby, how's Letty?"

"She's sorta okay. I shook her a little and her eyes opened, but now she's sleeping again. Can't you get us outta here?"

"We're going to try something right now. There's a tiny leak just above the opposite hatch. I know you can't reach it, but . . ." He explained what they needed Toby to do. "You understand?"

"Yeah; I'll try."

Curtis watched and cheered Toby on as his shirt repeatedly flew to the top of the hatch without catching. It finally caught, but he couldn't tell if it was snagged on the hatch's surface or being held by the vacuum. The green light continued to blink. After a few seconds, the shirt fell.

"My arm's getting really tired. This is kinda lame." Toby's frustration matched Curtis's.

"Keep trying, kid. It looked like you had it there for a minute." Two environmental staff had come up behind him, adding their words of encouragement.

The shirt flew upward twice more. The second time it caught and stayed. Curtis watched the blinking green light. It blinked, then held solid for two seconds before blinking again . . . held for several seconds, then blinked . . . intermittently holding and blinking. Curtis palmed the control pad and entered the override code over and over as fast as he could. On his fourth attempt the green light held long enough for the code to be accepted, and the hatch slid back.

Curtis reached into the airlock, grabbed Toby by the arm, and flung him into the corridor behind him. He clasped Letty by one ankle as another man crowded next to him and took hold of the other ankle. They fell backward, yanking Letty out as they went. When she cleared the hatch, Curtis commanded the hatch to close.

He sat up and knelt next to her, cupping the back of her head in his hand. Her hair was wet and sticky, but the bleeding appeared to have stopped.

"Letty, Letty, can you hear me?"

"T-toby?" She moaned, opening her eyes and quickly closing them again.

"Toby's right here. He's fine. We're taking you to med-lab. You'll be okay too."

One of the men had disappeared for a minute, returning with a stretcher which he laid next to Letty. Curtis helped them lift her off the deck and onto the stretcher.

"Wait a sec," Curtis said to the men. "Are you sure you're okay, Toby?" He held the boy by the shoulders and turned him around slowly looking for injuries.

"I'm fine, sir. I'm not hurt at all."

"That's good. Just to be safe, go along with Letty to med-lab and Doc will check you out."

"No," Toby said. His body posture and facial expression froze in defiance.

Curtis had seen his rebellious look before. The two men couldn't drop Letty to chase after Toby if he ran, and arguing with him would be a waste of time. He nodded to the men to go.

"Come with me then but stay close. If you get blown up, I'm not stopping to pick up your pieces."

Toby stepped next to Curtis and took his hand.

29 ESCAPE POD

Drew watched as E2 broke away while E3 kept the *Reagan* occupied. In quick succession, the station took three hits to dockside. A single energy pulse wouldn't breach a bulkhead, but repeated salvos would do the trick eventually, and the Diak ships were fast. Too fast for the Bin ships, though both appeared of a similar class, and three times as fast as the heavier-class ETOC ship. Even with its superior tracking capability, the *Reagan's* lasers racked up only near misses. Not one burst had hit its mark. E2 returned to take on the *Reagan* while E3 positioned itself for a new salvo dockside.

The damaged Bin ship had stopped firing altogether, conserving power for life support. Its partner stayed by its side, shields weakened but holding. Its lasers connected with E1. Colors rippled across the surface of the Diak ship. *How long can this last?* Drew wondered. The good guys weren't losing, but they weren't winning.

Jonesy monitored station damage reports at another terminal. He caught Drew's glance and wiggled his hand back and forth. They were holding their own for the time being. Still, if the attack continued, the station in its entirety would be at risk. This proved what he'd always suspected. The outer cells — ships — were the most vulnerable, and detaching and reactivating them was dangerous. It would take far too much time to offer a practical escape option. But then, no one had considered that the ships might need to be separated while the station was under attack.

He could evacuate everyone to the center of the station and was deliberating whether to go a step further and move them all over to Spud when the command hatch opened. Curtis entered with a shirtless Toby.

Drew took one look at Toby and raised his eyebrows questioningly.

Curtis nodded. "She's okay. Hit her head but was conscious and talking. I had her taken to med-lab."

Drew exhaled a breath he hadn't realized he'd been holding and returned his attention to his display.

Curtis joined Drew behind the monitor. "How long can we last?" he asked.

"Awhile yet, I think. But we'll be the worse for it. We're transmitting a mayday for any ship nearby, but no response. And they won't be any help if they're unarmed. Have dispatch order the staff to move people into the center of the station."

Curtis stepped to one side and tapped dispatch, relaying Drew's order. "Should we evacuate them to Spud?"

"I was just thinking that. Only the one armature is passable and getting there might be more dangerous than staying put. It's a two-kilometer trip and we'll lose everyone in the arm if it's breached. But, if this keeps up, Spud may be the safest place. And we need to act while it's still an option."

"Why don't I put together a team? We can take the women and children over in small groups . . . say a hundred at a time. Can we defend the passage?"

Drew shook his head. "If the *Reagan* repositions itself to protect the armature, it'll be even more vulnerable because it'll clue the Diak onto what we're doing. We could ask the Bin ship to put itself between the arm and the *Reagan*. To the Diak it would appear like reinforcement for the *Reagan*, but that would sacrifice the damaged Bin ship. Our best strategy is to move groups to Spud as quickly as we can without signaling our intent."

"Yeah, I ag—"

The room filled with cheers and applause. Simultaneously Drew and Curtis looked to the main viewer. New green squares entered from the top of the screen. First one, then three *Muck* ships appeared in frame.

A greeting came over the comm, "MCTT Zeta Quadrant Lt. Commander William William here. Do you mind if we join the fun?"

Drew responded, his voice wavering in relief. "Not at all, sir. This is Chief Cutter, good to see you again. Have at it."

As they watched, the green squares split up to engage the Diak. With the added fire power, in a matter of minutes, E2 and E3 were only fragments. E1 turned and ran with all three *Muck* ships in pursuit.

As the chase moved to the outer edge of the display, Curtis pointed to a piece of debris. It floated in the middle of the fragment cloud that had once been Diak E3. A red circle pulsed around it, with the side tag "E3: Escape pod."

Drew hailed the *Reagan*. "Can you send a shuttle to retrieve that pod?"

"We're on it, sir!"

~ ~ ∞ ~ ~

Curtis walked with Drew to the *Reagan*, which had docked on what remained of sublevel one. Having caught and destroyed E1, a *Muck* ship was assisting the damaged Bin vessel while another picked through the Diak debris. Commander William William and a handful of his men shuttled to the *Reagan* to join the pod examination, while his command ship took up patrol. The chief made an announcement letting everyone know *Muck* had destroyed their attackers and was now protecting the station. Residents and guests applauded, shouting words of thanks and praise as they passed.

Drew flashed a victory sign to a particularly boisterous group and spoke to Curtis. "I'll be surprised if that pod has an occupant, or at least a living one. There wasn't much time, but if it was undamaged, it should have cleared the debris zone well before the ship disintegrated."

Curtis nodded and glanced back over his shoulder just as Toby ducked into a side corridor. They'd ordered him to stay in HQ, but he hadn't expected Toby to obey. The kid was on his own now and had to get out of his own scrapes. Curtis didn't want to become his babysitter.

"Did you speak to Doc?" he asked Drew.

"Yes. Letty had a cut on the back of her head and a mild concussion, but otherwise she's okay. Doc wanted to keep her in med-lab for a while, but she wouldn't listen. Doc's got her hands full, but Letty's meeting us on the *Reagan*."

Curtis looked back over his shoulder again.

"Is Toby behind us?" Drew asked without turning.

"Yep. What are you going to do with him? Did Jonesy or Kyle find any relatives?"

"No. I'll speak to Letty. I think she'll want to take him back to Earth when she goes."

Curtis gave Drew a sideways look. "So . . . she's going back to Earth. Any chance you going with her?"

"Don't you wish."

"Maybe." Curtis wasn't eager to give up his new position. Things had finally gotten interesting, and he liked flying at the top of the pole instead of half-mast. Besides, he was good at it, even Drew had to admit that. And the staff seemed to genuinely respect and trust him now, which surprised the hell out of Curtis. As day commander, he'd only garnered grudging respect. *Mattie must be gagging in her cell at my new standing,* he thought. *I'll have to stop by and rub it in.* He didn't have the background to continue as chief of administration. The position required an engineering degree, usually in space safety. He could angle for chief of security if Drew left the picture, but not without Drew's recommendation.

"I'm kidding, Chief. Everyone's glad to have you back, including me. I just think if you let the lady go, the distance might kill any chance you have with her."

"Day-by-day it seems less likely I have a chance," Drew confessed. "She hasn't shown any interest, and there's been plenty opportunities."

Curtis felt as forlorn as Drew looked.

~ ~ ∞ ~ ~

A group surrounded the Diak capsule on the shuttle deck of the *Reagan*. Letty was already there, along with Secretary Rostenkowski, Lt. Commander William, and a combined contingent of armed security crew from both ships.

"Well," Drew asked, "what have we got?"

Rostenkowski took the lead. "Nothing, as far as we can tell. Scans show no life signs, but the pod doesn't appear to be damaged."

"It's *something* though. More than we've had up to now," William William said with a soft hum.

"Have you tried to open it?" Drew asked, as he circled the object looking for an access latch or control panel of some type. The pod was ovoid, seven feet long, three wide and three high, a dull metallic gray, with a smooth, seamless surface.

Rostenkowski nodded to a woman with a handheld. She stepped out from behind two security crewmen. "This is our ship's engineer, Sarah Larsen," Rostenkowski said.

Larsen consulted her processor and shook her head. "There are no life signs because it's not a capsule. It's made of a metal alloy and solid through. There's nothing to open. Perhaps it's a ship part, but I can't imagine its purpose. I don't think it's dangerous."

"Why would the sensors have identified it as an escape capsule?" Drew asked.

"Most likely because it was intentionally ejected from the ship," Larsen said.

As the group stood silently contemplating the item, its surface undulated in a series of multi-colored ripples, then settled back to smooth, dull gray. In unison, the observers moved back several feet, and the security crew raised their weapons. A full minute passed without a word spoken or further change in the pod's surface.

Drew finally broke the silence. "How do you know it's not dangerous? Any possibility it could be a weapon?"

"Nanoids?" Rostenkowski interposed before Larsen could respond.

Larsen squinted at her screen and toggled her head from one side to the other. "I can only interpret the readings, which tell me it's a solid piece of unknown metal alloy." To Drew, Larsen didn't look that confident in her readings.

"I want it off my ship," Rostenkowski announced.

"Do you want to space it?" Commander William asked.

"No—I mean, maybe. I just don't want it on my ship. Any

suggestions?"

Without taking his eyes off the object, Drew offered, "Why don't we put it back on the shuttle and move it away from the station. Larsen can share her readings with my engineers and Commander William's. If there's a consensus — or not — we'll decide what to do from there."

Rostenkowski looked reluctant. "My ship only has the one shuttle."

"Likewise," Commander William said.

Drew shook his head. "We only have a two-man maintenance craft. It's too small for the pod." He considered moving it to Spud, when Curtis spoke up.

"What about the screamer cell?"

Letty glanced from Curtis to Drew. "What's a screamer cell?"

Drew hid his annoyance. He didn't want the Diak object on his station any more than Rostenkowski wanted it on her ship. Though it was a perfect example of what the cell had been designed to hold. "It's a cross between a maximum-security detention cell and an ejectable airlock," he said. "Plus, we can introduce an anti-contaminate or knock-out mist if either's called for. We've used it twice. Once for a screamer that Doc refused to sedate, and once for a nut case who insisted on smearing feces on herself and anything else in her reach. Neither were dangerous, but the cell was designed to hold anything that could threaten the station. When it's occupied, it's under twenty-four-seven scan."

Curtis refused to meet his gaze. The others gave Drew accusing looks. He reddened, remembering why Curtis always seemed to annoy him so much. "Yeah, okay. We'll move it to the screamer cell while the engineers examine it. It'll be a tight fit though."

Commander William stepped to one side to answer his comm. After a minute, he rejoined the group. "My crew completed scans of the debris from all three Diak ships," he announced. "They found no traces of biological matter."

30 SAR MODE

Infiltrating the primary targets proved more difficult than Sar Mode first calculated. The Diak transmitters had been detected and many disabled. Fortunately, the desire to reproduce would always win out, and the implantation would continue. Sufficient devices dispersed across the populations of the five planets still transmitted. They were more than enough to maintain a strong link to the Mass. But the invasion must occur before exponential increases in the spread of devices, and the resulting mutation, turns the general populace. Those fully turned, would be of no value to the Diak as hosts. Though it varied with each alien race, the time between infection and turning had accelerated over the last century. It was disconcerting, but beyond Diak control.

Happily, there were billions of prospective hosts on the planets still untouched — biological data vessels awaiting transfer. And they required only a portion of those. The rest could be isolated, bred, and reserved to meet future demands. Colonists selected for these worlds were fortunate. They would form their own Mass and might survive for centuries before the need to rejoin the Spread. Sar Mode envied the settled lives they would lead. As the appointed principal she would never be so privileged.

That the targets had detected the Diak presented little problem. Even prepared, the targets' military defenses had proven insignificant. A few more rotations and the armada would be reequipped and assembled into strike divisions. They grew eager to explore this "Known Universe," as the aligned races called it.

Sar Mode allowed herself a small diversion. If she were a Diak colonist, which would she choose as her host among the five new races? Those called Bins were unappealing, small, ugly creatures. Earthlings were a physically strong, adventurous race. Their sense of wonder and discovery complemented her own. But they were weak minded and easily manipulated. Not the Earthlings then. The Fahdeens were angry and belligerent. Their development intrigued her, but no, not the Fahdeens. Her choice lay between the Bahdane and the Camdu.

Most perceptive of the group, the Bahdane were even-tempered. And they held enticing secrets. Sar Mode wished to explore those secrets. But the failure of the Diak to decipher the Bahdane language must first be overcome. The Camdu ... ah, the Camdu! Such beautiful creatures — an intelligent, forthright race not easily swayed. They would nod politely and listen but keep their own counsel. Yes ... certainly the Camdu — such an astounding shade of blue.

31 INTERLUDE

In the two weeks following the encounter at the station, the only new report of an attack came from a mostly evacuated Camdu outpost.

Dark Landing and the two Bin TSF ships held a moving, joint memorial over a live feed for the souls lost: eleven evacuees in the station corridor when it was hit, and eight Bindian crew members. Drew spoke for the evacuees, many of whom they had yet to identify. Letty spoke eloquently to the loss of the Bindians, who'd paid the ultimate price in coming to the aid of the station. And to the sadness of the entire Taleen Security Force in losing members who demonstrated such courage and selflessness. The Bindians felt particularly honored. Her presence at the service represented the only time any of their race had knowingly looked upon the head of the Taleen empire. After the memorial, the Bin ships limped back to their home world, where they would hold their traditional funeral rites. They towed their dead in a parade of brightly colored coffers.

With little forethought, the memorial feed was broadcast to the public. As a result, ready or not, Letty became a celebrity. She now required around-the-clock security and a host of assistants on Earth to handle the flood of inquiries that, once they began, would never let up.

The joint team of engineers was still studying the object, cautiously agreeing only that it didn't *appear* to present a threat, but without reaching a consensus about its function. In the meantime, it sat in the screamer cell, its surface periodically rippling without definable pattern or purpose. Drew was still annoyed at Curtis for it being on board, but overseeing station repairs offered a distraction.

They had a lot of work ahead of them. Drew focused on repairing the docks first, since four Taleen Security Force ships had arrived in the middle of the night, along with two heavily armed Earth Space Force battleships—half of the planet's fleet. They still hadn't fully evacuated all refugees from the station, but they'd made headway. Double-bunked, its public areas and cargo holds crammed full, the *Temperance* debarked with as many souls as it could carry.

Drew struck out for dockside to meet the new arrivals, ESF Rear Admiral, Jensen Sullivan, and the TSF Fleet Commander. He reflected that the station was perhaps the best supplied and, as of that moment, the safest location in Alliance territory. His thoughts moved to the briefing scheduled that afternoon with the newcomers and ETOC's Secretary Rostenkowski, MCTT Lt. Commander William William, as well as Drew and Letty. He looked forward to an entertaining alphabet soup of super egos.

As he entered dock sublevel one, where the ESF and TSF command ships were berthed side by side, he spotted Letty chatting with, judging by the uniform, Earth Space Force Rear Admiral Sullivan. Before he could join them, the senior dock foreman approached him.

Benny did not look happy. "Hey, Chief. I need to talk to you."

"What's up?"

"Just who the hell's in charge of these docks anyway?" Benny assumed a confrontational pose, feet apart, hands on hips.

Drew saw where the conversation was heading. He needed to make his expectations clear. "You are, but things have gotten complicated and nothing's changing in the foreseeable future. Dig deep, Benny. I know you'll handle things with patience and diplomacy. I'm counting on you to set an example for the men. Is there something specific I can help with?"

Benny relaxed his posture. "Well, for one, are any of these military ships supposed to pay docking fees—cuz they don't seem to think so. And every person debarked so far is carrying a weapon . . ."

While Benny listed his complaints, Drew watched a man in a TSF uniform exit his ship and head toward Letty. Evidently, the Fleet Commander--*fuck*, it was Travis Barnes! When she spotted him, she broke from her conversation with Admiral Sullivan and ran the distance into the commander's arms. He embraced her with a kiss on the lips, then picked her up and spun her in a circle. Their reunion continued with laughter and a series of shorter kisses and hugs.

Drew dragged his gaze away from the scene and refocused his attention on Benny. "Put your issues in writing for me. From now on, everything's on the record. In the meantime, I'll send a list of exceptions to the weapons restriction. I may have to consult with CoachStop for the rest. Unless it's something vital to the station's welfare, stand down while I sort it out. If you pick your battles wisely, I'll back you."

He left Benny stewing but resigned and returned to HQ without Letty knowing he'd been there.

~ ~ ∞ ~ ~

Upon arrival, the Earth Space Force sent a representative to question Mattie. *Muck* had already taken its turn at her and the hooker monks with the same results as Drew and the ETOC—not much. Drew wished fervently that things were different, and Mattie was still working by his side. He missed her organizational skills, dry humor, and the warmth of her friendship. Her assistant, Kyle, had stepped up to handle the day-to-day administrative tasks, but he was too timid and just *not* Mattie quality. On the other hand, he wasn't a traitor.

Drew entered the bazaar, less cluttered with refugees than before. He spotted Toby perched on the counter of an abandoned merchant stall and headed his way. Since Letty's unveiling, Toby seemed to always know her hiding spots. Drew had spoken to her about taking the boy to Earth, but they both avoided broaching the subject with him. He needed safety, schooling, and mostly to get out of Drew's hair.

Toby sat next to another boy close to his age. Drew thought of them as co-conspirators instead of children and wondered what they were plotting. "Have you seen Letty?" he asked.

Toby nodded. He held a voice-controlled model of a Camdu mountain lizard. It resembled an Earth-conceived dragon, but with a long muzzle covered in sharp spikes and the ability to turn various bright colors to blend with Camdu mountain flora.

"Where is she?"

"She told me not to tell anyone."

"Seriously, Toby?" Drew asked, his tone more a threat than a question.

Toby shrugged his lack of concern. "She and Doc are eating lunch in Doc's office."

"Thanks. Did she buy you that?"

Toby shook his head.

"Did you *steal* it?"

"No, I bought it myself."

"Where'd you get the script?"

"Curtis's been teaching me poker. He staked me in a game with some med-lab orderlies." His self-satisfied look said it all.

The orderly game was the softest game on the station. But an outsider could only bust it once. They'd never get a second invitation. The kid didn't realize it, but Walker was setting him up. Curtis was smart. The next game he staked Toby in wouldn't be so easy to beat. The kid's newly found confidence would shatter, and he'd be in Curtis's debt. Drew approved.

He veered off toward med-lab. As he maneuvered through the bazaar, he nodded to the TSF members spread out among the remaining refugees, collecting personal information and inquiring about desired final destinations. To a man and woman, Taleen Security Staff were professional and convivial, easily interacting with adults and children alike. Letty had said they could handle every possible situation. Drew wondered at their fighting skills.

A TSF member was talking to a large man who stood with his back to Drew. Drew would recognize that back anywhere. He approached the two men, interrupting their conversation. "Nikko, what the hell are you doing here?!"

Nikko looked down at him. "Queet *Demperance*. Vorking vor Valker."

"You're working for Curtis?"

"Da."

"Doing what? Wait . . . never mind. I'd rather hear Curtis's version." He continued to med-lab mumbling to himself. Curtis seemed to call the shots more and more lately. His brief love affair with the guy was souring. Though he had to admit, the added responsibility and Drew's outward show of appreciation for a job well done had wrought wonders.

He stuck his head in Doc's office. "Hey, Doc. Letty, when you're done here, can you meet me in HQ?"

"We just finished. I can walk back with you."

"Great."

Doc was clearing food containers off her desk. "I'll see you two later."

With two burly TSF staff trailing them, Drew took Letty on a route that avoided the bazaar.

"Why do you need those guys here?" he asked. "The station's full of military and security personnel."

"Our new CEO, Carl Evans, issued the order. I didn't want to make waves so soon. Besides, I guess I need to get used to it."

"I guess. I saw Nikko on my way to med-lab. Did you know he was here?"

"Yeah, he's 'vorking vor Valker.'" She smiled. "Didn't you know?"

"Evidently, when it comes to Curtis, I know *nothing*. But that's not what I wanted to talk to you about. Your people are doing a great job."

"Thanks. They're in their element. This is what they're trained for."

"As well as being an ace fighting force?"

She sighed. "Yes, as well as a fighting force."

"I've been kicking around an idea. I might want to apply for a job with the TSF," Drew announced. He needed a change — which was code for needing time to square his mythical self-image with reality. He wasn't the leader he once thought — far from it.

Thoughts of joining the TSF came to him days earlier and bore no connection to seeing Letty in Barnes's arms—though a mental image of them together played on an interminable loop. If joining the TSF provided a tentative link with Letty, well . . . so be it. It wasn't his goal to compete with the other man. Anyway, she'd made her feelings for him—or lack thereof—perfectly clear.

Letty stopped mid-stride. The two following them caught up and then backed off to give them privacy. "A job? What do you mean 'a job'?"

"Call it a change-of-career decision." They continued walking. "I'm not as good at this as I thought." He spread his arms to embrace his surroundings.

"I don't agree," Letty said. "But what type of job are you looking for? The requirements for the TSF would overlap those for a chief of security position. You might be trading one job for another, doing essentially the same thing but with less responsibility and pay."

"Honestly, I don't have an ultimate goal. I'll start on a bottom rung if necessary."

"What you're looking for is a place to hide while you figure out what you really want to do. Am I right?"

Drew thought about it. "Maybe." He'd misinterpreted his success at the academy and rapid advancement with CoachStop as proof of an aptitude for leadership, the ability to leap tall barriers and to look death in the eye and vanquish it. *Bullshit!* When he finally woke up and factored in the gen that most academy cadets were misfits and reckless daredevils, he'd stood out because he was conventional and steady. The only thing tested and proven at the academy was his ego, and he'd scored bigtime.

"I think you're making a mistake and underestimating your value," Letty said. "Besides . . ." She paused.

"What?"

"Well . . . the TSF spends much of its time in space, traveling, living, working, and in considerably closer quarters than Dark Landing. I couldn't help but notice, during our EVA, and even on the shuttle down to Bin, you have a . . . a *disinclination* . . . to appreciate space."

Drew bristled. "Not true. I'm just smart enough to understand the potential dangers. That's an asset."

Letty dropped it, evidently choosing not to argue with him.

"Okay. No offense meant."

In Drew's office, they continued to discuss his decision until it came time to adjourn their meeting for the next one.

~ ~ ∞ ~ ~

Letty contemplated Drew's surprising announcement as the others arrived at the HQ conference room. People milled around, chatting, served themselves drinks, and found seats.

All that'd happened obviously shook Drew's self-confidence. Letty hadn't confessed as much, but she harbored her own self-doubts. She owned the largest enterprise in the K.U. but had few qualifications to run it. Being an expert in company trivia didn't translate into being Chairman of the Board. Her dad had made the job look effortless while Letty dabbled in only what interested her, and that under an alias. Though she considered Drew's self-doubts groundless, they'd both arrived at personal crossroads on the same schedule.

As the only Earth political representative, Anne Rostenkowski called the meeting to order. "If everyone will please take a seat ..."

Letty continued to contemplate her shortcomings while Anne summarized what they knew about the Diaks.

"So ... wrapping up, tech contamination is easy to remedy once discovered, and we're confident we can locate and isolate humans infected with Diak nanoids, though we're still determining the parameters of such isolation. The ETOC's of the opinion that Diak strength is in their technology, not in their military ability. All we've seen is hit-and-run tactics comparable to guerilla warfare, and light-armored ships with the facility to change their shape but with fire power no more lethal than our own. And they've only targeted undefended outposts, primarily in the Zeta Quadrant, never home worlds." Rostenkowski sat and looked to ESF Rear Admiral Sullivan.

Sullivan cleared his throat, "With all due respect, Madam Secretary, you're assuming a dangerous position. The ESF feels strongly that the Diak are only testing our military strength with their forays. And our, Earth's and the Alliance's, response has been pitiful. It's as clear to the Diak as to our own leaders that, individually or combined, the Alliance worlds don't have the means to fight an enemy of equal force, let alone a superior one. And, under scrutiny, the Diak appears to be the far superior force. They simply haven't found it necessary to reveal their full military capacity. Remember, their initial strategy pitted Alliance members against one another by imitating our ship designs . . . showing superior strength wouldn't have served their purpose."

Muck Commander William William nodded. "The MCTT concurs," he said.

Letty wondered under what authority the MCTT concurred. As far as she was aware, the Coalition hadn't reassembled. But perhaps unsanctioned command of three heavily armed ships carried its own authority.

Travis Barnes stared at her. She'd told Drew the truth. She'd been friends with Travis since childhood. He was one of the trusted few who'd known her true identity. They'd had a brief fling while she was in college and would always be an important part of each other's lives. Travis appeared puzzled when she only smiled back at him. She realized he expected something more from her. As his superior, he was looking to her for approval to speak. She gave a weak nod.

Though a civilian employee in command of only a small corporate fleet, and lower in status than even Drew Cutter, Travis spoke with self-assured authority. "Along with many of you here, I was only recently made aware that Taleen research teams have been studying Diak nanotech for over a year. Before coming to Dark Landing, I sat down with the team leaders to brainstorm possible military approaches — tactics and weaponry, traditional or non-traditional — in controlling or eliminating the nanoid contaminants. They confirmed there was nothing we could do beyond what civilian authorities were already employing. However, there *was* a consensus on one aspect." Commander Barnes paused.

Letty wondered why she or Anne Rostenkowski hadn't received summaries of that meeting. Or, perhaps Anne had. Letty looked at Anne. She seemed just as interested in what Barnes was about to say as the others.

Barnes continued. "The Taleen research teams believe the Diak may rely too heavily upon their advanced nano-architecture. That reliance might also be their weakness. Secretary Rostenkowski may be right; perhaps our priority should be finding a way to exploit that weakness. We may not have to fight this battle solely with military personnel and equipment, and . . . ."

~ ~ ∞ ~ ~

Rostenkowski's mention of the Diak's shape altering capabilities reminded Drew to let Benny in on the answer to the mystery of how a Camdu ship could " . . . live in space twice."

Drew studied the TSF commander as he addressed the meeting. Some women would find Barnes's unsophisticated ruggedness attractive, and he was well-spoken. It seemed obvious to him that at some point, Barnes and Letty had had a relationship beyond friends or boss to subordinate.

His comm purred: *Acting Chief Curtis Walker*. Before the meeting, he'd requested alerts only for communication marked urgent. He excused himself and found Curtis standing outside the hatch.

"What's happening?" Drew asked. Curtis looked uncharacteristically shaken and even paler than usual, if that was possible.

"It's the object," Curtis said.

"Yes?"

"It's changed."

"And . . .?" Drew prompted.

"It changed into Fitz."

32 IT LIVES

Drew thought about informing those at the meeting of the new development, but he wanted to see the phenomena for himself first. Considering the unshakable Curtis's shaken condition, he steeled himself for whatever he was about to witness.

As they watched through the observation window, the figure sat unmoving on the edge of the cot in the screamer cell. It was Fitz all right, or at least a statue version of Fitz carved from dull, lead-gray metal alloy. No remnant of the original object remained.

"Do we have a vid of the change? Has it moved?" Drew asked.

"Yeah. The object seemed to disassemble and reform. It hasn't moved since. You'll have to view it for yourself. It just . . . just crawled up onto the cot and *became* Fitz. The whole process only took about ten seconds."

As Curtis spoke, the statue's eyes blinked. Drew and Curtis both took a step closer to the window, not sure what they'd seen. The statue blinked again.

"Holy shit!" Curtis said.

Drew nodded. He watched several seconds unblinking for fear of missing something, then pressed the speaker control.

"Fitz?"

Pastel ripples undulated across the statue's surface, settling back into dull gray stillness.

"Fitz, is that you?" Drew tried again with the same result:

ripples and then nothing. He laughed.

Curtis looked at Drew as if he was going mad.

"I can't help it, it's funny. Don't you think it's funny?"

"Hell *no*," Curtis said. "I think we should eject the cell."

"I don't know. Nothing has really changed except its shape."

This time Curtis's look echoed incredulity. "Are you kidding? It looks like Fitz and responds to Fitz's name—that's *different*."

"Yeah, yeah," Drew agreed. "Still, as much as I want to get rid of the beastly thing, I'm not sure I have the final word anymore. I'm going back to the meeting and let everyone know what's happened. I don't think it can leave the cell. But if it looks like it's trying to get out or disassembles again, go ahead and eject. I'll take the hit."

Drew called Fitz's name once more, and the statue rippled in response. "Tap if anything else happens." He left Curtis staring intently through the window, his head thrust forward like a turtle from its shell.

~ ~ ∞ ~ ~

When Drew reentered the meeting, Rear Admiral Sullivan was speaking.

"... and to that end, by executive action of President Mwanajuma, taken on behalf of Earth and its Provinces, we are appropriating all human TSF divisions, including ships, equipment, and supplies, to strengthen Earth Space Force until we recruit and train reinforcements to a level deemed sufficient to protect Earth and its colonies. In other words, indefinitely."

Letty and Commander Barnes jumped to their feet at once.

Letty sputtered, "Y-you can't do that—it's illegal. We'll get a court order to stay any action—"

Rear Admiral Sullivan cut Letty off. "It's not only legal, it's done. Your attorneys can file whatever they want, but under the *Fourth Amendment* to the *Global Constitution*, the action is justified by circumstances and supersedes civilian authority. As chairman of the board, you'll receive written orders within the next forty-eight hours and if you don't comply, members of the board, yourself included, can be held under military jurisdiction until the threat to Earth and its properties is ended. You might face charges of treason as well, but that's not for me to determine."

Drew cleared his throat. "Excuse me. As interesting as this is—and it's a beaut—I need to interrupt." Everyone turned and looked at Drew.

He grinned witlessly back at his audience, not sure if he was giddy with fear or inured to the fantastic by all that'd occurred over the past few weeks. "The Diak object has transformed into a metallic replica of the missing chief of administration for Dark Landing." He paused. No one spoke. "So . . . you wanna go see?"

As the group made its way to the screamer cell, Drew tapped Doc and asked her to join them. When they arrived, a mixed team of engineers stood with Curtis at the observation window. The newcomers crowded into the cramped space.

At Drew's nod, Curtis spoke Fitz's name, repeating it several times, and each time receiving colorful ripples in response. The room grew warm from the squish of bodies. After several rounds between Curtis and the statue, everyone except the engineers retreated to the corridor and back to the conference room.

Failing to reach a consensus of exclamations . . .

"What the hell?"

"Jesus *Christ*!"

"What the fuck was *that*?!"

. . . the meeting adjourned, and everyone rushed to report to their respective organizations.

As Drew left the room, he watched TSF Commander Barnes prop his feet on the conference table, then fortify his coffee from a flask retrieved from a pocket of his uniform jacket. Another prick to Drew's deflating ego. He was jealous of Barnes's unruffled demeanor, and reluctantly admitted he'd never achieve that level of cool.

~ ~ ∞ ~ ~

The following week brought no changes to the Fitz statue. A new scan now identified the nanoids the engineers failed to detect previously. In the meantime, the station experienced its own transformation. When Letty received Taleen Industries' *Notice of Appropriation* from Earth gov, Drew received a similar notice regarding Dark Landing, which also went to the station's co-op board and CoachStop Management. Most of the evacuees had found passage off the station. This left command, the security staff, and other essential station personnel, who were *asked* to stay and oversee the day-to-day management. Drew now reported directly to Rear Admiral Sullivan. He had leeway in what the rear admiral considered the mundane responsibility of keeping the station facilities and systems running efficiently. Since the station was to be armed and re-purposed as a military base and supply depot, Drew and his staff were basically reduced to janitorial status. Sullivan encouraged mezzanine and bazaar merchants still on the station to stay as well. They agreed since Dark Landing now enjoyed heavy defenses and a new crop of prospective customers

As Earth gov had no authority over *Muck*, Lt. Commander William William, in exchange for supplies and a weapons upgrade, dedicated his forces to transporting evacuees and escorting supply ships to and from the station. *Muck* also worked with ESF to rescue anyone still stranded on colonies or outposts, though the Diak made no further attacks, and many workers chose to stay in place. A few evacuees even returned to their outposts. An increased demand for raw materials to rebuild Earth's military meant huge incentives for experienced miners to return to their operations.

~ ~ ∞ ~ ~

With the influx of military personnel, Curtis's workload lightened by half. He revisited his plan to open a nightclub on Spud. He'd heard talk about Earth gov reopening the mine itself, but it had fizzled when they'd learned the existing mine was played out. Excavating a new one would further stretch Earth's dwindling resources.

Other than Nikko, Curtis's resources were nonexistent. He had to dismantle the monstrous ore crushing and separating equipment to make room for the club. He'd recruited Nikko for that purpose. The big guy could single-handedly break down the machines and, if he needed help, would have no problem coercing it. Later he would make a great bouncer. The problem was getting the bits and pieces off Spud. Shoving them out the airlock would create a hazard for the station and be unsightly. He would never get away with it.

Nikko came up with the solution. "Droop dem en meen."

"'Droop dem'? 'Droop dem en' ...? Ah, *drop* the parts down the mine. Of course! That's so simple. The mine is just a big hole now." Curtis's smile matched Nikko's. "Okay, buddy, one down. The big issue is finding cash for building materials and decor to remodel the place. I have an idea about where to start. We still have the package that—" Curtis stopped talking when Drew entered HQ.

Drew came up to Nikko and slapped him on the shoulder. He received a dangerous smile in return. "Nikko, Nikko, Nikko ... I'm reminded. Curtis, what the hell is Nikko doing here? He said you hired him?"

"I didn't *hire* him, he's my dependent."

"Your *dependent*?"

"Yeah, you know, I provide room and board. He occasionally runs personal errands for me."

"What type of personal errands?"

"Delivering and picking up my laundry, keeping my quarters tidy, that kind of stuff."

"Still, you could have run it by me."

"You know ... it wasn't my idea. He wanted to stay. What could I do? It's a free space."

"What's he doing in HQ?"

"Nothing. He stopped by to say, 'hi.' He was just leaving." Curtis flashed his well-practiced innocent look.

Nikko's smile broadened.

"There's a talk you and I still need to have," Drew said dryly.

Curtis nodded and shrugged. "Yeah, okay, anytime."

He delivered a warning glare at the two of them and headed to his office, shaking his head.

~ ~ ∞ ~ ~

Drew finished his logs and considered finding Letty for lunch when she and Toby showed up. The two had become inseparable.

"You busy?" Letty asked.

"No, I'm getting some lunch. You two want to join me?"

"Thanks, but we just had a bite. I was wondering if you knew that Anne and the *Reagan* are leaving in the morning."

"I learned a little earlier. Are you and Toby going with them?"

"Yes. Along with my dad, and those infected with the Diak nanoids. We're up to ten now, not including Mattie, and the half dozen from the *Temperance*.

"So, I was hoping we can get together tonight . . . maybe for dinner? You know, a goodbye . . . thing?" For once Letty seemed awkward.

Should I be encouraged? Nah. "Yeah. Sounds good. I'll be right here. Why don't you come by when you're ready — maybe around 1900?"

Toby had been following their conversation, his head swiveling from one to the other. As they left the office, he turned back to Drew with crossed eyes and a curled lip.

Drew mouthed, "Screw you," and immediately regretted it, even though Toby spent any time he wasn't with Letty hanging out with the men, learning to play poker, shoot pool, and swear.

~ ~ ∞ ~ ~

At 1800 hours, Drew's comm purred, *Katherine Taleen.* "Letty?"

"Surprise! Doc implanted me this morning. I got sick of the inconvenience. If you're free now, can we eat a little early? I have some last-minute errands. Plus, I'm a little stressed about the possibility Toby will try to ditch me tomorrow. I thought it would be best to move onto the *Reagan* tonight. That way I can keep an eye on him."

"Tell him if he doesn't leave on the *Reagan*, I'm going to space him."

Letty laughed. "Your threats are meaningless to him. I told you, he adores you."

It was Drew's turn to laugh. "We had this conversation before. Head over to the executive mess, I'll meet you there."

Drew and Letty arrived at the mess as Secretary Rostenkowski was exiting.

"There you are, Drew, I was going to tap you," Rostenkowski said. "We've been discussing what to do with the Diak object. A consulting team from Earth wants to come out and study it. Plus, we've received requests from other Alliance members. Some of

244

them think transforming into Fitz is their attempt to communicate with us. You'll be pleased to know we made the decision to move it to the far side of Spud in an ejectable airlock, like your screamer cell. Members can install their individual research domes in a configuration surrounding it."

"You're right, that makes me *very* happy," Drew said.

"We mapped a spot that should accommodate the size facility we anticipate. Commander Barnes is going out for a visual now. I thought you'd want to tag along and see for yourself."

Drew was shaking his head *no*, but before he could speak Letty piped up with an enthusiastic, "Yes."

"We can grab some sandwiches to take along. I want to go." She saw the look on his face. "Of course . . . *space* . . . if you'd rather not—"

Drew wasn't letting her play that card. "It's just . . . I was looking forward to a leisurely goodbye dinner with you."

"Well, me too, of course, but—"

"And there's nothing to see but a few rocks and some small impact craters. It's like the back side of the moon; it's pretty much the same as the front side." His argument sounded weak.

"Right, but—"

Rostenkowski interrupted their quibbling, "Great. Get your sandwiches. Drew, you can inspect your new shuttle."

"I have a shuttle?"

"Sullivan tried to commandeer mine for the station, but he doesn't have the authority. I donated it anyway. When I get back to Earth, I'll do some commandeering of my own and get one that's better appointed."

While they chatted, Letty entered the mess and returned minutes later with a box of sandwiches, a water pouch, and an eager expression.

.

33 THE MARIGOLD

Drew and Letty sat strapped into seats on the shuttle while Commander Barnes completed a seemingly unending pre-flight check and familiarized himself with the controls.

He's supposed to be an experienced pilot, Drew thought. *Maybe he's not so experienced after all, or he's never piloted anything as uncomplicated as a shuttle.*

Letty sat with their box of sandwiches on her lap, her impatience evidenced in her annoying foot tapping.

Drew stared out the window into the docking bay trying to ignore Letty and regulate his breathing in anticipation of the launch. The window wrapped around the bow of the shuttle and continued halfway down each side. A large skylight was set into the upper bulkhead, its external canopy retracted. The shuttle held ten passenger seats, all with good views. A tiny head was tucked in the back next to the storage lockers. Drew was struck by how utilitarian the shuttle was. He could see why Rostenkowski was willing to part with it for something a little more luxurious and suited to her position.

As the first of several announcements sounded to warn anyone still in the bay to clear out, Curtis, Nikko, and Toby clambered onboard through the still-open side hatch. They scrambled into seats and the hatch closed behind them. The second announcement came over the speakers.

Depressurization in five minutes. Anyone not appropriately suited must exit the bay.

The message would repeat each minute until launch.

"What are you guys doing here, Curtis?" Drew snapped.

"We're just coming along for the ride. Is that a problem?"

"I hope you checked with Barnes first." He wanted to add that protocol said to check first with your boss as well, but he held back.

Curtis only responded with an exasperated face.

Each day Drew dropped more of the pretense that he still ran the station. He made suggestions now instead of giving orders. Was it his mounting feelings of inadequacy or their very real circumstances that prompted the change? His men remained deferential to his *suggestions*, so it could all be in his head. They hadn't discussed his joining TSF again; it was one of the things he needed to talk to Letty about.

There was no bulkhead between the passenger area and the command station. Barnes swiveled in his seat to address them.

"Everyone strapped in? We're heading out. Curtis . . . you made it. Great! Hey, Toby, you want to come up here and give me a hand?"

Toby squealed and bounded to the front. When Letty laughed at the child's enthusiasm, Travis winked at her.

Drew, catching their exchange, called out, "Toby, dammit, don't touch anything."

Barnes spoke over his shoulder as he strapped Toby into the seat next to him. "No worries. Toby's training to be my navigator. Aren't you, bud?"

Letty elbowed Drew and hissed, "What is *wrong* with you?"

The last announcement sounded, and the dock lights dimmed. As the bay depressurized, the semi-opaque environmental shields shimmered and faded to reveal distant stars sparkling in the blackness. With a deft touch that spoke to experience, Commander Barnes activated the docking thrusters, and the shuttle moved gently into the void.

Drew's stomach heaved while Toby nattered away up front.

"What's the name of this shuttle anyway?" the boy asked

Barnes.

"The *Marigold*."

"*Marigold*! That's a lame name. *Lame name*. Hey, I just made a rhyme. We can call it *Lame Name*. That's still better than *Marigold*. No, wait, I know, we can call her *Thor's Hammer*. What do you think about that, Commander? Or, maybe *Thor's* —"

Drew tuned out and swallowed several times to settle his stomach. They progressed smoothly around the bow of the *Reagan* and away from the station toward the far end of Spud.

"Hey, Barnes, detour in closer to the armature," Drew ordered, needing to assert his authority in front of the man. "I want to see how the repairs are coming along space-side."

"Sure — not a problem."

As they neared the armature, the commander switched on the shuttle's floodlights to illuminate the damaged section. At the sudden assault of blinding light, several EMU-garbed workers twisted awkwardly about, swiping their gloved hands across their throats in the universal "kill" motion. Barnes cut the floodlights and increased the intensity of their running lights. The maintenance crew responded with grateful waves and thumbs up. They returned to the task of positioning a large panel over a portion of the hole created by the Diak laser blast.

Drew linked his comm to the foreman's, broadcasting the communication over the shuttle's speakers. "Shorty, it's looking good. We still on schedule?"

"Thanks, Chief. Yeah, we should be finished with the heavy lifting by tomorrow, then another week to refit the interior bulkheads and establish environmental integrity. I see we got a new toy."

"Yep. Courtesy of the *Reagan*. Carry on and let me or Curtis know if you need anything."

The shuttle pulled away from the armature and continued around the end of the pockmarked asteroid. Spud didn't so much resemble a potato close-up. Alliance-member and non-member planets had installed an assortment of scientific monitoring equipment and telescopes amongst the pockmarks. The sole condition required that the resulting data be shared equally among the represented races. Drew knew from talks with station-based scientists over the years, that Earth didn't adhere faithfully to that condition. He figured the others picked through their data as well before sharing.

As they drew closer to the backside of Spud, its distant sun—dubbed "Warvan," though the name was seldom used—shown brighter.

The attack came so suddenly, no one in the shuttle knew what was happening except, mercifully, Travis Barnes. He'd evidently spotted the Diak ship a split second before it spotted them. He activated their shuttle thrusters in alternating bursts that sent little *Marigold* into as close of a spiraling maneuver as it could handle, away from Spud and Dark Landing. Lacking weapons or speed, they had no other defense. Thanks to Barnes's save, Drew watched as a salvo of Diak's lasers missed them by a few meters.

Drew issued a mayday to security dispatch, while Barnes transmitted his own call for help to the TSF fleet. He held tight as Barnes put the shuttle through an array of thruster maneuvers, toward and away from the Diak ship, up and down, back and forth, narrowly evading each laser burst. Drew was amazed at the man's thruster choreography and his ability to anticipate their attacker's moves, especially since this was his first time piloting the *Marigold*. One successful hit would blow the fragile, unshielded craft to bits.

Muscles taut, anticipating the blast that would eject him into space, and dizzy from the erratic movement of the shuttle, Drew tried to orient to Spud and restore his equilibrium. Suddenly, the *Marigold* leveled off. The Diak ship was framed in their port window for one second before it disintegrated into particles. The cavalry had arrived just in time.

Barnes swore when a second Diak ship appeared starboard, but it turned away. Drew watched it retreat and then blink out of sight. There one moment, gone the next. Still trying to grasp what'd happened, he spotted yet a third enemy ship headed right at them.

Before Barnes could recommence thruster maneuvers, that ship passed by as well, its pulse streams directed away from the *Marigold*, probably firing at whichever ships had come to their rescue. Uncertain if they were clear of danger, the Commander continued with a new series of shuttle reorientations. Just when Drew thought they might actually survive the encounter, the chaos around them was suddenly augmented by the shuttle's shrieking proximity alert and flashing lights. With a head-snapping jolt, their thrusters stilled. The shuttle floated, alerts sounding, lights flashing, but unchallenged in a field of giant asteroids, none of which remotely resembled Spud.

Barnes cut the alarm and lights.

The sudden withdrawal of movement, light, and sound unnerved Drew worse than the chaos they'd left behind.

"Fuck!" Nikko said in perfect English.

~ ~ ∞ ~ ~

Drew took a breath and looked around the shuttle to be sure everyone was still strapped in and uninjured.

"Travis?" Letty's voice was plaintive. "What just happened?"

"I think we went through a wormhole."

"Not possible," Drew said. "I didn't see a wormhole. There weren't any buoys or other markers. Besides, we don't have wormholes this close to the station."

"That's the problem," Travis responded. "I'm pretty sure it wasn't one of ours. We were maneuvering erratically, but I never saw the edge distortion. It must have been shielded."

Toby broke the ensuing silence, "Wow! Look at the size of those *fucking* asteroids."

"*Toby!*" Letty reprimanded.

"What's that?" Curtis asked. "At about ten o'clock."

Drew looked where Curtis indicated. At first, he thought he saw a planet horizon, but the edge was spiked and irregular. He tried to piece together the bits he could see between the dimpled asteroids, many twice the size of domed sports arenas on Earth. As his gaze shifted from one gap to the next, he realized it wasn't just at ten o'clock, it was *all* around the clock. It was *big*.

"It's a ship . . . isn't it, Commander?" Toby asked in obvious awe.

Barnes navigated the shuttle through the field to a spot less dense that provided a better view of the object while still keeping the craft concealed. It was a space station, at least five times the size of Dark Landing. And a sea of ships surrounded it. The armada consisted of variously purposed spacecraft. Several thousand that Drew associated with Earth destroyer-class vessels were armed with projectile railguns as well as plasma accelerators. Thousands more were lighter gunships of the same type that had attacked the station. A few larger models he assumed were command ships. It seemed the Diak had learned all they needed about Alliance defense capabilities — or the lack of them — and was poised for invasion.

With a light touch on the port thruster, Barnes positioned them closer to the nearest asteroid, keeping the shuttle concealed but leaving a view of the station through an overhang. He issued a command that changed the window from normal to telescopic. Within a millisecond the small section of the station they saw jumped to fill the entire shuttle window.

Nikko reacted with a short, high-pitched scream, and Drew realized that Letty was holding his own hand in a vice grip. He might have found either action remarkable under different circumstances.

The magnified image revealed multiple levels with rows of large, oval viewing ports positioned equidistant on each level. At least they looked like viewing ports, but no light shone through. In between the neat, uniform levels jutted uneven, multi-shaped projections, many of which were cluttered with smaller, even more oddly shaped projections. Together they resembled abstract piles of scrap metal. Drew spotted a circular object he swore was a cog wheel, but its purpose escaped him.

As they scrutinized the station, a fast-moving Diak ship broke across their view. They watched the station and armada for more than an hour, and then Barnes moved the shuttle in to hug the asteroid as close as he dared, blocking their view. He unstrapped Toby and led him back with the rest of the group, putting him in the seat across from Letty.

"So, this is a pickle," Barnes said.

Drew laughed. As always, it was his go-to reaction in these situations, and he couldn't help himself.

Barnes continued. "Our only hope is to locate the reverse wormhole and warn the Alliance. It must be nearby. I suspect that's why the Diaks concentrated their exploratory attacks in the Zeta Quadrant. But this shuttle has no range. The oxygen generator will run pretty much indefinitely, well beyond our need for it. And I'll disable the gravity inductor to conserve power. But without water or food, we don't have a lot of time."

Letty half-heartedly held up her two-liter water pouch and

box of sandwiches.

Barnes nodded and smiled at her pitiful offering. "Any suggestions?"

While wormholes existed in clusters, when measured against the vastness of space, the distance between them would still exceed shuttle range.

Drew set aside his personal dislike of Barnes. "You're right. The Diaks obviously have access close to Zeta Quadrant. Our best bet is to follow one of the Diak ships. How we do that without being discovered — assuming we can even keep up — is a problem. Who knows how far we might need to travel? . . . which circles back to the food and, more importantly, water issue."

"What if we do locate another wormhole and it drops us somewhere outside the K.U.?" Curtis asked. "We'll be worse off than we are now."

"It's a risk we have to take. We'll worry about it when it happens," Barnes said, looking at Drew. "Chief Cutter, can I have a word with you up front?"

Drew squeezed past Letty and moved with Barnes to the command station.

Barnes kept his voice low. "Who's in charge here?"

"What do you mean?"

"Only one of us can be in charge. We need to agree whichever one of us it is, the other won't undermine him."

"You take it," Drew said. "You're the captain of the ship."

"Yeah, but you *own* the ship," Barnes countered.

"Not really. If anyone owns it, it's CoachStop or the Zeta Quadrant co-ops. I'm serious, Barnes, you take it. I promise not to challenge you if I can make suggestions along with the others."

"I encourage it. If you're sure, then . . . ?"

Drew nodded. "By the way, are the asteroids blocking the Diak scans? I'm surprised they haven't already picked us up."

"The asteroids should block us if we stay put and disable our instruments," Barnes said. "But I doubt they have their scanners activated anyway. In the middle of an armada that size, scanning would overwhelm their systems. Besides, what have they got to be afraid of here?"

Drew turned to find Toby in his seat next to Letty.

Curtis was scrounging around in the aft lockers. "There's

some kind of drink dispenser back here," he called out. "I don't know what it served, but there's probably a liter-and-a-half of stale water in its reservoir. And a box with about a hundred packs of peanuts too."

"Buckle up everyone. I'm cutting the gravity," Barnes announced.

Curtis returned to his seat. Drew took the seat Toby had vacated. As he adjusted the straps, a slow-moving shadow crossed the skylight.

34 TOBY'S PLAN

Everyone crouched low in their seats in an absurd attempt to duck from the ship that was passing above them. It moved in eerie slow motion. English letters appeared spelling "Reagan," along with her registration numbers, "404-E-132."

Diak nanoids doing what they do best, Drew thought. The chances of the Alliance surviving against an armada that large were insurmountable, but if Alliance defenses were unable to distinguish the attacking ships from their own, at least the end would come quickly. They sat in silence for a minute after it passed from sight.

"Maglocks," Toby whispered into the unnatural stillness.

"What, honey?" Letty asked.

"We can hang like bats upside down."

"Toby, you're not making any sense." Letty ruffled the boy's hair. "What are you trying—"

"Hush, Letty," Travis ordered.

She glared at him, but before she could retort, Drew spoke up.

"Toby, you're one smart little bastard."

"*Drew,*" Letty said, without her usual fervor.

"That eliminates the range issue," Curtis said.

"Would someone please explain to me what we're talking about?" Letty's head swiveled to include each of them.

"Da. Ken hung leek bot."

"Thanks, Nikko. I'll take this," Barnes said from his seat at the command station. "What our little genius is suggesting is that we attach the shuttle to the bottom of a Diak ship using its magnetic mooring locks and hitch a ride."

"Oh! Toby, that's brilliant." She bent down and kissed his forehead. Toby smiled sweetly back. As soon as she looked away, he turned to Drew, his smile transforming from sweet to smug.

Another shadow passed quickly across the skylight, a second ship, this one smaller and faster. The shuttle appeared to be lurking within an established flight pattern. If so, they might go unnoticed by departing ships. But to ships approaching the station in the same corridor, the shuttle's smooth, white exterior would make a striking contrast against the dark asteroid. Their chances of being discovered would increase tremendously.

"We might be able to pull it off if we attach to one of the larger ships," Drew said.

Barnes shook his head. "I'm not sure. It looks like they're in the final stages of preparation. I doubt one of the larger ships will go over now. More likely something smaller will make a recon run, hopefully a gunship. Anything smaller than that we couldn't hope to catch, let alone lock onto."

"Wouldn't any ship other than one of the largest feel something when the mags kick in?" Drew asked.

Barnes was studying the display on his console. "The shuttle's so light and its mags are self-regulating. They'll apply minimal hold, increasing gradually to accommodate low to no-gravity conditions. If I approach at the right angle, the result should be negligible to the host ship, but it's not going to be easy. We'll be trailing the ship for several seconds to match its thrust and accurately position ourselves for mooring. If there're other ships in proximity, they'll see us."

"You think we'll see the wormhole on approach? We may decide to drop instead of going through," Curtis said in a tight, measured tone.

When neither Drew nor Barnes responded, Letty asked, "Why would we do that?" She watched as the four men exchanged looks, finally settling on Drew. "What?"

"Even if this works, which frankly is a long shot, once we're back in Alliance territory and warn everyone, they won't be able to mount an effective defense against an armada that size. Don't you see?"

"No," Letty said, watching him intently.

"When that armada comes through, the first thing they're going to do is destroy Dark Landing and the ships defending it. Even if we forewarn the Alliance planets, not one of them could hold out against the numbers and firepower we just witnessed."

"So . . . if there's nothing we can do, at least we'll be home," Letty said, putting her arm around Toby. "We'll have a better chance there than we do here."

"Letty, there is *something* we can do," Travis said softly. "That's what Curtis means. We can try to collapse the wormhole so the armada can't get through. But it would have to be done from this side."

"*Oh*," Letty said, barely above a whisper.

"Besides the peanuts and some iffy water, there's a maintenance EMU in the back," Curtis said. "We could draw straws."

Letty didn't need an explanation this time. "I want to be included."

"No," Drew said quickly. "No one's going to agree to that."

"I insist. It's not fair —"

Barnes stopped her. "Drew's right, Letty, it's not going to be you. Besides, Toby needs you."

"There must be s-some other way," Letty's voice broke.

"I go," Nikko said firmly.

"And I'd start a petition to rename Dark Landing in your honor, Nikko," Curtis said. "But you'd never get that suit above your knees."

Barnes ended the discussion. "We're not drawing straws, and no one's going except me. I'm captain; it's my job. No arguments."

"But none of us can fly this thing," Drew protested.

"Letty can. But even if she couldn't, I can teach you what you need to know in a few minutes."

"How would you close the wormhole?" Letty asked, diverting the discussion.

"You learned how wormholes are stabilized in school," Barnes said.

"Well, I know it's held open by a ring of exotic matter but, truthfully, I can't remember much more than that."

"Close. Exotic matter appears in curved regions of space-time. Wormholes produce enough exotic matter to be self-sustaining, but that matter must be redistributed in order to expand and stabilize the wormhole. That's where the Blanchett ring comes in — it's a shell of infused exotic matter encircling the wormhole, holding it open.

Noticing Toby's rapt attention, Barnes directed his lesson to him. "A guy by the name of Thibault Blanchett developed the exotic matter *infuser*. It has a longer technical name, but that's essentially what it does. The direction in which the exotic matter is infused determines the direction of travel, which can't be reversed once it's established. Anyway, an infuser is a physical unit. If the exotic matter flow is terminated — by destroying the infuser, for example — the hole will collapse. But not immediately. It could remain open long enough for the Diak to detect the problem and correct it. But if we introduce ordinary matter into the ring, the hole will close in a flash, literally."

"And how do you —" Letty stopped. "There has to be another way."

"What if the Diaks use a different method than we do?" Drew asked.

"I don't see how they can. I mean . . . high school physics. It may look different, but it has to perform the same way. Regardless of mechanical engineering, the introduction of normal matter will do the trick."

Drew realized the success of the plan, from locking onto the Diak ship to closing the wormhole, fell squarely on Barnes. There was no way to distribute the responsibility equally. This was a suicide mission for Travis. Shame at the fleeting sense of relief he felt washed over him. *What the hell, Drew, be realistic. There's no chance of this working. We're all going to die.*

"I've had some recent experience with EMUs," Drew said. "If you'll restore gravity, I'll go back and check it out." Barnes hands moved on the control panel and Drew's ass settled into his seat. His body no longer pressed against the restraining straps.

~ ~ ∞ ~ ~

As Drew headed to the back, Barnes asked Toby to rejoin him at command. Toby sat on the edge of the seat next to him. "Listen, buddy," Barnes said, "you understand what we've been talking about, don't you?"

"Yeah," Toby's eyes filled, and his face contorted.

"None of that, now. I need you to be strong. Somebody has to take care of Letty."

"B-but Drew wants to take care of Letty," Toby said, squeezing his eyes shut to hold back his tears.

Travis smiled. "Just between you and me, I don't think that's going to happen. Even if it does, would that be so bad? Besides, you and Letty have something in common. That's why you need each other."

"What?"

"The two of you are orphans."

"Oh . . . yeah. She's an orphan too. I didn't think about that."

"So, things are hard for you both right now. Can I count on you?"

Toby lifted his head and squared his shoulders. "Yes. And when I'm old enough, I'll marry Letty."

Barnes tried not to laugh. "I wouldn't count on that either. But it makes me feel good to know you'll be there for her. Come on, let's go back and work out the details of your plan."

Barnes would exit the shuttle just before the host ship entered the wormhole. No point discussing what came next, he'd do whatever he needed to. "The moment the ship enters the wormhole," Barnes said, "Letty should cut the maglocks. Then just hang back. On the other side, stay in front of the wormhole until the Diak ship moves out of sight. The energy emissions will block their scanners if they enable them, but I doubt they will until they're clear. I'll wait for a count of one hundred."

"Sounds easy enough," Curtis said, with no attempt to conceal his sarcasm.

Barnes went on. "My guess is, if you come out in Alliance territory, it will be somewhere in the Schwarzschild Cluster. Regardless, as soon as it's safe, get the hell away from the wormhole and warn the station. They can send a ship to meet you."

"We could just as easily come out in Diak territory. What do you think our odds are?" Drew asked Barnes.

"Screw the odds. We just need a little luck."

"Remind me to invite you to our next poker game." Everyone looked away, including Drew. Barnes was sure he wished he could take back his words.

~ ~ ∞ ~ ~

Barnes repositioned the shuttle to view approaching ships and still maintain cover. He went over the controls with Letty. It'd been a while since she'd flown. The shuttle controls were straightforward, but timing their drop from the Diak ship was critical. Too soon, and they might not have the momentum needed to transverse the wormhole. Thrusters couldn't be activated inside its tunnel. Too late, and they'd be caught in the Diak's thruster blast on the other side or run right up its ass. After her briefing, Letty returned to her seat next to Toby.

Barnes would pilot the shuttle through the mag-locking procedure. Drew helped him into the EMU except for the helmet. He needed to be ready to go on a second's notice. They waited. Drew sat in the navigator's seat holding the helmet in his lap. The back of the shuttle remained quiet. Toby actually slept.

"You asked about the odds earlier," Travis said in a low voice. "I figure you guys winding up in Diak territory instead of Alliance space is about seventy-thirty, maybe greater. Whether I close their access to our territory or not, you can bet the ESF has already cut off their return route. At least the armada won't be able to go home triumphant. It's not much, but it's something."

"If they do get through and can't get back, they'll probably take one of our planets to colonize," Drew said. "But truthfully, I don't believe there are any Diak, at least not in biological form. Maybe at one time. Did you see anything resembling a supply ship in the assemblage?"

Barnes shook his head.

"They didn't find organic material in the debris of the ships we destroyed either," Drew went on. "I think the Fitz *thing* was an escape pod after all. The scanners were right; we just didn't recognize it for that afterward."

"Maybe. Have you considered what you'll do if you end up

still in the Diak universe?"

"I have. Assuming we're not spotted immediately, we'll scout around a bit. If no life-saving opportunity presents itself, and I don't expect it to, I'll look for a Diak target to ram. Short of that, I'll open the hatches," Drew said and shuddered.

Barnes nodded slowly.

"Can I ask you a personal question … just out of curiosity?"

Travis smiled and his response was on target. "About three years ago when we were both still in college. It didn't last long, and we haven't seen much of each other since then."

"Thanks."

"No problem." *Asshat.*

35 CATCHING A RIDE

They sat in silence, watching the armada through the shuttle window's telescopic view. In his head, Drew heard the ticking of a clock. He'd seen a vid of a drama made centuries earlier, restored from an old-fashioned data disk, and he'd been impressed with the use of a ticking clock as a device to mark the passage of time. He'd never heard a ticking clock before, and the sound had stuck with him.

Remarkably, Barnes yawned next to him. "You're kidding me," Drew said.

"Sorry, ' . . . those who are about to die . . .' are bored to — Oh *shit*, here we go."

The ships in the Diak armada were moving all at once but in different directions, resembling a bizarre, slow-motion dance. It took several minutes for Drew to detect a pattern.

Barnes spotted it at the same time. "They're lining up two abreast into battlegroups. The wormhole must be too narrow for whole units to go through together. This might take a while. Let's hope they send a recon unit out ahead of the main body because that's our only chance." He raised his voice, "Get ready, everyone."

"Sure as hell, they'll spot us," Drew said, tearing his eyes away from the discordant dance of the Diak ships to look at Barnes.

"If they do, they do," Barnes said, stoically. "And if they don't, we've got one shot. Miss it, and the only option left is to follow the armada and . . . *really* . . . what would be the point?"

Drew wanted to admire Barnes's resigned bearing, but he honestly thought the man was daft.

Twenty minutes later, the Diak vessels were still arranging themselves into neat lines when four gunships broke from the rest, quickly forming a diamond pattern. One in the fore, two side-by-side, and one in the rear, heading straight toward the asteroid shielding the *Marigold*.

Drew imagined the shuttle being split apart. He could feel himself freezing in open space, his consciousness holding out until the last nano-second—

Barnes tugged at the helmet in Drew's lap. "Come out of it, man. Change places with Letty, *now*."

He relinquished the helmet and rose. Letty stood behind him, ready to take the seat. He went to the back and sat in her still-warm spot next to Toby and pulled the restraining straps tight. Toby stretched to see over the seatback in front of him, but he was too short.

"They're coming?" he asked.

Drew nodded and pointed to the skylight. Toby looked up, pushing the hair from his eyes. *I should have taken him in for a haircut.* Drew laughed at the absurd timing of the thought.

Barnes brought the shuttle as close as he could to the top of the asteroid while still hidden behind its bulk. If the Diak ships kept to their current trajectory, they would pass directly over the *Marigold*.

When the first Diak ship appeared in the skylight, it started a slow roll to its starboard. Drew's breath caught. Its scanner had detected them, and the ship was moving in position to fire its laser cannon. When the roll continued out of sight, he realized it was the *Marigold* turning to acquire position for mooring to the underside of the trailing Diak ship.

From what he'd seen, the enemy ships were barely skimming the top of the asteroid, and the *Marigold* sat only twenty to thirty meters below. They were within collision distance, right where they wanted to be. Barnes was good, but from this point on they needed more than good; they needed the luck he'd spoken of earlier.

"Our proximity alerts!" Drew blurted.

"Disabled." Barnes barked. "Keep it down."

Drew bit his lip. "Sorry," he whispered. The shuttle's command display would give their position to the nearest centimeter. Barnes wanted no distractions while he concentrated on the job at hand.

Drew watched through the skylight for a sign they were still moving, but their distance to the target was negligible and his view of the asteroids and stars remained fixed. When Nikko sneezed three times in quick succession, Drew almost screamed. Then the shuttle's thrusters fired, and they *were* moving at a rapid speed. The asteroids flew past them and out of sight. Within seconds they reached empty space. With stars so distant, and without asteroids to mark their passage, there was no longer a sense of movement. Drew squinted to make out tell-tail blinks of light against the blackness.

He leaned into the aisle and looked forward. Barnes stood, his helmet attached. Barnes must have already moored the *Marigold* to the Diak gunship, though he'd felt no telling jolt. Letty moved into the vacated captain's chair. Drew closed his eyes and held his breath, anticipating the blast that would turn the shuttle and its passengers into fragments, forever expanding across the cosmos.

~ ~ ∞ ~ ~

Travis checked his helmet to make sure it was sealed properly and made his way to the back of the shuttle. *I'll be dead soon. Okay, that's weird! If it weren't for Letty and the boy, I'd aim the shuttle at the Blanchett ring and take the other three with me for company. Especially Drew . . . Jesus, that man is worthless. If Letty hooks up with him, at least I won't have to know.*

As he passed, he reached across Drew to pat Toby on the head and give him a gloved thumbs-up. The boy offered a teary-eyed thumbs-up in return. Travis avoided looking at Drew, afraid if he did, he'd smash him in the face. He avoided exchanging looks with Curtis and Nikko as well. He'd always heard that everyone dies alone. He could attest to the truth of the adage. He'd never felt so alone.

Once aft, he took a last look up the aisle before toggling the *extend seal* switch that would turn the back of the shuttle into an airlock. The environmental screen unfolded from its casing, following tracks set into the deck and upper bulkhead. Once fully extended, its seals engaged. The light on the control blinked green as the cabin depressurized. He pulled the drop seat from its niche and sat, waiting for Letty to signal when the edge distortion of a wormhole came into view. This was the part he'd dreaded the most . . . the waiting. If Letty didn't spot the distortion in time, he would go through with them and their plan would fail. The armada would cross into Alliance territory. At least he'd live a bit longer. Worse, if her timing was off and he exited into the wormhole tunnel, the plan would fail, and he'd have given his life for nothing.

Then there was also the possibility the Diak point ship would drop back and exchange places with the rearguard. It was a tactic he'd learned in training to keep pilots alert and apportion the higher risk of the point position. If the ships didn't stay true to their current positions, the shuttle team would all die together. Drew thought there *were* no pilots. But in the skirmish behind Spud, Barnes practiced eye noticed a slight difference in skill levels between attackers. The Diak may not be biological, but they weren't fully automated either. *Something* was physically piloting each ship.

As he fought to calm his nerves, Travis stared at the airlock control light. When it was time to go, Letty's signal was to toggle it from green to red and back. It occurred to him, if he got the signal and things turned to shit after he'd exited the shuttle, he might outlive Cutter. He smiled. *There's an upside after all.*

~ ~ ∞ ~ ~

Toby was visibly shaking. Drew undid their straps and pulled him onto his lap, extending his restraint to hold them both. Toby stopped shaking and snuggled into Drew's arms. Drew held him tight, grimacing at his tangy, musty odor. Apparently, no one had bothered to see that the boy washed occasionally. Letty was no more experienced in caring for a child than he was. Still, one of them should have thought to make sure the boy bathed. *Hell, has he even cleaned his teeth since he returned to Dark Landing? A little late now.*

All four adults watched for the characteristic edge distortion. Curtis and Nikko took forward starboard and forward port and

Drew took the skylight. Letty, having the least restricted view, scanned the expanse of space before them. She should spot the wormhole first. The Diak ships had formed up so tightly that, hanging from the rear gunship, they couldn't see the bellies of the ships ahead of them.

Drew spotted it first. "Letty . . ."

"Got it!" Her hand hovered above the control panel.

~ ~ ∞ ~ ~

Barnes watched as the *Go* light turned red then back to green. Without hesitation, he pushed the hatch release and slipped into space. For a moment, his stomach dropped, and he imagined the sensation of falling. It quickly passed.

He spotted the distortion about a kilometer ahead and below his position. As he watched, the four enemy ships disappeared into the wormhole with the little *Marigold* attached to the rearguard like a cosmic barnacle.

"You've gotta get this right. Release now, baby." he whispered into his helmet, knowing Letty couldn't hear him.

He started counting backward from one hundred and pressed the controls of his propulsion jets. As he closed in on his target, he searched for the device that he knew had to be there. All technology followed the same evolutionary pattern: it became smaller. Since the Diak enjoyed more advanced technology, he expected their infusers to be smaller than the K.U.'s twenty-by-twenty-foot standard. He'd traveled through wormholes hundreds of times in ships of all sizes, but he'd never seen one from his current vantage point. It was massive. The edge distortion was much wider than it appeared from the observation port of a ship.

At the outer edge, he thought he detected the narrow ring. He didn't *see* it as much as he envisaged it. The inner edge of the distortion feathered into the hole, but the outer edge seemed blunted by comparison, as if it was pushing up against something. It was an optical illusion. The ring kept the tunnel from collapsing inward on itself, not from expanding outward. He blinked rapidly to clear his vision, but the wormhole grew in size the closer he came. It was hard to see any detail beyond the distortion itself. He cut his propulsion jets, slowing his approach, and scanned the ring on its right side from the twelve to six o'clock positions, then began a reverse scan back to the top. Out of the corner of his eye he caught an inconsistency on the left at about seven o'clock.

There it was. Sure enough, it was smaller by half than the K.U. versions. The cube was camouflaged against the blackness of space, with the tiniest pinpoint of light twinkling from its center to imitate a distant star. It blended perfectly with the genuine objects. Forgetting his countdown, he strained to keep it in view, afraid to look away in case it disappeared into the backdrop.

As he approached, the wormhole grew larger still. To see even a small portion of the ring now he would need to crane his neck. He focused on the infuser. Instead of his normal reaction at the wonder of a bridge to another world, he'd beheld only a hole imbued with evil. He wanted to turn and run, but there was no place to go but forward.

36 BAD TURN

ETOC Secretary Rostenkowski, MCTT Lt. Commander William, and ESF Rear Admiral Sullivan, were joined in the Security HQ conference room by Travis Barnes's replacement, Makayla Liu, TSF next in command. The head of the Earth Defense Council, Sir James Hawking-Barstow, led the meeting over a live feed.

"We should close it while we have the chance," Sullivan said.

"I agree," William nodded.

"I don't," Rostenkowski voiced her opposition. "We should be prepared to close it on a second's notice, but for now, it's our only access to Diak territory."

"As I said," Sir James put an end to the dispute, "the council is equally split and still debating the decision. *And* it's for the Earth Defense Council and *only* the EDC to decide. For the short term, the question before you is the advisability of sending probes to try and locate their bridge into *our* territory."

"I'm sorry," Lt. Commander William cut in. "Shouldn't collapsing the wormhole be an Alliance decision, not just Earth's?"

"Perhaps, but it's in Earth's possession, and we're commandeering final judgment as to its disposition," Sir James said.

"Earth has displayed an exceptional talent for commandeering." It was the first time TSF Liu had spoken. The other four, having forgotten she was even in the room, frowned at the intrusion and ignored her.

Sir James went on. "Lt. Commander William, are you making

a formal complaint on behalf of the MCTT?"

William hummed his retreat. "No. As far as I'm aware, there is no MCTT. I'm in command of a rogue group that illegally *commandeered*," his whiskers rippled in a weak smile, "MCTT property."

"And we're thankful you did," Rostenkowski said.

"So," Sir James reminded them, "the probes?"

Except for Liu, the group nodded in unison. Sullivan spoke for them. "Since one of the Diak ships escaped through their wormhole ahead of the *Marigold*, they know we're in control of it now. Sending probes won't provide them with more information." Sullivan paused; no one had mentioned the *Marigold* to that point.

"My guess is your council thinks the Diak will take one of two possible actions: cease their attacks and stay at home since they no longer have a return route or send a larger force to take back their bridge. I'm in the camp that believes they have another return route. They managed to shield that wormhole from our patrols, but it couldn't have been there long. They knew we'd discover it eventually. It's too close to a heavily trafficked station. Yet their original plan included attacking us from within by spreading the nanoid virus across the aligned planets—a long-term strategy."

"The council hasn't told me what I'm to think yet," Sir James said, "but if they asked, I agree with you. It's worrisome to believe the Diak may have multiple ways *out* of our territory, but bone chilling to realize that they might also have multiple ways *in*. Admiral Sullivan, are you carrying the appropriate probe bundle?"

"No. But, as we speak, an ESF squadron is docking to reinforce our combined defenses. They're carrying one."

"We'll send another your way regardless. Hold launch until I get consent of the full council."

"Yes, sir," Sullivan said.

"Then that's all for—"

"Excuse me," Liu held her hand up. "We still need to discuss a rescue mission for the *Marigold*."

"There won't be a rescue mission for the *Marigold*," Sir James said. "Even if they weren't obliterated the minute they entered Diak space, they're defenseless, with little or no supplies, and no range."

"But . . ." Liu looked determined.

Sir James shook his head. "I'm sorry. *End transmission.*"

~ ~ ∞ ~ ~

After the meeting, Anne Rostenkowski stopped by Security HQ's front office. In the last few weeks, they'd lost four out five command staff and been hijacked by Earth military. Kyle Drubber and Mitchell Jones were still acting shift commanders, but Cutter's and Walker's positions had been combined and filled by an ESF officer. Capt. Murray seemed competent and fair, but he was insensitive to the emotional condition of security's rank and file. Anne felt they deserved a little more empathy. *On the other hand, the entire K.U. is suffering right now.*

Kyle sat at the shift commander's desk with as blank an expression as anyone still breathing could have until he noticed her approach. "Good morning, Secretary Rostenkowski."

"Hello, Kyle. I just stopped by to see how things were going. Any new crises?"

"No, but then it's early yet, sir."

She laughed. "If you and Jones have questions or need an advocate, you're free to come to me. I'm not sure I can always help, but I might be able to put in a good word."

"I appreciate it, sir. Can you tell me how your meeting went? Are we mounting a rescue mission?"

Her voice softened. "No. And I agree with the decision. There's no telling what's on the other side of that wormhole. It's sure to be guarded and maybe mined as well. Any chance of finding a way back is miniscule. We can't risk more lives on a mission without even a remote chance of success. But we're sending a probe package through."

"Yeah, we guessed as much. There is one other thing. Chief Cutter didn't want us talking to Mattie, and Capt. Murray is enforcing that. But she's overheard bits of conversation and knows something's up. I . . . all the staff . . . at least want to let her in on what's happened. Maybe she doesn't deserve it, but she was one of us once."

"I don't see a reason to keep her in the dark. But I don't want to countermand Murray's orders either. I have a few minutes now. I'll go back and speak with her myself."

"Thanks, sir."

~ ~ ∞ ~ ~

Mattie lay on her cot, eyes closed, arms crossed over her chest, one leg propped up with the other resting on its knee. Her foot made little circles in the air. Anne knew she'd heard her approaching the cell and guessed Mattie was trying to appear disinterested.

"Miss Freelander? It's Anne Rostenkowski of the ETOC."

"So?" Mattie said, without opening her eyes.

"You were scheduled for transfer to Earth on the *Reagan*, which was to leave this morning. But an unfortunate event yesterday evening has delayed the *Reagan's* departure several days."

Mattie sat up, no longer feigning her disinterest. "Is this about Chief Cutter? I know something happened."

"Yes. In a skirmish with the Diak, his shuttle inadvertently crossed into their space through a wormhole no one knew was there. Chief Cutter and several others were lost."

"So . . . Cutter's dead," Mattie said.

Anne thought she looked genuinely saddened by the news. "We assume—"

Mattie exploded like a detonated pumpkin before Rostenkowski could finish her sentence.

Anne stood perfectly still. She remained rational, noticing small details of the carnage around and all over her, but as if doing so out-of-body. As she watched, a tooth attached to a bit of skin slid slowly down one cell bar. She wondered at the almost total lack of red blood. The bit of tooth merged with a chunk of skull, its patch of hair still intact. Under their combined weight, both dropped to the deck with a soft splat.

The hatch opened and Kyle burst in. "Secretary Rostenkowski, something's happened!"

37 MAN DOWN

Travis Barnes approached the infuser. He easily made out the magnetically contained input and output conduits, which snaked between the infuser and the wormhole. One conduit captured exotic matter produced by the quantum vacuum fluctuations of the wormhole and the other infused it into the ring. The conduit lines were the circumference of a piece of straw.

The K.U. version had a much larger magnetic tube encasing the conduits themselves to provide further shielding. And K.U. units emitted proximity alerts to approaching ships, as well as safeguards to stop the exotic matter flow if the ship strayed too close. When the flow ceased from one infuser, a second — positioned on the opposite side of the ring — would reestablish the stream needed to maintain the wormhole. Barnes saw no second infuser. He doubted the Diak shared the safety concerns of the K.U. races, but it was odd they wouldn't want to protect the bridge if the single unit failed.

He hoped there was time to disable the infuser and take it permanently out of service. But the only way to ensure the ring collapsed before the Diak could re-stabilize it was to physically penetrate the ring. When *his* matter collided with the ring's exotic matter, the hole would close in a flash of brilliant light, taking him with it. He wouldn't feel a thing, but his natural instincts for self-preservation and pain avoidance kicked in. His heart pumped dangerously fast, and he sucked oxygen in large gulps. As he examined the infuser casing, he practiced breathing exercises he'd learned in training.

~ ~ ∞ ~ ~

The command console indicated the shuttle's hatch had opened, then closed and resealed. Travis was gone. Letty had no time to dwell on his passing. They were entering the wormhole, so large now that she'd lost sight of the edge distortion. For some reason the proximity indicator wasn't working. With sudden comprehension, she released the maglocks.

Travis had predicted only a five-second window to avoid dropping too soon or too late. She wasn't superstitious, but she hoped, willed, prayed, and cajoled whatever forces might be listening that she'd released the maglocks at the right time.

Though wanting to go back and comfort Toby, she remained at command. The viewport reflected the scene behind her: three adult heads floating above a row of seatbacks. Curtis stared through the shuttle window, his auburn hair pronounced atop a ghost-white face. Nikko sat ramrod straight in his seat, eyes closed. Across the aisle, Drew rocked slowly back and forth, his head tipped at an odd angle.

Letty returned her attention to the console just as the *Marigold* emerged from the wormhole.

~ ~ ∞ ~ ~

Travis looked for a latch or some other means to open the cube and access its interior drives. The sides were smooth, with no obvious panels or buttons. He ran a gloved hand across the top edge and down one side. The bottom corner protruded slightly. He moved down the box to inspect the bump at eyelevel and observed a raised lip about four centimeters wide. With all his force, he pulled outward. Not only did the side not open, but the box didn't budge. Somehow, it was anchored in place. Frustrated, he hit the side of the infuser with his fist. It popped open and slapped the front of his helmet.

He moved around the open panel to look into the interior. Inside lay a series of smaller black cubes, three to a row across and three down, each one a perfect miniature of the larger casing. The smaller cubes were set about five centimeters apart, with no apparent connections. He ran his glove around the perimeter of one, finding no bumps or indentations of any kind. He repeated the action on two others. Nothing. He grabbed hold of a cube and pulled on it.

With little resistance, it came away from the casing. He turned it over and over in his hands. It was smooth, six-sided, without seams or protrusions. He pressed on each side, duplicating the action that had opened the larger box. When nothing worked, he pushed it out into space, then did the same with the remaining boxes until he'd emptied the infuser case. Searching for the exotic matter conduits he'd spotted earlier, he realized there were none. Simply removing the interior cubes had successfully stopped the flow.

The wormhole yawned in front of him. He turned full-face toward a section of the Blanchett ring and activated his propulsion jets. *Shit!*

~ ~ ∞ ~ ~

They were through. The Diak ships that'd crossed ahead of them receded in the distance. They'd failed to detect the *Marigold*. Letty activated the shuttle's thrusters and moved it away from the wormhole and in the opposite direction from the retreating ships.

Drew slid into the chair next to her. The other three crowded behind them. She turned to Drew, her breathing labored from a combination of fear and relief. He reached out, cupping the side of her face in his hand, his thumb gently stroking her cheek, brushing the tears away.

"You did it, sweetheart."

Toby ducked under Drew's arm to hug Letty, pushing him away.

With a shaky breath, Letty said, "Now let's see if we're in friendly space."

All eyes looked to the map display on the control panel. In Diak space the caption for each object on the map within sensor range had read "Unknown." The captions now read "Devil's Gate," "Prosse," "Bin," "New Pryor," and a dozen other familiar appellations.

"*Locate Dark Landing,*" Drew commanded.

The display morphed to show the station's position one hop and three days out — well beyond the shuttle's range and ability.

Letty, not wanting to risk a live feed, dispatched a message with their coordinates to Dark Landing security, Secretary Rostenkowski, Rear Admiral Jensen Sullivan, and as many other names as she was able to spit out in her excited state:

> *Four Diak gunships headed your way; Diak armada amassing; results of attempt to close their bridge into Alliance space unknown. The* Marigold *could use a tow.*

Minutes passed before they received the terse reply: *On our way,* Marigold.

They each ate a package of nuts and divided the water pouch between the five of them, holding back some for Toby to drink later. They then settled in to wait the three days for help to arrive.

~ ~ ∞ ~ ~

His forward motion stopped by a gentle backward tug, Barnes opened his eyes and inspected his gloved hand floating weightless in front of him. Every nook and cranny, crease and seam was illuminated in sharp detail by a light beam originating from above and behind him. He pressed his propulsion controls without result. Something pulled him backward, away from the wormhole. And then he was consumed in a blazing white void.

~ ~ ∞ ~ ~

Sar Mode watched her display. The alien was snared in the repair craft's grip-net. As it backed from the wormhole to return to the command station, the ship was engulfed by a blinding flash of light. When her screen cleared, the bridge to far-off space had disappeared.

The appointed principal ordered new calculations. The secondary bridge would take time to create, and the chosen location lay many rotations from their current position. The cost to the Mass would be considerable. How many Diak would turn before acquiring new hosts? And, of those, how many would lose faith in their purpose and cease to be? On the five new worlds, they'd not only lost the advantage, but now the thousands of receptacles infused with Diak devices, set to detonate upon loss of transmission, were gone as well.

She was not programmed to handle regret or despair. It was a flaw in the system she'd often wondered about but could never explain. While a new assault plan was being generated, Sar Mode recalled a stored memory to dispel her melancholy. She'd grown curious about the small, six-legged creature with the cold nose and wet tongues to which the Paresee Captain had been so devoted. Of particular interest was how they reproduced.

~ ~ ∞ ~ ~

Kyle stopped short in front of Anne Rostenkowski but slipped and almost went down. He grabbed a bar of Mattie's cell for support, then hastily pulled his hand back and wiped it on his pant leg. He clapped the still sticky hand over his mouth in horror as he surveyed the macabre scene before him. Clearly Mattie had exploded. Parts of her covered the cell walls, the deck, the corridor, and Secretary Rostenkowski.

She turned to him. "Yes?"

His words came fast and clipped. "The Fitz statue disintegrated, and Capt. Murray ejected the screamer cell. Doc tapped and—"

Rostenkowski cut him off. "Please ask my aide to bring me a change of clothes. I understand there's a shower in the chief's office?"

"Yes, sir."

~ ~ ∞ ~ ~

Rostenkowski exited Cutter's, now Murray's, office in a fresh outfit, her hair tucked behind her ears, hanging straight, instead of its usual French twist. Every processor station in the outer office had two or three staff members in front of it. The air was filled with indistinguishable chatter. She caught Kyle's eye, and he came over.

"The *Marigold* is back, and there's a lot more," he said, then his smile turned into an expression of concern. "The others are waiting for you."

Anne nodded at Kyle and made her way to the conference room at a leisurely pace. Her approach to chaos was one of strategic detachment. She'd developed the unique ability to view chaotic events as an observer not a participant, as if she were standing outside, looking through a window. This perspective allowed her to maintain clarity and focus even when surrounded by turmoil. By mentally stepping back, she could assess situations objectively, make informed decisions, and lead with confidence. It was a skill perfected over years of experience, and the cornerstone upon which she built her illustrious career.

"Fill me in," Anne demanded, joining Rear Admiral Sullivan, TSF Capt. Makayla Liu, and ESF Capt. Murray at the conference room table.

"We got the following message from the *Marigold* twenty minutes ago," Sullivan said. He continued as Anne read the screen set in the table in front of her. "All ten ships of the ESF squadron that arrived last night are hunting the four Diak ships Miss Taleen warned us about, as well as watching for the armada. Pray the *Marigold* team's attempt to close the bridge from Diak to Alliance space was successful. My two battleships along with *Muck* and the TSF ships are patrolling the station and guarding the wormhole into Diak space. We're prepared to close it if our scouts spot the gunships or the armada."

Captain Liu relayed updated intel from her comm as she received it, "TSF dispatch reports there's a freighter, the *Essovius*, within hours of the *Marigold*. They've alerted her to the situation, and the ship will detour to get them." She glanced around the room. "That's good news. But Miss Taleen hasn't mentioned Commander Barnes. It's odd the message that they'd returned didn't come from him."

"There's a lot to wonder about right now," Capt. Murray said. "Excuse me." He tapped his comm to advise his EFS squadron they'd now be escorting both the *Essovius* and the *Marigold*. Then he addressed Rostenkowski. "Kyle told you they ejected the screamer cell, and we heard about the Freelander woman. Dr. Jameson reported four people waiting in quarantine for transport — the three women posing as monks and an infected evacuee–met the same end. She should be here any minute, and Sir James will be joining us as well."

38 LEAVINGS

At Letty's request, the *Essovius* sent its pilot over to dock the *Marigold*. He squeezed it into the tight space next to the *Essovius's* own shuttle with ease. When the doors closed and the bay pressurized, Drew relaxed. But he was exhausted; a sledge hammer pounded in his head, and every muscle in his body ached. As soon as the hatch opened, the five of them stumbled out. A nurse assistant escorted the group directly to the ship's small medical station where the doctor determined they were all somewhat dehydrated, but otherwise fine. The doctor wanted to keep Toby under observation, but the boy threw such a fit at being separated from the others, the only option was to sedate him. Letty wouldn't allow it. They were given water pouches with mineral supplements and told to contact medical if they felt nauseated or dizzy.

They sprawled on loungers in the ship's public area, eating hot soup and waiting for the live feed with Dark Landing. Toby had managed only a few spoonsful before falling asleep with his head in Letty's lap.

Letty looked calm, but periodically a tear would slip down one cheek. Drew knew she was thinking of Barnes; they all were. He'd never met anyone who cried as much as she did, but then he'd never met anyone who had as much reason to. Curtis and Nikko finished their soup in silence and sat unmoving except to take occasional sips from their water pouches.

Anne Rostenkowski's image materialized on the large

monitor. She was in the Security HQ conference room with Rear Admiral Sullivan and a man and woman Drew didn't recognize. The man wore an Earth Space Force captain's uniform, and the woman sported the equivalent uniform of the Taleen Security Force. The head of another man floated in the upper right corner of the screen, and he spoke first.

"Miss Taleen, Chief Cutter—everyone—welcome home. My name is James Hawking-Barstow; please call me Sir James. I know it sounds a bit presumptuous, but I've rather gotten used to it. I am the head of the Earth Defense Council. What a delightful surprise to meet you. I am sure you'll understand if I cut directly to the subject at hand. Would you please tell us what you know about the Diak armada?"

The female TSF captain sitting next to Secretary Rostenkowski broke in before Drew could speak. "Where's Commander Barnes?"

"H-he didn't make it," Letty said. Her voice rose as she struggled to maintain control. "Travis saved us all and probably the entire K.U. He stayed behind when we went through, sacrificing himself to close the Diak wormhole into our space. Are you sending someone to see if he succeeded?" The captain accepted Letty's news stoically, but her eyes glistened from the screen.

Sir James cleared his throat. "I am so sorry for your loss Miss Taleen . . . Captain Liu. An ESF squadron is on its way to meet the *Essovius*. One of its ships will continue to the coordinates you provided to learn if Commander Barnes was successful or not. We have reason to believe he was. In the meantime, no one has reported seeing a Diak ship, not even the four gunships you warned us about. Now, Chief Cutter, please."

"The armada is huge," Drew began. "Barnes and I estimated more than ten thousand ships, as well as a base station roughly five times the size of Dark Landing. It's sitting just beyond an asteroid field on the other side of the bridge we fell through. Their wormhole to Alliance space, if it's still there, is nearby; close enough to measure in kilometers. When we left, they were forming battle groups."

Drew and Letty alternated telling their story, starting at the point they crossed into Diak space. Curtis broke in a few times with an added detail. Somewhere in the middle of their rendition, Nikko started snoring.

~ ~ ∞ ~ ~

After ten hours sleep, the survivors were in the mess devouring their breakfasts when the ship's klaxon sounded. Except for Nikko, they all stopped eating and looked up.

"You've *got* to be kidding me," Drew said. Unexpectedly, Toby came around the table and climbed into his lap. Drew shrugged at Letty's amused look as an announcement came over the speaker:

> *All staff report to your stations. Everyone else stay as you are or return to your quarters. There are four Diak ships directly ahead of us.*

The ESF squadron was still more than a day out. As they braced in anticipation of the laser blast sure to come, the *Essovius's* second in command entered the mess. "They're just sitting there," he reported. "Our scan didn't detect life signs, but then our scanner isn't the most sophisticated either. The captain's talking to the ESF squadron commander now. He's afraid if we retreat, we might run into the full armada."

"You won't detect any life signs," Drew said.

They pushed from the table and found their way to the public lounge. Along with others already gathered, they watched an enhanced view of the distant Diak gunships on the big monitor. Most passengers and crew members who didn't have essential duties stayed in the lounge for the next twelve hours. The mess staff delivered a continuous supply of drinks and snacks, but little was consumed. Everyone spoke in whispered tones and jumped at loud noises. Doing nothing but watching the ships that, presumably, were watching them, was fatiguing. Nothing on the screen changed. The Diak ships did not move. Eventually, people started to drift to their quarters to sleep, or head to the mess for something hot to eat.

The audience reassembled when it was announced that the ESF squadron had arrived. One of the ESF ships broke off and escorted the *Essovius* further back while the remaining ships encircled the Diak recon unit. Thirty minutes passed without action and then, with no warning, the four Diak ships were blown to smithereens.

Toby jumped up, his arms and fists extended above his head. "Yes . . . yes . . . hooray!" he yelled, starting an avalanche of cheers and applause.

~ ~ ∞ ~ ~

The Security HQ conference room was full. Sir James led the meeting.

"At the exact time Commander Barnes—may he rest in peace—closed the Diak bridge to our territory, their recon unit seems to have become inoperative, and nanoid-infected individuals throughout the Alliance burst . . . or exploded . . . however you prefer to describe it. More than eight hundred thousand have been reported so far. I don't wish to minimize the gravity of the incident," he said, "but that is a *very* small number in relation to the combined populations of the Alliance worlds. First responders and others who came into contact with the deceased remains are being rescanned, though it's believed the nanoids were triggered to self-destruct upon loss of communication. I extend my condolences to anyone here today who lost a friend or loved one.

"Our home planets teetered on the verge of extermination. If not for the actions of one exceptional man, it's likely Dark Landing would be a memory, and the populations of the Alliance planets would be staring down the muzzle of a Diak laser cannon when they awoke this morning."

"We're sure the Diak don't have another bridge into our space?" Rostenkowski asked.

"The experts say no. When their wormhole closed, the link to their nanoids broke as well. If they had another bridge, it's thought their signal would have persisted. But we can't know conclusively."

"And going forward . . .?" Rear Admiral Sullivan asked.

"Going forward Alliance members and several of the non-aligned planets are forming a defense council along the lines of *Muck*, with the objective of building a combined military armada of our own. In the meantime, we remain on full alert."

"What are your plans for Dark Landing?" Curtis got the question in before Drew.

"Earth intends to maintain the station as a military outpost, at least in the short term. Obviously, we've not had time to discuss the details. I'm proposing the station continue as a trade depot and scientific base. And that we outfit Spud to house the military contingent until the Alliance can build a dedicated military post in the Zeta Quadrant."

Sullivan spoke up. "My orders are to keep the two battleships and the ESF squadron here." Sullivan looked at Lt. Commander William. He nodded. "Commander William's unit is going to remain as well while *Muck* regroups."

Sir James wrapped up. "Secretary Rostenkowski will return to Earth with the *Reagan,* and the Earth Defense Council will negotiate with Taleen Industries regarding TFS's continued level of participation. I'll stay in touch with each of you as matters progress. So . . . unless there are further questions . . .?"

With a few weak laughs, everyone shook their heads.

"*End transmission.*" Sir James' image faded from the screen.

~ ~ ∞ ~ ~

Drew, Letty, and Curtis reconvened in the mezzanine bar.

"We need to decide what to do with Toby," Drew said.

"*You guys* need to decide. I don't care as long as he's not underfoot here. Either of you want another drink?" Curtis entered his order for a refill, but Drew and Letty shook their heads.

"I contacted my legal department a few days ago," Letty said. "They found a great-great aunt, but she's unwell and lives in a retirement home, in no condition to care for a child. As I understand it, she's never met him. I've started the adoption process."

"Lucky kid. My parents are both dead. You can adopt me too," Curtis said as he retrieved his drink from the chute.

Letty laughed. "I overheard you speaking with your mother the day we returned to Alliance space."

"It's a miracle," Curtis quipped.

"Do you really want to take on that responsibility?" asked Drew.

"Yes, I do. I was too young to understand when my own parents died, and I was lucky enough to have a familiar and loving standby parent. Toby tries to hide it, but he misses his folks, and he's scared. I noticed you two have grown close, Drew."

"If you consider sharing a wet shuttle seat while we escaped from evil aliens *close . . .* yeah, sure." He changed the subject. "So, Curtis, how's the plan for your nightclub coming along?"

"It's on hold until I figure out what ESF has in store for Spud. If they turn it into a Space Force bivouac, I'll have to shelve my project for a while."

"And Nikko . . .?" Drew asked.

"Letty can adopt him too."

"I'm visualizing Letty taking her three kids, Toby, Curtis, and Nikko to Planet Disney, and buying you all mouse ears." Drew smiled at the image.

"Hell," Curtis said, "Letty probably owns Planet Disney."

Letty grew quiet and stared into her beer.

"You've *got* to be kidding me!" Drew said.

~ ~ ∞ ~ ~

After many delays, the *Reagan* was finally departing Dark Landing. Drew and Letty stood in a corner of the docking bay. They'd had a long, and for Drew disappointing, conversation the night before.

Letty wrapped her arms around his neck, laying her head on his shoulder in a sisterly manner. She pulled back and looked at him. "You know I love you, Drew, but ninety-five percent as a friend. As for the rest, if I'm being truthful, my feelings are messed up right now — we've been through so much together."

"So, five percent — I can work with that," Drew said, lifting his eyebrows boyishly.

"Sometimes you're an ass." She laughed. "We wouldn't last a day."

"Yeah, but I can't stop imagining what we could do in those twenty-four hours." Drew pressed his face into her hair; it smelled of orange blossoms.

When the *Reagan* was gone, Drew walked the station aimlessly, reflecting on all that'd happened and what he should do next. He couldn't stay at Dark Landing, but he'd lost interest in joining the TSF. Both would remain under the control of Earth military for the foreseeable future.

Like Letty, his feelings were a bit *messed up* as well. He

couldn't remember the last time he'd felt confident in his choices or proud of his accomplishments. Letty was the catalyst, not the cause for the insecurities he faced. To be honest, he didn't know how he felt about her anymore. What he needed now was time to himself.

Among the fears with which he struggled was his *bona fide* cowardliness. He felt deep shame for being glad Travis Barnes died instead of him. Maybe *glad* was too strong a word . . . *relieved*. Still, he didn't think he'd have the courage to make the sacrifice Barnes had made. And he couldn't shake the sense of uselessness he'd felt when Barnes left the shuttle, knowing he was a dead man. He was envious; he wanted to be like Barnes. *Hell, until now, I thought I was Barnes.* When Letty had taken control of the shuttle through the short, but harrowing, wormhole run, all he could do was sit in the back with the others, holding Toby. And space still terrified him. Neither time nor circumstances had cured the problem.

Then there was his poor judgement, his misplaced trust in Mattie and Fitz, and lack of faith in Curtis. *I'm a mess, all right. A cowardly, incompetent, fucked up mess.* He stopped walking, finding himself in front of the hatch to his quarters.

After a sleepless night, he made his decision. On the way to HQ, more light-hearted than he'd felt in months, he passed through the bazaar and noticed several early shoppers looking upward. The pigeon perched on the mezzanine rail. A small group to one side held signs reading, "Save Preston! Shoot Cutter!" He laughed and continued on his way, accompanied by boos from the demonstrators and fighting the urge to draw his blaster and turn the fucking bird into a shower of feathers. *Not my problem anymore.*

Kyle sat at the shift commander's desk. "Where's Curtis?" Drew asked.

"He's working out of Fitz's office this morning."

"Kyle, I think it's time we start calling it the admin office, don't you?"

"Good idea. Old habits die hard."

"Truer words . . . I've got some things to take care of this morning. Can you keep the universe at bay for a couple hours?"

"Can do."

Drew entered his office and commanded the hatch closed behind him. He started with a letter of resignation to CoachStop. He apologized for not giving notice, especially since the chief of administration position still remained open, but he emphasized that the staff, even short-handed, could and *had* handled anything thrown at them. He recommended Curtis Walker for the chief of security position, praising him effusively. Even though the praise was earned, he'd come close to puking his gonads as he dictated the words.

Not bothering with platitudes to Curtis, he included a script credit for half of his savings so Curtis might open his nightclub — or replenish his drug inventory. Whatever. It may have been a stupid move (it *was* a stupid move), but it made him feel *right* with Curtis somehow, and that was worth it. His note read simply: *Good luck. Try not to be a total ass.*

He struggled over his goodbye to Doc, finally expressing how he felt as frankly as possible:

> Doc,
>
> *You're too young to be my mother and way too smart to be my lover. Somewhere in the middle of that gooey mess, I adore you. We made a good team . . . the three of us. I refuse to believe that Fitz was anything but the friend and colleague we both admired. That other thing was simply a Diak-controlled look-alike. I'll miss you the most, but I know we'll see each other again. Keep up the good work and take care.*
>
> *Love, Drew*

He spent the next hour tidying up his records, leaving comments where needed and tagging items requiring follow-up. He'd packed his duffel and booked the presidential suite on the *Norwegian Princess*. The suite came with a real-water shower and a personal attendant. Finished with his last-minute errands, he left HQ with just enough time to pick up his kit and board before his ship debarked. On her six-month tour she would visit each of the Alliance planets. Her final stop was at New Las Vegas and coincided with a satellite tournament for a seat in the Multi-World Series of Poker main event.

He nodded to Kyle on the way out. "You're a good man,

Kyle."

"Thank you, sir," Kyle said, bewildered.

Drew smiled. He was taking a page from Curtis's book, and it felt surprisingly good.

EPILOGUE

Letty had delivered Toby to school and was in her office, where she'd spent much of her time since their return to Earth, catching up on the past three months. With some soul-searching, she'd decided to accept her position on the Board of Directors, but only after confessing her self-doubts to Carl Evans, the new CEO, and naming him co-chairman. She needed someone she could count on for guidance.

The Alliance markets were proving slow to recover from the Diak scare. The nanoids that infected their technology were easy to disable, but the fact that their tech had been breached in the first place shook the Alliance members to their core. Rebuilding military forces gone fallow for more than a century also exacerbated economic recovery for each race. And, worse, Fahdeenians were demanding a secession vote, though no one believed it would come to that.

She was concentrating on financial reports, not her strong suit, when her assistant entered the office with a perplexed look.

"This is interesting," he said. "Someone using the David Jacobs' alias charged passage on the *Norwegian Princess* against Jacobs' expense account. Finance flagged it. That was the alias you assigned to Drew Cutter, wasn't it?"

"Yes."

"Do you want me to have accounting deny the expense and

close the account?"

Letty didn't answer immediately. She gazed out the penthouse window at the distant Golden Gate Bridge, closed for the last two hundred years to all but foot traffic.

"No. Tell accounting I approve all charges without limit but have them send me weekly activity statements."

He must have known she'd find out—or maybe not. *That's ballsy, Drew. Good for you.* She smiled and returned to work.

AUTHOR NOTE

Book reviews are crucial to all authors. I hope you enjoyed *Transmuted*. Please take a moment to write an honest Amazon review. It doesn't have to be lengthy or involved and can be as simple as one or two sentences. I will be forever grateful.

If you liked *Transmuted*, you'll love the continuing adventures of Dark Landing and its cast of characters in book two, *Mass Primary*. The prologue to *Mass Primary* follows.

Thanks for reading,
Robin Praytor

MASS PRIMARY
DARK LANDING SERIES, BOOK 2

PROLOGUE

E. D. 2519
Screamer Cell
The edge of Zeta Quadrant
The Known Universe

Hoping to slow the nanoid devices devouring him, Ekis ran multiple diagnostic routines in concurrent loops. His structural body was gone, only cells remained, and precious few of those. *The devices* would never tire. When the last biological cell transmuted, the devices, their objective achieved, would disintegrate and Ekis would cease to be.

The stars visible through the observation window were so distant, he could perceive no sense of movement or change. When they had ejected the airlock from Dark Landing, he'd watched the station grow smaller and smaller until even his imagination could no longer sustain its image.

His thoughts drifted, and his concentration lapsed. *What point to continue?* In answer to his question, the airlock jolted as if it had bumped into something. *Impossible!* One did not *bump* into something in space. One smashed into it, or it smashed into you.

www.ingramcontent.com/pod-product-compliance
Lightning Source LLC
Chambersburg PA
CBHW020438270626
47155CB00022B/628